Prov
By Diana Kane

Providence

Dedication

To those who encouraged me, pushed me, rode my ass, and sometimes verbally slapped me to get in gear…this one is for you. You know who you are.

Table of Contents

Chapter 1

"Finally in the home stretch ladies, let's finish this up." I make a mental note to talk to my schedulers. Putting a bilateral breast reconstruction with immediate implants on with a pedicle flap to follow is a bit much for one day. It's nearing 8 pm, my stomach is starting to eat itself, and I'm so thirsty I could drink a gallon of water. Typically I would break scrub and let Abby close, but I really want to finish this case as soon as possible. "You two planning your usual Friday night dinner and drinks tonight?" Abby and Alex stop what they are doing and look at each other. I've seen these silent conversations many times, yet have never figured out how to interpret them. It's only a matter of seconds before they refocus on closing.

"Yeah, we're still going. Want to join us?" Abby never looks away from the abdomen as she finishes the closure.

"Yes. Tonight is my treat though. You've earned it after our long day today. Thanks again Alex for staying late with us."

"No problem. If we're making it a group outing, do you mind if I invite Catherine?"

"Not at all. If you two want to finish up, I'll break to dictate, put the orders in and speak with the family. Should get us out of here faster. Send me a text when you're ready to go." I break and immediately head for the doctor's lounge where I can get a much-needed glass of water and dictate. I'm not surprised to find it deserted at this hour on a Friday evening. I switch off the TV and down my first glass of ice water, the relief immediate. With a fresh glass of water in hand, I sit down to dictate and put the post op orders in, my aching feet welcoming the rest.

Once finished, I call the surgery lounge and ask to have my patient's family placed in one of the consult rooms. I finish my third glass of water and head toward consult room three, where the family should be waiting. I update the husband and daughter letting them know that the surgery went well, answer their questions and direct them back to the family lounge. I check my phone and am surprised that Abby hasn't texted me yet. Curious, I head back to the OR. I'm happy to see that the patient is on the hospital bed, waiting to be extubated.

"Everything ok?"

"Just waiting for her to wake up a little more," the CRNA informs me. I peek at her vitals and check her drain output just to be certain we didn't miss a bleeder. Everything looks good.

"Great. I'm going to take care of a few more things. I'll be ready to leave when you two are." I leave the room and head towards the main surgery desk. I hear the commotion just before I'm nearly run over by the staff wheeling the gurney down the hall. The brief glimpse of the patient is enough for me to know that it isn't good. Dr. Andrews, the trauma surgeon, is right behind the patient. At the desk I see Dr. Hastings talking with a distraught woman, she looks familiar. My mind quickly flashes to the bloody face of the patient and finally connects the dots. The trauma patient is a former patient of mine, and the woman Dr. Hastings is speaking with is her partner Katrina. I recently finished treating Jill for reconstructive surgery following her treatment for breast cancer. Over the course of Jill's multiple surgeries and appointments, I had grown quite fond of their bond. They seemed to be one of the few genuinely happy couples I've encountered in my life. They were a couple that could give you hope, hope of finding the same for yourself, even if by the age of 41 you weren't truly sure if you've ever actually been in love. Katrina's eyes lock onto me, and I realize that I've likely been staring.

"Dr. Hudson?" Dr. Hastings heads toward the OR where they have taken Jill. Katrina shakily makes her way towards me.

"Katrina. Is…what…" I have no idea what to say. I almost asked if everything is ok; clearly, it isn't. Asking what happened also seems inappropriate.

"Jill went out for her evening run. They think she was hit by a car. I don't really know much other than she needs brain surgery and she has internal injuries they're operating on." She begins sobbing, so I do the only thing I can think to, what I feel is expected, I pull her in for a hug. The few people who pass by the desk look questioningly at us. I need to direct Katrina out of the area and back to the lounge, yet part of me wants to give her some privacy. I know from my time with them that aside from their friends they are largely alone. I know Jill's parents passed away in an auto accident when she was a child, and she was raised by her godmother. My phone chirps causing Katrina to pull away from me.

"I'm sorry, you're probably busy. I shouldn't keep you." She futilely swipes at the tears streaming down her cheeks.

"Not at all. I just finished up for the day." I move behind the desk and retrieve a couple of fresh tissues for Katrina. "Let me walk you back to the lounge, or I could put you in one of the consult rooms and let the volunteers know where you are."

"The lounge is fine; I don't need any special treatment." I guide Katrina in the direction of the family lounge, wondering what support I can offer her.

7

"Can I call anyone for you?" On the way to the lounge, we pass the women's locker room, where Abby and Alex are waiting for me outside the door. I subtly motion for them to give me a few minutes.

"No, there isn't anyone to call. Her parents are gone." We get to the lounge, and I direct her to check in at the desk. Check in complete, she takes a seat, and I get her a few more fresh tissues and a glass of water. I can't leave her alone to deal with this. I'm not a neurosurgeon, but even I know that things did not appear favorable.

"I can sit with you, unless you'd rather be alone." Katrina forces a quarter smile, I know it must require a great deal of effort on her part.

"That would be nice, but please don't feel obligated to." Her voice is a subtle whisper that seems to be pleading for me to stay.

"I'll stay. I need to take care of something though; it will only take a few minutes. If you're ok, I'll be right back." Katrina nods that she'll be fine. I head towards the locker room and find Abby and Alex still waiting for me.

"Was that Katrina? Is everything ok?" Abby remembers her as well. Not surprising since Abby seems to remember all of our patients.

"It was. Jill's been in an accident. I'm going to stay here with Katrina. She shouldn't be alone." I find my wallet and pull out some cash to give to Abby and Alex. "This should cover tonight. Go have some fun, you've earned it." Neither of them move to take the money, and they both try to protest over one another. "Stop. You routinely bust your backs for the surgeons in this place. Let one of us do something nice for you. Go someplace nice on me, please." Abby finally gives in; she knows that arguing would be useless.

I rejoin Katrina in the lounge and sit next to her in silence. I have no idea what to say. I struggle in social interactions with people I don't know very well.

"Thank you for waiting with me." She utters it in a hushed, steady voice.

"Sorry I'm not very good company." Katrina lets out a quiet laugh when I say this. "What? I'm not good at small talk, not that this seems the appropriate time for it."

"Nothing, just that I should probably be the one apologizing for being poor company."

"Shall we agree that neither of us is very good company at the moment, no apologies necessary?"

"Sounds fair. So Dr. Hudson, what shall we talk about?"

"Please call me Sara." Katrina nods but says nothing. "Why don't you pick the topic?" I will defer this all night, knowing I'm not the best at starting conversations. I'm perfectly content sitting quietly, losing myself in my thoughts.

"Alright Sara, since we don't know each other very well, why don't we focus on that. I'll ask you a question, which we both have to answer. Then you can ask me something. Fairly easy and hopefully it will keep me distracted to some degree."

Katrina's idea sounds as good as any. "You go first then."

"Alright. Favorite movie."

"I can only pick one?" Katrina gives me a look, I'm sure she's trying to convey a degree of annoyance, but the look is comical, and I can't help but giggle.

"You aren't going to make this easy, are you? I suppose I'll allow you to pick a series."

"Still impossible. I enjoy movies, but it depends on my mood. *Star Wars* and *The Godfather* are classics of course. I enjoy Tarantino's films as well."

"You aren't going to pick are you?" This time Katrina smiles a little, a sharp contrast to the worry evident in her eyes.

"Impossible for me to pick one. You can pick a single movie out of all the movies in existence?" I'm skeptical, with all of the options out there how can anyone identify a single one as better than the rest?

"*The Rocky Horror Picture Show.*"

"Seriously?"

"Yeah. You don't like it?"

"I do. When I was in undergrad, we used to go to the live shows as often as we could. The participation was always so much fun."

"Which is why it's my favorite. Plus I met Jill at a live show." Katrina goes quiet, fresh tears threatening to spill from her eyes as she loses herself in her thoughts. One question into our chat and I've already failed to distract her. I stay silent and focus on the basketball game on the TV. After a few minutes, Katrina finally breaks the silence. "Your turn."

"Are you sure you want to continue?" Katrina nods that she does. "Ok. What do you do for a living?" I'm certain that Abby knows the answer to this question, she always gets to know our patients better than I do.

"I'm co-owner of an accounting firm. It isn't as exciting as your career, but I get to work from home most of the time. I also have the freedom to chose how much I'm going to work at any given time."

"How so?"

"Well tax time is obviously my busiest time of year. The rest of the year I have the ability to delegate most of the work. If I ever feel like I need to work more, I do. I enjoy the freedom."

"The freedom does sound nice. Do you enjoy the work?"

"As I said, it isn't exciting by any means, but yes I enjoy it for the most part. Starting the business was trying, that's for sure. I don't miss those days. Now we're well established, and I have people to do the day to day stuff for me." Katrina answers in an autopilot fashion, her eyes focused off into space, making it clear her thoughts are elsewhere. I know I can't change that, but at least I can try to help her feel less alone right now. "What about you, do you enjoy your work?"

"I do. It has meaning for me. I like that I'm able to help women regain a sense of self or a small amount of self-confidence after their mastectomies. For some women, it means a great deal. I don't think it's as exciting as you believe it is though. If I have an exciting day, things have probably gone very wrong."

"What made you go into plastic surgery?"

"My mother was diagnosed with breast cancer when I was eight. She had neglected her own healthcare and it was too late by the time the diagnosis came back. She was gone just after my 10th birthday. Oncology never held my interest, but I enjoy helping the women who elect to have reconstructive surgery. I also perform a few other procedures, but I enjoy the reconstructions the most."

"I'm so sorry about your mother. I didn't know." Katrina looks at the floor, clearly uncomfortable with where the conversation led.

"It's ok. There's no way you could have known. It was 31 years ago. I've made peace with it. I try to honor her memory with my work. I hope she would be proud of me."

"I'm certain she would be. I know Jill felt more like herself after her reconstruction was finished. She felt like she had lost a vital part of her gender identity, you gave that back to her." The silence between us returns. It isn't uncomfortable by any means. I can only imagine what is going through Katrina's mind at the moment. I try to remember what it was like going through everything with my mom. The years combined with my age at the time have made the events fuzzy at best.

"Favorite book?" Katrina's question pulls me out of my struggle to remember.

"Which genre? I enjoy reading a bit of everything."

"I'm starting to think that variety is the spice of life is your personal motto."

"I have a lot of interests. I have favorite authors like Katherine V. Forrest and Harper Bliss, but what I read depends on my mood." I look at Katrina as I wait for her to protest my refusal to name one book, but all I see is confusion set in.

"I apologize if I'm being too forward, but are you gay?" I can't help but laugh. I've been out for so long that I don't ever think about it anymore. It's a fact that I forget isn't obvious or known to everyone. I've never made it a point to keep my sexuality hidden; I simply cannot care less what people think about my private life, so I forget that there are people who don't know.

"I am."

"Wow, didn't see that coming. Huh. Normally my gaydar is pretty accurate."

"Sorry?" I'm not sure what response she is looking for.

"I should apologize, I'm not exactly being graceful." Katrina shakes her head slightly.

"No need. I don't think I fit the typical stereotype and I don't broadcast it. I don't even think about it if I'm being honest. At this point it is just a fact about me, similar to how I have green eyes and brown hair. You haven't offended me."

"Well, I'm glad I haven't offended you. You don't go out much, do you? I mean we've never seen you at Velvet or anywhere else." I've been to Velvet before; I'm just not a regular there.

"No, I don't go out much. On evenings that I operate, I can end up being here quite late. On clinic days, I'm often so busy that I don't have a minute to myself from the second I get to the office until I leave in the evening. If I'm honest, I have too much available business for the time that I have to work in. But these women all come to me looking for help, I can't turn them away. So I make the time."

"It's admirable that you're dedicated, but your work can't be the only thing that defines you." I've heard this time and again from women I've tried to date. I work too much. I know that I do. I always promise that I will limit my case load once we find a new partner to share the reconstruction cases, we just haven't finished the search yet.

"I promise you, it isn't. I just prefer activities that I find to have more meaning. So I work out, volunteer, relax at the movies, —." The phone rings, interrupting my spiel, the lines I constantly tell myself to justify the sad state of my personal life. I know that I allow my social awkwardness to govern a lot of what I do. I become highly uncomfortable in large crowds, especially if I don't know most of the people around me. I also have a tendency to prefer to stay home once I get there. I'm aware that I've grown increasingly disconnected from the community as I've poured more and more of myself into my work. I seldom date anymore and truthfully, have pretty much given up on the idea that I will ever find myself in a real, stable relationship again.

"Should we answer that? We're the only people here." I look around and realize she is correct. It's well after 9, and the volunteers have left for the day.

"Yeah, we should. It's likely for you anyway."
Katrina makes her way to the phone and answers it. I'm
unable to hear her end of the conversation, so I refocus on
the basketball game. It's a blowout, but better to focus on
that than where our conversation left off. It isn't long
before Katrina is making her way back to our seats.

"Just the nurse letting me know that they're still
working. She said she will call in an hour if they're still
going, before if one of the doctors is ready to speak to me."
I nod that I understand. Katrina sits lost in thought for a
few moments. "You know when Jill was having her
mastectomy and reconstruction surgeries, those phone
calls were nice. They almost feel cruel now. I hate the not
knowing. The nurse didn't tell me anything, didn't give me
any details. It's driving me insane." Katrina's anguish is
written plainly on her face.

"I'm sorry. I can't begin to imagine. If they're still
working, maybe that's a good thing." Katrina doesn't
respond, so I allow her to contemplate her own thoughts.
The first game of the night has finally ended and it looks as
though tip off is mere minutes away on the second of the
triple header.

"When you left earlier, did you check on her?"
Katrina is eyeing me; as if her near silver eyes can discern
the truth by seeing my thoughts.

"No." Honestly I could have and did think about
doing so for a minute, but I would have only been in the
way or an unnecessary distraction. I already knew enough
from seeing Jill on the gurney earlier. The outcome isn't
likely to be favorable.

"You didn't?" I can't tell if Katrina doesn't believe
me or if she simply refuses to believe that I do not have the
answers she's seeking.

"I went back to the locker room. I don't know if you noticed, but Abby and another woman were waiting outside of one of the doors we passed on the way here. I was going to take them out for dinner and drinks tonight, to thank them for all of their hard work. I went back to let them know I was going to stay here and to give them some money to cover their evening. I came straight back here afterward." I see the resignation set in, her acceptance that I don't have any information for her, causing her shoulders to sag.

"I'm sorry, I didn't mean to put you on the spot, I'm just terrified. I know that Dr. Andrews said she has a ruptured spleen that has to be removed and that they needed to check her for other internal injuries. Dr. Hastings seemed very concerned about her head trauma. I don't know what I'm going to do if…" Katrina begins to sob anew as the possible outcomes play through her head. Unsure of how to best comfort her, I place my hand on her shoulder. In less than a second she is sobbing on my shoulder again. The second game tips off as Katrina works to collect herself.

"I'm sorry, I think I've ruined your lab coat." I look at my shoulder and take in the black stain her mascara has left. I look up to find her watching me, so I shrug.

"No biggie, I have others if it doesn't wash out." Katrina refocuses her attention on the game, so I do the same, giving her the space I feel like she may need. The reality of my long day and the late hour hit me as I feel exhaustion start to kick in. I try to hide the yawn, but fail miserably. Katrina's attention is pulled back to me and I give her a small smile.

"You should go home. I'm sure you've had a long day. You aren't obligated to stay with me."

"I know I'm not obligated, but no one should be alone at a time like this. I'm going to run upstairs to the coffee shop. Can I get you anything?" I know it could be quite a while before Katrina has any news. I also know that it isn't likely to be good news and don't want her to be alone for that either.

"I don't think I have any cash, hold on."

"Don't worry about it." My words don't stop Katrina from searching her small purse.

"I'm good, thanks though." I frown slightly and make my way upstairs to the Biggby coffee shop in the lobby.

The chipper barista greets me and I can't help but wonder if she is naturally that lively or if she's simply over caffeinated. I order a Caramel Marvel and a White Lightening, hoping that Katrina will like one of the two. Lattes in hand, I head back downstairs to the lounge. I arrive to find Katrina pacing around the perimeter of the lounge, her head down, her shoulders visibly tense. I hang back, allowing her space, despite the uncomfortable heat from the cups searing into my palms. In my haste to get back, I foolishly neglected to grab a pair of cup sleeves. Her route eventually brings her close to the entrance and she stops in her tracks when she sees me, eyeing the cups I carry. "Caramel Marvel or White Lightening?" Katrina smiles and shakes her head.

"Honestly, you didn't have to. Either one is great though." I look down at the cups and realize my second mistake, I didn't bother paying attention when I put the lids on.

"I honestly have no idea which one is which. Right hand or left hand?"

Katrina laughs. "I'll take the left hand then. Thanks." She takes the offered latte and risks a small sip. "Mmm. White Lightening. I love white chocolate."

"Me too." I smile, secretly relieved because I was hoping I could keep the Caramel Marvel. We reclaim our seats and refocus on the game, another boring blowout. "Are you particularly attached to this game?"

"Not at all. Can we change it to something else?" Happy to hear her agreement with my unspoken sentiment, I make my way around the volunteer desk and locate the remote. I hand the remote to Katrina, putting the burden of making the choice on her. I'm thrilled when she stops on *The Empire Strikes* back. "Look, you love these movies."

"You don't?"

"I do, I never get to watch them though because Jill isn't a fan." She turns the volume up a little and takes another sip of her latte. "So, next travel destination?" I inadvertently snort while attempting to hold back my laughter. Katrina starts to laugh as I burry my face in my hands, my cheeks burning with embarrassment. "What was that?"

"Just me being me. I was actually trying not to let my own laughter at the thought of a vacation become audible."

"Why is thinking about a vacation funny?"

"I haven't taken an actual vacation in at least a decade. I've traveled for conferences and I go on a mission trip every year, but not a real vacation." Katrina is still eyeing me, disbelief written all over her face.

"Why?" I let out an audible sigh but don't answer. I work too much, I know. Other people fail to understand the work I do, how busy it keeps me, and how much I hate to let people down. "Wow, you're a workaholic aren't you?" Katrina asks when I fail to answer.

"Yeah, I guess I am. I just have a hard time setting a luxury like a vacation as a higher priority than helping someone dealing with the lingering effects of breast cancer. I would love to travel to Iceland and to see Rome. Iceland first though, I hear it's beautiful."

"It is. I'd love to go back sometime. I think it's great that you're so dedicated to your work, but you really need to allow yourself some downtime. You're going to be burnt out by the time you are 50." I can tell Katrina's words are sincere.

"I know. Someday soon." I've been telling myself this for the past three years. Abby has been saying it even longer. I promise myself that I'll put more pressure on my partners to get the search for another surgeon taken care of sooner than later. I take another sip of my latte and inadvertently inhale it as the ringing of the phone startles me. I become torn between answering the phone and my struggle to free my windpipe of the hot liquid. Still coughing, I wave my hand towards the phone letting Katrina know I will be alright. The call is brief and I have only just regained the ability to breath normally when Katrina returns and stands in front of me.

"Are you alright?" She examines my features, checking to see if I'm still choking.

"Yeah, just inhaled instead of swallowed." Katrina is fidgety as she stands before me.

"Can you show me to consult room two, please? That was the nurse calling to let me know Dr. Andrews will be out in a few minutes." She is becoming increasingly nervous as the seconds tick by.

"Sure, follow me." Katrina falls in behind me as I exit the lounge, turn right and then make a quick left. "This is consult two. I will be in the lounge when you're done. Can you make it back there?" Katrina looks at the floor and then back at me, her frazzled nerves causing fresh tears to form.

"Actually, would you mind staying in here with me? I know this isn't your specialty, but you've had training. Maybe you'll think of a question that I should ask or can just act as a backup memory for me."

"Of course." I hear the airflow regulator kick on as the doors leading into the surgery department open. I know Andrews will be here in seconds.

A short tap on the doorframe announces his arrival. "Ms. Beaumont?" Andrews shakes her hand and eyes me. I nod my head slightly acknowledging his silent greeting. He closes the door and takes the seat across from Katrina. Her nervousness reverberates off of the four corners of the room as Katrina clutches my hand, crushing my fingers in her palm. I place my free left hand over the top of hers and pat it a few times, hoping she will realize what she is doing. She eases her grip, but doesn't release her hold entirely. She never takes her eyes off of Andrews as she waits for him to start cluing her in on what's happening.

"A few things to talk about. Ms. Gilbert's spleen was ruptured as we suspected, so we had to remove it.

She can live her life without it, but the spleen plays a large role in maintaining the immune system, so she will likely be more susceptible to certain types of infections. She also had a few liver lacerations that we were able to repair. Her kidneys are fine as well as all of her other abdominal organs. We will have to leave the chest tubes in until the fluid around her lungs clears. She also has a broken femur that I'm placing an orthopedics consultation for. Dr. Hastings is still working and will be out to speak with you when he is finished. Do you have any questions that I can answer for you?" Katrina sits in silence as she processes everything Andrews has told her. I always thought he is a down to earth kind of guy, and I can appreciate how he communicated the circumstances in as plain of language as he could. When Katrina doesn't speak he looks at me. I don't have any questions so I gently squeeze Katrina's hand hoping to get her attention.

"Will she live? Can she recover?"

"From the injuries I have discussed with you, yes. I didn't have an opportunity to speak with Dr. Hastings, so he will have to fill you in on his findings. When he's done we will send Ms. Gilbert for another CT scan before moving her upstairs to intensive care. She will have a room assigned to her by the time she leaves the OR for her scan. You'll be able to wait for her there after speaking with Dr. Hastings." Andrews pauses for a few moments, giving Katrina time to soak up the new information. His eyes shift back and forth between us, my gut telling me there is something else.

"What is it, Dr. Andrews?" For someone so lost in her thoughts, Katrina is still incredibly observant. He continues to eye both of us before finally settling his attention on me.

21

"Dr. Hudson, I was planning on consulting you."
Now it's Katrina's turn to watch the two of us as I try to
silently determine if the consult has to do with Jill.

"If it has to do with Jill can you please just do it
here?" Whether she's tired of the silent conversation
between Andrews and me, or simply tired of being in the
dark, Katrina is not about to be left out of the conversation.
I nod my consent to Andrews, permitting him to continue.

"Well, it looks as though her left implant has
ruptured. I know that you're not on call, but the nurse
checked the record and saw that you were the care
provider, so my plan was to contact you." I knew that this
was a possibility and had hoped that on top of all her other
injuries that Jill would not have to deal with this as well.

"Thank you for letting me know. I will take care of
it."

"Thank you. Any other questions I can answer for
you Ms. Beaumont?" Katrina shakes her head no as she
keeps her gaze focused on me. I instinctively know she
has many questions for me. Andrews takes his leave,
closing the door behind himself. I stop Katrina before she
can ask anything.

"Everything with the implant situation will be fine. If
we used a saline implant, her body will absorb it without
causing any harm. If it was a silicone implant, her capsule
should hold the leakage. If it doesn't, the new silicone is
more cohesive, meaning she will be fine for the time being.
Since Andrews picked up on it, I'm guessing the shape has
changed enough that it's noticeable. Let's go back to the
lounge and wait for the call from Dr. Hastings. I'll log into
Jill's chart and look up what implants we used. Either way,
I will eventually have to operate to remove and replace the
implant. This isn't life threatening and can wait for another

day." Katrina squeezes my hand and releases the breath she seems to have been holding. "You holding up ok? Any questions?"

"I'm ok. She's going through so much. All I can do is sit here, powerless."

I squeeze her hand and feel my lips form a slight frown. "Just try to stay positive. Dr. Andrews did say she should be able to make a full recovery from her abdominal injuries. The broken femur can be repaired, as can the ruptured implant." Katrina nods her head. "Ok, let's head back to the lounge where I can log in and check her implants."

"They were saline." The conviction in Katrina's voice is convincing, but I still have to check. I look back at her and nod. "She preferred the feel of the silicone implants but was paranoid about a potential leak, so she chose the saline ones." I know Katrina is right, her words have jogged my memory. Either way, I still have to check.

Katrina paces the lounge as I log in at the computer behind the desk and check Jill's chart. Katrina's memory is solid; Jill opted for the saline implants. Curiosity gets the better of me, and I check the status board to see if Hastings is still operating. The in room time shows two minutes, meaning he finished closing two minutes ago. I feel my stomach turn in anticipation of the phone ringing, and the news the conversation with Hastings will bring. Fifteen minutes later the phone rings. Katrina, who is still pacing the lounge, rushes over to answer it.

"Back to consult two, then she will be in neuro ICU 7."

"Would you like me to come with you or wait here?"

"With me please, I don't have a good feeling about this." *Neither do I;* I think to myself as I follow Katrina out the door. About five minutes later Dr. Hastings is knocking on the door. It takes all of my will power not to shake my head at him as I immediately notice the blood staining his shoe covers and his scrubs from the knees down. I silently hope to myself that Katrina doesn't notice. Hastings takes a seat without closing the door. I realize that it's the middle of the night, that the OR is a ghost town, but his lack of consideration for Katrina's privacy irks me.

"Ok. The findings from the CT that I discussed with you earlier were pretty accurate. Her hemorrhaging was significant. I had to do a left frontal lobectomy and leave her bone flap off to accommodate brain swelling. She has a pair of drains in, and we will evaluate their output and remove them when her drainage decreases to a minimal level. She's going up for a CT scan now and then will be heading upstairs. Did the nurse give you her room number?" I've heard rumors about Hasting's poor bedside manner, but he has set my blood boiling. It takes every ounce of restraint I have not to snap at him. One look at Katrina tells me she doesn't understand half of what he just told her.

"Lobectomy?" Her voice is barely above a whisper.

"Yes. We had to remove her left frontal lobe. It was damaged by the bone fragments and bleeding heavily. Removing it also allows the rest of her brain more space to swell." His answer is so flippant and unenlightening that my anger starts to boil over. Horror quickly spreads over Katrina's face.

"You cut out part of her brain?"

"I had no choice. It was the left frontal lobe. Controls a lot of elements involved in personality. It's likely that if she recovers there may be parts of her behavior you won't recognize."

"I don't understand." Katrina looks at me for help.

"Ok. Right now it's a waiting game. Her brain needs time to recover before we have a clear picture of how much of a recovery you can hope for. Let's just take it a day at a time and cross bridges as we get to them."

"Ok, I guess." I physically have to bite my tongue. I can feel the coppery tasting blood as it connects with my taste buds. As soon as he's gone, I plan to call Catherine and beg for a favor. Ethically it's wrong on several levels, but Katrina deserves some clarity, and I cannot offer her much on this subject. Hastings leaves, and I close the door a little too forcefully behind him. I sit back down next to a visibly shaken Katrina who immediately latches onto me and starts sobbing on my shoulder. I comfort her as best I can until she finally calms down a measure. "I don't understand what's happening. I can't take it."

"I know. I'm going to try to call in a favor. One of my close friends is another one of the neurosurgeons here. I'm going to see if she can take a look at Jill's chart, Hasting's op notes, and the scans and talk to you. Ok?" Katrina nods her agreement as she pulls a fresh tissue from the box and dabs at her eyes. "I'm going to step outside to make the call. I'll be right back."

I pull out my phone as I step into consult room one and close the door. I select Catherine's name from my contacts list and listen as the ringing stops on the fourth ring, intercepted by voice mail. It's after midnight. I know that the three of them have long since called it a night. I redial Catherine's number, determined to make her answer. Again her voice mail takes the call. This time I leave a message telling her I need her to call me as soon as possible. Not wanting to leave it at that, I redial her number a third time. A breathless Catherine answers on the third ring. I immediately know I've interrupted her quality time with Alex.

"Sara?"

"Sorry to interrupt, but I need a favor." I briefly explain the situation to Catherine and ask if she can come in.

"That man is an ass, a good surgeon, but an ass. Hold on just a second." I can hear the noise as Catherine attempts to cover the microphone. I hear Alex groan in the background and ask if everything is ok. The sound of the microphone being uncovered comes through again. "I'll be there in half an hour."

"Thank you. I'm going to owe you one." A modicum of relief surges through me as I disconnect the call and exit consult one to rejoin Katrina.

True to her word, Catherine is in the lounge 25 minutes later. As she pulls me in for a welcoming hug she whispers, "Sorry, had to freshen up." I chuckle softly as we pull away from one another.

"I figured I interrupted. Sorry again." Catherine shifts her glance to Katrina and then to me. I nod to confirm that's who I need her to speak with. Without missing a beat, Catherine makes her way over to Katrina.

"Hello. I'm Dr. Waters." Catherine extends her hand and shakes Katrina's. "May I sit for a moment?" Katrina nods, and Catherine takes the seat on her right. "Sara has briefly explained the situation to me. I'm sorry Dr. Hastings was so unclear. If you'd like, I can take a look at Jill's chart, her scans, and any notes to try to clear some things up for you."

"Would you please?" Katrina's voice is a whispered plea, her demeanor that of a broken woman.

"Absolutely. Give me a few minutes to see what I can learn, then we can talk." Catherine rises from the chair and heads to the computer behind the desk.

"Your close friend?" Katrina eyes me; I know what she is thinking. I can't help but laugh a little.

"Not that close. Catherine is madly in love with her partner." I glance in her direction and see the small grin play over Catherine's lips.

A few minutes later Catherine calls over the counter, "Katrina, would you come here please?" I join them to find that Catherine has Jill's first CT scan pulled up. "This is the CT that they took when Jill was brought in." Catherine manipulates the mouse over the scan and begins circling it around an area of the skull. "If you look here you can see part of the skull over the left frontal lobe had been shattered." Catherine scrolls down a few images and stops, circling the same area on a new image. "Some of those bone fragments were displaced into Jill's left frontal lobe. They would have damaged the tissue and likely caused a great deal of bleeding. The common course of action would be to perform a lobectomy, or to remove a portion of the brain. Your frontal lobe controls a lot of emotions, memories, motor functions, impulse control and a variety of other things. While you do have two frontal lobes, damage to one can lead to changes in a person's typical behavior. We really have no way of predicting the extent to which these changes will occur. Questions so far?"

"Not yet, thank you."

Catherine switches to a slightly deeper view, this time of the brain's surface. "If you look here, this is the midline of the brain. Ideally, you would see this align down the middle of the skull. As you can see, Jill has what we call a midline shift of 9 millimeters. This shift indicates how much pressure is on the brain. The higher the pressure, the greater the need for surgical intervention. With a midline shift of 9 millimeters, Jill would have absolutely needed a craniectomy to attempt to alleviate some of that pressure." Catherine scans further, the damaged brain tissue of the frontal lobe is easy to identify. "This is the brain tissue that would have been below the point of impact. As you can see it is bright white, which indicates that it's severely damaged. I'm unsure how familiar you are with anatomy, but Jill's ventricles aren't visible due to the large shift and the high pressure." Catherine switches the scan to bring up Jill's post-op images. "These images were taken after surgery. If you look at this scan, you can see that Dr. Hastings was able to remove a majority of the damaged brain tissue. It isn't necessary to remove it, but with the bone fragments involved, I'm going to guess he had to in order to establish some level of control over blood loss. You can also see that the midline shift is still at 6 millimeters, which is still higher than we would like it to be. However, you can begin to see her right ventricle again, which is a positive." Catherine shifts the view from deep to superficial and stops on what looks like half a skull. "This image shows what bone structure was removed and frozen. As you can see a majority of the frontal bone, as well as the anterior two-thirds of the parietal bone, are gone. Given the severity of the shift and the location of the injury, I would have done the same thing. When you see Jill, she is going to have a great deal of bandaging around her head as well as something indicating that she is missing a bone flap." Catherine turns to Katrina and looks at her.

"Please just tell me," Katrina whispers her plea.

"There is no way to predict outcomes correctly 100% of the time. Jill's Glasgow Coma Scale rating was a 3. That is admittedly low. If a patient can score an 8 or above, they have a very strong likelihood of making a full recovery. I've seen people make full recoveries from GCS 6. I've also seen people with GCS 6 not recover. I've seen patients make partial recoveries from a GCS 3 score before." Catherine's words hit Katrina hard.

"So you're saying?" Catherine exhales slowly. I know she is trying to break the terrible news as gently as she can.

"In my professional opinion?" Katrina nods. "I would advise you to be cautiously optimistic. Honestly, it isn't an exact science. The human body tricks us all the time. You can see a healthy 40 year old who exercises every day suddenly die from a heart attack or an aneurysm. Likewise, there have been instances where individuals smoke a pack of cigarettes a day and drink heavily and live into their 90's. This is no different. A GCS 3 is low, but I've seen partial recoveries from it. Should you hope for a full recovery? Absolutely. I would caution you though to be prepared for less, much less, unfortunately. Sadly this is something that's just going to require time." Catherine pauses to give Katrina a moment to process. She looks up at me and shakes her head slowly. I know then that there is little to no hope for Jill making any type of recovery. "Can I answer any questions for you?"

"Can I see her? Am I allowed to see her?"

"Of course. Come, Sara and I will walk you up there."

A few minutes later Katrina, Catherine and I stand in neuro ICU 7 around Jill's bed. Visitors are limited to two in the ICU but given I'm still in my work attire and Catherine's presence is familiar on this floor, so no one objects. As we stand there watching Katrina holding Jill's hand and crying, I see Catherine grow visibly uncomfortable.

"Still difficult to think about?" I put my hand on Catherine's shoulder as I mutter the question under my breath.

"Even after all this time. It reminds me of when it was Alex. How scared I was that I lost her. Maybe that's part of the reason our bond is so strong. I know how it feels to almost lose her. I don't ever want to let anything go unsaid or undone." Catherine shakes her head slightly; like the movement will clear away her emotional cobwebs.

"Understandable. Katrina, would you like to ask Dr. Waters anything else?"

"No. Thank you very much for taking the time to help me understand. I'm sure Sara pulled you out of bed just to come here." Catherine manages to stifle the grin that threatens to spread across her face, but not the gleam in her eye as she remembers whatever she and Alex were doing when I interrupted.

"No problem. Would it be alright if I check in with you tomorrow?"

"Yes."

"Do you need anything before I go?"

"No, I think I just want to be alone with Jill for a while, if that's alright." I nod my head that it is and write my phone number down for her.

"Call me if you need anything, no matter the time." Katrina nods that she will. Catherine and I take that as our cue and make our exit. "Thanks again. I really do owe you one."

"What are friends for? No bill for this one," she tells me as she throws me a quick wink.

"She won't recover will she?" I press the button for the elevator, the doors opening immediately.

"It's highly unlikely. Right now she isn't even breathing on her own. That would be the first step. Never say never though, I guess. Are you ok to drive?"

"I'm fine. I just feel bad for Jill and Katrina."

"I don't think I've met them. How do you know them?"

"Jill was a patient." I shake my head, unable to believe how one person can go through so much in the span of a few short years.

"Are you close to them?"

"Not super close, but I work with my patients for quite a while. You get to know them." Catherine nods her understanding.

"I'm going home to wrap my arms around Alex extra tight. If you need anything or if she has any more questions, I'm only a phone call away."

"Or three." We both laugh as we get into our cars. I switch on the heat against the mid-February chill and wave to Catherine as she pulls out of her parking space.

Chapter 2

I wake up just after 5 am, despite getting to bed much later than I'm accustomed to. I guess some habits are not so easily broken. I try to go back to sleep, but give up after 15 minutes, figuring that I'll be able to get to bed early tonight. The sound of sleet steadily tapping against the window makes it clear that I won't be running outside this morning. I check my phone as I head downstairs to the gym I've set up in the basement. No messages from Catherine or Katrina wait for me, and I leave the rest to deal with later. I switch on Netflix and hop on the rowing machine to warm up my core. 15 minutes on the rowing machine, 15 minutes on the treadmill and then arms and shoulders with the free weights. I make it through two episodes of *Grace and Frankie* in the time it takes to complete my routine.

Sweaty and high on endorphins, I push my burning muscles up the stairs and head toward the kitchen to see what I can throw together for breakfast. I put together a grocery list and clean up my mess while I eat, my habit of being as efficient as possible ruling my actions, even on a day off.

My phone rings as I'm pushing the cart to my car. "Morning Abby."

"Good morning. I just wanted to get an update on Jill and Katrina." I take a deep breath and exhale before giving Abby a quick summary of the situation. "That doesn't sound good."

"Catherine said she very likely won't recover, and if she makes any recovery at all, it won't be a full one."

"When did Catherine get involved?"

"I called her last night and asked for a favor. Hastings's bedside skills are unimpressive, and Katrina had questions. Catherine was kind enough to come in."

"I can't believe you got her to answer the phone," Abby manages through her peel of laughter.

It's my turn to laugh now. "Only took three back to back calls." Abby laughs again. "I'm going to go up there in a little bit to see how Katrina is holding up. I need to take care of my groceries but can meet you outside of the Biggby in the lobby in about half an hour."

"Sounds like a plan. I'll see you then."

"See you then." I disconnect the call. Abby learned a long time ago that I never end calls with the typical good bye. Good bye just seems too final, so I don't use it.

Half an hour later I've put in an order at the coffee shop and am waiting for the lattes and Abby's Chai tea. I see Abby coming towards me as the barista places the three drinks in a carrier for me. Unlike last night, the cups are labeled with their contents. As Abby draws near, I extract her tea from the carrier and greet her with it.

"Thank you! What a dreary day." She takes a tentative sip of her tea. "This is perfect."

"Shall we?" Abby tilts her head towards the elevator as she takes another sip of her tea. We board the elevator and head upstairs to the ICU. "Did you guys have a good time last night?"

"We did, thanks again. Catherine insists we try again when you can make it."

"Absolutely." The ding of the elevator alerts us to the fact that we have arrived at our destination. We knock to announce ourselves and wait to be told to come in. Katrina looks back at us as we enter, her eyes puffy and red.

"Sara, Abby. Thank you for coming." Abby, always a hugger, pulls Katrina into her arms. I see Katrina struggle to keep it together as Abby offers her the typical platitudes and comforts you hear in these situations. Katrina gives me a small smile as she pulls away from Abby. I move towards her and extend the drink carrier, allowing her to take her pick. "I'm going to owe you a franchise at this rate." She takes the carrier from my hand and sets our drinks on the small tray table found in every patient room. She pulls me in for a hug and surprises me as she continues to fight off her emotions.

"You won't owe me anything. Do you need anything else?" I whisper to her. Abby gives me a small smile of approval before turning to make her own assessment of Jill.

"No, thank you. Thanks for coming back."

"Of course. You could have asked me to come back at any point, and I would have. You don't have to face this alone."

"Thanks. I plan to let our friends know what happened later today. I'm just not ready for the inevitable traffic and the questions that will come along with it. I'm not ready to explain this time and again."

"So don't. Take the time you need. Ask for some privacy. The only people you need to be strong for right now are yourself and Jill. Abby and I can leave if you'd like. We just wanted to check in." Katrina pulls away from me and looks me in the eye.

"No, you can stay. I wasn't throwing you out. I don't know, it feels easier with you. You know the situation, I don't have to explain it to you, try to answer your questions, or deal with your emotions instead of worrying about mine." Katrina looks back and forth between us before settling her gaze back on Jill. "Does that sound terrible?"

"Not at all. Why don't you sit back down? Did you sleep at all after I left?"

"Not really. I might have dozed for a few minutes here and there, but if I got an hour, I'd be surprised." I figured as much. I pick up her latte and hand it to her. She accepts the offered cup and takes a sip. Abby and Katrina start to talk a little, and it becomes clear to me how much closer Abby allows herself to get to our patients than I do. I enjoy my latte as I silently watch their interaction, not hearing a single word they are saying. A slight pang of jealousy hits me as I wish that I possessed the social ease that Abby does. I've never seen her struggle when conversing with a stranger, nor does her self-confidence ever seem to waiver. Suddenly I realize that Abby is staring at me. Katrina turns to look at me seconds later. I have no idea how long I've been lost in watching them, criticizing my own inability to be more like Abby. I gauge the fullness of the cup in my hand; as if I could measure time by how much of the rejuvenating beverage I've consumed. My cup is almost empty, and Abby and Katrina continue to stare at me.

"Sorry, I zoned out." Abby simply shakes her head, a knowing grin plastered on her lips.

"Typical. I have to get going so I can get to the shelter for my volunteer shift. Are you leaving with me?" Am I? I have no idea if I should leave or if Katrina would rather I sat with her for a while. I look at Katrina, searching for an answer. Her eyes quickly shift to the vacant chair and then back to me.

"I'll probably stay a little longer." A little of the tension eases out of Katrina's shoulders when she hears my answer.

"Ok." Abby gives Katrina another hug and writes down her phone number. "Feel free to call me if you need anything."

"I will. Thank you for visiting." Abby says goodbye and makes her way out the door. I take the seat that Katrina indicated moments ago.

"Did you want me to go? I will if that's what you want, I wasn't sure."

"No, please stay." Katrina never takes her eyes off of Jill. We sit there in silence, and I find myself once again tuned out as I stare off into space. The sound of Katrina's chair sliding over the tiled floor pulls me out of my trance. "Do you want to go for a walk? I've been sitting in this chair since we got here last night." I think about this for a second and realize that this means Katrina hasn't eaten.

"Sure. Have you had anything to eat?" Despite my breakfast, I feel my own hunger starting to settle in. Katrina must be famished at this point.

"No, but I'm not really sure how much I can eat." I'm relieved that she's at least open to the idea.

"If you're comfortable going downstairs, we could head down to the cafeteria and get a little lunch?" Katrina shifts her focus from me back to Jill for a few minutes.

"Yeah, we can do that." She squeezes Jill's hand before she releases it and heads toward the door. Our elevator arrives, thankfully empty.

"Has Dr. Waters been in today?" I assume she hasn't since I haven't heard from her.

"No. Is she really going to come back today?"

"She said she would. Catherine is a woman of her word. I think this is all just a little too familiar for her." Katrina furrows her brow as she looks at me. I remember then that she doesn't know Catherine or Alex. "Sorry, long story short is that her partner was involved in an accident a few years ago. While they weren't together at the time, Catherine was the on call neurosurgeon and had to operate. She refused to leave Alex's bedside. I didn't know Catherine that well when all of this happened, but it was easy to see that last night brought back a lot of bad memories for her." I grab a tray as we enter the cafeteria. "Have you been here before?"

"You said her partner. So she lived?"

"She did." I see many emotions cross Katrina's face as she processes all of this. "I can't imagine how she managed to operate on someone she cared about like that."

"Neither can I." I give Katrina a few seconds, but she says nothing more. We take an exploratory lap around the cafe to see what each station is offering today. Not wanting anything too heavy, I order a turkey and cheddar wrap and an order of vegetables with hummus. Katrina

38

orders a club sandwich and a cup of chicken gumbo soup. At least she is willing to try to eat. At the register, I block her from paying.

"I've got this. I get a monthly food allowance." Katrina tries to protest, but I swipe my employee badge before she can. Sale complete, I direct us towards the back corner of the dining area, relieved to find it empty. "Booth or table?"

"Booth please." I settle us into a nearby booth and Katrina slides in across from me. "Big plans for the day?" I'm relieved to see Katrina take a bite of her sandwich.

"Not really. I tend to use Saturday as a catch-up day. So I work out like I always do then I grocery shop, clean, run errands, take care of laundry, finish up my charts from the week. If I'm lucky, I can have everything taken care of and just relax on Sunday. I know, I live a thrill packed life."

"So what do you do for fun? You have to do something to unwind." I can't help but chuckle. I'm certain that Katrina thinks that I work every day of the week.

"Depends. On Thursday evenings I work with a private trainer. I typically have dinner with friends at least once a week. On Sundays we have brunch. In the winter I like to ski, in the warmer temperatures I like to go hiking. I go to the movies and read a lot too. I don't work all the time, but I do run around enough that sometimes it's nice to just stay home on a Sunday, you know, have a pajama day."

"Those are nice for sure." The message alert on my phone interrupts anything else Katrina might have said. I look down to see a message from Catherine.

"Catherine is here. She's going to meet us in a minute," I inform Katrina as I respond to Catherine's message. Katrina stops the spoonful of soup that now loiters half way to her mouth. She thinks twice about it then continues to eat.

"I hadn't realized how hungry I was. Thanks for lunch."

"You're welcome. Sorry, it isn't anything special."

"It's good actually. I'm surprised, given that it's hospital food."

"Yeah, they revamped it all recently." I hear a pair of familiar voices nearing us. Catherine and Alex are here, their arms wrapped around one another as they search the dining room for us. They walk right by us, so absorbed in whatever they are discussing that neither of them notice us sitting here.

"I see what you were talking about last night." Katrina doesn't seem rattled or upset by their affectionate display so far, a small relief given I wasn't sure how she would react.

"They've been through a lot together." I watch them for a second longer before finally deciding to pull them back into the real world. "Hey you two, over here." They take a second to finish whatever discussion they're having before Catherine quickly kisses Alex's forehead and pulls away just enough to direct them towards our table.

"Dr. Waters, thank you for stopping by."

"Please, call me Catherine. This is my partner Alex, Alex this is Katrina." Alex shakes Katrina's hand as they exchange hellos. I slide out of my side of the booth and reseat myself next to Katrina. Catherine and Alex take the unspoken cue and seat themselves opposite us.

"Thank you for checking in."

"Has Dr. Hasting been through today?" Katrina nods her head as she finishes the last of her soup. "What did he have to say?"

"Not much, just that there haven't been any changes." Catherine nods.

"It's early still. How about you, how are you holding up?" Katrina takes a deep breath to steady herself.

"I'm trying. I'll be ok for a while, then the smallest thing will trigger something and I'll lose it. I don't know." Katrina looks down at the table; like she is ashamed of being emotional.

"I understand, I remember it well." Alex reaches up and squeezes Catherine's hand that is resting on top of the table. Catherine allows her to relocate it back onto her lap. "You're doing great, really. Remember, one breath at a time. It's good that you ate something, you probably hadn't realized how much energy you are expending."

"I hadn't. Sara has been great, keeping me company, caffeinated, and fed." Catherine's eyes quickly glance at me before resettling on Katrina.

"Any questions I can try to answer for you?" Catherine gives Katrina time to consider.

"None that I can think of."

"Well, if you think of anything Sara knows how to reach me." Katrina doesn't notice it, but I can clearly see the amusement in Catherine's eyes as she alludes to last night. "Do you need anything?"

"I'm all set thank you. The offer alone means a lot." We sit in silence for a minute or two, they feel like much longer.

"You two have plans today?" Alex and Catherine both look at me, it's Alex who finally answers.

"We're headed to Chicago for the night. Shopping and meeting up with some of Catherine's friends for an evening out. First a late lunch though, we got a later start than we anticipated." Both their cheeks flush, I didn't need that clue to know why they got a late start. Anyone who knows them could guess why.

"Well, safe travels and have a good time."

"I mean it, Katrina. If you have any questions please have Sara contact me. It won't be an inconvenience." Catherine reaches across the table with her free hand and gently squeezes Katrina's forearm.

"Thank you, really. Have a nice time in Chicago."

"Thank you. Should we go, baby?" Alex nods to Catherine, and they extract themselves from the booth. "Sara, call me if anything changes."

"I will, thanks Catherine. Alex, I'll see you next week." With that the pair make their exit, leaving Katrina and I alone once again. "Shall we head back upstairs?" Katrina doesn't answer, so I slide out of the booth and take care of our tray and trash. She finally speaks once we are on the elevator back upstairs..

"That's never going to be Jill and I again, is it?" I don't need clarification, I know what she's asking.

"You don't know that, it's early days still."

"I don't know it, but I feel it all the same. I'm not even honoring her wishes. She never wanted to have machines keeping her alive. I just can't let her go though." Just like that, the subtle nuances between Catherine and Alex have reopened Katrina's floodgates. Tears slip out of her eyes and quickly make their way down her face. There's nothing else I can do so I simply place a supportive hand on her shoulder and allow her to cry.

When we're back in the room, I find myself at a loss for what I should do. Katrina is still upset. I have no idea if she would like me to stay or if I should leave to give her some privacy. She takes her seat at the side of Jill's bed and grasps her hand again. I find myself loitering near the entrance of the room, my feet seemingly glued to the floor, my mind wanting me to act, yet not being able to decide how.

"Do you need to leave?" Katrina has noticed my lingering near the door despite never taking her eyes off of Jill.

"I don't have to leave. I honestly don't know what I should do. Part of me feels like I should leave to give you some privacy. Another part says that I should stay to keep you company and offer support. What would be best for you?"

"I know I'm not great company right now, but selfishly, I don't want to be alone. If you have stuff you need to take care of I understand." Without saying a word I make my way around the bed and take a seat in the chair across from Katrina's. She stares at Jill, absorbed in her thoughts, so I sit silently, pulling out my phone to find a book to read.

"Do you think I'm being selfish?" I'm halfway through the second chapter and already fully engrossed in the story when Katrina interrupts my focus.

"I don't think that's for anyone else to say. Do I personally? No, but would it really matter if I did? Or if anyone else does for that matter? I think that this is a unique situation that very few people would ever be able to fully come close to understanding the emotions involved."

"What about with your mom?"

"I was young so I'm not sure how much I trust those memories. I don't think I comprehended that she was sick for the longest time. She still fed me and made sure I was ready for school, all the little things you take for granted. Towards the end though, when we knew she didn't have long, I remember her suffering. She tried so hard to be strong, to not let me see it, but I remember. I asked my grandmother why we weren't doing something to help my mother. I think she thought I meant something to help her get better since her answer was that there was nothing else to be done. I asked her why we couldn't take her to the doctor like we took Sadie to the vet. Sadie was our dog. When she became old and ill we had to have her euthanized. I thought surely we did the same for people who were suffering. I guess my point is this, if she were suffering would this decision be easier for you?"

"I wouldn't let her suffer," Katrina answers without hesitation.

"Right, but she isn't suffering, and the outcome is unknown at this point. Personally, I don't see the harm in waiting for more information to become clear, but it isn't my decision to make. I can't imagine how heavy of a burden this must be."

"Thank you." She flashes me a shadow of a smile before returning her attention to Jill. Sensing our conversation is at an end, I refocus on my book, diving back into the story. Sometime later I glance up to find that the emotional toll has finally proven to be too much, Katrina is asleep. I quietly get up from my chair and make my way to the nurse's station where I ask for, and am given a couple of warm blankets. I return to the room and gently cover Katrina up, hoping that I don't accidentally wake her. Mission accomplished, I settle back into my chair and resume reading my book.

Chapter 3

Sunday morning finds me back at the coffee shop and on my way back up to the ICU. Katrina's message this morning put an early end to pajama day. This is the first time she has asked for anything, so even though I don't know what it is, I am happy to help her if I can. I enter the room to find her pacing along the length of the bed, an episode of Law and Order airing quietly on the TV. She doesn't notice my presence immediately, but stops when she finally does. I hand her one of the cups of coffee without saying a word.

"Thanks," she says as she takes the offered cup. She sits down in her customary seat but still seems antsy.

"Are you alright? You seem agitated." She continues to fidget, her knee bouncing and her fingers picking at the sleeve around the coffee cup.

"Yeah, just starting to get cabin fever I think."

"Understandable. Did you sleep at all last night?" The dark circles around Katrina's eyes tell me that even if she did, it wasn't much.

"A little off and on I think." She shifts her focus to the TV. "I have no idea what's even happening in this one, I just had it on for some background noise and momentary distraction." She's so fidgety that it's starting to make me anxious.

"Is there anything you need? Do you want to go for a walk, get outside of this space for a few minutes?" Maybe she will finally tell me what it was she messaged me about this morning. If not, I hope she will at least go for a walk and hopefully settle down a little. She turns away from the TV to look at Jill and then me.

"Actually, I need to go home for a little bit." Now I know why her anxiety is so high.

"Would you like me to stay with Jill? Or I can take you to your house if you'd like."

"I hate to leave Jill here alone, but I have no idea what walking into our house is going to feel like. Plus, I need to let a few people know what's happened. Most of all, I need a shower and fresh clothes. I feel disgusting."

"I can take you. If anything changes with Jill's condition the staff will contact you and we can rush back." Katrina stands up and grabs her coffee. "Now?" She moves towards the door, letting her actions serve as the answer to my question.

Katrina tells me where she lives and gives me rough directions as we take the elevator down. "I have to say, this is not what I pictured you driving at all." She laughs a little as she opens the passenger side door and climbs in.

"What did you think I'd be driving?" I have an idea what her answer will be, but am curious nonetheless.

"I don't know, something sporty and expensive. An Audi, BMW, Mercedes, something along those lines."

"And what exactly is wrong with my Jetta?" I feign anger.

"Nothing, it's just—," Katrina is stammering, clearly not picking up that I was messing with her.

"Relax, I'm not upset. Just messing around a bit. I like my Jetta. It gets me where I need to go and doesn't cost a small fortune every month. I tend to be practical when it comes to most things. I could easily afford any of the cars you thought I would drive, but they all do the same thing that my Jetta does."

"I suppose that makes sense. I've never understood having an overpriced car either. Guess I just had the rich doctor stereotype going on in my head. Sorry."

"No need to apologize. I can't wait to see your reaction if you ever see my house."

"Why? Big and fancy?"

"Hardly. Admittedly it's probably bigger than I need, but it isn't a mansion by any stretch of the imagination. Just a place that I really loved the exterior design of and the location. It sat vacant for quite a while and was very outdated. I picked it up for next to nothing and had it gutted and remodeled."

"So no pool, hot tub, movie theatre, tennis court and extra large garage filled with luxury cars?" She laughs to let me know she is joking.

"Well, I do have a hot tub. Catherine has an indoor pool that I've grown quite jealous of, so I have someone working up a few ideas and getting me the estimates. Otherwise no, none of that other stuff. What would I do with it? Seems like such a waste of money. At least if I end up adding on to accommodate the pool it will add value to my investment. I'd rather save money for other things, like retiring before I'm 80. I'm one of the few surgeons I know that has already paid back their student loans. I lived in a cheap apartment for a few years after graduation just so I could take care of those. I'm not a fan of being in debt."

"Wow, sounds very responsible. I wish Jill was more like you in that sense. She likes to spend money like crazy."

"That must drive you a bit insane, being an accountant and all."

"It does, but sometimes it's impossible to say no to her." Katrina's expression relays her sadness letting me know that our casual conversation is at an end. She stares out the window looking at the landscape that she has to have seen countless times. She's silent the remainder the trip and sits glued to her seat when I switch the car off. I use this time to take in the Cape Cod before me. The blue-grey siding set over stone veneer, the ample windows, the perfectly manicured lawn with it's flowers and bushes along portions of the house, the attached garage. The house is beautiful and inviting, it feels like a home. The sound of the car door closing pulls me out of my assessment. I quickly scramble out of the car and meet Katrina as she unlocks the front door.

"Can I get you anything to drink?" I take off my shoes and follow Katrina through the house, trying to take everything in as we pass by it.

"Water would be great, thanks." We reach the kitchen and I'm still struggling to take everything in as Katrina prepares a glass of ice water for me. I hear Katrina chuckle and move my focus to her. "What?"

"Nothing, just that look you had a few seconds ago. It's overwhelming isn't it?" Busy was the word that came to mind right away, but I don't want to be rude.

"A little." I feel my cheeks flush slightly as I make this small admission, which feel like an insult.

49

"I told Jill it's too much, but you can't argue with her when it comes to interior decorating." Katrina looks around and shakes her head.

"Well, that is what she does for a living. I would imagine it wouldn't be a winnable argument."

"No, it wouldn't. She likes things a bit busier than I do. Anyway, I apologize, but I'm really not in the mood to give a grand tour. Would you mind if I just settle you in the den while I take a shower?"

"Not at all."

"I'll probably need about an hour to shower and send out a few messages. If you're hungry help yourself to whatever you can find. Feel free to watch whatever is on TV." She leads me to one of the rooms we passed on the way to the kitchen. The light moss green furniture on the beige carpet all complimented by various pieces of art is a lot to take in, yet somehow it all works together. "The remote for the TV is on the coffee table. I'll be back in a little bit." Katrina leaves me on my own, allowing me to dive back into my book.

"You're always on your phone." I look up to see Katrina, her swollen red eyes betraying how she is doing being back in their home. I didn't hear her coming down the hall, nor did I have any idea that it's already been 45 minutes since she left me to my own devices.

"Just reading a book."

"Anything good?"

"Some lesbian romance novel. Quite good so far."

"Come to the kitchen with me." Katrina glances back at me, flashing me that look again, the same look of disbelief I received earlier.

"What?"

"Are you reading a thrust and bust?" I laugh because I haven't heard a romance novel referred to as a thrust and bust in a very long time.

"It gets steamy, but it has a plot."

"Oh my god, you're totally reading a thrust and bust." Katrina is laughing, the laughter a sharp contrast to her still puffy eyes.

"I swear it isn't a thrust and bust. When you have no love life…" Katrina's laughter immediately stops, and she eyes me skeptically.

"None, really?"

"Not for a while."

"Let me guess, too much work."

"It isn't that. Ok, I'm sure that's part of it. Aside from that, I don't make the best choices in partners, or at least historically I don't. I really dislike the person I became with my last girlfriend. I allowed myself to be manipulated by her and gave her control of everything but my work. She was materialistic and selfish, yet I stayed with her. I don't want to be that person again."

"So you're just going to be celibate for the rest of your days?" She opens the refrigerator door and starts to rummage through it. "Hungry?"

"I could eat a snack." I take a deep breath and prepare to answer her first question. "I don't plan to remain celibate, I just don't want to make the same mistakes again."

"Yeah, but if you don't try…"

"It isn't that I'm shut off to the idea of trying, I just want to know that she's going to be worth the risk. I don't want to dive in head first without knowing how deep the water is."

"Fair enough. We don't have much food in the house right now. I could maybe scrape together a salad, I have some fruit. I have no idea what this was at some point, as if that isn't embarrassing." I watch in amusement as Katrina puts the unknown item back in the refrigerator.

"We can stop some place if you'd like."

"Nah, I'll just fix up a salad and cut up some fruit. Plans today?"

"Nothing really, just relaxing. Probably would have read, watched a movie, something. Do you want some help with that?"

"Nope, I have it. So what does your typical week look like?" Katrina busies herself depositing her chosen rations on the counter.

"I work out every morning, first thing. On Mondays, Wednesday and Fridays I operate, so depending on my caseload for the day, I can finish up as late as 7 or 8 pm. Tuesdays and Thursdays are office days, I usually wrap those up between 5 and 6. Thursday evenings I work with my trainer. I keep things open every other evening so I can fit whatever I need to in. Exciting, I know."

"I don't think anyone's life is that exciting. Life is mostly routine anyway."

"Perhaps. So I can stop up first thing in the morning and between cases if you'd like. Catherine operates the same days that I do, so I wouldn't be surprised if she and possibly Alex check in at some point as well. Did Hastings stop in this morning?"

"He did, no change." She retrieves a pair of plates and two sets of silverware and takes them over to the dining room table. I grab the salad and the fruit and follow her. We eat in relative silence, making me wish I hadn't asked about Hastings. After we finish we clean up the mess and she packs a bag to take with her. The return trip is quiet, except for the few times her phone goes off before she gives up and silences it.

"Would you mind if I went back up alone?" She doesn't bother tearing her gaze from the view when she asks.

"Not at all, whatever you need."

"You sure? I don't want you to feel like I just used you for a ride."

"I'm sure. Do what you need to do."

"Thanks." I drop Katrina off and remind her to let me know if she needs anything. She promises that she will. When I haven't heard from her by 7 that evening, I send her a quick message to make sure she's still doing ok. She responds about an hour later letting me know that she is. A few minutes after that another message comes in, this time Catherine asking for an update. I send her one, and she lets me know that her plan is to stop up

before her first case in the morning. I tell her I'll meet her
at the coffee shop at 7.

Chapter 4

Jill continues to show no sign of changes or improvement as the week passes. Her drains and chest tubes are removed, but she remains on the ventilator. Catherine continues to check in every evening and becomes more certain with each passing day that Jill will not recover. Katrina's demeanor shows the slightest changes throughout the week, and I find myself wondering what's happening. By Wednesday she starts to allow their friends to visit. Friday morning as Catherine and I check in, the mystery is solved.

"I have to take her off the vent." She doesn't look at either of us as she says it.

"Katrina, you don't have to." She finally looks at me, but all her expression shows is finality. "I need to honor her wishes." She waves her hand at the vent and then over Jill in general. "This isn't it." Catherine and I look at each other, both knowing we're going to be late for our first cases.

"Katrina, you understand that if they take her off of the vent that Jill might not make it. There's also the chance that she could breathe on her own. There is no certainty."

"I do, but it's what she wants. We talked about it when we found out she had cancer. No extreme measures and she wanted to donate her organs." Catherine and I look at each other again. "I know, as a cancer survivor she can't donate. I still have to do what's right, and that is to honor her wishes. I've thought about it all week."

"What do you need?"

"I already spoke to Dr. Hastings about it yesterday. It's going to happen this evening. Can you be here?"

"Of course, I'll be here." Catherine nods that she will as well. Catherine heads towards the door, I know she will wait for me in the hallway. I move toward Katrina and place my hand on her shoulder. "I only have one case today, a long one, but just the one. If you need anything just text my phone and I'll have Abby break scrub and come up." Katrina places her hand over mine and nods. "I should be done by 4. I'll be up as soon as possible."

*****

My case goes smoothly, and I find myself finished before 3:30. I'm thirsty and starving, so Abby finishes closing and applying the dressings while I dictate, put in post op care orders and speak with the family. I head upstairs to the cafeteria to get something to eat, but find my appetite quickly dissolving as Katrina and Jill push to the forefront of my mind. Knowing that I won't be eating dinner tonight, I manage to force a protein bar and an orange down before I head back downstairs to meet Abby in the locker room. I text Catherine that I'm done, and she lets me know that she and Alex are in the back of the dining room. Abby in tow, we head upstairs and find Alex and Catherine embracing, only this time not an ounce of sexuality is oozing off of them. This is purely for comfort. Neither one of them sees us as we approach, allowing me to easily over hear their conversation.

"It could have been you."

"It wasn't."

"I know, but it could have. I feel for Katrina, I know what it's like to sit in that chair, but I can't imagine how it must feel to make this decision."

56

"I know baby, I—." Alex finally spots us. Catherine, realizing they are no longer alone, pulls away enough to see who the interlopers are. They separate with a quick kiss and head toward us. We ride upstairs in silence, knowing what we're about to witness.

We enter the room to find Katrina alone. The four of us look at one another trying to figure out what is happening. "Katrina, where is everyone?"

"I had everyone say their goodbyes earlier this week. They don't need to see this, and I don't want to worry about other people right now." Now everything makes sense, suddenly allowing visits, the slight change in her demeanor throughout the week, she has been preparing for this for days. I try to pinpoint when she could have made this decision and realize it must have been Sunday, when she wanted to be alone.

"Ok. We came to be here for you, but if you'd like us to leave we can." Katrina shakes her head.

"No, stay. I appreciate it."

A few minutes later I'm surprised when Dr. Preston enters followed by Dr. Hastings. Dr. Preston typically works in the OR, meaning Catherine has called in a favor. I look at Catherine, and she nods slightly confirming my suspicion. I'm grateful to her for it. Dr. Preston is about as compassionate as they come, a stark contrast to Hastings. Hastings turns and finally notices Catherine, the look on his face comical; like someone has slapped him with rotten fish.

"Catherine?"

"She's a friend John." The look on Catherine's face is enough, he doesn't say another word.

Dr. Preston introduces herself and explains what's about to happen. I appreciate her thoroughness and for ensuring that Katrina understands that Jill will be kept comfortable throughout. When she's finished, she asks Katrina if she is ready. Katrina indicates that she is and Dr. Preston begins the process of taking Jill off of the ventilator. Once the tube is out Katrina takes her hand and tells her that she loves her and that it's ok to go, that she will be ok. She kisses Jill goodbye and waits in silence. By the 28 minute mark, Jill's respirations are shallow and infrequent, I know it won't be much longer. Katrina must know as well, because she kisses her one last time and tells her she loves her. By the time Dr. Preston calls time of death at the 34 minute mark, the only dry eyes left in the room belong to Dr. Hastings. He makes his exit as quickly as he can. Dr. Preston stays long enough to spare some words of comfort for Katrina then exits, leaving the five of us alone. Abby moves to Katrina's side and whispers something, then pulls her in for a comforting embrace. They continue to whisper back and forth. I look over and notice that Catherine has a death grip on Alex's hand, her knuckles as white as fresh snow. I know what's going on in her head, the imaginary scene she's playing out. She finally notices me looking and relaxes her grip, leading Alex closer to Katrina. Abby breaks their embrace and signals that she will be in the hallway. Catherine and Alex each take a turn consoling Katrina before making their exit. Katrina throws her arms around me and begins to sob. I hear the door quietly click shut and am thankful for whichever of my friends had the presence of mind to close it. I let her cry without saying a word, nothing I can offer will change anything for her. My heart breaks for her as I hold her trembling form. Ten minutes pass like this before Katrina regains enough composure to pull away from me. I grab a pair of fresh tissues for her and let her know that I'm going to wait outside while she says her final goodbye. She nods that she understands.

In the hallway I let Abby, Alex and Catherine know that Katrina is saying goodbye. It's clear that Catherine is still shaken. I tell Alex that she should take her home and Alex agrees. We hug goodbye, and they ask me to let them know what arrangements are made. I promise them that I will. Abby loiters with me, but I know that she needs to get home to her kid. I tell her to go and enjoy the important things, that I plan to wait for Katrina and give her a ride home. She tells me to call her if Katrina needs anything. I promise that I will, and am left alone to wait. Twenty minutes later Katrina finally emerges, belongings in hand.

"I'm ready."

"You're sure? You can take all the time you need."

"I've been saying goodbye all week. I need to go." I can't imagine how difficult this week has to have been for Katrina, and the strength that she must possess to have gotten through it largely alone.

"Would it be ok if I drove you home?" I'm hoping that she doesn't object, I really don't think she should be driving.

"Probably a good idea." We take the elevator down one last time, and I find myself feeling guilty for being grateful that I won't have to see the inside of that room again.

The drive back to Katrina and Jill's is silent. Katrina stares out the window again, but her disconnected gaze makes it clear she doesn't really see anything. I pull into the driveway and shut off the engine, but Katrina doesn't move. She sits and stares at the house as panic slowly engulfs her. "I can't stay here tonight."

"It's ok. I can sleep on your sofa if you'd like. Or I have a guest room you can use. Or I can get you a hotel room somewhere." Katrina silently ponders my offers, her panic mildly dissipating.

"You sure?"

"Yes. Which would you prefer?" Katrina stares at her house and silently weighs her options.

"Guest room please."

"Alright. Do you want to go in and pack some fresh things? I'm off until Monday, but you're welcome to stay as long as you need to." Katrina stares at the house, debating.

"Can you come in with me? It will only take me a few minutes."

"Of course, take all the time you need." She finally exits the car, and I follow. Once inside, I get it. Jill is everywhere in this house, she did all the decorating, their shared memories. Sleeping here would be like sleeping with her ghost.

"I'll be right back." I wait for her in the entryway, certain we will not be here any longer than necessary. She returns in less than five minutes, and we make the short trip to my house in more silence. I park in the garage and escort Katrina inside. She follows me but says nothing. I kick off my shoes in the mud room and lead her to the guest room. She still says nothing but starts to open her bag, so I leave her to it. I head to the kitchen and put the kettle on and locate the tea in the cupboard. I make her a cup of tea and pour her a couple of fingers of whiskey. She still hasn't left the guest room, so I take them to her and let her know that I'll be in the den if she needs anything. I put another basketball game on the TV and settle in on the couch with my newest book.

"Another thrust and bust?" I didn't hear her enter the room, despite the TV being muted.

"It wasn't a thrust and bust and no. This is some monthly freebie, a spy thriller this time." Katrina seats herself on the opposite end of the couch, setting her tea and whiskey on the end table. She stares at the TV. I can't tell if she's nearly catatonic or if she's really watching the game.

"You're welcome to turn it up or change it to something else. I have a bad habit of turning the TV on, even when I plan to read."

"This is fine." I know then that she is seeing it without really seeing it. I don't bother turning it up, I know it won't make any difference to her. I go back to my book, and when I look up a chapter later, I notice Katrina shaking. I go to the hallway closet and grab a pair of blankets. I drape one around her shoulders and sit the second on the couch next to her so she can place it over her lap. I notice that she has consumed all of her whiskey and most of her tea. Hopefully, she will get some sleep tonight.

"Thank you." She takes the second blanket and curls up underneath it.

"Of course. Can I get you anything else? More tea? Whiskey?"

"No, but I have a weird favor to ask." Thrown off a little, I wait for her request. "Do you think you could sit in the guest room with me until I fall asleep? I don't think it will take long." Her voice is meek; like a child's after a nightmare. I shut off the TV and Katrina takes this as consent. She heads down the hall to the guest room and curls up in bed. I place the extra blankets on the foot of the bed, just in case, and seat myself on the floor where Katrina can see me. She watches me as I try to refocus on my book. My concern for her pulling my focus away time and again. I look up to find her watching me.

"It's ok, I'll be here. I'm not going to leave you alone. If you need anything, my room is down the hall on the right."

"Thank you."

"For what?"

"For looking out for me. You barely know me and yet you've been a rock this week."

"It's fine. Get some rest." I refocus on my book and manage another chapter. When I look up Katrina is finally asleep. I tiptoe quietly out of the room and down the hall to my bedroom. I brush my teeth and change into a pair of shorts and a tank top. I fall into bed and continue reading, knowing that the emotional wear from the day won't allow me to stay up too much longer.

Chapter 5

I wake up a little after 4 am, a product of going to bed extra early last night. I try to fall asleep again, but my effort is fruitless. Sticking to my routine, I get ready to work out. On my way down the hall, I stop and look in on Katrina to find her cocooned in the blankets, seemingly sound asleep. I fill up my water bottle and head downstairs for cardio, core and arms day. I start an episode of *Penny Dreadful* and get going on the rower. I follow that up by blowing through my run on the treadmill. Feeling like I have extra energy to burn, I decide to add some extra core and abdominal work. I quickly whip through 50 sit-ups and follow that up by planking for 3 minutes. I do another round of 50 sit ups and am in the middle of my second plank when I realize that I'm no longer alone. I still have a minute left on this plank that I'd like to finish, so without breaking my form, I address Katrina.

"Sorry, did I wake you?"

"No, I've been up for a few minutes now. You do know that it's barely 5 am right?" 20 seconds to go, I'll wait to answer her until I finish. When the timer goes off, I stand and grab my towel. I turn and catch Katrina staring at me, a shocked look on her face.

"I know what time it is. I work out every morning." Katrina is still staring.

"Yeah, I can see that." I realize then that I'm only wearing my sports bra and a pair of gym shorts.

"You alright?" I towel off and pull my t-shirt on, hoping that I'll still be able to get my extra arms routine in.

"Yeah, I just…" Katrina trails off as she averts her gaze and looks around the basement. "What's with the mats?"

"Sparring practice. The trainer I work with does a lot of mixed martial arts training. I had a buddy in the class with me for a while. She'd come over and we'd practice, that is until she moved away." I feel the slight smile on my face as I think about sparring with Mel, and how one evening sparring evolved into something else entirely. I miss my no strings attached sexy time with Mel. I miss sparring with her as well.

"Something tells me she was more than just a sparring buddy," Katrina emphasizes the last two words, making air quotes with her fingers. I'm busted. I feel my cheeks flush slightly and I find myself hoping that my face is still red from working out.

"No, in the end, she wasn't just a sparring partner. It wasn't serious, just sex."

"How evolved of you." I can't tell if she is being sarcastic or serious.

"Yeah, well I had just gone through a messy breakup, and we both knew she was leaving. It had an expiration date before it even began."

"Makes sense." Without another word, Katrina turns and heads back toward the stairs.

"Hey, did you need anything?"

"Oh, no. I just woke up and you weren't in your room, then I heard the TV so I followed the noise. I didn't realize you were busy."

"It's alright. You can join me if you'd like. I still have to work on arms, but feel free to use anything down here." I already know she will refuse before I finish the offer.

"That's alright. I'm going to go back to bed." She heads up the stairs before I can respond. I push through my arms routine, seeing Katrina's sadness has sapped some of my energy away. Routine complete, I call it a day and head back upstairs for a quick shower. As I pass by the guest room I can hear Katrina's sniffles. I'm torn between giving her privacy and checking on her. I decide to give her space, hoping that if she needs anything she will come to me.

Showered and famished, I head to the kitchen. Hoping Katrina will eat if I prepare something for her, I fry up some turkey bacon, scramble some eggs and cut up some fresh fruit. I toss a few slices of toast in as I finish preparing the eggs. Breakfast ready, I head to the guest room where I am greeted by silence. I knock softly, hoping if Katrina is sleeping that it won't wake her. She calls for me to come in and I enter the room to find her lying in bed, staring at the ceiling.

"I made breakfast, if you feel up to eating. There's coffee as well. Or I can make you some tea."

"Yeah, ok." I have no idea what she is agreeing to. She finally tears her gaze away from the unremarkable ceiling and looks at me. I arch an eyebrow at her, hoping she will elaborate. "I'll try to eat." She doesn't move an inch. Instead, she reverts back to staring at the ceiling. I think back to when I lost my mother, how I wasn't allowed to wallow. I have no idea if I should try to keep Katrina busy or if I should just let her lay in bed all day if she chooses to. Making my choice, I step further into the room and approach the bed.

"Come on, breakfast is ready," I inform her, extending my hand. She eyes it for a moment as I wait for her to tell me to get lost. Surprisingly she takes it, and I help pull her from the bed. She squeezes it once, a silent thanks, before releasing it.

We eat breakfast in relative silence. Well, I eat my breakfast while Katrina pokes at hers absentmindedly, taking a small bite here and there. At least she is eating something. I gaze out the window, looking around my back yard for any traces of the deer that have been appearing on a fairly regular basis. I'm about to give up when I see a small movement at the edge of the woods. I keep my eyes glued to the spot and sure enough the huge 10 point buck makes his way into my backyard. Typically he's followed closely by a doe. I search for her but see no other movement. About a minute later she breaks through the edge of the forest with a fawn in tow. I watch them for a second before tapping Katrina on the hand and pointing, as if using my voice would startle our guests. She watches the trio with me and manages a little more of her breakfast.

"Do they always get this close?"

"From what I've seen they're fairly brave. They're out there pretty much every morning."

"It's nice. I love this view, it's relaxing."

"Yeah, I like to gaze out the window while I'm eating breakfast. It always provides a nice relaxing start to the day, the calm before the storm." The deer retreat back into the woods leaving the scene void of movement once they fade into the foliage. I look over at Katrina and find her slightly more animated, her once fixed eyes roam around the room taking it in.

"Didn't you say you gutted this place and remodeled it?"

"I did. I liked the Victorian frame, but wanted it modernized. I had the kitchen opened up and larger windows installed. The basement wasn't finished, so I had them take care of that as well. Aside from having the wall separating the kitchen and dining rooms removed, I really didn't alter much structurally. I did have everything converted to be as green as possible though. It took quite a while, but I feel like it was worth it."

"I think it looks wonderful. I love the darker and neutral hues and how you've decorated it enough for it to be interesting but not overwhelming."

"Thanks, but truthfully I let an interior decorator do a lot of it. I told her what I wanted and what I absolutely didn't want, and she came back with her ideas. I'm absolute rubbish when it comes to that sort of thing, hell I can barely dress myself, if I'm being honest."

"She did well. To me it's what a home is supposed to be, warm, inviting and relaxing. None of the bright colors and extreme amounts of art that—," Katrina cuts herself off as she thinks about Jill. Her eyes and shoulders drop, fresh tears roll down her cheeks, but somehow she manages not to break down completely. She swipes at the tears with her hands and takes a deep breath. "I'm sorry, this is ridiculous, I can't even say her name without falling apart."

"You have nothing to apologize for. I think what your feeling is most likely perfectly normal. No need to worry about how I will react, just do what you need to do. Ok?" Katrina nods that it is. "So it's supposed to be a little warmer today. I was thinking of going for a walk later. Would you like to join me?" I'm hoping she will at least think about it, getting some fresh air and moving around might help in some small way.

"That might be ok. I think I'm going to go back to bed for a while though." I have a suspicion that Katrina is really going to cry in private, but I say nothing, opting to just nod my acceptance.

"I'll check in with you before I decide to head out, but if you need anything before then, please don't hesitate to find me." Katrina nods and puts a hand on my shoulder. I accept this as a silent thank you and watch as she leaves the dining room and heads back down the hall to the guest room. I clean up the mess in the kitchen, and as I'm putting the leftover fruit away, I realize that I need to go grocery shopping soon, like before lunch soon if we're going to eat. Mind racing, I throw together a quick grocery list. I head down the hallway and pull a set of bath towels for Katrina to use. I knock at her door, somehow knowing that I won't wake her. In the moments before she calls for me to come in I can hear her blowing her nose. My earlier suspicion was correct, and now I feel guilty for disturbing her. I slowly open the door and enter. "I just wanted to bring you these and see if you want or need anything from the store. If I don't get some groceries, we won't be having anything for lunch." Katrina is sitting up, her back against the headboard, her arms holding her knees to her chest. She doesn't look at me or respond, the expression on her face distant. I set the towels on top of the dresser and move to the foot of the bed and sit down. She still doesn't move, not even her eyes. I gently place my hand on her forearm and she jumps, startled by the touch even though I'm sitting two feet in front of her. "Hey, what is it?"

"She's gone. I killed her. I gave up and I killed her and nothing I do can ever change that." She still stares ahead, looking at, but not seeing a thing.

"You did not kill her." I have no idea if my words register with her. Her unblinking gaze is still directed elsewhere, despite the fact that I just spoke to her. "Hey." She still doesn't look at me. Becoming a tad irritated, I move my fingers from her forearm to her chin. Using my thumb and my first two fingers I force her to turn her head and look at me. "You did not kill her. The vent was breathing for her. You didn't do this, you're not responsible for this. The driver of the car is the guilty party, not you. Do you hear me?" She nods that she does and I let go of her chin.

"You're right, I know you're right. I just feel so…"

"That's grief, your mind processing, trying to make sense of it. You've just gotta give it time and remember that you did nothing wrong. Talk to people if you need to, don't shut everyone out. I imagine you have a lot of friends that are pretty worried about you right now."

"I know." Katrina looks down, a mask of shame takes over her face.

"Sorry, I didn't mean to lecture you. What can I do?"

"Nothing, you've been great. I feel bad being in your space and begin such a mess," she motions her hand up and down her body.

"No need to worry about any of that. You haven't kept me from doing anything I would've been doing. You have a right to feel however you're feeling at any particular moment. Don't forget that." She nods her head in agreement but says nothing. "Now, I do need to go to the store. Can I get you anything? Favorite comfort food?"

"Ice cream."

"Flavor?" At this point, I'll buy her anything so long as she'll eat it.

"Tin roof."

"Alright, done. I'll probably take that walk when I get back; if you think you want to join me."

*****

Later that evening I sink into my couch feeling exhausted. Between waking up extra early, the added sets during my morning work out, the two-hour walk we took through the woods and trying to help Katrina get through this, I feel justified in having a mindless movie night. I'm perusing the selection via on demand and nearly leap off the couch when Katrina speaks.

"Mind if I join you?" I thought she was asleep. She retreated to the guest room a short while ago and hadn't made an appearance or a sound since.

"Sure," I say as I flip the trailing end of my blanket off the other two-thirds of the couch. Katrina sits down, wrapping one of the spare blankets from the guest room around herself.

"What are you planning to watch?"

"No plan, just seeing what's available. Can I get you anything? Want some of that ice cream?"

"That sounds great actually, I can get it though."

"No, you pick the movie, I'll get the ice cream." I return from the kitchen a few minutes later, two bowls in hand. "Did you find something," I ask as I hand one of the bowls over.

"Yes, you're going to love it." She doesn't tell me what it is, so I settle in for whatever surprise she has in store. I know what it is before the Paramount logo is off of the screen, *The Godfather.*

"Good pick."

"I hope so." Katrina raises a spoonful of ice cream to her mouth. My own spoon sits frozen midway between my bowl and my own mouth.

"You've never seen it?" I ask in disbelief.

"Nope, never." I don't answer as the movie gets underway. About an hour into the movie I can feel eyes on me, that Katrina is staring at me.

"Not getting into it?"

"No it's good, it's just…" I give her time to formulate her thoughts, put them into words. "Never mind, it's weird." I grab the remote and pause the movie, wanting to know what's going on. I look at Katrina expectantly, and she finally relents. "I just…" her look turns sheepish as she continues, "was wondering if we could cuddle." She was right, it sounds like a beyond weird request. I try to keep this judgment off of my face, but I feel it contort and know I've failed. "Not in a sexual way…I just feel like, I don't know…there is this void, like I'm empty, and I just need some human contact, some kind of tether. I'm sorry, forget that I asked, it's weird." I think about it for a minute, in a way it makes sense, I know I've felt similarly after a bad breakup, I can't imagine how it feels for her. Without a word, I lift the edge of my blanket and wait for her to slide across the couch. She hesitates for a moment, but accepts the invitation. She presses herself against my side and relaxes against me. I pull the

71

blanket up over both of us and resume the movie before wrapping my arm around her shoulder. As the tension slowly eases out of her body I realize that she's right, human contact is nice. How could I have possibly forgotten?

Chapter 6

Katrina informs me over breakfast that it's time for her to go home. A mixture of sadness and resolve radiate from her, so I don't question her decision. I drive her back to the hospital to pick up her car. She insists that she will be ok. I tell her I'm only a phone call away if she needs anything, and head home to get my to do list done. I catch up on my charting, do some meal preparation for the week, get the laundry done, have brunch with a group of friends, and take a look at my cases for tomorrow. I'm just settling in on the couch, waiting for my gaming system to boot up when my text alert goes off. I hit the home screen button to see if it can wait, but the preview shows the message is from Katrina. It's just after 7 pm. My *PlayStation* waits for me to pick an activity as I type in my security code to check the message. Katrina's message asks if I can come over. I look at the time again, knowing that the day is winding down, wondering what her message doesn't say. Would this be a quick visit or does she need someone to spend the night in the house with her? I power down the *PlayStation* and send a quick reply letting her know that I'll be there soon. I pack a small over night bag just in case, grateful that tomorrow is an OR day and I won't have to make myself fully presentable like I would if I were in clinic.

Katrina answers the door, and it's clear that she is shaken. "Thank you for coming. I didn't want to bother you, hadn't planned to, but…" Katrina trails off and shakes her head as she looks at the floor.

"It's alright." I follow Katrina to the kitchen where I see she has a bottle of whiskey sitting on the counter and a tumbler with a few fingers in it.

"Can I pour you some?" Apparently, I eyed the whiskey a little too closely.

"Sure. Could I trouble you for a water as well?"
Katrina turns to the cupboard and pulls out a tumbler and a
glass, fills the glass with ice water from the refrigerator and
returns to stand opposite me. Her hand is heavy as she
pours the whiskey and I easily have three to four fingers
sitting in front of me. Katrina says nothing as she downs
hers and pours herself another. She turns away from me
again, walking back to the refrigerator and opening the
door.

"Can I offer you anything to eat? Apparently,
everyone thought I was starving or that I should eat my
feelings." While Katrina is trying to be polite, I can sense
the anger starting to build-up below the surface, seeping
out in her mannerisms and her tone.

"Have you eaten anything?" I'm not particularly
hungry, but I'm worried that Katrina hasn't eaten since
breakfast this morning, especially if she is drinking like this.

"Breakfast."

"Why don't you eat with me?" Katrina opens her
mouth to protest, but closes it when she sees the look of
disapproval I give her. She pulls two bowls out of the
refrigerator, puts one in the microwave and sits the other
on the counter near me.

"Soup and salad?" She takes another deep drink
from her tumbler.

"Sure." She tries to turn her back to me again, but I
stop her by grabbing her arm. "Hey. What the hell
happened today?" I can see some of the fight go out of
her, she knows I will make her talk.

"Nothing really. My phone has been blowing up since Friday evening, people asking if I'm ok, wanting to know where I am, if I need anything... As soon as I told one person I was at home, everyone seemed to know. People have been in and out of here all day. That would have been exhausting by itself, but to top it off they show up, and I have to deal with their grieving, their sadness and I had to look at the pity in their eyes all day. I just wanted to be alone today, to deal with being back here with her ghost haunting me in every inch of this damn house." Katrina is nearly shouting by the time she finishes. The microwave beeps but neither of us move to retrieve the soup.

"Feel better?" Katrina looks at me, questioning my meaning. "Well, do you? You obviously needed to get that off your chest. That isn't the answer," I say pointing to the bottle of whiskey. Katrina takes a deep breath, releases it and drops her head. The microwave beeps again; as if it's impatient to have the contents removed.

"You're right. I know you're right. It's just that...I don't know." Katrina turns her attention to the microwave, finally relieving it of the imaginary burden.

"Hey, you can unload on me if it helps. Tell people you need your space if that's what you require. Just don't sit here trying to drown your sorrows." Katrina sits the bowl of soup on the counter in front of me, a slight smile playing at her lips. A small chuckle escapes her, and I wonder if she has started to crack.

"Sorry I unloaded on you, it isn't you, please know that. You've been great. I don't ever see those pitying looks, I don't have to worry about you breaking down...you know?"

"You don't have to apologize for your feelings. Just try to remember that those people today were friends with both of you. They've lost someone too, not on the same level that you have, but they have. You have a right to feel everything that you're feeling, just be careful not to take it out on those trying to offer you support." Katrina looks ashamed as she stirs her potato soup. "Don't feel ashamed, I'm not scolding or judging you. You asked me to come over here, I assume for a reason, I just want to ensure that you're alright, or as alright as you can be." Katrina nods and takes another bite of her soup. As we eat the small meal, Katrina asks about my day after we parted company. I'm happy to see that she neglects the remaining whiskey in her glass opting to switch to water. She stays quiet as she cleans up, this time the silence between us is uncomfortable, the heavy silence between two people when both know that one person needs to ask for something that they haven't worked themselves up to requesting yet. The clock reads that it is approaching 8:30, nearing my usual bedtime. I'm still waiting for the real reason Katrina asked me over to come out, but don't want to push her. She invites me into the den to watch a movie, a movie I know I'll likely never make it through, yet I agree to watch. She starts up *Fight Club,* and I feel her staring at me.

"This an ok pick?"

"Yeah, it's a classic in my book. I'm going to be honest though, I might not make it through the whole movie." Katrina laughs.

"Past your bedtime? Need a blanket?" Well, at least she is joking around a little bit, better than when I first arrived.

"More like approaching my bedtime. I'm fine without the blanket, thanks." We continue to watch the movie in silence. I try to become fully immersed in it, but thoughts of why Katrina called me over still weigh heavy on my mind. About halfway through the movie, I feel myself start to doze off. I look over to find Katrina fast asleep. I look around the den for a blanket but don't see one. I debate with myself whether or not I should start searching the nearby closets for one or if I should just stay where I am. Finally deciding that Katrina's warmth outweighs the guilt I'll feel looking through her closets, I extract myself from the comfortable sofa to begin my search. Katrina's eyes snap open at the slight movement, the visible disorientation only lasting a few seconds.

"Are you leaving?" It seems like the question is laced with a little bit of sadness.

"No, I was just going to look for a blanket for you. You fell asleep. I didn't want you to get cold, and I didn't want to wake you. I probably should get going though, I have surgery in the morning."

"Actually, I..." Katrina looks at her hands, seemingly unable to make her request.

"Do you need me to stay?"

"Would you mind? I have a guest room you can use, I'm planning on sleeping on the couch."

"Why would you...right." It takes me a few seconds to connect the dots. Katrina can't bring herself to sleep in the bed that she and Jill shared for so many years. I know that I'll likely regret it tomorrow, but the part of me that always wants to help people can't say no. "Why don't you take the guest bed and I'll sleep on the sofa."

"Are you sure, you have to operate tomorrow. You'd probably sleep better in the guest room." She's right on all counts, but I know I'll be fine.

"I'm sure, besides I'll likely be up and out before you wake up. I just need to get the overnight bag from my car." Katrina gives me a look that conveys her shock.

"You knew what I needed?"

"I suspected, yes." I head towards the entrance, slip on my shoes and retrieve my bag from my car. When I return to the den Katrina is arranging a pillow and some blankets for me. I set my bag down next to the sofa and Katrina surprises me by pulling me into a big hug.

"Thank you. Thank you doesn't begin to cover everything you've done for me the last couple of days, but thank you."

"You're welcome. If you need anything I'll be here, don't be afraid to wake me. I'll check on you between cases tomorrow." Katrina nods and makes her way upstairs.

*****

A sharp clatter rouses me from my sleep. I sit up, briefly disoriented as to where I am. Reality sets in when I hear Katrina's expletive emanate from the kitchen. The smells of breakfast hit me then, coffee brewing and bacon frying. I fold the blankets and leave them and the pillow in a neat pile on one end of the sofa before making my way towards the heavenly aromas.

"Morning," I say as I stifle a yawn. Katrina nearly jumps out of her slippers and one hand shoots to her chest. "Sorry, didn't mean to startle you."

"Shit. Sorry, I didn't mean to wake you." She grabs a coffee mug and pours me a cup. "There are a few different creamers in the refrigerator. Help yourself."

"Thanks. What's all of this?" I ask, indicating the multiple frying pans Katrina has working on the stove. I find the french vanilla creamer and dilute my coffee, hoping I can get enough caffeine to jump start my workout free morning. Katrina turns and looks at me briefly, I can see the dark circles under her eyes. Either she didn't sleep at all, or she slept fitfully.

"I wanted to make you breakfast. You were nice enough to stay here last night, on my couch. I know this isn't how you typically start your day. I put some towels in the bathroom if you'd like a shower." Katrina quickly forces each sentence out as she shifts her focus between frying pans.

"Thanks, that would be great." I head down the hallway to the bathroom, coffee in hand, hoping that the combination of coffee and a shower will get me moving.

Loaded up on bacon, eggs, pancakes and two cups of coffee, I thank Katrina and head for the hospital. Halfway there it's apparent that my body misses getting the endorphins going. I know I'm going to need a double shot from the coffee shop to really get myself through the morning. I make my way to the doctor's lounge to review my cases, happy that my first case is a quick fat grafting case to finish filling in a few areas around a set of bilateral implants. I also have an exchange of expanders for implants case and an implant exchange for reduction case. I silently hope that I have a good tech, or today could easily become a long day. I'm thankful when I find out I have Alex in my room today. Her relationship with Catherine is the best thing to happen to my surgery rotation in a long time.

We knock out the first case, and I head out to manage my usual post op activities. Once finished, I send a text to Katrina checking in. She responds quickly letting me know she is doing alright. It occurs to me that I might actually be bothering her with the texts, so I message her again asking her if it does. She assures me that it doesn't. I let her know I'll check in again after my next case and head back down to the OR. Alex has the room turned over in record time, and my patient is being intubated when I arrive. An extra bit of luck falls into my lap when Dr. Yates, a fourth-year resident, shows up, enabling Abby and me to operate on both sides simultaneously. We finish up the case, I do my usual post operative tasks and head up to grab a quick lunch in the cafeteria. Sushi and a soda in hand, I find a vacant seat and check in with Katrina. She responds that she's ok and asks if I am done for the day. I let her know I have one more case, but should be done by four at the latest. I also ask again if she needs anything. She assures me she's ok, so I shrug it off, inhale my food and head back downstairs. Abby and company are prepping the patient when I return. I'm happy to see that Dr. Yates is joining us again, meaning this case should go pretty quickly.

I break scrub at 3:30 and head out to take care of my required tasks. Tasks completed, I head upstairs to check on the one patient I have staying in house. Everything seems fine with her, leaving me free to head home. I pull into my driveway and am surprised to see an obviously upset Katrina sitting on my porch. I park in the garage and sneak under the door as it starts to close, making my way over to Katrina.

"Sorry to ambush you like this, I just didn't know where to go or who I could deal with talking to." I unlock the front door and let us into the house.

"It's alright, what happened?" I stop just inside the entryway, sensing that something isn't right.

"When you texted me after your second case I was speaking with a detective that had stopped by. They caught the guy, the guy that..." Tears start streaming down Katrina's cheeks. I don't need her to finish the sentence, I know what's happened. I give her a hug before leading her to the kitchen. I put on a kettle of water to make us some tea and join Katrina at the bar while I wait for it to boil.

"You could have told me this earlier. I could have figured something out if you needed someone there."

"No, you can't cancel your cases for this. Besides I wasn't sure how I felt, I still don't know how I feel or am supposed to feel about it. Am I supposed to feel happy because they caught the guy? Relieved? Angry?"

"How do you feel about it?"

"Like all those things are in a bag that someone keeps shaking up. I'm happy that they caught the guy, and that he confessed. Apparently, he had his license taken away last year because of multiple drunk driving offenses. I'm relieved that he won't have an opportunity to do it again, at least not for a long time. More and more though I'm angry. Angry about all of it. That he was given so many chances, that I had to make the decision to remove life support, that she's gone long before she was supposed to be, that our time was cut short." The tea kettle goes off as Katrina becomes increasingly animated; like her anger is responsible for heating the water. I turn the stove off and assess Katrina. It's clear that she's angry, but her jeans and t-shirt aren't ideal for what I have in mind.

"Wait here a second, I'll be right back." I head to my bedroom and change into a pair of gym shorts and a t-shirt. I grab a second set for Katrina, estimating her to be similar in size. I return to the kitchen and hand them to Katrina, who eyes me with a quizzical look. "Go put these on and meet me in the basement." To my surprise, she doesn't argue. I head downstairs and turn on my iPod. The Yeah Yeah Yeahs start up, good for working off some angst for sure. Katrina joins me and looks at me expectantly. "Are you angry?" She gives me an are you kidding me look, she's clearly not amused. "Well, are you? Are you pissed off?"

"Yeah, I am!" Her voice booms over the music.

"Good. Own it, admit it. You want to hit something?" This time she looks at me like I've lost my mind. "Not me. The bag maybe," I wave my hand at the punching bag hanging from the ceiling. Katrina nods, the anger still blazing in her eyes. "Ok. Do you know how to properly make a fist and throw a punch?" She balls up her fist, and I'm pleased to see that she isn't amongst the many who tuck their thumb inside of their curled fingers. "Good." She moves to punch the bag, and I have to physically restrain her. "Whoa, whoa, whoa! Hold on there. Just one second." If I thought she was pissed before the fire in her eyes burns threefold now. I quickly make my way to the storage closet and pull out a set of gloves. "Use these, you'll thank me later." I help her put the gloves on and watch as she gets used to how they feel. "Go ahead and hit the bag when you're ready." I barely get the sentence out before she takes a swing at the bag. Her form is sloppy. I try to correct her, but she is going to town. Knowing that this is what she needs, I allow her to take her emotions out on the bag. After a minute or so she stops and I think it's because she has tired, only I quickly realize that she is sobbing, her mood swinging in an entirely new direction. She struggles with the gloves, fighting to get them off but gives up and slumps against the wall before I can help her. I cross the room to her and sit down on the floor at her feet, freeing her hands from the gloves. She wraps her arms around her legs and rests her head on her knees as she cries. I sit uselessly in front of her, waiting for her to calm down or let me know what she needs. When she finally looks up I know, she needs a tissue, something I don't keep down here. I get up and grab a towel from the storage cabinet, knowing anything she throws at it will wash out. I hand it to her and she looks at me, but uses it when I nod my head to let her know it's ok. She stands up and her eyes dart between me and the bag. "You want to try again?"

"Yeah, I do. I don't even understand why. I've never been an angry person, but every day I feel it taking me over, bit by bit."

"Let me show you a few things." I slip the gloves on and show Katrina the proper way to throw a jab. After I demonstrate one in real time, I take it step by step, telling her to mimic my actions. I go over the proper stance with her, ensuring her feet are the appropriate distance apart, her hips remain inside her feet and her knees are slightly bent. I also tell her that it's important to keep her hands up and her elbows pointing toward the floor. She looks tight, so I remind her to relax, that tightening up early will slow down her speed. When I'm confident she understands everything up to this point, I show her an actual jab in slow motion, making sure she understands the extension and rotation of the arm. We go over this a few times, and I have her demonstrate a few to me. When I'm confident she has it, I slip off the gloves and assist her with them one more time.

"How do you know all of this?"

"I had a friend in high school whose father trained Golden Gloves fighters. He was worried about me going off to college and wanted to make sure I could defend myself. So he gave me lessons." Katrina gets into her proper stance and tries a few basic jabs. Once I'm confident she has it down, I show her how to expand on it. She practices until she's out of breath and markedly more relaxed than she was before we started. I shut off the iPod, and we head back upstairs for some water. "Feel any better?"

"Yeah, actually, I do feel a little better."

"If you want to come to a training session with me on Thursday night you are welcome to. It can be intense and kick your butt, but it's great stress relief."

"I can't this Thursday, maybe the following week though?"

"Sure, but it'll have to be in three weeks." I must have shown a small measure of disappointment at her answer, even if I didn't intend to.

"Jill's memorial service is Thursday. Why three weeks?" Sadness takes over her features. I feel like an ass for not even thinking about the fact that there would be a service and Katrina hadn't told me the date yet.

"I'm part of a mission trip to Ghana. We leave a week from Saturday and we'll be gone two weeks." With everything that's been going on, the trip is quickly sneaking up on me.

"I hadn't pegged you as being religious." I nearly laugh out loud but manage to contain myself at the last second.

"I'm not, at all. The trip is to provide surgical services to those who would otherwise not have access to them. We'll operate for roughly 12 hours a day, each day we're there. I'll be there primarily to take care of the cleft lips, cleft palates, and such. I'll also help out with breast cases as needed."

"I'm beginning to think you're some kind of saint." I can't tell if she is being serious or sarcastic. "Seriously, you've taken care of me, you travel around the world and provide free services to those who need them. What else do you do?" This time I do laugh.

"I assure you, I'm no saint." My stomach grumbles, so I check the clock to discover it is almost 6. "You hungry?"

"Yeah, I am."

"I made some Chicken Salad yesterday. I have lettuce you can put it over, or you could make a sandwich with it. Sound ok?"

"Sounds great actually." We eat dinner and discuss a variety of topics. Katrina asks more questions about the mission trip, our most embarrassing moments, things that very few people know about us, and views on religion and politics. By the time Katrina leaves it's nearly 9. I head to the master suite and get ready for bed. I melt into my bed and am fast asleep before I can open my book.

Chapter 7

Thursday afternoon Catherine and Alex meet Abby and me outside of the funeral home. We enter the parlor to find it packed. I scan the faces in the room looking for Katrina. Several faces look familiar, former and current patients. It makes me realize how closely knit the community is here, and how I have largely failed to become a part of it. I locate Katrina near the front of the parlor, surrounded by people who are likely expressing their condolences. To my surprise, she looks as if she's holding up fairly well. Aside from a few brief text messages, I haven't spoken with her since she left my house Monday evening. A few people greet us as they pass by, and for some reason, I'm surprised to see how many know Catherine. The appointed hour arrives, and the hushed din that previously consumed the room abates as Katrina and Jill's friends find their seats. We maintain our place at the back, not really feeling like we belong here, yet wanting to show Katrina support.

The service is non-denominational and brief. One of their friends reads a letter written by Jill, reminding everyone to live their lives to the fullest, act in ways that make a positive change, and to love one another like it's their last day. She also asks her friends and loved ones not to spend their time grieving for her, that she lived a life that made her happy, tried to help those in need and could move on without any regrets. I realize as I listen to the reading that Jill must have prepared this when she was diagnosed with cancer. I hear Abby sniffle on my right and look over to see Catherine and Alex leaning on each other on my left. Another friend reads a eulogy that she prepared, her words turning to a muffled drone as I scan the room. Katrina swipes at the tears trying to roll down her cheeks. I admire the strength she possesses to not break down completely. People suddenly begin to stand, breaking me out of my reflections. The service is at an end. I see people queue up near the closed casket to pay their final respects and speak with Katrina. I cannot fathom how exhausting this must be for her, yet she stands there, hugging each person as they convey words that I'm certain do nothing to fill the emptiness she must feel. I remember my mother's service, this same line, the pitying looks, the hushed whispers about my being so young, being forced to stand there listening to each person's condolences as they hugged me and assured me that everything would be ok, that they were sorry. I don't recall how it made me feel then, but thinking about it now leaves me feeling irritated. Katrina eyes the four of us and breaks with tradition, excusing herself from the people waiting to speak with her. She disappears into the mass of people waiting to pay their respects before breaking through and joining us in the back.

"Thank you for coming, I really appreciate it." She hugs Catherine and Alex before allowing herself to be enveloped by Abby. I see her face tighten a little as Abby whispers something to her. She breaks free from Abby and turns her attention to me, pulling me in for a hug. "Please get me out of here. I can't listen to one more person tell me they're sorry," she whispers as she locks her arms around me.

"Ok, but don't you want to say goodbye?"

"The casket is empty. She had arranged for her ashes to be repurposed into one of those coral reef things."

"Ok. Anything we need to grab before we leave?"

"No." I look around the room at the people still milling about. I have no idea where Katrina wants us to take her, but I know if we don't get her out of here soon, people will flock to her back here, effectively blocking any chance of an exit.

"Alright, come on." I make my way towards the exit, hoping Catherine, Alex and Abby follow suit. I push my way out the door and quickly head around the corner, near the side street where we parked. I'm happy to see that our entire party is in tow.

"What was that?" Catherine eyes me, questioning our rushed exit. I shake my head at her, and she allows the matter to rest. "Ok, anyone feel like getting a drink then?"

"Yes," Katrina is quick to answer the offer. "Somewhere that people won't think to look for me." We all look at each other; as if we can communicate and deliberate silently.

"The brewery?" I make the suggestion knowing we need to get out of here if we're going to escape without being spotted. Catherine and Alex exchange a look, then look at me. Alex shrugs and Catherine nods. Brewery it is. "Meet you over there?" Everyone agrees, and we head towards our cars.

"Can you drop me to pick up my car before we get to the brewery? I don't think I'll be able to stay as late as you guys will." Abby's request will take us a few miles out of the way, but isn't an issue. We make the drive back to the office in silence. Abby has never really been able to tolerate silence, so she attempts to make small talk. I've never been a fan of small talk and Katrina is clearly not in the mood for it, so Abby's attempts fall on deaf ears. Abby starts her car and heads out of the parking lot towards the brewery. I should follow but leave the car in park as I look over at Katrina.

"You ok?" She doesn't answer me for at least half a minute. I give up and move to put the car in drive when she finally speaks.

"I'm trying, I really am. It's just this anger, I can't get rid of it. Then at the funeral home, everyone telling me they're sorry, that she loved me, going on and on. The more people said those things to me, the angrier I could feel myself getting. If I didn't get out of there I was going to blow a gasket, just start screaming, throw something…I don't know. I'm trying, trying to stay calm, but it gets harder every day." Katrina draws a deep breath in through her nose and releases it out her mouth. She repeats this as I pull my phone out and send Catherine a quick message that we will be another 5 to 10 minutes, to start without us. I put the car in drive and pull out of the lot, heading towards the woods a mile down the road. I park on the shoulder and shut off the engine.

"What are we doing here?"

"Come on." I open my door and get out of the car, but Katrina just eyes me like I'm crazy. "Trust me." She relents and exits the car, following my lead. I guide her into the trees just far enough that I can barely see the outline of my car along the roadside. "You want to scream? Scream!" Katrina gives me a look like she officially knows I've lost my mind but says nothing. "Scream damn it! Let it out!" I'm yelling at her, trying to get her to just let it go. She finally does, screaming as loud as she possibly can. As she repeats it, I look around and find a smaller fallen tree branch. It is fairly lightweight, but seems sturdy enough. She looks at me as I hand it to her. "Want to hit something? Go to town." This time she doesn't hesitate. She starts swinging the branch at a nearby tree, screaming in frustration with each connection. When the branch finally snaps she looks at me like a kid that has broken a new toy. "Throw it!" She does, and we both watch as the branch sails end over end before connecting with another tree, causing it to drop lifelessly to the ground. I look around and find a small rock. I pick it up and give it to her. She needs no direction, this time hurling it out into the thicket of trees before us. I kick aside some fallen pine needles and find a few pinecones, not ideal but she can throw them. I hand them to her one at a time, and she hurls them as far as she can. "Better?" She draws in successive breaths, but nods that she is. "Ok, let's go then." We get back in the car, and I head to the brewery. "I'm going to put you in touch with my trainer, see if he can't give you my time slot while I'm away, or get you in at another time. You need something to help you vent, maybe it will help. Until then I'll get you a spare set of keys to my place. Feel free to use the basement or the woods whenever you need to."

"Thanks. Why is it you never tell me you're sorry for my loss, or I never see that pitying look in your eyes?"

"Honestly?" I see her nod in my peripheral view. "Well, that's a multi-part thing. One reason is that I remember when my mom died, people would say those things to me or I'd see their looks, and it was irritating and exhausting. Second, if I said those things or gave you those looks, would it even be believable? I mean I didn't really know you or Jill, and if events hadn't panned out exactly as they did, we probably wouldn't be in this car right now. For instance, if I hadn't had an unusually long day in the OR I could have been long gone and wouldn't have had a clue what had happened. I guess my point is that we really aren't friends, so would my saying those things to you even be believable?" Katrina allows my words to soak in for a few seconds.

"But we're friends now, or at least becoming friends, aren't we?" My turn to deliberate. I guess we must be, I mean I did just offer her a set of keys to my house.

"Yeah, but my point is would it even feel real if I said those things to you. Do I feel sorry about what happened? Absolutely. I can't even begin to imagine how you feel, nor will I pretend to. Have I felt some degree of pity for you? Yeah, I probably have. But I've also seen how damn strong you've been, and I know that you're going to be ok. Maybe it will be a while, but I know you're going to get there." I can feel Katrina staring at me, yet my sideways view doesn't allow me to discern her expression. Never a red light when you need one. "What?"

"That might be the most honest thing anyone has said to me since the accident. Thank you."

"I don't exactly have anything to lose do I?" I pull into the parking space and shut off the car.

"Well, we are friends now." Katrina at least smiles a little as she says it.

"I suppose so. Before we go in, are you planning on getting blitzed in there?"

"Would it be an issue if I were?" Honestly, I'd prefer she didn't, but I have no right to tell her not to.

"It would be understandable. Just want to know what I should be prepared for."

"Honestly, I have no idea."

We enter the brewery and find the table occupied by Catherine, Alex, and Abby. Katrina heads directly for the bar and Catherine gives me a look. "She needed to blow off some steam, so I stopped and let her get some of her frustrations out." This time Alex gives me a look. "Not in the way you're thinking. Not everyone thinks that sex is one of the key food groups like you do." Catherine and Alex start laughing as I head towards the bar.

"...heard. Sorry I couldn't make it today. Sara! I was wondering where you were when those three walked in."

"Hey, Nate." I look from Nate to Katrina and back again. "You two know each other?"

"For years. I met Katrina when we were in some of the same undergrad classes. I didn't know the two of you were friends though."

"May I have my usual?" I ask, opting to ignore getting into whether or not Katrina and I are friends.

"Food, drink, or both?"

"Did they order anything to eat yet?" Nate shakes his head. "Just the drink then. How's Jeff?"

"Oh you know Jeff, he'd tell you he's fabulous. Honestly, he is. He should be back soon, he's taking a delivery over to a VIP customer." Nate sets two whiskey sours on the counter. "On the house ladies." Katrina and I take our drinks and make our way back to our table. I quickly pick up that the topic of conversation is the mission trip and why Abby is not joining us this year.

"So Sara, when will we be intruding on Friday night dinner and drinks again?" Catherine wears a hopeful grin as she poses the question.

"It will have to wait until after my trip. Maybe in a month." I watch her grin transform into a frown and shrug in response.

"Sorry, Friday night dinner and drinks?"

"Alex and Abby have been friends since the beginning of time. They have a custom of going out after work together on Friday nights, just the two of them. Catherine and I invite ourselves along now and again."

"Wait so you two," Katrina points to Alex and Abby, "used to and now you two?" She looks at me and then Abby. The four of us all start laughing in unison.

"No, Abby has never been a vagatarian."

"Alex, really?" Catherine pokes her in the side. Nate saunters over to our table and sets a drink in front of Abby.

"What's this?" Abby eyes the drink and then joins the rest of us, focusing on Nate.

"Gentleman at the bar sends his regards. Anyone else need another?" Katrina indicates that she does. I look over and realize that she's made her way through her first one before I'm halfway through mine. I can see where this evening is headed already and ask Nate to bring me a water when he returns. As he walks away, we all start giving Abby a hard time, trying to figure out which of the men at the bar bought her the drink. We make our picks so we can force it out of Nate when he returns. When he does, we discover that Catherine was right, not surprising since she seems to possess a 6th sense when it comes to reading people. Abby pumps Nate for some information on the man, trying to decide if she should go talk to him. Nate says he seems like a decent guy, used to come in with the same woman but he hasn't seen her in months, that he never gets drunk, usually just has a drink or two before leaving, and, most importantly, he says, that he is a good tipper.

We order food while Abby continues to deliberate. By the time it arrives, Katrina is on her third drink, and Abby has decided to go for it. Abby takes her time returning, she doesn't have to hurry, she ordered a simple Caesar Salad. I prepare to eat my buffalo chicken wrap while I observe Katrina, hoping she will eat at least half of her burger and fries. Thankfully she does, and we somehow manage to keep the conversation lively enough as we watch Abby interacting with the stranger. Twenty minutes later Abby practically bounces back to our table.

"Clearly that went well," Alex teases Abby.

"It did, only, I sorta need to bail on Friday night dinner and drinks tomorrow. Is that OK?" Alex looks at Catherine and grins.

"I'm sure I'll find something to occupy the time." Abby looks slightly embarrassed before looking at me.

"Oh, uh, I don't think it should be an issue but—." I cut her off.

"I'll let you go if it gets too late. One of us should have some semblance of a love life." I notice Katrina signaling for another drink. Everyone looks at me, and I realize that I'm not the only one keeping tabs on her consumption. I subtly shake my head and shrug my shoulders. Thankfully, no one says anything. At this point, I'm grateful that she ate a little over half of her food. Sensing where things are heading for Katrina, my companions have the wherewithal to ask for their tabs when Nate brings Katrina's fresh drink to the table.

"What tabs?" Nate winks as he walks away from us. Catherine and I look at each other and both start digging cash out at the same time. Abby takes off first, needing to get home to see her kid. Catherine collects the cash from me and tells me to focus on getting Katrina to the car. I thank her as she heads up to the bar to stuff Nate's tip jar.

"Ready?" I watch as Katrina downs the remainder of her drink and slowly stands up, clearly wobbly on her feet. Alex notices. and we each take a side in an effort to get her out to my car. Once she's safely deposited in the passengers seat, I close the door and give Alex a hug goodbye, thanking her. Catherine joins us and we hug as well. They both look at Katrina then back at me.

"What are you going to do with her?" Catherine asks as I sigh and run my fingers through my hair.

"I can't very well leave her alone. I'll probably take her back to mine. I have things I need to take care of."

"Be careful." Catherine doesn't say anything else. She and Alex clasp hands as they walk away, leaving me to deal with Katrina on my own. I climb into my car and start it, letting it idle as I try to figure out what I'm supposed to do. Resigned to my fate, I back out of my spot and head home.

"Hey, this isn't my house," Katrina slurs as I wait for the garage door to open. How very observant I think to myself as I put the car in park. I scold myself for becoming irritated, she has every reason to drown her sorrows, I just never had a high tolerance for drunk people.

"No, it isn't. I have things to get done and I don't think you should be alone right now." I open my door and climb out of the car. Katrina opens hers and practically falls out, saved by the seatbelt I insisted she fasten before we left the brewery.

"No, I need to go get my car," she protests, causing me to shake my head.

"Not tonight you don't. I'll take you in the morning." I pull one of her arms over my shoulder and wrap mine around her waist, basically hauling her into the house. Once inside I deposit her at the dining room table and head back to the kitchen to get her a glass of water. "Drink this," I order setting it in front of her. I quickly grab my laptop from the den and join Katrina at the table. I remotely log in, hopping I can get some charting done while I work to sober Katrina up. We sit at the table for an hour as I work on my charting, only pausing to refill her glass. She remains quiet the entire time. I'm not sure if she is simply brooding or if I should be concerned. I finish up my final chart and check the clock. I'm late for class, which I knew back at the brewery I was going to miss. I send a quick message to Jason apologizing and asking for a favor. He lets me know not to worry and asks what I need. I briefly explain the situation and give him Katrina's name, asking if he has room to work her in. He assures me he does, to pass along his number to her. Those things taken care of, I refocus my attention on Katrina who appears to be half asleep while sitting at the table. I stand up and look at her.

"Come on," I order, extending my hand. She stands up, a little steadier on her feet, but takes my hand anyway. I'm glad that I brought her back here, where the bedrooms are all on the main level. I lead her down the hall to the guest room where she promptly flops down onto the bed. I pull her shoes off, my irritation growing. I cannot stand it when guests wear shoes in someone's home. I take advantage of Katrina already being half asleep to retreat to the kitchen to refill her water. I return to the guest room and deposit it on the night stand. "Get up." She stirs a little, so I grab both of her hands and start pulling her to her feet. I hold her up long enough to fling the comforter and sheet back, then redeposit her in the bed. She curls up in the fetal position, so I flip the bedding back over her, knowing her suit is going to be rumpled beyond belief in the morning. I switch the bedside lamp on and Katrina's hand darts out and grabs mine, startling me.

"I'm sorry I'm such a mess." A tear rolls down the side of her nose as I look at her.

"Don't worry about it. Get some sleep." I exit the room, leaving the door slightly ajar as I do. It's too early for bed, so I change into a pair of shorts and a t-shirt and curl up on the sofa in the den with a new book. I'm in the middle of the third chapter when I hear Katrina shuffling down the hall. I feel her eyes on me as she stops short of the sofa, as if she is debating whether she should join me or just go back to bed. I turn and look at her as she deposits herself on the end of the couch.

"I can't sleep."

"That suit probably isn't helping. I'll grab you something a little more comfortable." I head back to my bedroom and grab a pair of shorts and a shirt for Katrina to sleep in. I turn around to return to the living room and nearly scream aloud. Katrina is standing in my doorway, I hadn't heard her following me. "Good grief, I'm starting to think you're determined to give me a heart attack tonight." Katrina looks ashamed as I hand her the clothes. "Change into this, see if it helps." I head back to the den as Katrina closes the door to the guest room. I pick up where I left off and by the time I reach the end of the chapter Katrina has not returned. I assume she's finally fallen asleep.

Ten minutes later I am alerted to the fact that I'm wrong as Katrina plops down onto the couch next to me. "What can I do?" She doesn't say anything, she simply scoots away from me, then lays her head on my thigh, focusing her gaze on the blank TV screen. I have no idea what to do. I know that I need to get to bed soon, so I can't allow her to fall asleep like this. As I try to figure out my strategy, I feel the cool moisture start to soak through my shorts as Katrina lays there silently crying. Without thinking, I start to slowly stroke her chestnut hair. She sniffles and swipes at her eyes, so I give her the silence she needs and go back to my book. After another chapter, I look down to discover she's fast asleep. I set my book down and slowly extract myself from under her head, replacing my thigh with one of the decorative throw pillows, that up until now I've questioned its purpose. I head to the hall closet and grab a pair of blankets and return to the den to drape them over Katrina. I shut off the lights and head down the hallway to prepare for bed. I've just drifted off to sleep when a soft knock on my door pulls me back to an alert state. I switch on the bedside lamp, wincing at the sudden brightness. "Come in."

Katrina opens the door and stands in the doorway. "I don't think I can be alone right now." Without a word, I flip the bedding back on the far side of the king size bed. Katrina shuffles her way around and climbs in. *What am I doing?*, I think to myself as I switch the lamp back off. I shake my head in the dark, knowing I likely won't be sleeping much tonight, I seldom sleep well when sharing a bed with anyone.

Chapter 8

I don't hear from Katrina at all over the weekend. I'm not sure if I expected to, but by Monday I'm concerned enough that I plan to stop by her place on my way home. My second patient arrives to pre-op and is found to have a fever and elevated cell counts, causing me to have to reschedule her surgery. I can't risk placing implants in someone with an existing infection coursing through their body. I hate that she will have to wait a few more weeks to have the next step in her reconstruction done, but being safe is the best course of action we can take. Wrapping things up in the OR just after noon, I find myself excited at the prospect of having a little extra free time before I leave for Ghana on Saturday. I run a few errands and then pull into Katrina's driveway. I ring the bell, but she doesn't answer. Given that her car is parked in front of mine, I assume that she's home and that she doesn't want to see me, or maybe anyone. I send her a text letting her know that I stopped by to check on her and ask her to let me know if she needs anything. I head home and park in my customary space in the garage. The sound of blaring music greets me as I enter my house and panic momentarily sets in. It takes me a few seconds to realize that the music is coming from the basement and to recall that I gave Katrina a set of keys Friday morning. I kick off my shoes and make my way down the basement steps, making no effort to be quiet, Katrina won't be able to hear me over the blaring din of her music anyway. I stop at the base of the stairs and watch Katrina attack the bag, mixing uppercuts and hooks in with her jabs, or at least the semblance of those punches, her form on each needing refinement. She's breathing heavily and sweat seems to be oozing out of her every pore. Oblivious to the fact that I'm here, I move over to the iPod connected to my system and pause the song, bringing a welcome respite from whatever angry music Katrina had playing.

"What the fu—," Katrina pants as she turns around. She shrieks when she sees me. "What are you doing here?" I raise a single eyebrow at her, is she seriously questioning what I am doing in my own home?

"It's my house." Katrina bends at the waist, putting her hands on her knees as she tries to catch her breath. "You really should stand up straight and put your hands on top of or behind your head if you're trying to catch your breath." She heeds my advice and adjusts her posture. I make my way over to her, stopping an arm's length away. I'm still in my dress slacks and blouse, not the appropriate attire for this, but it should allow me the freedom of movement to show her the adjustments she should make. "Who taught you the uppercut and the hook?"

"I watched a few videos on the internet. Why?"

"No reason, other than you should consider making a few adjustments to your form if you wish to properly utilize those punches. Do you?" Katrina nods that she does, so I spend the next few minutes going over them with her. She demonstrates to me that she understands the changes and can maintain them while switching her punches up. "How long have you been at it?"

"I don't know. I met with Jason this morning and had my first class. I still felt full of energy, so I biked over here. What time is it?"

"Going on one."

"Really? I hadn't realized. I've been down here at least an hour already."

"You had a class with Jason this morning, and now you've been down here for over an hour?" My tone communicates my concern as Katrina eyes me warily and nods. "Be careful, don't over do it."

"Well, it's either this or drink."

"Why? Do you usually spend your time drinking?" I see the anger flash in her eyes.

"Don't. Don't psychoanalyze me!" She grits her teeth as she barks her command.

"I'm just concerned. Maybe talking to someone would help. I could make some calls about grief—."

"I DON'T WANT TO FUCKING TALK TO ANYONE!" Rage surges through her silver eyes as she screams at me. I refuse to participate in this conversation, if that's what this is, anymore. I throw up my hands before turning around and pressing play on her iPod, her music of choice now appealing to the surging anger I feel. "Sara. Sara wait!" I ignore her and head back upstairs. The sun is shining, and the weather is warm for this time of year, so I change into a pair of sweats, make myself a glass of lemonade, and take a seat on the patio on the back side of the house. My Kindle sits in my lap ignored. I'm unsure why I bothered to bring it with me. In my vexed state, I won't be able to focus on, much less enjoy, reading anything. Instead, I stare off into the woods, hoping the sounds of the birds chirping and the feel of the warm sunshine will calm me down. I have no idea how long I sit there, listening to the sounds of nature when the sound of the slider door opening sends a new wave of irritation coursing through me. I don't bother to look at her or acknowledge her presence.

"Sara—." I quickly hold up my hand, silencing her.

"You will never speak to me like that again, most certainly not in my own home. Understood?" I still refuse to look at her, opting to let my icy tone convey my sentiments.

"Yes," she murmurs. "I'm sorry."

"Aren't you sick of having to apologize for your behavior? I'm sick of hearing it." I'm being unduly harsh at this point, I know, but it's my turn to lash out it seems. "I was only expressing concern for your well-being and offering a possible means of assistance."

"I know." I hear her release a deep breath. "May I sit?" I flip my hand at the chairs I know exist to my right, still refusing to take my eyes off of the woods. Not content with this, Katrina seats herself across the table from me, trying to force me to look at her. "I just feel angry all the time, and when it isn't anger, it's a fire fueled rage. I hate everyone, even the people I know I actually care about. I hate seeing everyone going happily about their lives. I hate people I've never even met. To answer your question, the drinking is new. I was a social drinker at worst before, maybe three drinks a week. Now all I want to do is hit things and drink."

"You're spiraling out of control. You need help. Help that I'm not able to offer you. You need to talk to someone."

"I know, but I'm not ready." I close my eyes against the anger I feel flare up inside of me, like being near Katrina has infected me with the poison coursing through her veins. I want to toss the chair I'm sitting on against the house, I see myself doing it in my mind's eye. Instead, I take a deep breath, and as I let it slowly slip past my barely parted lips I open my eyes, refocusing on the woods stretched out a few hundred yards away. I hear the sound of Katrina's chair scraping across the paving stones and the opening and closing of the patio door as she heads inside, presumably to leave. I don't try to stop her, despite the fact that I know she will likely head home and drown herself in a bottle of her choosing. I don't try to stop her because I know no matter how badly I'd like to keep her from self-destructing, nothing I can say or do will dissuade her from this path she does not wish to abandon. I don't try to stop her because I know that I can't keep putting myself on the front lines of a battle that cannot be won.

*****

I arrive at class Thursday night, happy that my early day on Monday allowed me to prepare for my trip and keep my usual appointment. I walk in and toss my bag on the floor in the corner, pulling off my shoes and sweats. I make my way over to the rack and grab a bar to use during my normal stretching routine.

"Hey Sara," I hear Jason call and find his reflection in the mirror. I feel a fresh wave of irritation spread through me as I see Katrina's reflection as well.

"I thought I'd combine your classes on Thursdays, since you're friends. She's still green, but she's been coming in every day and working hard. You ok with that?" Tonight I'm not, but what choice do I have? I nod that I am and continue my routine. I study my reflection in the mirror as I stretch and wonder if I'm the only one able to see the anger in my features, my tense shoulders and clenched jaw. I join them and Jason fills me in on Katrina's progress. He has me work on the bag while he goes over some grappling and counter moves with Katrina. I set to work on the bag, hammering it mercilessly time and again, alternating between jabs, hooks, and crosses. My pace is frenetic, and I quickly feel the sweat soaking through my shirt.

"Ok Golden Gloves, now you're just showing off." That wasn't my intent, but it probably looked that way. "I'm going to have you spar with Katrina for a little bit. Just take it easy on her, she hasn't been doing this as long as you have." I nod that I will and follow him to where Katrina waits for us on the mats. Jason signals for us to begin and I immediately take the defensive, always preferring to attack an opponent when they're vulnerable. Katrina moves in, and I easily evade her attempt, sweeping her legs and taking her down. I allow her to get up as Jason gives me a cautioning look. Katrina comes at me again and I effortlessly counter, this time slamming her into the mat a little more forcefully than I should.

"Shit!" Guilt surges through me as Katrina takes a moment to get up. I look up at Jason and can tell he is equal parts confused and pissed. "I can't do this tonight, I've gotta go." Jason furrows his brow at me but nods a silent dismissal. I return to my bag in the corner and take off my gloves, stuffing them back into the bag, before pulling on my sweats and shoes. I pull the hood of my sweatshirt over my head and make my way outside. Knowing that I'm too angry to drive right now, I toss my bag in the car, before locking it up and starting on what I hope will be a mind clearing walk.

"Sara!" Katrina's voice calls to me as she exits the gym. "Wait!" I ignore her and keep walking, despite the patter of her footfalls on the sidewalk as she runs to close the distance between us. Hood up, head down, hands in the pockets of my zip-up sweatshirt, I keep walking, knowing that I likely won't be clearing my head after all. She catches up and wraps her hand around my bicep, pulling me against my intended direction. My anger surges and I stop myself before I swing. The aborted motion and the tensing of my bicep have a look of terror mixed with shock registered on Katrina's face.

"That," I say lowering my eyes to her hand, "is a singularly bad idea right now." She releases my arm and backs up a step.

"Just talk to me. You're pissed off at me, I get it." I shake my head at her and start walking again. Persistent in her pursuit, she follows.

"Angry at you, yes. You seem hell-bent on bottoming out. You refuse any effort I've made to talk to you or to assist you in finding someone you can talk to. You scream at me in my home and drown yourself in a bottle every chance you get. I could have easily hurt you three different times in the last half hour because of that anger, now I feel guilty about that. Worst of all though, now I pity you. I pity you because of all the ways you could cope, could choose to combat everything you're going through, you're taking the easy way out and finding solace in a bottle." Her fists clench and rage flashes in her eyes. She wants to hit me, I can see it clear as day, and if she did, I know I wouldn't hit her back.

"You have no idea what I'm going through," she says through clenched teeth. Her fists unfurl, and her muscles relax. "Do you think this is easy or something? That I'm enjoying this? Do you?"

"No, but you need to admit that you need help. Help that I, nor your friends, can give you." She briefly stands in defiance before the fight goes out of her. Her shoulders slump and her head drops down, shame taking over her body.

"I know. I'm going to find a grief counselor." Her voice morphs into a quiet mumble as she admits this.

"Good." I think about my next words and loathe them before they leave my mouth. "Katrina, I'm not big on ultimatums, but I'm going to give you one anyway. I leave for Ghana Saturday morning. I will be unreachable while I am away. I don't want to see you again until you get help. My natural instinct is to try to help you, and I know I won't stop trying, even as you spiral further downward. You'll get help when you're ready, but I'm asking you not to contact me until you do. This is your journey, but if the trajectory of your path is only a downward slope, then I can't continue on it with you." The blood in my veins turns to ice as shock settles itself across her features. I have to walk away when I notice tears starting to pool in her eyes. At that moment I know that I am a terrible human being, that I'm walking away from her when she likely needs support more than ever. Self-preservation trumps self-sacrifice at times, no matter how shitty it makes you feel. I get in my car and find myself wishing that tomorrow were Saturday, and I would be getting on the plane to Ghana.

Chapter 9

I step off the plane and plant myself on familiar terra firma. I'm exhausted, but filled with a sense of fulfillment from having helped the patients in Ghana, grateful for the luxuries that I have and take for granted, but most of all I feel a renewed sense of spirit, I feel at peace. My colleagues and I pile into our shared ride and make our way out of long term parking. Right now I want nothing more than a long hot shower, the comfort of my bed and 12 hours of uninterrupted sleep. I can almost feel the pulsing warmth of the water on my neck and shoulders, that is until I see Katrina's car in my driveway. The pinpricks of irritation I start to feel only intensify as I pull my suitcase from the trunk of the car. By the time I slip my key into the lock, the peace I had been feeling is gone. I drop my suitcase by the door and kick off my shoes before following the sounds emanating from my kitchen. I discover Katrina preparing food of some sort, headphones in, completely oblivious to my presence as she sings and dances along to whatever is playing. I'm not sure how long I stand there, watching her while I process my conflicting emotions. Irritation and anger vie with exhaustion and the amusement I feel watching her dance around. She turns to make her way to the refrigerator and finally sees me leaning against the wall. Her fright quickly transforms into perhaps the first genuine smile I've seen her wear since Jill's accident.

"You're home! Welcome back!" Seeing her smile is nice, but I'm exhausted and questioning why she's in my home. Has she forgotten my simple request or is she just choosing to ignore it?

"What are you doing here?" I ask, managing to keep my voice even.

"I wanted to do something nice for you, so I picked up some groceries and I'm making you dinner."

"Ok, but what are you doing here? I thought I made my feelings clear the last time we spoke." Despite my even tone, my words wipe all traces of the smile from Katrina's face. She looks at the floor, and for a few seconds, I'm certain she has no intention of responding.

"You did, and I heard you. I didn't want to, but that Friday night I got blackout drunk. I woke up Saturday afternoon in my bathtub with a blood stained towel wrapped around my forearm and an empty bottle beside me. I had no idea how I ended up there or what I'd done to my arm. A quick tour of the house clued me in on a part of the evening's events as I discovered several destroyed pieces of art, the pieces Jill had acquired that I never liked. Paintings, sculptures, blown glass, all of it was fair game. I worked on cleaning the place up as I fought my pounding hangover. I realized then that you were right, I needed help. I messaged Catherine and asked if she could put me in touch with anyone. In under fifteen minutes I was on the phone arranging an emergency meeting. Not only did she recommend someone, it seems she called in a favor. I've been seeing Dr. Sutton twice a week. He has me trying all sorts of stuff, journaling, meditation, writing letters to Jill, stuff like that." Catherine did well, Sutton is well known for being one of the best. I make a mental note to thank her the next time we speak. "You're still upset, I get it. I'll just clean up and write down directions for everything, then I'll be gone."

"I'm not upset, just exhausted. I know that none of that could have been easy for you. I should apologize though. I had no right to treat you like I did or to lay down that ultimatum."

"You were right though, I was self-destructing and probably wouldn't have stopped. You've done nothing but try to look out for me since Jill's accident. I know I took advantage of that at times and I'm sorry. I won't lie though, it isn't easy, but I'm trying."

"I never thought it would be easy. I'm glad you were able to find some help. I'll still be here if you need anything." A partial smile returns to Katrina's lips.

"You will?" I nod and return her smile. "Thank you," she utters as she pulls me in for a hug. I look over her shoulder as she wraps her arms around me.

"What is all of this?" My eyes sweep over the litany of items strewn along my counter top. Various vegetables, sugar, assorted spices, and a lot of dirty dishes.

"I told you, I'm making you a meal. I wanted to repay you for all the kindness you've shown me. Catherine told me you were due back today but wasn't sure when. I figured it would be sometime this evening."

"What can I do?"

"You can march down the hallway to your room and take a nap. You look spent. Things won't be ready for a couple of hours anyway."

"I'm fine really, how can I help?" Katrina doesn't answer. Instead, she takes a glass out of the cupboard and fills it with ice water using the dispenser on the front of the refrigerator. Thankfully she turns and hands it to me. I finally see the long cut down the length of her forearm as she presses the glass into my hand. Grabbing the glass with my right hand, I wrap my left hand around her wrist and gently push upward, eying the remnants of the wound.

"I know, I'm lucky it wasn't super deep, I could have been seriously injured. I'm ok though, really." I could easily lecture her about her near miss, but her words feel genuine, so I don't. "Alright you, take your glass of water and go to bed." I open my mouth to protest but before I can say anything Katrina grabs me by the shoulders, spins me around and pushes me out of my kitchen. "Take a nap. We can have dinner when you wake up." I want to argue, but my exhausted body begs me not to. My feet feel like they're encased in concrete as I trudge my way down the hall. I close the bedroom door and unceremoniously strip as I cross the room to my beckoning bed. The last thing I recall is the soft caress of the Egyptian cotton sheets against my newly bronzed flesh as I quickly drift off.

*****

I roll over and inhale the tantalizing aroma that permeates the air in my bedroom. My salivary glands kick into overdrive as I take a deep breath and look at the clock. 6:30! I've been asleep for nearly four hours. I kick off the sheet and roll out of bed. I still want a hot shower and debate taking one before checking in with Katrina. Instead, I pull on a fresh pair of sweatpants and a comfy t-shirt and head towards the kitchen.

"Hey sleepy head, I was wondering if you were going to sleep all night." A smirk plays at Katrina's lips as she teases me.

"I probably could have. It smells amazing in here!"

"Thanks. Dinner will be ready soon."

"Can I do anything?" I look around, the dirty dishes seem to already be in the dishwasher, the table is already set.

"No. I've got this." She eyes me, and that grin is back.

"Ok. Do I have time for a quick shower?" Katrina turns away from me, and I see her shoulders shake as she stifles a chuckle.

"Good idea." I hear the small giggle escape her as I walk away. I enter the master suite, catching a glimpse of my reflection in the mirror. No wonder Katrina was so amused. My hair looks like birds have nested in it, creases from the pillow still line my face, and I'm sure if I looked closely enough I'd find traces of dried drool around my mouth. I shake my head at my reflection, switch on the water and strip off my comfortable attire. I feel like Pigpen as I step into the hot stream and convince myself that if I look down the water will be cloudy with the grime it rinses off my body.

Fresh from the shower, I realize I'm famished as I make my way back to the kitchen. "Perfect timing." Katrina grins as I take in the spread on the table. Chicken and steak fajitas with all the fixings, rice, refried beans, chips, pico de gallo, guacamole, and a pitcher of margaritas. "Catherine and Alex told me it's your favorite meal."

"It is. You made all of this?"

"Yeah, well not the chips or the tortillas, but everything else. Here, sit." She motions to one of the chairs and pours me a drink as I take a seat. She pours one for herself and takes the seat across from me. Her expression turns serious as she eyes the drink and then me. "I swear that I haven't had anything to drink yet and promise I'm not going to get drunk." I shake my head, knowing I can't deny that both thoughts had crossed my mind.

"It's ok. I don't have the right to police your behavior, but that doesn't mean that I won't worry." Katrina looks at me, her thoughts unreadable, the silence threatening to become uncomfortable. "This looks amazing, shall we?" We both start preparing plates for ourselves. "That's a lot of guacamole." Katrina laughs, seemingly relaxed once again.

"Catherine warned me that you have a tendency to go crazy with it. I argue that it's nearly a food group on its own. I figured it would be better to make too much than not enough." Curiosity about the unknown connection between Catherine and Katrina is taking over my brain.

"I didn't know you had been in regular contact with Catherine." Katrina eyes me momentarily, trying to assess what I'm really asking her.

"I hadn't. When I called her that Saturday afternoon, it was the first time I spoke with her since we were all at the brewery. I didn't even know if she would respond to my message since we had our falling out, or whatever you want to call it, before you left. She messaged me that evening to see if I wanted to join Abby, Alex and herself for dinner that night. The invitation surprised me, but I accepted." Katrina pauses as she takes a sip of her margarita. "She's quite shrewd, isn't she? At dinner, the cut on my arm busted open and bled through the dressing. She didn't make a scene or say anything at the time. When Alex and Abby went to bathroom together, she interrogated me. I was shocked that she was unaware of how I'd been behaving, that we had fought. Anyway, she examined my wound and reprimanded me, explaining the numerous ways I could've caused serious injury to myself. That woman can give quite the lecture. She cleaned it up and put some glue on it that burned like mad. The three of them just sort of kept tabs on me these last two weeks. I thought it was because you asked them to, but you didn't, did you?"

"No, I did not. I don't make a habit of broadcasting other people's private business. That's just how they are though. We look out for one another." Katrina eyes me; like she's trying to see if I've spoken the truth. Her brow furrows suddenly, and I can tell she is debating whether she should ask the question plaguing her mind. "What?"

"Why the questions about Catherine and I? You don't think that we…" I laugh uncontrollably, nearly choking on a grain of rice as I do.

"God no!" My reaction stings Katrina in some way. She looks down, and a frown settles over her lips. I realize then that she thinks I've insulted her. "It isn't that. I mean come on, surely you've seen how she and Alex are with each other. Neither of them has even thought of another woman sexually since they got together. It's nauseating on the one hand and jealousy inducing on the other. No one stands a chance of coming between those two." Katrina's mood shifts back to relaxed.

"It's impossible not to notice isn't it?" She chuckles to herself before going quiet. I wonder what's on her mind, but don't press her. "I wonder if people ever felt that way about Jill and I."

"I know they did. I admired your relationship every time the two of you came to her appointments. Some of our other staff did as well." I can see Katrina's eyes turn glassy and know she is fighting the tears.

"Thanks." She sniffles and clears her throat. "Ok. Tell me about your trip, if you're allowed to talk about it." I laugh again as I wonder what kind of trip she thinks I went on.

"Well, it wasn't exactly a top secret mission for the CIA." She smiles and laughs as she refills our glasses, emptying the pitcher. We did somewhere around 180 procedures in the 10 days we operated there." Katrina's mouth drops open, the shock evident. "I didn't scrub every one of them. I did scrub and assist on cases that I wouldn't typically do here, but the staff and supplies there are so limited. We have top of the line everything, fresh supplies, and all the hands we can use during cases here. There the equipment is almost always donated from a company or hospital because it's outdated. Skilled assistance can be even harder to find. But in some ways the work is more rewarding, you know that the people you're helping wouldn't likely receive treatment if you weren't there to offer it. Cleft lips, cleft palates, mastectomies, hernias, so many procedures we take for granted here, that we assume to be basic medical care, are luxuries there. The people there are always so welcoming and kind. I love going to the market and seeing the produce stalls with all the fresh fruits. The chickens in the cages throw me off every time, I hate thinking about how the animals that we get our meats from are treated, but it's just so different than the markets here are. Winneba Beach is spectacular, I went as often as I could. The weather was beautiful, always in the upper 70's but the humidity was stifling at times. There was another plastic surgeon there that I got to work with, it was nice trading ideas with her, being reminded that there are many ways to approach a case." I start to lose myself in my memories of the last two weeks.

"Is that it?"

"Huh?" I'm not sure what Katrina is asking me, yet she looks a bit perplexed.

"It seems like you just spaced out in the middle of telling me about your trip. I was just wondering if that was it." Katrina looks at me expectantly, and I feel my cheeks flush. I certainly don't have to tell her about that part of my trip. "Oh, that's so not it! Now you have to tell me, whatever it is!" More blood rushes to my face, and I know she isn't going to let me get away with not telling her. "You met someone there, didn't you?"

"Yes…no…not how you're thinking. I had a lovely, but brief fling."

"The other plastic surgeon?"

"Yes." Katrina grins at me, her eyebrows arching up. "What? It was the accent, ok! I'm a sucker for a sexy accent. It was just a little fun though, we both knew it. It was fun while it lasted, but it's highly unlikely that I'll ever see her again."

"You really aren't going to give me any details are you?"

"No, I'm not." Katrina looks disappointed but doesn't press me any further.

"So is that all you are after? Just a little fun?"

"No. Why are you asking me that?"

"No reason really. You mentioned before that you had that fling with your old sparring partner and now this one as well. Do you have a habit of avoiding relationships?" I'm starting to feel like I'm being psychoanalyzed.

"Why do I feel like I'm being slut shamed?" Katrina looks properly taken aback, but I don't give her a chance to protest. "Have I had flings? Yeah, I have. I don't actively avoid relationships though. I do approach them with a high level of honesty and try to be as realistic as possible. In both of the instances you know about, a long term relationship was never going to happen, the circumstances wouldn't allow it to even be a possibility. That doesn't mean that I didn't have desires that couldn't be fulfilled in those moments. For the record, I've never cheated on a partner, have never knowingly slept with someone who already had a partner, nor do I go out looking for the flavor of the week." Dinner is suddenly losing its appeal.

"I'm sorry, I really didn't mean it like that, I just worded it poorly." I take a deep breath and let my irritation out with it. We resume eating, the silence gradually becoming unbearable.

"So what are your plans for the remainder of the weekend?" I'm so anxious to be rid of the silence that I'm resorting to small talk.

"Honestly, I don't really know. Some of my friends invited me to meet them at Velvet tonight, but it doesn't even sound close to appealing. I'm not ready to be in that space, with all the noise and the strangers. I don't want to be there and lose control and either blackout or breakdown. I don't have any idea what I'm up to tomorrow. I've honestly just been taking it one day at a time." I nod my understanding as I stuff the final bite of food from my once full plate into my mouth. "What about you?"

"Nothing really. I might go biking tomorrow if the weather is nice. I took Monday off as well so I could have the extra day to recover and readjust to life here. I'll probably end up seeing what's playing at the movies. Tonight though, if it doesn't involve my sweatpants, a blanket, and my couch then it isn't going to happen."

"That sounds nice."

"Which part of it?"

"All of it, I love relaxing nights at home. I didn't know you're into biking. Who do you go with?"

"I'll go alone, sometimes Catherine and Alex join me, other times Abby and her daughter. I have a few other friends that enjoy it as well. Just depends on who's available when I go. Why do you bike?"

"I do! I haven't been out yet though." This isn't surprising since it is still cool out.

"If you want to go tomorrow you are welcome to join me."

"That'd be great." Katrina looks at my empty plate and then me. "More?"

"I couldn't if I tried, thank you. It was delicious. You really didn't have to do all of this, but I really appreciate it." Katrina stands up and starts to clear away the dirty dishes. "Let me do that, you already did all of the hard work."

"I've got it. You just go get your blanket and settle in on your couch. From the sounds of it, you've earned it." I try to ignore her suggestion and grab one of the dishes to wrap it up and put it away, but Katrina swipes it out of my hands. "I mean it, you go and relax. I'll get this cleaned up and be on my way."

"You don't have to go. The only exciting thing happening here is going to be a movie night, but you're welcome to stay."

"You sure? I don't want to intrude on your plans."

"Of course I'm sure. I don't have anything grand planned, hell I don't even know what I plan to watch yet."

"Alright. You go get settled and find a movie, I'll finish up in here."

I'm still searching for a movie when Katrina joins me in the den. "You still haven't picked something?" I look over and find Katrina wearing a teasing smile.

"Work in progress. Let me know if you see anything." I can always find something to relax to, the issue is I have no idea what Katrina will enjoy. I scroll through the options, checking the details of the titles I'm unfamiliar with.

"Ooh, *Kill Bill* is always great." I remember mentioning to Katrina that I enjoy Tarantino's work, so I wonder if she really does like it or if she's saying so for my benefit. "You don't agree?"

"I do, I just know that his style isn't for everyone."

"Yeah, Jill was never a fan of his, she hated the violence and the blood. I've always had to see his films with friends or on my own." Sadness mars her features as she thinks about Jill, but she keeps it together. "Do you want a glass of water?"

"I can get one."

"I'll get it, you just start the movie." I want to argue but realize she might just need a moment to herself. As she rises from the sofa, I stop her.

"I should warn you, I don't see volume one and two as separate entities. If we watch one, we have to watch the other." She turns to face me, a smile plays at her lips but never reaches her eyes.

"Of course. I had a nap earlier, I'll be fine."

Katrina rises from the couch as the credits roll on volume one. "Brief intermission, I'll be right back." Knowing I could use the bathroom, more water and to simply stretch my legs, I head down the hall to the master suite. When I enter the kitchen to refill my water I find Katrina with her back to me, working on some task in front of her.

"Need some help?" She jumps a little and looks over her shoulder at me, never fully turning around or giving me a glimpse of what she's up to.

"No. Almost finished. Go get the second half started, I'll be right there." I can feel my eyebrows contract of their own volition, and a frown settle in, but I simply refill my glass and return to the den. A few minutes later I hear Katrina approaching and look over to discover her holding a pair of plates, their contents just out of sight.

"Intermission seemed like a good time for this." She hands me one of the plates and my eyes bulge as my salivary glands go into overdrive.

"Is this what I think it is?" Katrina grins at me.

"White chocolate cheesecake with fresh strawberry topping? Yes, yes it is." I hear Katrina giggle, but can't tear my eyes away to figure out why. "I take it from the look on your face that you approve." Unable to resist any longer, I greedily take the first bite. The intensity of the flavors flawlessly blend together as the sweet treat melts on my tongue, making me release a low moan.

"Oh my god, this is amazing." I close my eyes as I savor the flavor. "Please tell me that there isn't a whole cheesecake in my refrigerator. I'm not sure I have the willpower not to eat all of it." I shovel another bite into my mouth enjoying every ounce of richness it has to offer.

"Well there is a whole one, yes, but it's only an eight-inch cake. I have a smaller pan that I used." I pause with the third forkful halfway to my mouth.

"You made this?" Small wrinkles begin to crease her forehead as she flashes me an incredulous look.

"Of course I did. Where did you think it came from?"

"I don't know, a bakery somewhere. Seriously, I'm going to have to work out extra all week because of this, but it's so worth it." I stuff another bite into my mouth, starting to feel sad that my plate is nearly empty.

"Speaking of working out, what about training with Jason? Can we do Thursdays together? I've been going a few times a week still. It totally kicks my ass, but I really enjoy it."

"Sure." I can't think of a reason to object, plus I do miss having someone I can spar with once or twice a week. Picking up new moves and learning to think faster during actual combat is much easier if you have an opportunity to practice more than once a week.

"You know, his Tuesday nights opened up, if you want to go then too." Is she reading my mind?

"I think I can make that work. I should warn you that when I'm on-call I still try to make it, but sometimes I have to bail at the last minute or even in the middle of class." Katrina smiles, and I see something shift slightly in her eyes.

"Maybe I should warn you that I'm going to be better than you soon."

"Is that so?" I ask as I arch an eyebrow at her.

"Yes, it is." A suppressed giggle escapes her pursed lips, spoiling the conviction she tried to put behind her bold talk.

"I think I should start the movie now." I let a slight smile work at the corners of my mouth, just enough to let her know that I'm joking. All the while I can feel my overly competitive spirit kicking into gear.

Chapter 10

"Do you have everything that you need? Swimsuit, something a little warmer for later?" Catherine and Alex are hosting another warm weather get together at their place. Grilling dinner, games, swimming, music, drinks, and good company all enjoying the wonderful weather together. It's early August, which means that we're running out of opportunities for these gatherings.

"I think so. How many people are going to be there?"

"One never knows. At least six but probably less than 30." Katrina's look shifts marginally. I can't tell if she's nervous or scared, perhaps a little bit of both. "You'll be fine. You can follow me over there if you'd like so you can leave whenever you want. I just thought it would be easier to pick you up."

"No, I'll be fine. I think I have everything. Can you carry my bag while I grab the dessert?" I take the offered bag from her and look around as I wait for her to return from the kitchen. The once overwhelming interior is gone, boxes litter the den and the dining room, the colorful furniture hidden behind them. Katrina returns, and I hear the sound of her steps halt. She's caught me taking in my surroundings. I wonder if my face has betrayed any of the sadness I feel for her situation. I look at her, and she arches an inquisitive eyebrow at me.

"Do you want to talk about it?" I doubt she will, but I still feel obligated to offer.

"Not really, but I feel like you want to talk me out of it. Just know that I feel like this is the right thing to do. She's been gone for six months. We bought this place together, built our life together here and now this place is haunted by her ghost. It doesn't feel like home anymore. This isn't an impulsive decision that I've made. I feel like I needed to sell the place for some closure. I'm doing the right thing for me, I promise."

"Ok. For the record, I don't want to talk you out of it. I just hope that you won't regret it someday. I trust that you've thought it through." Katrina has been doing very well in the months since my mission trip. I initially worried that it was because she always seemed to be busy doing something. Tuesdays and Thursdays we have class, we typically spar, kayak and hike one day out of the weekend, I know she spends time with her other friends, and she and her business partner are in the process of expanding their business to accommodate some billion dollar corporation. Her anger now seems minimal, and her drinking appears to be well under control. I know she continues to meet with Dr. Sutton every other week, but I never press her on what they discuss. When she told me she was putting their house on the market, I thought she was backsliding, that she had lost her mind. It sold in three weeks though, and she's been surprisingly steady about the decision.

"Good. Can we go have some fun now?" She smiles at me as she turns me in the direction of the door and playfully pushes me toward it.

We arrive at the house and make our way onto the porch and ring the bell. I'm shocked when Taylor answers the door. We give each other a hug, and I see her eyes run up and down Katrina's body as I introduce them. That flirty look I've seen and received from Taylor in the past is ever present on her face. I look around for Nikki and see her just down the hall, fully immersed in conversation with Kevin and Derrick. I feel Katrina lean into me as we walk down the hall, followed by her warm breath near my ear.

"Ok three things. One, it looks like there are more than just a few people here. Two, Catherine and Taylor look so much alike it's sorta creepy. Three, why do I feel like I just got molested by Taylor?" I laugh heartily, I can't help it.

"Shall I address those concerns in order? First, there are a few people here, but everyone is great, so don't worry. You already know Catherine, Alex, Abby, Nate, Jeff, and myself. Maybe even one or two others. Just relax. If it gets too overwhelming, we can leave. Second, yes Taylor and Catherine look quite similar, but I assure you that their physical similarities are where it starts and stops. Personality wise they're nothing alike. Third, yeah, she was checking you out. She's a massive flirt. Unless something has changed, she's here with Nikki, so you should be safe. If she isn't, just make it clear you don't want her attention. She may be a flirt, but she does listen." Catherine approaches us from the kitchen, bag in hand.

"Hello!" She leans in and gives me a hug. "You know the drill, keys in the bag."

"Seriously?" I don't even need to ask, I can see the collection she has already amassed. Without further protest, I surrender my keys and am rewarded with a wink and a smile from Catherine. She turns to Katrina, hugs her in greeting and looks at her expectantly.

"Oh, we rode together."

"Very well then. Fix yourselves a drink, dinner should be ready soon. Are you planning on crashing here? I'm sorting out rooms for people if you are, but you would have to share." Katrina shoots me a surprised look. I just shrug. "You know the rules, Sara. If you're drinking, you're staying or getting a sober ride home."

"Yeah, yeah, I know. Just keep my keys and hold a room until we figure it out. Mind if I give Katrina a tour?"

"Of course, sorry I can't be a proper host and do it myself. I'd avoid the guest apartment, I'm pretty sure I just saw Taylor and Nikki head down there." We both laugh and Catherine heads back into the crowded kitchen. We follow and deposit our dinner contributions on the bar with the rest of the food.

"Shall we?" I look at Katrina and feel a sense of uneasiness; like there is an elephant in the room we can both see but refuse to acknowledge.

"Let's." I lead Katrina through the house, hoping to find a quiet spot to address the issue of drinking.

As we make our way down the hall, Alex exits the master bedroom and wraps me up in a welcoming hug. "Mind if I borrow your bedroom for a second," I whisper in her ear as we embrace. I pull away and watch as she greets Katrina with a similar hug. She gives me a questioning look but slightly tilts her head toward the door giving me permission. Anxiety takes over my stomach as I prepare to broach a subject that might result in an argument between us. Since my return from Ghana, I haven't seen Katrina drink much of anything. That doesn't mean I know what her plans for tonight are. Katrina looks around the room, taking it in while I try to figure out a way of broaching the subject without setting off an argument.

"So, uh, this rule Catherine has, is she serious?" I am relieved to know that I'm not the only one wondering what we should do about the situation.

"Yeah, she is. I forgot about it. I usually just crash here. Were you planning on drinking?"

"I was planning on having a few." She looks at me for a second. "Not getting wasted or blackout drunk." She says it like it's an afterthought for her; like I need some reassurance. "Were you?"

"Same as you, not planning on getting trashed, in all likelihood I'd still be ok to drive."

"But Catherine won't allow it, will she?"

"No, it's a firm rule for her. Honestly, with the trauma work she does, I can't blame her."

"So we have a good time, or we stay sober and get to leave."

"Yep." I'm deflecting, I know I am, but I don't want to force Katrina's hand on this matter.

"Good time then?" She smiles at me, seemingly at ease with her choice. I have to trust that she will control her drinking, she hasn't given me any reason lately to doubt her.

"Sure. Now that we have that settled, want to finish the tour then get a drink?" Katrina's smile is radiant, clearly settling the dilemma has made both of us happy. "Ok. Just one last thing to show you."

"The pool?" I nod and grin, her excitement is contagious. I lead her to the pool, the smell of chlorine giving its existence away before we actually get to it. I watch as her eyes expand and her mouth gapes open when she finally sees the pool. "When are they breaking ground on yours?" I laugh, her question and her expression are too much.

"I have to finalize the plan this weekend. There are two options. I've been stuck on the fence when it comes to choosing one. I should get someone else's input I think."

"I'll take a look if you want." My face must register the shock her volunteering has levied on me. I've never found looking at design plans to be that interesting, and frankly given some of her comments regarding Jill's profession, I never thought she did either. She starts to chuckle, and I begin to think she has been messing with me. "Of course I'll take a look at them. The sooner yours is built, the sooner I'll have access to a pool as well." Of course, I laugh and shake my head, unable to believe how I could've forgotten that fact.

We rejoin the rest of the party and make our way to the bar. I make myself a whiskey sour and Katrina makes something that looks quite fruity. I'm determined not to keep track of how many drinks Katrina has, to trust her to know her limits. We start making our way around the party, and I introduce her to the people she hasn't met before. I'm drawn into catching up with Shannon when I notice Katrina is no longer with us. Shannon and I chat for a few more minutes before she excuses herself to use the bathroom, the exasperated look she wears tells me she's already tired of being pregnant. I look around for Katrina and see her talking to someone I don't recognize from behind. She catches me looking and smiles, never disengaging from her conversation.

"So, new girlfriend?" I recognize Taylor's voice coming from behind me. I turn to face her and discover that Nikki is with her. We greet one another and fill each other in on life as we know it. "Why aren't you telling her about your new girl?" Taylor doesn't like it when she isn't the center of attention.

"She isn't my girlfriend. She's a mutual friend to a few of the people here, your sister included. Besides, if she were my girlfriend we'd be having a discussion about you eye fucking her before she made it through the front door." Nikki looks at Taylor and shakes her head, but doesn't leave her side. "Sorry, Nikki." I feel bad for putting Taylor on blast like that in front of Nikki. At least Taylor has the grace to look a little embarrassed about the situation.

"Oh, I know how she is. I don't know what she's going to do when I'm out there full-time."

"You're moving to San Fran?"

"Yeah. Taylor flew out to visit Catherine and help me move my stuff across the country. We've been doing this whole long-distance thing for too long. Time to figure out if it's legit or not. I've got a job lined up, waiting for my arrival." I stand there in a stunned silence, certain this day would never happen.

"Well congrats you two, I hope it works out." I truly do wish them the best. I look over again and find Katrina still chatting away with the unknown woman. Curious as to her identity, I excuse myself from Taylor and Nikki and make my way across the room.

"Hey, I was wondering if you were ever going to come over here. Allow me to introduce you to—."

"Hello, Brenda." I know my voice is flat, entirely void of any warmness. If I'd realized that Katrina has been speaking to Brenda this entire time, I never would have joined her. Now I find myself trapped in six degrees of lesbian hell.

"Sara." Brenda's tone lets me know the feeling is mutual. Katrina quickly picks up on the fact that there's something off.

"Katrina, I just came over to see if you needed a refill." I don't have a clue what she's drinking, but I have no desire to spend another second with Brenda. Katrina looks at her glass, still a third full, then up at me, trying to figure out what she's missed.

"Yeah but I'll come with you. You know I'm particular about my cocktails." She wraps her hand around the back of my arm and leads me towards the bar. "What was that?"

"Nothing. She worked in the OR a few years ago, before she made some big career change. Let's just say that things got out of hand at a party one time and that lead us to discover that we have nothing in common, nor do we even like each other." Katrina starts laughing uncontrollably. "How do you know her?"

"Our firm handles the books for her business. I don't work with her directly, she's my partner's client, but we've had a few pleasant enough conversations over the years."

"Ah, it looked like you were old friends or something."

"Were you watching me?" I feel the blood leave my body and rush to my cheeks. I hadn't felt like I had been watching her, but maybe I was. "Anyway, I learned something vitally important tonight." The relief I feel that Katrina didn't force me to answer her previous question is quickly replaced by curiosity.

"What would that be?"

"That you have a nickname." I feel myself cringe reflexively. I've heard it before. It was funny the first few times but has long lost its appeal. All I can do is shake my head. "What, you don't like being known as the Breast Whisperer?" That was not what I was expecting. I can feel the confusion instantly register on my face. "Oh my god, there's another nickname isn't there!" Katrina is enjoying this, far too much. I drop my gaze to my feet, knowing she will pester me until I tell her.

"There is. Honestly, I hadn't heard about being called the Breast Whisperer. I think the other name is better though. If Alex dubbed the new one as well, then she's losing her touch."

"Alex gave you your first nickname?" I nod to confirm that it's true. "So are you going to tell me or should I go ask her." Katrina tilts her head to the right, she's already located Alex, ready to interrogate her if I don't crack quickly enough.

"The Wizard of Tatas," I lean in and whisper as quietly as possible into Katrina's ear. She completely loses it, stopping in her tracks to let her laughter take over. I try to close the remaining distance to the bar, wanting to put some space between me and my newest embarrassment. Katrina's hand shoots out and grips my arm once again, forcing me to wait. When she finally composes herself, she forces me to face her.

"Alex's name is better, but I can tell that you don't necessarily enjoy it. I'll try not to bring it up again." I nod my appreciation, wanting to drop this subject as soon as possible. "So how about that drink?"

"Sounds good." We refill our drinks at the bar and join the line of people preparing plates of food. We find ourselves seats outside, choosing to sit in the grass under a large oak tree. It places us at the edge of the party, giving us a distance from the noise and allowing us a prime vantage point to people watch from. I watch Katrina as she cuts her burger in half before trying her first bite as I cut into my bacon wrapped stuffed chicken. Catherine and Alex haven't held back tonight. I catch Katrina eyeing me as the first bite practically melts in my mouth. "Trade you half a burger for half of that chicken." I think she's joking but quickly realize she isn't. My face must betray my skepticism about her offer. "I'm not kidding. If that chicken put that expression on your face, then I have to try it." I cut the chicken in half and offer it to her. Having initially debated between the two, I'm fine with having a little of both. She takes a small bite and closes her eyes as she chews.

"Ok, I don't think I enjoyed it quite that much." She instinctively laughs and nearly chokes as she tries to swallow. "Sorry, you ok?" Despite her face being red, she nods and clears her throat.

"Yeah, I'm good." We sit and watch people interacting with one another, I've always found people watching to be fascinating.

"They really are adorable together aren't they?" I have a feeling I know who she's referring to, so I look around and see Catherine and Alex feeding one another.

"They are. I think it's because—." I cut myself off, not wanting to finish the thought, not wanting to remind Katrina of Jill by mentioning Alex's accident. Katrina looks at me, waiting for me to finish, her eyebrows arched in a mix of anticipation and expectation.

"Because of Alex's accident?" I look down at the grass, upset with myself for bringing up something I know will likely remind her of all the pain surrounding Jill's death. I feel the warmth of Katrina's hand as she places it on my shoulder. "It's alright." I turn my head to look at her, to assess if she really is ok. "I can't lie, it makes me sad to think about it, it probably always will. I'm ok though. I'm not going to breakdown or get super angry for no reason. I'm making peace with it I guess." Katrina's hand still rests on my shoulder. I reach up and place my hand over hers and give it a slight squeeze. I feel her squeeze my shoulder in return as I examine her face. She's telling the truth, her expression reflects peacefulness marred by a tinge of sadness in her eyes and at the corners of her mouth. I feel relief and happiness for her, it's been a difficult road, I'm glad she's finally finding some sense of peace.

We finish our meal and make our way back to the bar for another drink. Catherine joins us and looks at me, a satisfied look in place. "That's at least your third drink, you're staying." How she manages to keep tabs on everyone is beyond me. I look at Katrina and shrug, receiving a shrug from her in return. We know we can't argue. Catherine's grin is triumphant, she knows she has won, and she loves it. "Good. I've allocated you the guest room at the far corner of the house. You know the one right?" I nod that I do. "Great. I know you don't sleep soundly, so I figured being further from the party and everyone else would be best." She smiles and saunters her way back outside. I turn, intending to show Katrina where our assigned room is, but find her immersed in a conversation with Abby. I head outside, stopping and having conversations when prompted. Eventually, I find myself standing near the fire pit, its warmth a bit much for the late evening hours. I stand and watch the flames, hypnotized by their movements, my mind clear of all thoughts. I hear footsteps approaching but don't pull my gaze from the fire.

"I thought you said she isn't your girlfriend." Taylor stops at my side, her gaze as fixed on the flames as mine.

"She isn't. Where is this coming from? You looking for permission or something?"

"Nope. You shouldn't get irritated when someone asks you about her, I mean one of you always seems to be watching the other, your little private dinner under the tree, I saw that moment the two of you shared. If you don't want people to know that's fine, you should just be a little more discrete." I finally tear my eyes from the entrancing flames.

"There isn't anything to know!" I have no idea if I hiss it or shout it. Taylor has often rubbed me the wrong way with her innuendos and insinuations. "That moment you think you saw? We were talking about her partner who passed away six months ago. There was no moment." Taylor's look shifts slightly, but doesn't give anything away.

"Interesting," she mumbles as she walks away. I retrain my focus on the fire, trying to find the meditative state I had just a few minutes ago, but it's gone. I can hear the party around me, people making their way closer to the fire.

"There you are! I've been looking for you." Katrina takes the spot formerly occupied by Taylor. It makes me wonder why people always take the space on your right, even if the space on the left is equally unoccupied. "Your drink is gone. Want a refill?" I can hear in her voice that she's having a good time, one that I don't want to spoil. I take a deep breath and let it out slowly. "What's wrong?"

"Nothing, just Taylor being Taylor. I'm fine. Still want to get that drink?" We head back to the house and are stopped by Kevin and Derrick asking if we want to play a game of cornhole. We agree to return after we refill our drinks.

Several games of cornhole later, the attendance at the party has dwindled markedly. Catherine and Alex are snuggled together on one of the benches by the fire. Taylor and Nikki occupy the bench opposite Catherine and Alex. Abby and Blake, the guy from the brewery, are sitting under the oak tree where Katrina and I ate earlier. Derrick, Dahlia, Shannon, and Kevin are all playing a game of cornhole. I head towards the fire and sit on one of the vacant benches, not even attempting to insert myself into the existing conversation. I stare at the flames and realize how tired I am. I shouldn't be surprised, it's after one in the morning, long past my usual bedtime. I once again find myself staring at the flames as they move like they're dancing to music only they can hear. It's relaxing, so relaxing that I don't even realize that Katrina has joined us, sitting down on my right and holding another whiskey sour for me.

"So Sara, how is the search for the new partner going?" Catherine means well, I know, but this is the most frustrating thing in my life right now.

"I feel like it'll never be over. Who knew getting someone to move to the midwest was going to be so difficult? We have some new options, but it's hard to meet to interview or discuss candidates because we're only all available on the weekends. Someday though, it has to happen, right?" I can see the sympathy in Catherine's eyes, she knows I've been working too much, that I've made the job my life, that I have one foot dangling over the edge of the abyss that is burnout. I know that I'm the only one to blame.

"I didn't know you were still looking." Katrina gives me a look; like she feels hurt that I haven't shared this information with her.

"We are. There's one candidate I'm hopeful would make a good fit. I've felt that way before though, so I'm trying not to get my hopes up." Thankfully the conversation moves on to talk of Catherine and Alex's upcoming vacation to Italy. I try to remain focused as I sip my drink but I know I need to head to bed. Katrina stifles a yawn, and I realize she's right there with me. Tired of listening to the never-ending drone of conversations I'm not a part of, I stand up and excuse myself, telling everyone goodnight. Katrina rises and does the same causing Taylor to shoot me a look; like she just received confirmation that all her suspicions are true. I cast her a warning glare and shake my head slightly, watching as she receives the message.

We walk back to the house, and as we pass through the kitchen, I stop and grab two glasses of water. While we've both done well pacing ourselves tonight, I know that a headache in the morning is an all too real possibility. We make our way through the house and open the door to the guest room. I'm relieved to discover that Catherine has set out two sets of gym shorts and t-shirts, knowing something comfortable to sleep in would be nice. I deposit the waters, grab a set of clothes and head back down the hall to the bathroom, closing the door behind me so Katrina can change. I drag my feet, trying to ensure she will be decent when I return. I slowly open the door and when I'm met with no protest, enter the room to find Katrina already curled up in bed. Her back is to me, so I have no idea if she's still awake. I quietly make my way to the vacant half of the bed and try to climb in without disturbing her.

"I hope you don't mind that I opened the window a little. You can close it if you think it'll be too cold or the light will bother you." I have no objections, it's still a nice night out, and the bedding will be more than enough to stay warm. I take a deep drink from my glass of water and switch off the lamp.

"Goodnight." I should fall asleep quickly, but naturally, I don't. Instead, I find myself staring into the faintly moonlit room. I'm not sure what's keeping me awake. Katrina's breathing has been steady for a few minutes, yet does not work as a focal point for me to relax to. She suddenly rolls over, taking position on her other side, now facing me. I continue to struggle against my insomnia, staring into the dimness; like I will find the answer written on the ceiling if the moonlight hits it at the right angle.

"Can't sleep?" I jump a little at the sound of her voice. "Sorry. You alright?" I flip from my back to my side, facing Katrina in the darkness. The moonlight illuminates her eyes, intensifying the silver.

"Yeah, I'll sleep eventually I'm sure. What about you? I thought you were asleep already."

"Not yet. I've just been thinking."

"About?"

"I don't know, the future I guess. What mine looks like now. You ever do that?"

"Sure. I'm guessing most people do. I keep picturing a vacation in mine, sadly it seems to move further away."

"You should just take one. You're no good to those women if you are beyond exhausted." She goes quiet, but I can still see her eyes, watching me. "Do you ever see yourself settling down?"

"What do you mean? I'm not exactly a wild child over here."

"No, I mean, I don't know. Just seeing all those couples tonight, Catherine and Alex, Derrick and Dahlia, Shannon and Kevin, Abby and Blake, even Taylor and Nikki…their relationships are all so different and yet they all seem so happy. Do you ever see that for yourself? I try, but I haven't been able to imagine it."

"I think you'll be able to see it someday; when you're ready to. I've tried to see that, but I'm just never able to. I know I'm difficult to date, I have such limited time, I'm stubborn and probably at least a dozen other undatable things."

"Stop. You've only ever painted a general picture of how things were with your ex, but you're not undatable. I think once you free yourself up from work a little, you'll be able to focus on putting yourself out there a little more. Then it will happen."

"Are we making a bet? It'll happen for you before it happens for me. I'm willing to make that bet."

"Sure, what should we wager?" I can see the moonlight bounce off of Katrina's teeth as she smiles.

"I don't know, I'm sure we'll think of something eventually."

"Yeah." Katrina rolls onto her back and closes her eyes, so I ease myself back onto mine as well. "I think I just miss having sex."

"Yeah, I do too," I whisper back, thankful that she can't see the shock that's registered on my features. Without warning, she starts laughing, a genuine, out of control, infectious burst. I can't help but join her, a few minutes passing before our room becomes quiet once again. "Goodnight Katrina."

"Sweet dreams Sara."

Chapter 11

"Are you going to dinner and Velvet Friday night for the moving away party?" Katrina and I circle each other, both breathing heavily. I wait for her to try to attack me but she has long since caught onto my strategy, often forcing me to be the aggressor.

"Yeah, I should be done operating in time for dinner, at least I hope I will. I didn't know you were going." I feint like I'm going to jab but drop to go for a leg sweep. She deftly evades the maneuver, forcing me to admit she has gotten much better in a short period of time. I bounce up quickly, anticipating a counter attack.

"Alex invited me. Do you mind?" This time she tries to throw a jab at me, but I easily side step it, quickly wrapping one arm around her neck and the other under her extended right arm. Hands locked together, I twist my hips and flip her onto her back. As she tries to recover, I unlock my hands and quickly lock my legs around her arm. She instinctively tries to push my feet apart, but my ankles are locked. I know I have her now. I relax my arms just enough to lean back and capture her left arm, locking her into an arm bar. I lean back, but don't fully engage the submission move, I don't want to hurt Katrina, I just want to make her tap. "Is there a way out of this?"

"Tap out. I don't have it fully engaged, or you'd be in quite a bit of pain as your elbow would be hyperextended a little more every second. Eventually, it could dislocate." I apply just a little more pressure, and Katrina quickly taps. We both get back to our feet, and I see Katrina flexing her elbow. "You ok?"

"Yeah, all good. You going to answer my question though? I won't go if you don't want me to."

"You should, I think it'll be fun." I also think about who else is likely invited and realize something that does not sound like a lot of fun for me. "Besides, if you don't come I'll probably be the only single person at dinner."

"I take it your date Sunday night didn't go well." We continue circling one another, each waiting for the other to make a move. Remembering the disastrous date distracts me momentarily. Arranged by one of the anesthesiologists, I grudgingly agreed to meet his sister if for no other reason than to get him to stop pestering me about it. He booked a reservation for us at a nice Italian restaurant for Sunday evening. I arrived a few minutes early, while she arrived fifteen minutes late. Already annoyed by her inability to show up on time, it quickly became apparent that we had next to nothing in common. We both quickly ate our meals in silence and split the bill. I don't think either of us could get out of there fast enough. I focus again just in time to see Katrina coming at me. I have little time to react. I attempt to backpedal but end up tripping over my own feet, taking myself down. I'm not sure if she tried to catch me or if I trip her as well, but somehow I find myself laying with my back against the mat, Katrina on top of me with my legs locked around her, just above her hips. She squirms in an attempt to break the leg lock, and every nerve ending in my body ignites as she inadvertently grinds against my sex. I audibly inhale through my clenched teeth, my back arches upwards into Katrina and I feel my eyes roll back and close of their own accord. When the sensation passes, I open my eyes to find Katrina's face a few inches from mine, staring at me. She knows what just happened. Her silver eyes bore into me, and I stare back at her. My now throbbing sex is demanding I close the short distance between our lips and try to get some more of the attention it so desperately craves. My brain is sounding alarms like it's at Defcon 1, telling me taking it any further might be one of the worst ideas in the history of mankind. Katrina's eyes search my face, and I see her bite the inside of her lower lip. I wonder if her mind and body are fighting the same war that mine are. I feel Katrina's hand tap against my thigh, and instinctively unlock my ankles to release her. She carefully elevates herself off of me before standing up. She helps me to my feet, but I can tell that she is avoiding making eye contact with me.

"I gotta get going, a lot of stuff to get done at the house. See you Friday night?"

"Won't you be at class tomorrow night?"

"Tomorrow is moving day remember?" I did remember because I had tried to clear my schedule to help her, but she insisted that I not, that the movers were going to do all of the work anyway.

"I remembered," I say as I watch Katrina jog up my basement steps. A few seconds later I hear the front door close. I stand in the basement dumbfounded, unable to sort out everything that just transpired. Katrina? Really? Have I been ignoring some building attraction to her or did I simply consider kissing her because of proximity and sexual frustration? Are things between us doomed to be forever awkward now?

*****

Friday night I find myself filled with anxiety as I shower and prepare to meet everyone for a night out. I haven't heard from Katrina since she left Wednesday evening, nor have I tried to contact her. I nearly called her to see if she wanted to share a ride, but chickened out as I stared at her contact information on my phone.

The driver deposits me near the entrance of the restaurant, and I find myself standing outside staring at the door, hesitant to go in. I finally dial up my courage and head inside letting the hostess know that I'm here for the Waters party. I follow her, as requested, and am glad to see that they have placed us in a private room, knowing we have a tendency to get a little loud when we all get together. I look around to discover that only Catherine, Alex, Taylor, and Nikki are present, thus far. For some reason I feel a sense of relief settle in, Katrina's actions when she arrives will speak volumes about where things stand between us. I walk around the table and take a seat opposite the door, near Catherine and Alex. I order a margarita and watch the door anxiously.

"A tequila kind of night?" Most people who know me know I tend to stick to whiskey, so the question doesn't surprise me.

"The weather is warm and I plan on dancing later. Why not?"

"Why not indeed. Shots then?" Taylor's suggestion actually sounds like a good idea. When the waitress returns with my margarita, I order a round of Patron shots for the five of us. We finish our toast, and I'm in the middle of taking my shot when the hostess escorts Katrina into the room. I nearly choke as I fight to properly swallow the sharp flavored liquid. She's wearing a form-fitting shirt with an extremely plunging neckline. I follow the neckline down to its end, showcasing the top of her breasts, which seem to be threatening to tumble out at any moment. My tongue reflexively runs over my lips. The sound of someone clearing their throat brings me back to earth. I look away, refusing to make eye contact with anyone.

"You alright?" Alex leans in and whispers so only I can hear. I nod that I am, still waiting to see where Katrina sits. I see her do something on her phone before she makes her way around the table and sits next to me, that plunging neckline monopolizing my peripheral view. Taylor shoots me a look from the other side of the table, but I ignore her, refusing to be goaded or add to the tidal wave of emotions I feel myself starting to drown under. Catherine catches my eye and gives me an inquisitive look. That's when I know that they all saw my reaction to Katrina's entrance. The hostess returns with Katrina's drink, and I take advantage of the opportunity to ask where the restroom is, even though I'm quite familiar with this establishment. I stand up and excuse myself.

"Want another shot, Sara?" Catherine practically purrs as she asks the question.

"Sure," I answer as I walk out the door. I don't need the bathroom, just a few minutes away from the knowing looks I'm getting and the distracting view of Katrina in that shirt. I can still clearly picture it when I close my eyes. I turn on the cold water and splash some on my face, happy that I never wear makeup. I feel my phone vibrate as I'm patting my face dry. The message is from Katrina, asking if we're ok. I send her a response that I think we are and head back to face the firing squad. Abby, Blake, Derrick, Dahlia, Shannon, and Kevin have all joined us in my absence. So has the next round of shots. I take my seat as Katrina checks her phone, probably reading my response.

"Did you drive?" I can feel her eyes on me and see the distracting view in my sideways glance.

"Took a Lyft. You?"

"Same." We hoist our shots and toast to having a great night. I open my menu and immediately search for carbs, something to soak up the bottle of alcohol it seems I'm going to be drinking tonight. I feel a mounting pressure for things to be normal between Katrina and me, I need to start a conversation with her, to not feel awkward talking to her.

"How did the move go?"

"Good, I'm mostly settled into the condo. Somehow the movers and the cable guy all showed up on time. I finished unpacking late last night. Slept half the day today."

"I meant to message you but…" I trail off realizing I should have come up with an excuse before I opened my mouth.

"Yeah, it got a little…" Ok, this officially feels awkward, something I've only felt around Katrina a few times. "It wasn't intentional you know. I was trying to break the leg lock when I saw your reaction. Full disclosure, I wasn't sure what to do. I've been so concupiscent lately that I thought about trying my luck. But then you were looking at me, and I realized that you had seen the look on my face, I was sure you had read my thoughts, so I had to leave." I chuckle, unsure if knowing we were having the same thoughts makes this any less awkward or not. "Why are you laughing?"

"No reason. Concupiscent isn't a word you hear every day. I'm not sure I've ever heard it used in a sentence actually." We both start laughing then.

"What are you two whispering about over there?" Derrick's voice carries across the table, all other conversations stop, waiting for our answer.

"Just one of those had to be there moments." It isn't a lie, but I'm not sure I want anyone else to know. Katrina starts laughing again, and I can feel the air between us shift back to the familiar atmosphere we shared before the incident in my basement.

It's still relatively early when we arrive at Velvet, meaning it's easy for us to procure one of the few tables the place offers. Unable to drink, Shannon claims the table for our group as the rest of us line up at the bar to order. "Do you play pool?" Katrina asks as we step away from the bar.

"Sure." We head upstairs and find one of the empty tables, the rest of our group electing to pass. "Traditional game, 9-ball or something else?" Katrina eyes me warily. "Traditional it is. Who's breaking?"

"All yours." She racks the balls properly, earning an unspoken kudos from me. I chalk the tip of my cue and place the cue ball in my preferred breaking spot. The crack of the cue ball making its connection is music to my ears. I watch as the balls scatter around the table and see the 14 drop into the corner pocket. "Stripes are yours." I assess the situation before me, trying to think at least three shots ahead. Confident in my game plan I align my shot on the 15 and call the side pocket. I gently tap the cue ball with the proper English to send it in the down the table toward the 10. I watch the 15 drop and head around the table to line up on the 10. I call the far corner and line up to strike with back spin, trying to ensure I'll be in place to play the 11 next. I take my shot and watch as the cue ball heads to where I hoped it would. "I'm in trouble here aren't I?"

"Maybe, I've never seen you play." I line up my next shot and call for the corner that Katrina is standing at. As I draw back my cue, she bends over, flaunting the view of the plummeting neckline at me. I lose my focus and hear the embarrassing sound of my cue glancing off the cue ball. "That was dirty of you."

"Maybe, but you never told me you're a hustler. Gotta use the weapons you've been given." Touché I think to myself. I watch as Katrina goes to work, easily sinking the 3, then the 6, followed by the 2. Who was she calling a hustler? I scramble to think of a way to turn the tables and finally remember how she looked at me the morning she saw me in my basement those many months ago. Luck would have it that I'm already standing near the pocket she calls for her next shot. I wait for her to lean over and line it up then slowly lift the lower edge of my shirt, revealing my toned abs. She catches me a split-second before her cue makes contact, her movement enough to change the angle of her strike. Neither of us watch as the ball caroms off of the side rail. Katrina's silver eyes gaze hungrily at my abs, and I stare lustfully at her cleavage. The alarms in my head go off again, so I lower my shirt and silence them with another drink. "Who's the dirty one now?"

"You said it yourself, gotta use the weapons you've been given." Why am I flirting with her? Sure she's attractive, smart, kind and a hundred other great things, but we're just friends. I've never thought of her as anything other than a friend.

"Touché," she replies. Is she flirting back? What the hell is happening? I focus on the table, needing this game to be over. My dry spell, the memory of the near miss two days ago and that plunging neckline have me wanting to take Katrina on top of this table. I dial in, using all the focus I have in my body. I quickly sink the 13, followed by the 11, and then the 12. Katrina tries her dirty trick again, but I see it coming and block it out. I watch the nine ball roll into the corner pocket and line up on the eight. Admitting defeat, Katrina steps back and watches as I end the game. "Well played, next drink is on me."

"Thank you. We should check in downstairs, be a part of the party."

"Sure," she says, sounding a little dejected. She crosses the room to the bar and buys our next round. Her fingers brush against my hand as she gives me my victory drink. I feel that light connection course its way to places that it shouldn't. I've sparred with her several times, our sweaty bodies connecting in all sorts of places, and have never felt this response before. I need to stop this, now. Katrina leads the way down the steps to join our friends on the main floor. I follow her, but break off to head to the bathroom without saying a word. I lock myself in the stall furthest from the door and lean against the wall. I'm wound so tight that I could scream. A short-lived debate takes place in my head before my throbbing sex claims its victory. I unbutton my jeans and slip my hand inside my black lace panties and start to massage my outer lips. The music grows louder as someone enters the bathroom. My hand stills as I worry about getting caught, but I decide to turn that risk into a fun game, the danger adding fuel to the fire. I massage my outer lips over my clit in a slow circular pattern. The response is immediate, my body begging for more. Knowing I can't be gone for too long, I give in, parting my lips and rubbing my first two fingers up and down the inside of my folds. The sensations reverberate through my body, I know I'm ready for more. I slide my fingers further back and gently circle the tip of my middle finger around my opening as my palm massages my pulsing clit. I slip my middle and ring fingers inside and start moving slowly in and out, grinding my clit against my palm with each movement. My breathing is heavy but quiet enough I'm confident no one knows what I'm up to. The door opens again, and I hear Katrina call my name. I freeze for a second, my fingers buried deep inside myself, until the image of Katrina in that shirt flashes into my mind, followed by the sensation of Katrina grinding against me the other day in my gym. It's all I need. I focus on those images and get back to working myself. A moan escapes me as I approach my climax. I flip myself around, resting my weight on my forearm against the wall. Knowing I can't hold back much longer I bite down on the supportive forearm and work myself into a frenzy. My inner walls contract as I fuck my own hand, thinking of Katrina the entire time. My impromptu gag works well enough to silence the noise as I finally climax. When the spasms finally stop, I pull my hand out of my pants, wiping my juices on some of the cheap toilet paper. I relax for a minute before cleaning myself up and exiting the stall to wash my hands. My flushed face greets me as I look in the mirror. I splash some cold water on it for the second time this evening and hope that the dimly lit bar will hide the discoloration until it fades.

I exit the bathroom trying to come up with an excuse to explain my absence. I know I'll be questioned. "What happened to you?" I barely make it back to the table before Derrick begins the interrogation.

"Ran into a former patient." I hate telling the lie, but it's the safest one I can come up with, knowing that I won't be obligated to introduce them to this imaginary person.

"I tried to find you, must have just missed you somewhere." Katrina eyes me, I can see the speculation written all over her face. She looks me over and her eyes freeze, locked on my forearm. That's when I remember bitting down on it to stifle any noise. I look down to see the imprinted outline of my teeth still clearly visible. I try to nonchalantly cover the mark with my right hand but when I do Katrina looks back to my eyes, a knowing smile playing at her lips. I feel my face flush as I look around the bar, like I'm searching for the rescue boat to throw me a lifeline. The bar is filling up and people are starting to dance.

"I'm going to dance," I announce, hoping to escape the situation. I quickly down my drink and turn for the dance floor.

"Finally, someone else is ready." Taylor, Nikki and Alex get up to join me. I have no idea what song is playing but it's up tempo and has a good beat. The four of us easily carve a space on the dance floor and forget everything else as we start our carefree movements, smiling and laughing. Song after song we dance as the sweat starts to seep out of our pores. I sneak glances back at our table when I can. I see Catherine hungrily watching Alex dance while the rest of the table seems to be having a good time laughing and joking around. A few songs later I see Catherine rise from her seat and stalk towards the dance floor, her eyes never leaving her target. She skirts her arms around Alex from behind and pulls Alex's ass into her hips. They fall into a seamless rhythm, giving everyone watching a glimpse of what their sex life is like, not caring where their hands land or who might be watching. I decide to take a break as the music changes to something slow. I head to the bar and order a drink and a shot.

"Buy a lonely lady a drink?" I turn toward the voice to see Katrina standing next to me.

"I'm not sure how much of a proper lady you are in that top, but sure. What'll it be?" She smiles at me and I cringe inside, chastising myself for flirting with her again.

"I'm glad you noticed. Whatever you're having is fine." I ask Sandra to double the order and give her the cash and a nice tip. Katrina and I step to the side and take our shots before heading back to the table. "I didn't know you can dance."

"I didn't know you were watching."

"Is there anything you aren't good at?"

"Plenty." I down half of my drink in one go, wanting to dance as soon as the music changes. I notice Katrina's eyes examining my arm again and look down to see the faint bruising occupying the space. I quickly down the rest of my drink and head to the bathroom without a word. The music switches to something up-tempo again while I relieve myself, meaning I can head straight for the dance floor and avoid sitting through another song at the table. I rejoin my friends and continue dancing the night away. The music has a little more sexual energy, but I've had too much to drink to care. I dance with my friends, with a few random women who join us, former clients, and by myself. At some point, Katrina joins our little dance party. I try not to watch her, by forcing myself to focus on any and everything else. The song switches to something slow and sexual, so I turn to leave the floor to get another drink. The sensation of someone pushing up against me and a pair of hands on my hips stop my escape.

"That was you in the bathroom earlier, wasn't it?" I don't need to turn around to know whose hands are locked on my hips, but I make an effort to anyway. Katrina prohibits it, closing the small gap between us. I can feel her warm breath on the back of my neck as her hands force my hips to move in time with hers. Within seconds my body joins her movements. I can feel the soft caress of her nose as she slowly moves her head from the base of my neck around to my ear. "Were you thinking about me?" I freeze as she whispers the question, her breath tickling my sensitive ears. I feel the pressure of her hands on my hips as she forces me to turn and face her. Her silver eyes ooze something I've only glimpsed there before. She pulls me closer to her and wraps her arms around my waist. I feel my arms wrap around her neck, wondering where the command came from. We continue grinding against one

150

another, our eyes locked, unwavering; as if we're challenging each other to make the next move. The two halves of my brain fight a war with each other, half wanting the next song to have the same tempo, the other half hoping it's something upbeat so I can escape this without further damage. I have no idea where our friends are, the only person I see is Katrina, and all I feel is lust surging through my body. Katrina licks her lips and draws my attention to them. I close my eyes trying to shake the image, but all I can think about is what it would feel like, her lips on mine, running my tongue over her lower lip. I feel the pressure of Katrina's lips on mine and fleetingly wonder if I'm imagining it. She runs the tip of her tongue over my lips, and I feel my body tremble as I part my lips to respond. Our lips collide and our tongues tentatively probe one another's mouths before the kiss intensifies, our need for one another growing at a fever pitch. I pull out of the kiss slightly as I suck on her lower lip before forcing our mouths back together. The song ends and our lips separate. I look at Katrina and see a barrage of emotions cross her face as she looks at me, shock, horror, mortification, sadness, but none of the desire that had been present. She backs away from me, and I see her dart into the crowd. I stand frozen, unable to process what just happened. When I can finally move, I try to follow her trail through the crowded bar, knowing she must have gone outside. I head out the door looking for her, but she isn't there. I walk around the building, but don't see her. I call her, but she doesn't answer. I send her a text while I stand at the entrance waiting for her response, one that never comes. I have no idea what just happened or what it means.

"Are you ok?" I hadn't heard the door open, but Abby stands in front of me. Everyone witnessing the kiss only makes this worse, they will expect answers, answers that I don't possess.

151

"I've gotta get out of here." I pull up the app and arrange for a ride home.

"If you leave now everyone will think you left together." Abby is right, I know she is, but I can't go back inside and deal with my friends right now.

"It doesn't matter. You should go inside and have a good time."

"Ok." She turns to head through the door, but stops before opening it, turning back to me. "Sara, you didn't do anything wrong. I know you're telling yourself that you did, but she went after you."

"I know, but I should have walked away. Part of me didn't want to." Abby shakes her head as she opens the door and heads back inside.

My ride arrives, and I ask the driver if she has time to make a quick stop. She assures me she does, so I give her Katrina's address. Her condo is closer to the city than her house was, but still on the way to my place. I try to call her again, but this time I go straight to voicemail. Now I know she's avoiding me. The driver pulls into her driveway, and I ask the her to wait a minute. I feel like a stalker as I knock on her door. There are lights on, and I catch the movement of the blinds out of the corner of my eye. She won't be coming to the door. I have no other option but to give up and go home.

Chapter 12

Saturday morning I get up and drag myself into the three interviews we have scheduled. I'm not mentally focused enough to do this today, but I have no choice. I check my phone only to see that I have no missed calls or messages since I last checked it 15 minutes ago. I shower and change into business professional attire, wishing I could just wear the scrubs that I wear more often than not. I step out of the house into the early morning sunshine, thankful that I was able to drink enough water last night to eliminate any chance of a hangover today. I send Katrina another message asking her to talk to me, but hold out no hope of getting a reply. I leave for the office, stopping to pick up bagels, fruit, and juice on the way.

The interviews go well enough, I think. I'm honestly so distracted by waiting for my phone to vibrate that I can hardly focus. One candidate seems to standout above the rest though, and my partners seem to agree. Not wanting to lose this candidate like we have others before, we call and ask if she'd like to come in to discuss things some more. Given that she currently lives in California, we agree to meet with her in an hour. I grab a bagel and head to my office, closing the door for a little bit of privacy. A knock at the door wakes me. I lift my head from the desk as the door opens. One of my partners informs me that Dr. Westland is back. He pauses and looks at me, I know he wants to say something else but thinks better of it and closes the door. I check my hair and face in a small mirror I keep in the top drawer. I make a few minor adjustments to my hair and quickly eat half the bagel I grabbed earlier. Time to get this over with.

I leave the office telling myself one month. Westland will be starting in one month, meaning that by the holiday season I should have some of my workload lifted, allowing me to take a vacation. It's all that I've wanted this last year, to have a new partner committed to joining us, reducing my caseload. I should be happy, but I'm still distracted. I check my phone to see that I have several new messages and missed calls, none of them from Katrina. I ignore all of them and head home.

I have a lot to get done, but it isn't going to happen today. Instead, I change into a pair of mesh shorts and a t-shirt, order a pizza and put on *Closer*. I binge on pizza and wallow in my growing emotional whirlwind. When the credits roll I start *Great Expectations*. Noticing a trend, I shut it off and start *The Silence of the Lambs*. I wake up on my couch to find the movie over so I shut off the TV and crawl into my bed.

I wake up early Sunday morning recognizing the manic state I get in when something unresolved is bothering me. My emotions are in complete chaos, my burnout, sexual frustration, confusion about the Katrina situation and a litany of others pulverize the damn that usually holds everything back. I want to scream, cry and hit something all at the same time. The bad thing is that Katrina still has not contacted me, the good is that I always get a lot accomplished when I find myself like this. The sun isn't up yet, but the grocery store is always open. I make a list of what I need and am home before dawn. I look around the house to see if anything needs cleaning, but the service always does an excellent job and the house is spotless. I round up any laundry that needs to be done and get that started. I get caught up on my charting between loads. I prep some meals for the week and get everything cleaned up. I'm fully caught up and out of things to do before noon. Still wanting the distraction of busy work, I back my car out of the garage to detail and wash it. With nothing else left to do I jump in the shower. I hear the doorbell ringing as I step out, so I toss on clean shorts and a shirt without toweling off. I open the front door to find Katrina standing on my porch. She stares at me, and I'm keenly aware of the shirt and shorts and clinging to my skin, showcasing the fact that I am not wearing a bra or panties. I really don't care at this point, so I walk away leaving the door open.

"You have a key you know." I hear the sound of the door closing behind me but don't bother turning around to see if she's here or has run off again.

"I didn't know if you'd want to see me."

"You didn't know if I wanted to see you? I called and messaged you several times. I even stopped by your place Friday night. I know you were home, that you know it was me. I've tried, and you've been avoiding me." There is an edge to my voice, I can feel the anger building up inside.

"I know. I needed time to process." I wait for her to continue, but she just stands there staring out the window. I refuse to beg her to talk, so I open the refrigerator and look for something to drink. Finding nothing, I close the door and settle for a glass of water. I offer the glass to Katrina. She takes it, so I fill another. "Can we sit down?" She heads into the den before I can respond. I find her seated on one end of the sofa, so I plant myself on the ottoman, not wanting to be too comfortable. I listen to the sound of the clock on the wall ticking the seconds away, waiting for Katrina to finally speak. "So, things got a little crazy Friday night."

"Was that before or after you kissed me then ran away?" Katrina flinches, and her eyes shift to the floor.

"That's fair. Both I guess. Please don't take it personally." Katrina seems to have lost some of the life that she's shown the last month or so, but it doesn't stop me from being angry.

"Don't take it personal? You came after me, you flirted with me, you started shit with me on the dance floor, you kissed me and when I responded you ran away and ignored my existence. How do I not take that personally?"

"I ran because I felt like shit after it happened!" She shouts, but I can't tell if it's because she's trying to get through to me or if she's becoming angry herself. She takes a deep breath and blows it out slowly. "You're right, I flirted with you, I watched you dance, I thought about you in the bathroom, I pursued you on that dance floor, and I kissed you…all because I wanted to. I wanted it, and I enjoyed it…but somewhere in the mix of making out with you and the alcohol, Jill came to mind, and it was like having a bucket of ice water tossed on you as a means of waking you up when you're sound asleep. I felt like I had betrayed her, that I cheated on her, that I shouldn't be enjoying myself with you. I couldn't breathe. So I ran. I hid in the parking lot across the street. I watched you when you came out looking for me, you walked around the building, and then Abby checked on you. I used her distraction to sneak out of the lot and down to the corner. I caught a cab and went home. I was there when you arrived a short while later but couldn't see you." She looks at me, wanting a response but I can't give her one. I feel like I've been punched in the gut, I want to breathe but I can't. "I'm sorry, this isn't fair to either of us."

"What do you want me to say?" I can't yell at her, argue with her, or anything really. I've never been in her shoes before. It's clear that the situation has been bothering her as much, if not more, than me.

"I don't know, tell me something, anything. Don't you feel anything right now?"

"I feel, I don't know…confused I guess." This conversation hasn't clarified any of my confusion regarding what happened between Katrina and I. I still am unsure if I harbor genuine feelings for her.

"What does that mean?"

"It means that I need you to leave." Katrina drops her gaze from my face to the floor as she stands up. She heads for the front door, and I follow her down the hall. She opens the door to leave, but turns to face me after she steps out onto the porch.

"Are we ever going to be ok? I really don't want to lose you." I see her eyes become glassy, know that there are tears there, threatening to make their presence known. She looks miserable, and her sadness weakens my resolve.

"We will be." I have nothing else to say, so I close the door, leaving her standing there. I feel insensitive and foolish, but mostly I wish I could just not feel. Thankful that I'm not on call, I shut off the ringer, plant myself in my reading chair and stare off into space.

Chapter 13

I don't see or really speak to Katrina for two weeks. I message Jason excusing myself for missing our sessions due to work. I have no idea if Katrina showed up, I just know I couldn't see her, much less spar with her. Katrina messages me but I either neglect to respond, or I keep my responses as short and uninviting as possible. I resort to living on autopilot, moving from one commitment to another, trying to not feel anything, but the emotional whirlwind persists. Everyone tries to get me to talk about it, but I don't care to, so eventually, I stop talking to everyone. This is how I cope, how I deal with problems. It isn't healthy, but it's how I work.

I pull into my driveway late Friday evening to find Katrina sitting on my porch, a takeout bag sitting next to her. I should be irritated that she's here without an invitation, but I can't deny that I miss her. I park my car in the driveway and make my way to the front door. I slide my key in the lock and enter the house, leaving the door open behind me. I hear the door close and Katrina's footsteps behind me in the hall.

"What are you doing here?"

"Alex said you were going to have a late day, so I brought you dinner...and I miss you." I have to admit to myself that I've missed her as well. Two weeks and I still have no idea what my feelings toward Katrina are.

"Please don't say things like that to me." I see the confusion on her face.

"That I miss you? Why not? I do miss you." She still doesn't get it. I close my eyes in frustration.

"Don't you get it? I have no idea how I'm supposed to feel about you or our situation." Katrina is still confused, and if I'm honest, so am I. I still don't have answers for how things got so out of hand, but the fact that what happened is still bothering me is answer enough.

"What do you mean?"

"It means that I think I might have feelings for you that I either didn't know existed or that I ignored until everything blew up. You either don't or can't return those feelings. I don't want to lose you as a friend, I'm just struggling with sorting out my emotions right now. So I can't have you showing up here telling me that you miss me because I miss you too, I'm just not sure on what level." Katrina processes my words, giving them time to sink in. I busy myself getting a glass of ice water, not wanting to see any signs of hurting on her face. I take a drink and deposit the glass on the counter. I want to change into something lighter, so I head towards my bedroom. Katrina blocks my path, the look on her face isn't one of hurt.

"You know that I care about you too, right?" She takes my hands in each of hers, my body involuntarily responding to the contact. I close my eyes and breathe, not wanting to say something harsh or do something foolish. When I open them again Katrina has moved a step closer, the lust filled look back in her eyes.

"Please don't look at me like that."

"Why not? I want you, you want me. We could have some fun."

"Where is this coming from? Why would you even suggest it? Do you enjoy seeing me like this? Do you want to humiliate me more?" She recoils at my words and

159

the site of two weeks of repressed emotions threatening to streak down my face.

"No, it isn't that. I enjoyed what happened at Velvet, I thought you said you did too. We could enjoy each other some more, if you want."

"Why so you can run out of my house like your ass is on fire the same way you did at the bar? No thanks, I'd rather not invest in something so I can get hurt in the end."

"But I didn't mean to hurt you. I just thought that maybe we could keep this casual, you know, one of your no strings flings you've told me about." I know my feelings are more evolved than lust when this doesn't even sound remotely appealing.

"If you came over and told me you were on the same page, that you weren't going to freak out and run then maybe we could try again. But you want casual sex and I know I can't give you that." I pull my hands free from Katrina's and move around her to escape down the hall. I slam my bedroom door and grab a clean pair of shorts and a t-shirt. I drag my feet hoping Katrina will leave, but I find her sitting in the den when I finally emerge from hiding. I head into the kitchen and hear footsteps as she follows me.

"I do care about you, more than you realize it seems. There's just this horrible guilt that I feel when I think about that. I don't want to feel like that with you, the guilt I mean. I'm trying to sort it out, I really am, I just hate not seeing you, not talking to you."

"What do you want me to do with that? Am I supposed to just sit around waiting for you to figure it out? Feel like I'm the other woman while you sort out your guilt complex? That isn't fair to me, and I refuse to put myself in that situation. Come back when you've sorted it. We can talk then." I storm back down the hallway and slam my bedroom door for the second time since I arrived home. I sit on my bed and stew, waiting to hear the sound of the front door closing. After fifteen minutes there is a knock on my door.

"Sara, please come out and talk to me." I can hear the pain in Katrina's voice and fight the urge to give into her, ignoring her plea. "Sara, I wouldn't be here if I didn't care, please open the door." After ten minutes of her pleading, I realize she isn't going to leave. I fling open the door and block her entrance. She looks at me but doesn't say a word. Without warning, she takes my face in her hands and kisses me. I want to pull away but feel my body melting into it. The images of Katrina's face at Velvet flash through my mind, and are enough for me to break it off and back away from her.

"Please just leave. I'm begging you to please just leave now. I can't watch you run away from me again, so please, if you care at all, just go." I curse the hot tears as they free themselves and roll down my face. Katrina opens her mouth to say something but changes her mind. I watch her walk down the hallway and hear the front door as she closes it behind herself. I curl up in my bed and cry, wondering how I can put all of it away again, the stress, confusion, exhaustion and now these newly acknowledged feelings. The sound of my phone chirping catches my attention. I retrieve it from the nightstand and check it to find a message from Katrina. *I wouldn't have run tonight; just so you know.* I type out a quick response: *Not tonight, but you would have tomorrow, and that would have been worse.* My hope that the conversation is at an end is fruitless though as my phone chimes a few seconds later. *We don't know that.*

I can't take anymore. I leave my bedroom and locate my laptop in the den. I open up the web browser and check the going rate on last-minute flight and resort deals. I need to get out of here, now. I find a cheap flight and resort deal for a two-week trip to Punta Cana. Good enough. I check the flights and find that I can leave on a red-eye in the morning. I check my calendar and discover that I don't have any cases in the next two weeks that can't be delayed. I send a message to Abby claiming a family emergency. I ask her to reschedule my OR cases for when I return, booking them in a manner that will allow us to catch up as quickly as possible. I also ask her to reschedule my new office consults, including having me stay late on office days. I finally ask her to take care of my rechecks for me by seeing them in the office when we would normally be in the OR. I apologize to her for the chaos that it will cause, but promise her a nice bonus when I return. That handled, I book the package and start packing. I don't need much to sit on the beach for two weeks and try to forget about my problems here. My phone chimes again and I check to see a text from Abby: *I know you don't have any family to have an emergency to run off to. If you need to get out of here, do it and don't feel guilty. I'll take care of things while you're away.* Yes, Abby will be getting a big bonus indeed. I send Abby another message thanking her and giving her the contact information for the resort if there's an emergency. I tell her that I won't be taking my phone, but I'll check my email from time to time.

I run down a mental checklist making sure I've packed everything I'll need. Satisfied that I have, I grab my laptop and toss it in my carry on before getting ready for bed.

Chapter 14

I drop my bags on the floor and flop down onto the unfamiliar bed. It's early afternoon, and the cool air inside my suite contrasts sharply with the hot, sticky air outside. The entire trip to the airport I was racked with guilt for abandoning my responsibilities. I nearly didn't get on the plane, but when I thought about going home, I remembered why I had to leave in the first place. I needed to get away, to have the time and space necessary to figure out how this mess I currently call my life happened. I take a deep breath and open my eyes before sitting up to thoroughly examine my accommodations.

The walls are primarily white but are broken up by a few light gray accent walls. The queen bedding is your typical hotel white with a light gray duvet that features some leaf and vine design done in black. In place of a headboard is a saltwater aquarium set in the wall above the bed. Several fish that I can't identify swim in and around the coral within its confines. The length of the room is divided by two steps that lead down to a small sitting area. A gray sofa and two matching arm chairs are separated by a small light blue area rug and a small circular table. The bathroom is separated from the bedroom by two thick glass walls, one of which slides to close off the small space from the rest of the room. I look at the thick translucent glass. You can't see clearly through it, but it would definitely allow the silhouette of anyone using to shower to easily be observed. The private terrace outside of the sitting room's glass door seems to be composed of plant covered walls. In the center of the open space is a small two-sided structure, the wooden sides meeting at one corner. Privacy drapes dangle from the roof of it, but are pulled up enough to reveal the large cushioned reclining space and pillows within. I take it all in again and realize that it's wasted on me. This isn't a place you come to forget about someone, this is a place you come to be with someone. Good thing I don't plan to spend much time in my room.

I put on my black bikini and a pair of black mesh shorts with an orange tank top. I slip into my flip flops, stuff my key, Kindle and a few other necessities into my small shoulder bag and head out to explore what the all-inclusive resort has to offer. Everything is white and wood and should seem nondescript, but it somehow works together well enough to look classy. I take note of the locations of the open-air restaurants and the fitness center. I may be on vacation, but I have no intention of not working out. I step outside to find perhaps the largest swimming pool I've ever seen. I know the water is warm, and it looks inviting as I stand here in the humid heat, but I also know the ocean is just a short distance away. I look around and locate the open-air bar, time for a drink and then the beach. I sit down on one of the vacant stools, the bartender smiling and welcoming me. The greeting sounds rehearsed, but her eyes travel up and down my body a bit more than they politely should. Her voice is soft and her accent sweet like honey. She is quite possibly the most beautiful women I've ever seen. Not wanting to be caught staring, I look around again, wondering where the heavy crowds I expected are.

"Not very busy." I'm on vacation and attempting small talk, surely these are warning signs of an impending apocalypse.

"Product of the slower season. Would you like something to drink or are you waiting for someone?"

"Just me." Her smile shifts slightly as I look over the variety of bottles lining the shelves. "What do you recommend?"

"Depends, why are you here?" It's a bold question. I sit in silence, wondering if I've misunderstood her. "Bad breakup or running away?" I can feel the shock register on my face.

"Are you a bartender or a psychic?" She laughs and smiles at me genuinely this time, highlighting her perfect white teeth, a sharp contrast to her deeply bronzed skin and ebony hair.

"Both, I suppose. Or maybe it's just that this is the first second you haven't looked lovelorn since you stepped into my bar." Her words make me think of Katrina, of how even now I'm unsure how I feel for her. I force the unwanted thoughts from my mind and clear my throat. "Running away then?"

"I suppose that works." She tilts her head slightly as she continues to appraise me.

"I have just the thing." She turns away from me and I watch her go to work, pouring the various liquids into an ice filled shaker. Her long black hair cascades over the white resort top that hugs her curves in all the right places. She's tall, with wide shoulders, a slender midsection and larger breasted than I would expect for her build. Her toned arms lead down to long slender fingers that deftly work at creating the fruit garnish for the top of my drink. She places the drink on the bar between us. I pick up the glass and take a tentative sip. It's initially sweet and fruity but mellows, leaving a slightly sour aftertaste.

"Mmm. That's really good. What is it?" She smiles again, and I can't help but stare at her, she's the definition of breathtaking.

"Thank you. It doesn't have a name. Just something I tried mixing up one night." She shrugs like it isn't a big deal and wipes down the counter out of habit. "So, tell me what brings you here, what has you running away from this man you clearly care about."

"Woman," I blurt out without thinking. She arches her perfectly sculpted eyebrow at me, the only reaction my correction yields. "It's a long story, I'm sure you don't want to waste your time listening to it."

"I have nothing better to do," she says as she uses her hands to gesture around the sparsely populated bar. I take a drink of the nameless beverage while I debate whether I should share my sad tale with her.

"Sara," I say as I offer her my hand. She accepts my offered appendage, and I feel her long fingers wrap around my palm as she firmly shakes my hand, the contact with the alluring woman sending pulses through my body.

"Isabella." A beautiful name for a gorgeous woman, I think as she releases my hand, the odd sensation our brief connection yields lingering after our hands part. She has high cheekbones, slightly pouty lips, and deep brown eyes. "So are you going to share your story with me or should I pretend I have something to do?" I like her boldness and doubt many people ever deny this woman anything.

I launch into my recollection, stopping only when Isabella has to wait on the few patrons that straggle in. Isabella sits a fresh drink on the bar in front of me as I finish. "Do you doubt that she has feelings for you?"

"I don't know," I say shaking my head. "I'm not exactly an objective observer here. I just couldn't watch her run away like that again."

"What do your friends think?"

"Couldn't tell you. I've avoided talking to them about it. I only told one person that I'm here." I see surprise register on Isabella's face as she releases a low whistle.

"When you run away, you really run away." I give her a pointed look and she holds up her hands. "No judgment. I have no idea what I would do in your situation."

"Yeah, well I don't exactly have a plan either, sorta flying by the seat of my pants." Isabella nods and leans back against the counter behind her. I take another drink of my cocktail and see her eyes assessing me again.

"So you're a fighter?" I nearly choke on my drink.

"No, I'm a plastic surgeon. Why would you think that?"

"Just the part about sparring and you're…" She doesn't finish the sentence with words, but I see her eyes checking out my viewable physique, I know what she's thinking. She shakes her head quickly; as if she's trying to clear away some mental fog. I wonder if she's embarrassed that I saw her looking at me, or if I would even be able to tell if her face reddened through her deeply bronzed skin. I finish my drink and place the empty glass on the counter. "Another?"

"No, I should get going. Thanks for listening." Isabella nods her head and turns her attention to the remaining patrons at the far end of the bar. As she walks away, I leave a large tip under my empty glass.

*****

A few hours later I'm settling into what I'm hoping to make my new routine. A swim in the ocean followed by air drying under the hot sun on the beach. Once it becomes too hot or sticky, I repeat the process. I lay there under the sun's receding rays, drying off. The relatively empty beach offering me the peace and quiet my mind will not.

"A little over-generous aren't you, doctor?" Her voice is like honey, and I have no idea if she's upset or not. I open my sunglass shielded eyes and look at Isabella. This is the first time I've been given a view of her long shapely legs, clad in short black shorts. As my eyes wander up the length of her body, I catch her looking at my bikini-clad form.

"You earned it, listening to me." Isabella sits on the white sand, less than an arm's length away. She leans back and props herself up on her elbows, crosses her legs and looks out at the water. I realize at that moment that this is a woman who takes what she wants.

"I did ask you to share, twice, if I recall." She smiles but doesn't take her gaze away from the water.

"So what brings you out here?"

"I'm on my way home."

"This is the route you take home?" I envy her, the view of the water and the salt-scented air are relaxing, despite the heat and humidity.

"Sometimes." She turns her head and looks at me. "Where are you from?"

"Michigan." She looks over at me again and raises her sculpted eyebrows. I watch her eyes slowly drift down

168

the length of my body and back up again, leaving a trail of sensations in their wake.

"Aren't you afraid you're going to burn?"

"Not really. I had a decent tan when I got here. We do have sunshine this time of year."

"Yes, I can see the tan lines." Her gaze fixes on my two-toned thighs and she giggles. I feel my cheeks flush with slight embarrassment. "How long are you here for?"

"Two weeks. This is the first vacation I've taken in at least 10 years."

"Dios mío!" I have no idea what Isabella has said, but her tone indicates shock. She stands up and brushes the sand off of her shorts. "Well doctor, maybe I'll see you around."

"Sara," I call as she walks away. She turns back, looks at me and smiles.

"See you, Sara."

*****

The next morning I wake up early as usual. I could blame a number of things from the unfamiliar bed to emotional exhaustion, but I simply accept that I'm awake. I brush my teeth and grab a bottle of water before making my way out onto the terrace. The temperature is in the mid-70s and the humidity bearable without the sun pounding down. I decide to go for a run on the shoreline followed by a swim. I put on my bikini, a sports bra, shorts, and a tank top, grab two more bottles of water and head to the beach. I push myself hard during my run, knowing it's because of all the stress I've experienced lately. Surfers work the swells against the backdrop of the sunrise. The water is choppy enough that a great swim isn't possible, so I toss my belongings onto some dry sand and settle for a soak instead. Once cooled, I make my way back to my belongings where I watch the surfers as I drink one of the bottles of water.

The sun is well over the horizon, and most of the surfers have packed it in as I pull on my tank top and shorts, deciding it's time for a shower. "You're up early." The morning sun prohibits me from seeing anything but the shadowed outline of the person approaching me. I don't need to though, the silky voice with the sexy accent tells me who it is, not that there's anyone else here that knows me. She approaches, and finally her form blocks enough of the sun for me to see her. She is clad in a bright blue bikini and drops of water bead and roll off of each one of her curves as she stands in the sand about a foot away from me. I watch one of the drops start at her neck and follow it as it rolls between her breast and down her abdomen before being absorbed by her bikini bottom. I return my gaze to her face and find her grinning at me.

"You surf?" She laughs, knowing that I've been checking her out.

"Yes. Ever try it?"

"No. Not much call for it where I live."

"Right. Well, let me know if you want to try it."

"Thanks, but I'd probably end up hurting myself." I've been accused of being many things, but graceful was never one of them. Isabella shrugs before raising her arms to wring out her hair.

"Well Sara, I've got to get home. Perhaps I'll see you later," she says as she turns to leave.

*****

Showered and changed, I head to the restaurant for breakfast. I order an omelet, toast and a fruit smoothie. I look around and find that I'm the only person here alone. I make a mental note to remind myself to ensure my next vacation destination isn't typically a romantic couples getaway.

Appetite sated, I head back to my suite and realize I have nothing to do. I grab my Kindle and curl up in the canopied enclosure on the terrace. I wake up during the early afternoon and curse myself, knowing that I probably won't sleep much tonight. I head inside and grab another bottle of water and the brochure detailing the activities the resort has to offer. Scuba diving, parasailing, golf, various classes, the list goes on and on. I make a mental note of things I might look into and decide to head back to the bar for a drink.

I seat myself on a stool with a view of the ocean. A well groomed young man approaches, flashing me a cocksure smile. I'm sure with his dirty blonde hair, ice blue eyes and chiseled features it works more often than not. "What can I get you?"

"Whiskey sour please." He flashes me that smile again, pours my drink, then loiters, trying to make small talk. I take out my Kindle and start reading my book, hoping that he will take the hint. He backs off a little, but not enough for my liking. I focus on my book, determined to ignore him until my drink is gone. The plot picks up, and I lose track of time or what's happening around me.

"Hello again." Her sultry accent makes it sound like she is purring the words. I look up at Isabella standing before me. She wears a similar top to the one she wore yesterday, but her hair is up in a messy bun today.

"Hi." I can feel the smile spreading across my lips.

"Sorry I interrupted your reading. I have to check in with Matt." I watch her approach the other bartender, who must be Matt. They chat briefly, and I realize that it must be shift change. I go back to my book and am pulled away from it by the sound of another whiskey sour being placed before me, one that I didn't order. Matt smiles and tells me to have a nice day as he winks. I go back to reading my book until I feel Isabella standing before me.

"Was he bothering you?" I give her a look indicating my confusion. She slides the second drink towards me, and I really look at it for the first time. There on the napkin is Matt's name and number.

"I didn't ask for either of those," I say, shifting my vision from the drink to Isabella.

"What is this anyway?"

"Probably a whiskey sour."

"Oh no, that won't do." She takes the drink and dumps it out before I can protest. "I have something better in mind." I try to read my book while she prepares my new drink, but find myself drawn to watching her instead. She places the concoction before me and waits. I half expected the same drink that she made me yesterday, but it isn't. I take a sip and let the cool liquid settle on my tongue. It's initially sweet but slowly shifts to just a touch of tartness as the alcohol finally reaches my taste buds.

Isabella dons a satisfied grin and I know I've been treated to another one of her secrets.

"Let me guess, another one of your creations."

"Yes but this one has a name." I look at her expectantly, waiting for her to share.

"Well?"

"I call it Forbidden Fruit." She smiles and makes her way around the bar, checking on the other patrons scattered around it. I watch her interactions, trying to figure out if she's flirting with me or if she has the same mannerisms with all customers. Deciding that it's the later, I go back to reading my book until her rounds bring her back to me.

"What are you reading?"

"I honestly have no idea what it's called. Just some free lesbian romance novel I downloaded ages ago."

"And you picked now to finally read it? Are you some kind of masochist?" I see embarrassment flash across Isabella's features, a complete u-turn from her normal in control, composed self. I can't help but laugh.

"I know, it doesn't make any sense does it?" I release a small chuckle as I think about it. "Maybe I just need a little hope or something."

"I shouldn't have asked you that, I apologize."

"Don't worry about it, really. I'm not bothered." She eyes me, and I can see her nervousness abate when she sees that I'm being sincere. A new couple seats themselves at the bar, commanding Isabella's attention.

She's gone for a while this time as she serves the new additions and checks on the other patrons as well.

"So has it gotten good yet? Isabella leans on the bar in front of me, allowing me a clear view down the front of her shirt. *It just got much better*, I think to myself and feel my lips curling into a telling grin.

"Compelling, yes." My eyes remain fixed on the view down Isabella's shirt.

"But not juicy yet?" Isabella arches her eyebrow when I finally look up at her.

"Not yet, but sometimes you have to build up to that, you know, invest in the characters first."

"And sometimes you don't." Now I'm certain that she's flirting with me. There's no denying that she's a beautiful woman and that her sexy accent only adds to her appeal. Thinking about her certainly gets the juices flowing.

"I assume you teach the bartending classes offered in the brochure." Isabella's demeanor changes from playful to confused back to business as usual.

"Sometimes. Would you like a private lesson?" She arches an eyebrow and grins at me. This woman never misses an opening.

"Perhaps," I stammer. I cannot deny Isabella's attractiveness or that her boldness has me reeling. Her eyes are locked on mine, her lips slightly parted, like she is weighing her next move. I sit there waiting for it, but Isabella's attention is required elsewhere, there are other patrons to serve. I see her slightly parted lips close and her eyes shift back to their blank business as usual facade before she turns away from me. I go back to reading, trying to keep my eyes off of Isabella's form as she works her way around the bar.

"Something tells me your book is more than compelling now." I look up, straight down the cleft of Isabella's breast. She leans low on the bar in front of me, waiting for some response on my part. She leans back, changing my view. I look her in the eyes, and she smiles knowingly. "You hide it well, most people wouldn't see it, but your lips were parted, your pupils kept dilating, your breathing increased and you started fidgeting a little." I feel the blood rush to my face and look down, hoping she won't notice. "No need to be embarrassed. I am curious though." Without hesitation, I flip a few pages back to where the scene started and hand Isabella my Kindle. I watch her as she reads the words that turned me on moments ago. I wonder who she imagines herself doing those things with. I see her lick her lips, her eyes dilate, and her nipples harden slightly, just visible through the tight shirt she wears. "That could be fun," she whispers as she passes my Kindle back to me. She pours herself a glass of ice water and takes a deep drink of it.

"There's a musician playing here tonight. She sings in Spanish, but her voice and the music hypnotize you. You should check it out."

"I don't speak Spanish."

"It won't matter. It will be free for you, so nothing to lose."

"I'll keep it in mind." She didn't specifically ask me to join her, but I know I would have said yes if she had.

"Just a suggestion." She leaves me to make her rounds, and I go back to my book. Several minute pass before she circles back to me. "Would you like another?" I look at my drink and realize it's gone. I gaze at the water and the sun reflecting off of it, debating if I should have another drink or move on.

"Another time. I should get some sun."

"Right, those tan lines," she looks downward like she can see my lap through the bar. "If you change your mind," she smiles at me. I reach into my bag to leave her a tip. As I move to place it on the bar her hand grabs my wrist. "Not today. You were already too generous last time." I open my mouth to protest but all my mind can focus on is the warm flesh still circling my wrist. "You let me read the story, consider that tip enough." She winks at me and walks away, trailing her long delicate fingers over the back of my hand as she does. The soft caress elicits gooseflesh despite the sticky warmth of the day. I stand there dumbstruck for a moment and nearly sit back down before realizing that there will only be two hours or so of sunlight left.

*****

Sunbathed and showered, I sit on the foot of the bed wondering what I should do. My stomach audibly suggests that I should feed it, that I haven't eaten since breakfast. I put on my navy blue sundress, the spaghetti straps and low v-neck preventing me from wearing a bra. The dress is long and flowing, with a slit that stops mid-thigh. It's lightweight and perfect for the muggy weather. I make my way to the restaurant offering authentic Mexican cuisine and order the beef, chicken and pork tacos and a margarita. It's after 8 pm, but the restaurant is still reasonably busy. I read to pass the time I spend waiting for my meal to arrive. When it does, I force myself to consume it slowly, to take the time to enjoy the flavor. Authentic cuisine is scarce at home, I need to enjoy it while

I can. I try to people watch as I eat, but see nothing but couples once again. I finish my meal and leave, intending to go for a walk on the beach, but the sound of music stops me. A woman's voice joins the music, her timbre is like silk gliding over your skin. I follow the sound and enter the performance hall. It's surprisingly full, divided by couples seated at their tables and others dancing with one another. I stay toward the back and listen, realizing Isabella was right, it's hypnotic. I order a drink at the bar and seat myself at one of the vacant tables near the entrance, with my eyes closed and my body gently swaying to the sultry voice crooning from the front of the theatre.

"You took my advice." My eyes snap open and find Isabella standing beside me, her long legs wrapped in a black sarong, a tight white tank top complimenting it. The outfit is simple, yet compliments her body perfectly. I stare at the small gap that flirts with me between the low slung sarong and the lower hem of the top, feeling my tongue slowly run its way over my lips. Isabella sits down in the empty seat without invitation and glances around the room before turning to me. I close my eyes and let the music take over once again, letting my body sway in time, despite feeling the weight of her eyes on me. "Dance." I'm not sure if it's a request or a command, but when I open my eyes, I see Isabella rising from her seat and feel my body follow her.

On the dance floor, I close my eyes and let the nuances of the music control my movements. I occasionally risk glances at Isabella and each time find her watching me. I sneak glances at her body moving in time to the music and resist all temptation to stop and watch like she's dancing for me in private. Midway through the third song, I feel the heat of Isabella's body pressed against me, her breasts against my back and her hips resting against my ass. Her left arm wraps around my midsection, one hand resting against my stomach as she slowly trails her finger tips up the length of my thigh, accessible via the slit in my dress. Our bodies meld together like this as we move as one in time to the music.

"This song is beautiful, what's it about?"

"Breaking up. She is telling the lover that plans to leave that he will regret it." The song sounded so romantic, in a tragic sense I suppose it might be. We continue to dance together as one song moves on to the next. I can feel Isabella's nose as she nuzzles the back of my ear and the sensitive nape of my neck. I want to turn around and press my lips against hers, but the feeling that we are being watched stops me. I open my eyes and discover that an attractive pair of women watch us from a few feet away, neither looking particularly pleased.

"Who is that?" I lean back and whisper in Isabella's ear. She hesitates momentarily but doesn't answer my question. Instead, she slowly turns us so that our backs face our unwanted admirers.

"Want to get out of here?" I feel her warm breath caress my ear when she makes the suggestion, sending shivers along my spine. I clasp the hand held against my stomach and move us toward the exit. Once outside of the theatre, I hesitate, unsure where I should lead us. I look to Isabella for guidance and see that her mood has shifted, something seems to be bothering her.

"Want to go for a walk?" Walking isn't near the top of the list of things I want to do. It's been months since my mission trip, and my body is begging for attention, especially the ministrations of the beautiful woman who still clasps my hand. I nod that I do and Isabella leads us down to the shore, keeping my hand in hers. We walk in silence, and I can tell that despite her physical presence, Isabella isn't completely with me.

"Care to talk about it?" I make the offer, curious to discover what's bothering her. She remains quiet for a while. I don't press further because somehow I know she won't answer.

"I'm sorry, but I'm not very good company now. I will say goodnight." She gently squeezes my hand before letting it go. I watch her as she walks away from me, her shoulders slumped and her head down. With nothing else to do, I turn around and crawl into bed with my book, the feeling of Isabella pressed against me a fond memory.

Chapter 15

An unexpected noise wakes me the following morning. Disoriented, I roll over and look at the clock to discover that it's just after 9 am. I roll onto my back and stare at the ceiling, realizing that it's my third day on vacation and I've already destroyed my normal sleep pattern. I hear the noise again and realize that it's a thunderclap. Curious, I slide out of bed and open the door leading to the terrace. Rain cascades from the gray sky, the scent of the fresh water falling different from the salt tinged air I've quickly grown accustomed to. I stick a tentative hand out the door and discover the water is warm, not shower water warm but pleasant enough. I close the door, brush my teeth and get dressed to head to the fitness center, plugging my earbuds in, letting my gym mix start to get me pumped up.

I step into the fitness center and look around. It sits on one of the corners of the main building. The two exterior walls are composed of untreated glass from floor to ceiling, offering a view of the beach front and some of the bungalows that sit along the resort's outskirts. It hits me as I take in the view, not only has the torrential downpour stopped, but the puddles have already dried up as well, removing any evidence that it had rained. I shake my head in disbelief and seat myself on one of the rowing machines. I'm nearing the end of my interval when I realize that I have an audience. Isabella stands on the path outside of the gym's glass wall, watching me sweat. When she realizes she's been caught, she keeps her eyes locked on me instead of averting them in embarrassment. I stop rowing a minute early and make my way to the glass that separates us, not caring that the only thing covering my sweat soaked body is my sports bra and a pair of mesh shorts. I stare at her as she rakes her eyes over my body before flashing me a lascivious grin and moving on. I guzzle half a bottle of water before jumping on the elliptical machine to crank out another interval. I watch the crashing waves as I ignore the burning in my legs, realizing that if I want to swim it will have to be in the pool. I finish the bottle of water as I make my way back to my room where I change into my merlot hued bikini and my black sandals. I wrap one of the hotel's towels around my waist and make my way to the pool.

I deposit my towel and sandals on one of the pool side chairs and lower myself into the water. It's cooler than I expected, a byproduct of the rain. The decorative shape of the pool isn't conductive to swimming laps, but I make do and push myself as hard as I can. When my body tells me I've had enough I make my way to the shallow water near my belongings, content to soak while my body cools down. Despite the rain abating, the sky remains overcast. I lean back and close my eyes, happy to have a clear mind and the ability to just be at peace in the water.

"You should drink this." I open my eyes at the sound of the water muffled voice and discover Isabella standing at the edge of the pool offering me a bottle of water. I instinctively plant my feet and slouch down, like the crystal clear water will somehow cover my modesty. Isabella's face betrays her amusement before she sits the bottle down and makes her way back to the bar. I down the bottle in two long draws as I climb the stairs out of the pool. I look towards the bar and find Isabella watching me, her lips parted slightly, her eyes focused on the twin spaghetti straps that curve around my hips. The sensation of the water slowly trickling down my thigh reminds me of the sensation of Isabella's fingertips last night. I wrap the towel around my waist and slip into my sandals before making my way to the bar. I watch as Isabella fixes me a glass of ice water and places it on the bar, anticipating my presence or perhaps commanding it. Either way, I willingly join her, even if nothing more comes of this, she's still a welcome distraction from everything I came here to escape.

"Thanks," I say taking a seat and the water. She smiles as her eyes linger a little too long on my breasts. I feel the grin playing at the corner of my lips as she tears her gaze away.

"It will likely rain most of the day, I hope it doesn't spoil your plans."

"Well I don't see myself swimming in the ocean or deepening my tan today, but I'll survive." Frown lines crease her forehead as she absorbs what I've said.

"You really didn't make any plans?"

"Nope, I told you, this was all spur of the moment." She shakes her head and looks at me.

"Perhaps a massage then. I'm sure you could use it after this morning." Her voice lowers during the second sentence, despite the fact that we are basically alone. I nearly choke on my water. *Smooth Sara, really smooth.* I watch as she grabs the chrome drink shaker. "Drink?" she asks arching one eyebrow in my direction. With every movement she makes I can't help but watch the white fabric of her snug shirt hug the curves of her upper body. My stomach chooses this window to release a painfully loud gurgle, raging because I haven't eaten since dinner last night. Isabella laughs, and I feel my blood defy gravity, torrenting to my face.

"Later, perhaps. I should get something to eat." She closes her eyes and nods slightly, the smile leaving her face. I briefly wonder again if the flirting is an act for the tourist, but then remember the feeling of her pressed against me, her fingers trailing their way up my thigh, and the contrast of her soft hand in mine versus the firm hand she held against my stomach. *It can't be an act*, I think as I walk away from the bar. I risk a glance over my shoulder and find Isabella intently watching me walk away. *No, definitely not an act.*

Showered and fed I watch the second storm of the day, the rain coming down like sheets of glass and quickly disappearing. I read for a time while my meal digests before taking out my laptop and logging into my email. Several messages await my attention, so I scan the list of senders, picking out the important ones. I open a message from Catherine, received only minutes ago. The subject line is *You're where?!?!.* So Abby has told her, which means Alex knows as well. I click the link and the message appears: *Katrina has been asking after you. Alex and I had no idea you were gone. Abby told Alex after much pressure was applied. I assume this has to do with a specific someone. Try to enjoy yourself, your secret is safe with us.* I send her a brief reply: *Sorry, the trip was last minute, I needed to get away so I could rest. I appreciate your confidence. We'll talk when I get back. Please don't blame this on Katrina, we're both at fault. Love to you both.* I scan further and read the generic messages from my partners telling me to take whatever time I need and they are here if I need anything. I've always preferred keeping my business and personal lives separate from one another, so they know very little about my private affairs. Abby has sent me two messages, the first with my reworked schedule when I return. I won't be getting many lunch breaks or finishing up in the OR before 7 pm anytime soon, but I needed this. Her second email is to warn me that Catherine and Alex pressured her into revealing my location. I send Abby a quick response thanking her for the new schedule and telling her not to worry about telling Catherine and Alex. With no other messages that look urgent, I shut my laptop and decide to follow Isabella's suggestion.

*****

The sensation of water hitting my toes wakes me from another nap. The hour long deep tissue massage coupled with some time in the sauna turned me into a useless puddle. I vaguely remember slinking my way back to my suite and laying down in the enclosure on the terrace. Another rain shower steadily falls, but I know it will be brief. I stretch and end up further exposing my legs to the cascading water. I sit up and realize that I'm parched, hungry and that it's nearly dark. I tread the short distance inside and down another bottle of water. Despite the rain, it's still warm and humid. I catch a glimpse of myself in the mirror and take in my wrinkled clothes and messy hair. I exchange my shorts for my black sarong and an emerald green tank top that fits me like a glove. I brush out my hair but give up on taming it and pull it up into a messy bun. As I make my way to the restaurant, I'm stopped by a familiar song. I stand there, sifting through my brain for the reason that it holds my attention. I struggle with the elusive memory before finally catching it. It's the song that was playing when Katrina kissed me. The scene replays in my mind, and as she flees, she takes my appetite with her. No longer wanting to eat and not wanting to be in the confined space of my suite, I do the one thing I can think to, I head to the beach. The combination of the unpredictable rain showers coupled with the lack of daylight results in the beach being eerily abandoned. I amble along, wandering further than I have to this point. When I reach what I'm sure is the end of the resort's shoreline I turn around and slowly stroll in the other direction, wracking my brain, trying to decode my feelings for Katrina. I near the bungalows for the first time and take in their cookie cutter design. They all bear the same glass paneled walls overlooking the ocean, the same off white exterior paint, the same balcony style patio and the same thatch roof. Trios of palm trees separate one mirror image from the next. All they are missing are the inspected by operator 123 stamps. I continue to wander the shore, the waves licking at my feet, the edges of my sarong soaking up the salt water. The ocean offers a certain serenity, so I sit down with my feet planted on the tide line and my arms wrapped around my knees, staring out into the empty void in front of me. I don't know how long I sit there staring into nothingness, but for the second time today I'm brought back to consciousness by a thunderclap that gives a five second warning before the downpour commences. There's nothing I can do, so I stand up, extending my arms and tipping my face up to the unseen clouds.

"You're insane!" The din of the falling rain slapping the ocean leaves me unsure if I heard the words or imagined them. I look around but don't see anyone. Then I hear laughter. I may have felt like I was losing my grip when I started this walk, but I know I did not imagine that. I follow the sound and find Isabella standing under the thatched overhang of the last bungalow in the line. I saunter away from the shoreline and pause at the base of the stairs leading up to her deck. I can't see her, but she voices no objection, so I ascend them, feeling my desire for her coming to life all over again. She waits for me at the top, standing in the threshold of the sliding glass door, towel in hand. I stand there in the rain as she drinks me in, I can feel the already tight tank clinging to my curves and the sarong hanging just a little lower on my hips. "Come in," she commands as she offers the towel. I take it, unsure what I should do with it. I can hear the rainwater pooling on the floor as my over saturated clothes shed their excess. I dry off my face and then drop the towel, trying not to cause a flood. I watch her as she gathers another towel and motions to the bathroom as she hands it to me. I'm keenly aware of the familiar translucent glass walls, but know she really won't see more of me than she already has. I close the door behind me and wring out my clothes in the sink. A knock at the door startles me, as I

stand there fully naked. "I have some dry clothes for you."
I feel guilty taking them, but if I don't my only real option is
to go back to my suite. I wrap myself in the towel and slide
open the door to accept the offer. I watch Isabella as her
collected facade is betrayed by the slight sound of her
breath catching, her lips parting and her pupils dilating.
Leaving now isn't an option.

I slip into the backless sea blue sundress and
fasten it around my neck, the small knot the only thing
securing the fabric to my body. I stand there and listen to
the softly playing music, as a touch of nervousness settles
in. I slide open the door and find Isabella in the small
kitchen, preparing what must be a pitcher of sangria. She
pauses when she sees me and a small grin curls at the
corner of her mouth as she resumes her work. "Drink?"

"Thanks." I unglue my feet from the floor, slowly
approaching her as I take in my surroundings. Aside from
the larger space, the addition of the kitchenette and the
absence of the bed, the decor is quite familiar. "This is
your place?" She nods as she places the orange, lemon
and lime garnish on our glasses. "No offense but how can
you afford it?" My gaze quickly shifts away from Isabella
as soon as the words leave my mouth. Embarrassment
surges through me, and I want nothing more than to dart
back to my suite. "Sorry, sometimes I lack a filter."
Isabella laughs, much to my relief.

"Not to worry. My family owns the resort." The
shock must be painted on my face because Isabella
chuckles again before offering one of the finished drinks to
me. "It's not a big deal. Most of my family work here in
some capacity. I do not care for the business side of
things, I don't enjoy working with numbers or the monotony
of financials and meetings every day. I prefer creativity
and people. Come, sit." She grabs the pitcher of sangria
and leads me to the identical arm chairs, claiming the far

one for herself. She sits across from me, close enough that I could slowly run my foot up her leg if I tried to. I watch her as her eyes fix on something. I turn slightly to see what it is and realize she can see my discarded clothes drying on the side of her bathtub. I should feel a modicum of modesty that she's now aware of my nakedness below the borrowed sundress, but I don't. "What were you doing out there?" I close my eyes and enjoy the music. I can't understand the words but something about it grabs my soul, I can't help but love it.

"Walking. Thinking." I keep my eyes closed, and my mind focused on the music. I feel myself start to gently sway in time with it.

"About her?" I open my eyes and fix my gaze on Isabella's.

"Amongst other things." She hides her reaction, if she has one. I continue to enjoy the music and my drink. The song changes and I realize that somehow I've heard it before. "Isn't this the woman from last night?" I feel her voice wrap around me, the sadness in her tone and the melody feel familiar.

"It is," she says as she stands up and extends her hand to me. "I believe we were interrupted last night." I take her hand, and she leads me to the small open space between the kitchenette and the sitting area. I feel her body press against my back, her left hand rest against my stomach and her right hand begin trailing along my thigh again. We easily fall into a rhythm with the music, like someone pressed pause last night and is now resuming the feature. I can feel my body respond to the contact with hers. I lean my head back as her luscious lips softly caress their way over my bare shoulder and up my neck. "I want you," she whispers, her hushed words caressing my ear. Sheer animalistic lust courses through me as the

187

hand on my abdomen slowly inches its way towards my breast. I break free from her and turn to face her, placing my hands on her hips.

"I can't offer you anything. I still have to leave at the end of next week." I don't want any confusion, as badly as I want Isabella there has to be transparency.

"I know," she whispers as she trails a finger down the side of my face, under my chin and down my sternum, stopping near my heart. "And I know that this belongs to another. But you are beautiful, how could I not want you?" Her words are exactly what I need to hear. My hands forcefully grip her hips and pull her to me as our mouths clash against each other, tongues swirling around and darting in and out at a fever pitch. The hand that held a finger near my heart shifts over and aggressively grabs my breast. She lowers herself and ministers to the other through the fabric of the dress. As she teasingly bites down on my nipple, I feel my legs threaten to give and let out a loud moan.

I grab her by the hair and pull her head back, "Where's the bedroom?" She rises and pulls me to her, pressing her mouth against mine once again as she carefully guides us down a short hall into her bedroom. My hands snake under the thin fabric of her shirt and find her bare breasts. I brush my thumbs over her erect nipples before pinching them between my fingers. She emits a soft growl as I tug upward on her shirt, trying to remove it. She lifts her arms long enough to allow me to, and I stare at her exposed torso, the bronzed skin, her taut stomach, her perfect breasts with the expresso colored areolae and the erect nipples begging for my mouth. She takes advantage of my momentary distraction to turn me and pin me against the wall. Her lips lock on mine again as her hands greedily knead my breast, taunting my nipples with every pass. My excitement builds, and she pulls back, staring at me with fire in her eyes. Without breaking eye contact, she reaches behind my neck and undoes the lone knot keeping the dress in place, looking away to watch it fall to the floor, drinking in my nakedness. Her eyes lustfully fixate on my breasts and as I attempt to remove her shorts her head dashes in, greedily sucking my nipple into her mouth before biting it and rolling her tongue over it. It sends shockwaves to my core causing me to groan.

"Fuck!" Her eyes look up at me as she does it again to my other breast and trails her fingers up the insides of my thighs. She lowers herself and my hips buck against her as she sucks on my throbbing labia. Her hand presses on the back of my thigh and guides my leg onto her shoulder, giving her better access. She presses down on my hips, pinning me against the wall as she slowly runs her tongue along my sex, circling my swollen clit when she reaches it. I watch our reflection in the mirror as she latches her mouth onto me. Her tongue teases my entrance before she sucks my clit again, causing me to rock against her. She repeats her pattern, this time inserting her tongue a little further and swirling it before pulling back out to swipe at and suck my aching sex. Her hand finds my breast, and the dual sensations are nearly too much. I start riding her face as hard as my position allows me to, my fingers tangled in her hair pushing her into me. "Oh fuck," I scream as I climax, Isabella keeping her rhythm until I force her to stop.

She runs her tongue up my midsection as she rises from the floor. My body is still trembling from its release, but I don't hesitate. I pull her to me, claiming her mouth with mine. I can taste myself as our tongues clash and my hands finally free Isabella of her shorts. I push off the wall and guide us towards her bed, pushing her down onto it when we finally get there. I rake my fingers along the inside of her thigh as my mouth claims one of her nipples, circling it with my tongue before sucking and nibbling it.

My fingers roll over her sex as I bite her nipple again, causing her hips to rise up off of the bed and her to release a low hiss. Her motion forces firmer contact with my fingers and I can feel her juices as they begin coating my digits. Wanting more, I spread her lips and slowly circle her entrance before running my fingers up to circle her clit. I bite down on her nipple again as I insert one finger to the maximum depth. She pushes down against me, silently asking for more. I withdraw the finger and repeat the process with two fingers, this time massaging her clit with my thumb when she presses against me. I pull back and repeat the motions and devour the groan she releases with my mouth. My thumb continues to circle her clit as I kiss her, but my fingers stay in place, gently massaging her g-spot. She tries to pull me back to her as I stand up, but I deny her, wanting to watch her body as she gets closer to the edge. I gaze down at her as I move my fingers out and insert them again, flicking her g-spot with each passing. I start to increase the rhythm and intensity, enjoying my reward of watching her beautiful body writhe against the duvet as she pulls at her own nipples. I begin to piston my hand against her, and she starts bucking harder and harder. I can smell her sex. I have to know how she tastes, so I lower my mouth to her as she greedily fucks my hand. She groans something that I don't comprehend, but her body tells me all I need to know as I suck on her clit and finger her with reckless abandon. Her fingers grab hold of my bun and press me against her gyrating hips as her walls begin to tighten. She screams out as she climaxes and her walls clamp down on my fingers, her juices running down my palm. She pulls my head away, and I remove my fingers when she finally relaxes enough. I lay on the bed next to her and stare at the ceiling as we both try to catch our breath, the ache in my arm quickly subsiding.

"So is this your thing?" Isabella turns to face me.

"My thing?"

"I don't mind if it is, but do you make a habit of seducing tourists?"

"Not for many years." Her eyes seem to go dark from what the dim light creeping in from the hallway allows me to see. She slides herself fully up onto the bed, resting her head on one of the pillows there. I'm curious about what she isn't saying, but am starting to feel as though my question has worn out my welcome. As I stand up to leave the sound of her voice stops me. "The women that were watching us last night. That was my ex and my former best friend from childhood. We were together for three years. I left work early one day to find them in bed together. It had been going on for well over a year."

"And that's how you ended up living here." She nods, and I take it as a cue that I can stay. I lay down next to her, trying to imagine how she must feel seeing them. "I'm sorry you went through that."

"It was over a year ago. I'm over it." I understand now, our situations are different, but somehow we both need the same thing. "What are your plans tomorrow?"

"No plans, remember?" I watch the grin return to her face.

"You cannot stay here and not see some of the sites, take in the culture, live a little. I have tomorrow off if you'd like me to show you some things." Neither of us is going to fall for the other, we're both carrying too much baggage for that. We could give each other what we need though, and I've enjoyed her company thus far.

"That would be nice." Isabella rolls onto her side and smiles at me as she slowly trails her fingers up my thigh and over my hip before sliding up my stomach. Gooseflesh rises on my skin following her touch. When her fingers reach my face, she uses them to tilt it towards her.

"Are you staying?" The look in her eyes tells me she isn't talking about sleeping. I roll on my side and pull her to me, crushing her mouth with mine.

Chapter 16

Intensely vivid sex dreams are nothing new for me.
At least once a week I'll wake up extremely turned on and
have even experienced nocturnal orgasms before. So
when the sensations wake me this time, I open my eyes
and am momentarily confused. This isn't my suite, nor am
I alone. I can feel soft flesh pressed against my back and
the hand between my thighs slowly stroking the length of
my sex.

"Buenos dias," Isabella purrs in my ear before
taking my lobe between her teeth. The soft strokes of her
fingers cause me to press my ass into her hips.

"Mmmm, good morning." I slide my hand down and
press it against hers, silently asking for more pressure. I
can feel her grin against my neck.

"What would you like to do this morning?" Despite
my silent plea, she continues her slow, torturous teasing. I
try to press myself against her hand, but she pulls away,
denying me the increase in friction.

"I want you to fuck me," I pant, desperate for more.
She hesitates a second before finally returning her her
hand to my sex.

"We have time," she whispers before giving me
what I asked for.

*****

"Where are you taking me?" I left Isabella's
bungalow to shower and change with the plan to meet her
at one of the restaurants for a quick breakfast. From there,
we got into her Jeep, and she piloted us away from the
resort.

"You'll see." Thus far she had been stingy on the details, simply telling me to trust her. I stare out the window taking in the scenery. The sensation of Isabella slowly trailing her fingertips up the inside of my thigh pulls me back into the car.

"You know, if you wanted to do that we could have stayed in," I say as I part my legs a little further. Her fingers reach my apex and start to gently massage me, forcing me to audibly sigh.

"There's plenty of time for that," she informs me as she pulls her hand away, "but not now." She dons a devilish grin as she pulls into what looks like a cross between an outdoor mall and a flea market. The bright blue, green, and yellow buildings pull one's attention to them, the canopied stalls open to display their wares, a plethora of fresh fruits, live chickens, clothing and various hand crafted curios as far as the eye can see. The scents from different food stalls make my mouth water, despite having just had breakfast.

"Aww baby, I thought you'd never take me shopping." I laugh at the look on Isabella's face, my sarcasm hasn't translated.

"I see, you want to be funny. I will remember this," her smile assures me she's playing as well.

"I remember you teasing me first." My core hasn't forgotten either. Isabella simply grins at me.

"Come on," she instructs, getting out of the Jeep. "This can be a quick trip, I just need to pick up a few things." My steps must have faltered because Isabella pulls ahead of me a few paces before realizing I'm no longer at her side. I watch as she stops and turns to look for me, her confusion evident when her eyes finally meet mine. "Que?" I'm far from fluent in Spanish, but I at least know what she's asking.

"Do we have to rush out of here? I'd like to look around." If she wanted me to get a taste of the culture then what better place to start than the market? We haven't even really gotten into it yet, and already the contrast to American markets is quite evident. I'm curious and want to learn more. I watch her body language relax, and a smile spread across her face as she returns to me, extending her hand once she's close enough. I accept the offered hand and wonder if I missed something or had done something to give her the impression that I don't appreciate her effort to show me life off of the resort. Given that things seem fine now, I decide not to push the issue, to just live in the moment.

Our pace through the market can only be described as leisurely. Isabella and I chat when we aren't being interrupted, which happens frequently. It must be some combination of her being a regular here and her family being well known. She slips easily between speaking English with me and Spanish with the individuals who stop her. I have no idea what they discuss, but a few glances in my direction let me know that these people know her well enough to inquire about my identity. Each time she's pulled into one of these conversations I let go of her hand and look at the surrounding wares. Each time she finds me when she's finished and laces her fingers back through mine. With every repetition of this cycle, I feel an increasing sense of guilt. My mind keeps wandering back to Katrina each time I see something I'm certain she would like or something that simply reminds me of some memory of her. Then this beautiful woman that I know very little about, who is using her day off to basically take me on a date, will come and take my hand. Even though I've been clear with Isabella about the situation, I still feel guilty when

Katrina comes to mind. I can feel the first nagging signs of an impending headache as the tension in my shoulders and neck continues to grow.

I'm looking at the assortment of goods available in one of the shops as Isabella chats with a man I assume is the proprietor. The shop seems to offer everything from snacks to clothing to baubles. Isabella finds me and takes my hand again, but at this point the guilt is too much, and I immediately pull mine free.

"What's wrong?" I don't know how to answer her without sounding like a jerk, so I stand there staring at the rack of post cards like they're the most interesting things in the world. Isabella calls something across the store to the man and the next thing I know she is dragging me into the back room. She pulls me in behind her, closes the door and then pins my back against it. "What's wrong?"

"I..." I close my eyes, take a deep breath and exhale slowly, trying to find a way to tell her.

"Do you not want me to touch you in public?" The look she gives me is fierce, seemingly part irritation and part anger.

"What? No, that doesn't bother me at all. It's just..." I watch as Isabella's features soften, she's an intelligent, perceptive woman, and she has put it together on her own.

"It's ok to think about her."

"Is it? You're here, being wonderful, and my mind keeps wandering back to Katrina."

"Of course it's ok. I know who has your heart, you were honest about that. It's only natural that you think

196

about her. Sometimes it's nice to be reminded that there's someone who enjoys being with you. It makes the difficult times easier." As I marvel at the woman before me, I manage to connect some dots of my own.

"You haven't been here with anyone since…have you?" She doesn't have to tell me, the answer is immediate in her eyes.

"Not here or anywhere." I get it then. Isabella taking my hand has been as much a comfort for her as it is for me. The questioning eyes directed at me during the conversations I couldn't understand. This is her first public outing with someone since her ex, and it has to be much more difficult for her than my thoughts of Katrina are for me. Something possesses me as I look at the alluring woman before me and think about what the trip here has been like for her. I grip her by the shoulders and quickly switch our positions, pinning her back against the door as I lock my lips on hers. As my tongue dances with hers, I lift up her sundress, spread her legs with my knee and press my thigh against her. The sensation of her unimpeded sex gliding against my thigh causes me to bite her lower lip and her to hiss.

"You aren't wearing any underwear." She hasn't stopped grinding against my thigh either. "How well do you know the owner?"

"Well enough. We'll have to be quiet and quick, but he won't come back here." She continues to work herself against my thigh as her hand slips inside my shorts and underwear. Our eyes are locked as her fingers slip inside my folds, and I see she's pleased by the wetness she finds waiting. Her free hand grabs the back of the leg between her thighs, and draws it more firmly against her. My hands go to her breast as our lips reconnect. Both of our breathing picking up as our excitement builds. Isabella groans as she bites my lip and I pinch her nipples. "I'm close, are you?" Just knowing she's close is enough for my body to catch up with her, I can feel the start of my own orgasm. Isabella can too, and she pulls my thigh even tighter against her as she bucks harder and faster over it. Our mouths meet again and swallow one another's release, hers seconds before mine. When she finally calms enough to withdraw her fingers and release my leg, I sink down and slip under the dress to delicately lap up the juices from her lips and thighs, savoring her sweet tanginess. She moans as I finish and pull the dress back over my head in time to see her pulling her fingers out of her mouth. I'd take her again if we didn't have to leave this storage room. We quickly right ourselves and reenter the store proper. Isabella grabs two bottles of water and exchanges a short conversation with the man while she pays. If he knows what we were up to and said something, her face never betrays any embarrassment. This time when she takes my hand I don't feel any guilt, not because she told me I didn't have to, but because the scent of her is still on my lips making me think of no one but her.

"Is there anything you want to double back to?" We made it through the market, Isabella picking up the various pieces of fruit she was after, while I purchased a new sarong and another sundress.

"I think I'm all set."

"Very good, I have other plans." Her words cause a mild sense of disappointment to pass through me, even if I have no right to feel that way. As we walk back to the Jeep, I try to figure out if I had said or done something wrong, but her hand still clutches mine, so I don't think I have. She owes me no explanation though, so, like earlier, I decide to continue living in the moment.

When the Jeep pulls out of the market, she turns in what I believe is the wrong direction to return to the resort. Then again, Isabella lives here, so I figure I have the directions turned around in my head. Five minutes later, as Isabella asks me about life at home, I know my initial sense was correct, we aren't heading back to the resort after all. A few minutes later we arrive at Isabella's next destination, the zoo.

"You like animals?" I ask her as she puts the car in park.

"Yes, don't you?" She has a mild look of concern on her face, wondering if she has made an error bringing me here.

"More than people most of the time." She smiles at my answer, erasing all sense of doubt I had seen there seconds ago.

"On this, we agree."

We take our time going through the park, not bothering to rush from one show or exhibit to the next. It's nice just walking with her, getting to know her, comparing life on the island to life in the midwest. Watching the exotic birds, iguanas, sea turtles and other species provides a temporary distraction from what I'm enjoying more, just being here with Isabella.

It's mid-afternoon by the time we finish seeing the park. I stifle a yawn and try to suppress the gurgling in my stomach, but Isabella notices both. "I would like to show you something tonight, if you will let me."

"Of course." Isabella's lips curl into a smile at my answer.

"Perhaps a nap and dinner first." The mere mention of the word nap has me yawning again, causing Isabella to smirk. She parks the car and I help her carry her bags to her place, intending to retreat to my own suite for a nap.

"What time do you want to meet for dinner?" I ask as I place the bags I carried on the counter. She tilts her head to the side slightly as her brow furrows together.

"You're leaving?" Isabella closes the small space between us.

"I thought—."

"You could stay," she interrupts me, using a fist full of my shirt to pull me to her and kissing me forcefully. I slide my hands around her hips, down her toned ass and around the back of her thighs, pulling upward. I pick her up, and she wraps her long legs around my hips, locking them against the small of my back. I carry her back to her bedroom, our mouths never separating. There's no more debating if I plan to stay, I want more than the sample I had at the market, much more.

*****

For the second time today, I wake up in Isabella's bed, the difference being I know where I am this time. Isabella still slumbers next to me, her arm lazily draped over my hips as I stare at the ceiling. Dusk seeps in from the windows, and a look at the clock reveals it's nearly 8 pm. I'm thirsty, and my stomach is starting to protest loudly. I try to slip out of the bed without waking Isabella, but she stirs as I lay her arm back down on the Egyptian cotton sheets. I quietly pad down the hall to the kitchen to get a glass of water. I find a glass, fill it and down it in one long drink. I fill it again then set it on the counter next to the sink, I need something to eat. As I turn away from the sink, I feel Isabella's arms wrap around my waist, her naked form pressed against mine, her lips hovering a short distance from my ear.

"Dinner and then we can go," she whispers, her breath caressing my ear, sending chills along my spine.

"I should shower first. What should I wear?" She hasn't told me where we're going, I know she won't, so I don't bother asking.

"I like what you have on now." She runs her hands over my exposed abdomen and up my sides.

"I'm naked and I probably smell." I feel her face as she nuzzles in against my neck, the rise of her chest as she inhales and the warm torrent of air that brushes over my neck as she exhales.

"I like how you smell."

"I smell like sex." I feel her grin against my shoulder.

"Isn't that the best smell? You may shower if you'd like, but there's no need. The clothes you wore today will be fine." Isabella drinks the glass of water I had neglected and releases me, making her way back to the bedroom. I follow, watching her bare ass sway from side to side, knowing she's putting a little extra effort into it to entice me.

Somehow we manage to get dressed and make it to dinner. Our conversation is effortless. We discuss our families, hobbies, pet peeves, why I became a plastic surgeon, what I love about my career, and countless other things. We laugh and share stories, and as I sip my margarita I realize that if this were a first date, it would be going perfectly. Maybe it's going so well because we've already had sex or because if we hated each other, it would be easy to walk away. Whatever the reason, I find myself enjoying being in her company.

After dinner, we leave the resort in the Jeep. Try as I might to get Isabella to tell me where we are going, she refuses, each time grinning and reminding me to be patient, trust her or to wait and see. We travel a short distance before stopping at a security gate. Isabella keys in a code, the gate slowly opens and we continue up the drive, parking outside of what can only be described as a mansion.

"Where are we?"

"This is my family's estate." I immediately grow tense and nervous, I'm not prepared to meet this woman's family. My unease must be written all over my features because Isabella laughs at me. "Relax, we're not going inside. We have to walk from here though." Isabella exits the Jeep and pulls a bag out of the back. I release the breath I didn't realize I'd been holding and open the door, wondering when she put the bag back there. I meet Isabella at the front of the Jeep and she takes my hand as we follow a well tended path away from the house. Isabella leads us as the trail changes direction or branches off, never hesitating, her familiarity with the trail making it clear that this is where she grew up. Eventually the path leads to a set of wooden stairs leading down. I follow Isabella, freezing once I see where we are headed. Before us is a freshwater lagoon, the transparent water glowing from the moonlight. The stairs leading down to a deck that overlooks the water, holding a patio furniture set and two lounge chairs. The two sides opposite the deck are enclosed by what looks to be a cliff face, one of the faces receding inwards to what may be a cave, the other host to a small waterfall. The final side, adjacent to the deck, tapers off into land covered in trees and plants. It's peaceful and secluded, a paradise all its own. When I look back down the stairs, I see Isabella, five steps lower, smiling at me. She continues her descent, so I follow. When I catch up to her, she's placed the bag on the table and is removing its contents: towels, two bottles of wine and several bottles of water.

"This is really beautiful. When did you do all this?" Isabella smiles and pulls me to her.

"You fell asleep before I did. I called the desk and arranged the bag. The waiter let them know to put it in my car after he brought us our meals."

"Sneaky." She grins at me before giving me a soft, chaste kiss.

"Red or white?" Wine has never been high on my list so I don't really have an opinion.

"You're the expert, you chose." I watch as she uses the corkscrew to open the bottle of white.

"I'm afraid we don't have glasses."

"You're pure class, aren't you?" I say grinning. I can't help but tease her, we're well past worrying about drinking out of the same bottle. She laughs before kissing me and offering me the bottle. I take a drink, and she does the same when I return the bottle to her. She kisses me more intently, and I break it off when I feel her trying to remove my top. "What are you doing?"

"I thought it was obvious," she whispers in-between the soft kisses she peppers down my neck. Her hands are still under my shirt, and I put space between us when she tries to remove it again.

"What about your family?"

"They will not interrupt us, I told them I would be here tonight." As if to prove her point, she unties her sundress, allowing it to slide down her body and pool at her feet. I feel my body respond to the sight of her standing naked before me, the moonlight illuminating her skin. She stalks over to me, a predator closing in on its prey, her eyes locked on her intended target. She pulls me against her and kisses me again.

"Wait, so they know?" I ask as our lips part when she pulls my top up over my head. She sighs, I know I'm frustrating her, if not flat out irritating her.

"Of course they do, I think they were just happy I finally planned to spend time with someone." I don't need Isabella to tell me I'm not the first woman she's brought here, I have no illusions on that front. Her hands slide up my abdomen and over my breasts before reaching around to unclasp my bra.

"So they know what you're doing out here, and they're ok with it?" Isabella abandons her task as she growls against my neck.

"I want to be naked with you in that water, but if you would prefer, we can get dressed and go see my family." She takes another drink of the wine before kissing me again, the remnants of the wine on her lips and tongue seeping into my mouth.

"Sorry, I just find it intriguing." This time Isabella pulls away, my bra still firmly in place.

"Why? They want me to be happy."

"I don't know. I guess because I never had the chance to tell my mom, she was gone. It makes me wonder how she would have reacted; if she would have treated me differently."

"What about your father?"

"I don't know. He was a firefighter. He died shortly after I was born, trying to save a child during a house fire. My mother and grandmother raised me after that, until my mom passed. Then it was just my grandmother and me." I've totally killed the mood, I can feel it. Isabella stands with her hands on my hips, lost in thought.

"Did you tell your grandmother?"

"Yes, she was great about it. Told me I had to live my own truth and that she just wanted me to be happy."

"She raised your mother?" I nod to confirm. "Then perhaps there is your answer. If she felt that way then surely she instilled those same values when she raised your mother."

"Yeah, that makes sense." I take another drink as I ponder this theory, wondering if I can accept it as truth, even though I know it can never be proven.

I feel the gentle touch of Isabella's fingers under my chin, bringing my focus back to her. "Are you ok?" Her eyes and the tone of her voice let me know that her concern is genuine.

"Aside from the fact that I've completely killed the mood, yeah I'm ok."

"That can be fixed," she smiles as the fingers resting on my chin slide to the back of my head and she pulls me in for a searing kiss. I feel her unhook my bra as the kiss intensifies and lower my arms as she tugs down the straps. Shivers course through my body as she slowly trails her fingertips down my spine, hooking them into the waist of my shorts and panties, pushing them down. She presses her body firmly against mine, and I can't suppress the grin as an image comes to mind. "What are you smiling about," she asks barely disrupting our kiss.

"You'll see," I grin again as I suck her lower lip into my mouth. I feel her smirk as I lower my hands to her hips, hook my discarded bra with my foot and guide her to the railing of the deck. When I feel the soft bump of her back meeting the rail, I lace my fingers with hers and guide her arms up over the rail. I can feel her full blown smile as we kiss and my own excitement knowing she isn't going to fight my urge. She obediently keeps her hands where I leave them as I squat down to retrieve the bra and bind her hands. She parts her legs as I work, ensuring I smell her excitement. I close my eyes and inhale deeply as the sweet scent hits me, causing Isabella to chuckle, two can play this game. I slowly trail my tongue up the inside of her thigh, starting just above her knee and stopping just shy of her core. She arches into me, but I deny her, repeating my teasing on her other thigh. This time as she arches towards me I slowly start to rise, running my finger tips up her legs and digging into her ass as I reach full vertical. A low growl escapes her as I rake my fingers across her toned cheeks. I push my hip against her sex as I lean in to kiss her and roll her taut nipples between my fingers. She moans and tries to push against me for more contact, but I deny her and pull back completely. I slowly back away, watching as she writhes against the rail and struggles against the bra securing her to one of the spindles. She focuses her lust drenched eyes on me as I pick up the wine bottle and take a long drink.

"What are you doing?"

"Committing this to memory, comparing it to what I thought it would look like." I grin and take another sip of the wine.

"And?"

"This is better."

"See something you like then?" I know she is trying to turn the tables on me, trying to get me to satisfy her needs, and I will, when I'm ready. I lick my lips and let my eyes drift over her. "Tell me."

"The hollow of your throat and the way it meets your clavicle, your strong shoulders, and your muscular arms." I pause to take another drink of the wine. "Your long, toned, supple legs, slender hips and flat stomach." She spreads her legs and arches her hips upwards.

"What about this?" I feel my resolve waiver and lick my lips again. I know how she smells and how she tastes. My mouth waters thinking about it.

"Your perfect, hairless pussy and how the moon is highlighting your juices." I silently curse the moon as I feel the majority of my restraint flee.

"Is there something wrong with my breasts, doctor?"

"Your breasts," I stammer as my eyes fix on her perfect, full breasts with the coffee colored areolae and firm nipples.

"Yes, surely *you* know what those are, *doctor*." Isabella has turned the tables, and she knows it. "Is there something wrong with them?" Her taunting me pulls me out of my trance. I slowly saunter towards Isabella with the wine bottle in tow. I tip some wine into her mouth before slowly trailing the lip of the bottle from the hollow of her throat down to her navel and back up again. I slide it over to her left breast and gently circle her nipple with it before rolling it over her nipple three times. I repeat the pattern on her right breast before dumping a few drops of wine down its slope, licking and sucking it off of her heated skin. She groans loudly when my tongue connects with her nipple, so I repeat my actions on her other breast. Her hips arch out, and her sex brushes against my hip, leaving a trail of her excitement in its wake. I tip the remainder of the wine into Isabella's mouth before forcefully kissing her, finally allowing my body to press against hers. I cast the empty bottle aside as my hands find her breasts, roughly kneading them before pinching and pulling her nipples. She grinds against my hip when I do, so I break off our kiss to tease one of her nipples with my mouth, trailing my now free hand down to tease her sex. She gasps when my fingers find her and I moan at how wet she is. I slowly run my fingers up and down the inside of her folds, coating them in her juices but avoiding direct contact with her clit. I can feel it pulsing as I skim the soft flesh next to it. I glide my fingers back and insert one, slowly circling her opening as I clamp down on her nipple.

"More," she pants as I withdraw my finger. I switch my attention to her other nipple, flicking it with my tongue before sucking it roughly into my mouth. I slide two fingers fully inside her as I suck on her nipple, and feel her push against them as I brush them over her g-spot. I pull out of her all the way and add a third finger into the mix, repeating my previous actions, picking up the pace with each stroke. When the pace becomes steady I lower myself and take her clit in my mouth. She wraps her legs around my neck and drives my face into her. She grinds against my face as my fingers pump in and out of her, her head thrown back, and the moon glistening off the sweat coating her body. "More," she instructs again. I falter, waiting for her to make eye contact with me to ensure I understand. I arch an eyebrow when she does, and she nods her consent. I pull back my fingers and slowly insert my hand, feeling her walls stretch and relax to accommodate the intrusion she asked for. I allow her to dictate the pace, letting her increase it as her body acclimates to the fullness, watching her hips begin to roll faster and faster. When her pace picks back up, I reposition my mouth on her clit and get back to work. She impales herself on my hand as I greedily lick, suck and nibble on her. It's only a matter of minutes before I feel her walls start to spasm and she unleashes a scream of ecstasy, making me grateful the lagoon is a decent distance from her family home. I wait for her spasms to stop before slowly withdrawing my hand. Isabella eventually plants her feet back under herself and I release the binding holding her arms. I stand up to massage the stiffness out of them, and she kisses me slowly and deeply as I do. I feel her legs tremble, so I carry her to one of the lounge chairs and grab one of the bottles of water for her.

"Are you ok?" She nods that she is, but the shaking continues and goose pimples cover her body. I collect the towels from the table before sliding in behind her on the lounger. She curls up between my legs as I drape the towels over her. I wrap my arms around her and pull her against my chest, unsure what else I should do. "Did I hurt you?" Isabella lets out a soft chuckle, and I feel relief wash over me.

"I'm good. I haven't had an orgasm like that in years." My body sags with relief as I continue to hold her. "I'm going to feel that while I'm at work tomorrow," she informs me when she finally stirs.

"I'm sorry," I whisper meekly, causing her to turn her head to me and kiss me.

"Don't be, that wasn't a complaint." She kisses me again before standing and offering me her hand. "Come on, I still want you in that water." She pulls me out of the lounger and into her arms. "Just so you know, I will find a way to repay you for that," she whispers against my ear before kissing me.

"Looking forward to it," I tease as our lips part. I pull away from her but keep her fingers laced through mine as I make my way towards the water. I stop at the edge of the deck and look down. I feel Isabella's heat as she presses herself against my back, her arms wrapping around me, allowing her hands to find my breasts. "How deep is it?" I ask as she massages my breasts and trails her tongue along the length of my shoulder. I lean into her as she teases my ear lobe and trails her hand down my abdomen to softly start stroking my labia. I sigh and tip my head back allowing our lips to meet. Her tongue flicks at my lower lip, and as I open my mouth to admit it, her lips are ripped from mine as she quickly shoves me off of the deck and into the water.

"Deep enough," she calls down from the deck as I surface, a self-satisfied grin plastered on her face. "I never said I would repay you tonight, you're just going to have to wait for it." I watch as she gracefully dives off of the deck and into the warm depths. I see her shadowed form dart towards me below the water's surface, even her silhouette is stunning. She coils her arms around me as she breaks the surface. I expect her to kiss me, but she just stares at me with a contented smile that melds into her chocolate eyes.

"Hi," I whisper as I brush away the wet strands of hair that have plastered themselves to her face.

"So what do you think?" I take everything in around me, the feel of her arms around my waist and mine around her neck, the smile that hasn't left her lips, the warm water wrapped around us, but most of all her eyes, eyes I can't look away from.

"Gorgeous," I whisper without thinking. Her smile broadens as she laughs.

"Not me, I was talking about all of this." I feel my own smile grow at the sound of her laughter.

"It's pretty perfect." Honestly, the whole day has been pretty perfect when I think about it. I gently draw Isabella's face to mine and kiss her slowly, setting aside sexual urgency, trying to convey my gratitude with the kiss.

"What was that for?" she pants when I finally withdraw my lips from hers.

"Just saying thank you for the amazing day." Her lips curl a the corners as we gaze at one another.

"That was nice." I feel Isabella's arms release me and watch as she swims away. "You coming?" I follow her into the depression in the rocks. It isn't deep enough to be an actual cave but the water is shallower and the moonlight dimmer under the slanted rock. I find a relatively flat rock in the shallow water and sit down on it, submerging my body to the top of my shoulders. I watch Isabella swim for a few minutes, enjoying the feeling of the warm water that surrounds me. Isabella swims towards me until she reaches the shallower water, where she switches to walking. I blatantly stare, my mouth slightly agape, as the water trails down her exposed flesh. I slide back on the rock as she nears me and she kneels down, straddling my thighs. "No one has ever looked at me the way you do."

"Then everyone you've met has been blind." Isabella cradles my cheeks in her palms, redirecting my attention from her body to her eyes. She smiles before kissing me, a kiss like the last one we shared. "What was that for?" I whisper as she rests her forehead against mine.

"I needed to thank you. Today has been a much better birthday than I thought it would be."

"It's your birthday?" Isabella nods that it is. "You let me use you like my own personal tour guide on your birthday?"

"You didn't use me, I wanted to. I thought it would help me to not think about it, but today has been wonderful. Thank you." She kisses me again, a seemingly endless kiss, the effects of which slowly trickle through my body until I can feel the euphoria in my toes. When our swollen lips finally separate, our foreheads meet as we both work to catch our breath.

"It might still be your birthday. What would you like to do?"

"Honestly, I just want to lay in bed and watch a movie or two. Not very exciting, I know."

"I think it sounds nice. Shall we?"

"You're serious?" I can see the hope in her eyes as she awaits my answer.

"Very. I thought that's what you wanted."

"Very much." The smile I receive is full and genuine, absent of any bravado. Her eyes seem to sparkle as she gazes at me.

"Good. You pick the movie though." She rises off of me and swims back to the deck, leading us away from the private paradise.

Back at her bungalow I strip off my clothes and recline against the pillows Isabella has set up for us. I watch her bare form as she curls up against me, her leg draped over mine, her arm slung over my hips and her head resting on my chest. She starts her movie of choice, sitting up to kiss me again as the opening title sequence begins. For the second time tonight, I can feel the kiss in my toes. As if sensing I'm on the brink of losing control, Isabella parts our lips and settles her head back on my chest, where I know she can hear my heart beating uncontrollably. I wrap my arms around her and relax against the pillows, focusing my attention on the movie as it gets underway.

Chapter 17

The next morning I wake up to find a note in Isabella's place, an impeccable looping cursive reading *Thank you for last night. I'll see you later — I.* I smile to myself, roll out of bed and get dressed, the smell of fresh coffee permeating my senses. I realize I must have just missed her, but as I pad down the hallway I spot Isabella curled up on one of her patio loungers, a cup of coffee in her hands. I grab a glass of water and step out onto the deck.

"You're still here." Isabella smiles at me and moves to get up. "Don't get up." She resettles herself and moves the half eaten plate of fruit that had rested at her feet to the side. She looks at me and pats the chair where the fruit plate previously sat. I follow her silent command, and she wraps her long legs around me and brushes a quick kiss to my lips.

"I have to leave soon. Are you hungry?" She grabs one of the grapes and feeds it to me before I can answer.

"Not really, I need to go for a run before I eat." Isabella laughs and feeds me another grape.

"You run every morning?"

"Unless I have a good reason not to." Isabella arches an eyebrow at me and grins.

"That sounds like a challenge."

"I thought you had to get going," I retort, grinning back. She sighs, and her grin fades.

"I do, another time though." She kisses me before standing up. "Walk there with me?"

I walk with Isabella back to the bar and head to my suite to change, determined to run on the beach before it gets much warmer out. The brochure detailing tourist activities catches my eye as I insert my earbuds, preparing to leave. I thumb through it and call to arrange parasailing today and a half day snorkeling outing for tomorrow. Satisfied with my plans, I head out the door, winking at Isabella as I pass by the bar on my way to the beach. I put in a couple of miles and decide to cool off with a swim. I could swim in the ocean, but teasing Isabella sounds like a lot more fun. I head back up to the pool by the bar and slowly strip off my sweat soaked tank top and shorts, revealing my powder blue bikini. I can feel her eyes burning into me as she prepares drinks for a couple sitting at the bar. I slowly strut my way to the stairs leading into the water and tentatively descend each one, even though there's a snowball's chance in hell the water will actually be cold. Once submerged, I turn around in time to see Isabella lick her lips. I flash her a sadistic grin and start swimming. Cutting my swim short so I'll have time to shower and eat before my parasailing adventure, I wait for Isabella's undivided attention and make my way out of the pool, drawing my ascent up each step out as much as I can. I wring the excess water out of my hair and pull my shorts back on before heading over to an empty section of the bar. She watches me as I approach, the water beading and running down my exposed flesh. I take a seat as she sets a glass of water in front of me.

"You're in a lot of trouble later," she leans over the bar and whispers to me. I arch an eyebrow at her, relaying my skepticism. "I can still feel you inside me from last night, and now you tease me like this."

"Nice to see you too," I whisper back, staring down the v-neck shirt that hugs her curves perfectly. I down the glass of water and stand up. "Thanks for the water. Gotta go though," I inform her before walking away.

*****

Parasailing still has my blood pumping. The rush as you're pulled up off the boat, soaring over the water giving you an aerial view, slowly descending as your feet reconnect with the water. It's something I may do again before I leave. I sit in my suite killing time by checking my emails. I never realized how many messages I get on a daily basis, how connected to this digital inbox my cell phone keeps me. It's too early for dinner so I decide to dredge through the flood of messages and address what I can, first going through and deleting the obvious junk mail, making my task seem less daunting. I send off responses about conferences, next year's mission trip, the women's health expo and a few other commitments. I read the updates from Abby and see that things are going well at the office. Another update from her informs me that the extension on the house is going well and they should be done with construction before I return. I'm midway through a memo from the hospital regarding the upcoming Joint Commission visit when there's a knock at my door. I haven't ordered room service, so I look through the peephole to see Isabella on the other side of the door.

"How did you—," I ask as I open the door. Isabella doesn't let me finish the sentence or wait to be invited in. She pounces on me, her lips crushing mine as she slams me against the wall and kicks the door shut. Our lips part as we pull off one another's shirts and Isabella deftly strips me of my bra, snapping the hooks apart and pulling it off before I even know she is doing so. She runs her tongue over my exposed clavicle and up my neck, pulling my earlobe into her mouth.

"Did you enjoy yourself today, teasing me like that?" Her hands are on my breasts, her thumbs and fingers teasing my nipples, sending ripples of pleasure through me. I try to thrust my hips against her, but she uses her leverage to keep me pinned against the wall. I can feel my panties getting wetter with each twist, pinch and pull.

"You didn't like it?" She loved it, I know she did, otherwise this wouldn't be happening right now.

"It made work interesting." Her mouth is on mine again, our tongues clashing, when I feel her hand leave my breast, slowly drifting down my abdomen. Instead of touching me, Isabella slides her hand down her own shorts and starts stroking herself. I wish I could see it, just being able to feel it happening is driving me wild. My hands instinctively find her breasts, pushing the bra up over them so I can access her nipples. Our kiss continues as she rubs herself and I add stimulation by toying with her erect buds. Isabella breaks off our kiss and brings her fingers up to my lips, the scent of her arousal too enticing. I greedily pull them into my mouth and lick and suck them clean, still teasing her sensitive breasts. Isabella groans as she frees herself from her bra and then disposes of my shorts and panties. I try to remove hers, but she stops me, forcing my hands above my head. Her mouth meets mine and swallows my moan as I feel her fingers against my throbbing pussy. I want to touch her, but she holds my hands hostage above my head as she gradually increases the pressure behind her touch. I push my hips forward, and without warning, I feel her bury her fingers inside me as deep as she can.

"Fuck," I pant, banging my head against the wall.

"I warned you that you were in trouble." She grins as she slowly pulls her fingers back and then slams them into me again, the pleasure and faint pain sending shockwaves through me. Her thumb brushes over my throbbing clit before she pulls back and slams into me again, my hips thrusting forward each time to take as much of her in as possible. Her hand pounds against me, my hips thrusting hard in return when I feel her tongue on my nipple. I lose myself at the combined sensations, shouting out in bliss, heedless of who might hear. Isabella kisses me, her fingers still clenched in my relaxing walls.

"Consider me punished," I tell her as she removes herself from me. She gives me a sadistic grin and kisses me again. With our lips locked, I push her further into the room, backing her up to the bed. When we're close enough, I tear my lips from hers, spin her around and bend her over the side of the bed. I pull her shorts and panties down and let them fall to her ankles, spreading her legs a little wider. I run my fingers over her sex to lubricate them and watch as she stretches her arms out above her head, her hands gripping the duvet in fists that tighten and relax with each of my caresses. When my fingers are coated to my satisfaction, I slowly slide them inside her, her head dropping as she groans. I move in and out of her, slowly increasing my pace with each stroke. When she starts to push her hips back to meet each stroke, I wrap her hair around my hand and gently pull back.

"Mmm. Fuck me, Sara." I pull back again, this time a little harder and she releases a loud groan.

"Touch yourself," I order her, my fingers still stroking her inner walls. I watch with satisfaction as her right hand releases the duvet and slides under her hip. I can feel her pussy twitch when she makes contact with her clit, my fingers still working inside her. Her hips gyrate faster and faster, torn between meeting her own touch and swallowing my fingers. She buries her face in the duvet as she comes, muffling the sounds of her orgasm. I release my grip on her hair and slowly withdraw from her. She slides the rest of the way onto the bed and lays there panting as I lick the sweat from the small of her back and kiss my way up her neck, draping myself over her as I climb higher. I lay on top of her and listen as her breathing returns to normal.

"How did you know which room?"

"Ownership has its privileges. I didn't know if you would come see me later and I couldn't wait."

"I'm glad you couldn't wait," I tell her as I roll off of her back. Without hesitation Isabella rolls over and nestles into me, her head resting on my chest. We lay and talk for a while, I can tell with each pause that Isabella is drifting closer to falling asleep. I'm not sure how long she's out before I join her.

I wake up in Isabella's arms, my hand wrapped around hers. I slowly extract myself from her embrace and use the bathroom. I pause to enjoy the sight of her naked beauty, as she lays oblivious to the world around her. I want to join her, to wake her and make her climax again, but decide to let her rest. I slip on my shorts and shirt, grab my Kindle and head out onto the terrace to take up residence in the enclosure. I lay there reading, occasionally stealing glances of Isabella's slumbering form.

"What are you doing out there?" I look up to see Isabella propped up on her elbows, looking down her body at me. She slowly opens her legs a little, an invitation, a tease, pure temptation. I resist the urge, wanting to see what she will do, hoping I'll see the show I wanted to so badly earlier. Instead, she climbs out of the bed and slowly sashays toward me, stepping out onto the terrace in the fading light, completely naked.

"What are you doing?" I ask looking around for uninvited eyes.

"No one can see us. Who cares if they hear us?" She slides on top of me and straddles my thighs. "Why are you dressed?" she asks as she pulls my top off. I wrap my arms around her waist and feel hers twin around my neck. Our eyes meet and I see the lazy smile take up residence on her lips and feel the one I give her in return. Slowly our lips come together, devoid of urgency, similar to the few kisses we shared at the lagoon. We kiss for what feels like forever, our tongues dancing with each other, her body pressed against mine, our arms wrapped around one another, the intensity building slowly. Eventually, my hands start caressing her torso, wanting to feel every inch of her, slowly mapping the contours of her body. I take her nonverbal cue to lay back when her hands move to my shoulders and push, never separating our mouths. She breaks the kiss, and I watch as she slides back, letting her hands caress my breasts and stomach until her fingers hook over the waist of my shorts. I lift my hips allowing her to pull them off and relish in the sensation of her naked flesh pressed against me as she returns her mouth to mine. We roll around, making out and pawing each other, the excitement building for each of us. When I feel like my body will spontaneously combust if Isabella doesn't touch me soon, I roll on top of her and slide my thigh against her sex. She moans into my mouth as we continue our sensuous kissing, and bends her knee, pressing her thigh against me. I grind against her thigh, and she matches the rhythm of her hips to mine, the tempo slow and torturous. Sweat rolls down my back as we continue working our hips together, the friction increasing our pleasure. I finally break off the kiss, my need to breathe winning, as our hips begin to work frantically. My face lingers just above Isabella's, our eyes locked, my nipples brushing over hers with each thrust.

"I'm close. Are you?" I nod that I am as Isabella presses more firmly against me and digs her fingers into my ass, holding on for dear life. I watch as Isabella's orgasm starts, her eyes rolling shut, just as my own begins. We lay there in each other's arms, legs entwined, sharing more tender kisses after we both come down. Isabella's stomach loudly protesting finally breaks the spell. I laugh as I pull away from her, knowing that it's usually my hunger that voices its opinion.

"Want to stay here, order room service and watch a movie?"

"I'd love that," she answers before kissing me again.

*****

I'm awakened in the morning by Isabella rising from the bed. "Good morning," I whisper as I stretch. She turns and smiles as she pulls on her shorts.

"Go back to sleep," she says as she leans over and kisses my forehead. I pull her down onto the bed with me and kiss her properly, trying to entice her to join me. She relents for a moment before flipping me onto my back. "I must go, I have a meeting. Come see me later." I groan as she laughs and leaves the bed. "I'll see you soon," she whispers as she runs her fingertips up my leg.

"Yes you will," I answer as she heads to the door. A look at the clock reveals that I've slept a later than anticipated, not leaving enough time to work out before my snorkeling adventure. A quick shower and trip through one of the breakfast buffets and I'm out the door.

It's mid afternoon when I return from my outing, brimming with energy. Despite the heat and humidity, I decide to go for the run I missed this morning. I pass by the bar to see it being tended by another man I have yet to meet, my workout mix already adding to the energy I feel threatening to spill out of me. I head down to the sand and start jogging, lighting the fuse that will have my legs pumping and my feet pounding by the end of the current song. By the time I've completed half a lap, I'm running at my usual pace, enjoying the feel of my muscles working and the adrenalin pumping through my veins. As I approach Isabella's bungalow, I spy her on the deck, focused on something I can't see. I'm tempted to abort my run and bolt up her stairs, but I stay focused enough to make the turn and head back to the resort. I keep making my laps, each time I approach her bungalow, the pull to run to Isabella becomes stronger. After twenty minutes I can't fight the urge any longer. I sprint down the beach toward the bungalow and jog up the stairs, finding Isabella working away on a large canvas.

"I didn't think you'd ever stop running and come see me." She continues her work, not looking away from the canvas.

"I didn't realize you saw me."

"Oh I saw you, it was very distracting seeing you continually approach and leave, wondering if you were ever going to come up here." Isabella puts down her brush and wipes off her hands.

"It wasn't easy to fight the urge." Isabella wraps her arms around my neck and kisses me. "Hi," I whisper when our lips part.

"You're all sweaty," she answers with a grin and slightly wrinkled nose.

"I thought you liked me all sweaty," I retort, pressing my forehead against hers.

"Mmm, there are times I certainly do. How was snorkeling?"

"It was fun, interesting, beautiful. What are you working on?"

"Just finishing a painting." She plants her soft lips against mine, and I pull her tighter against me.

"Can I see it?" I'd be lying if I said that I'm not curious. I know very little about art, but find myself wondering what she has created. She stiffens and pulls away from me slightly. "It's ok if you don't want me to, I'm just curious."

"It's ok." Her arms release me, and she takes my hand, leading me towards the painting. Before me sits a beautiful abstract piece, dominated by different shades of greens and blues, with hints of most of the secondary colors as well. It's beautiful and complex. One moment it makes me think of the ocean and the plant and animal life within, the next I feel like I'm looking at the physical representation of an emotional breakthrough, with the bright colors of hopefulness starting to bleed through the dark colors of despair and depression.

"I love it," I whisper as I continue to study it. That's when the signature on the painting catches my eye. I do a double take when I notice it, look to Isabella, then back to the painting. Disbelief sets in as I turn to Isabella. "You're Torres?"

"It isn't a big deal." Her tone is matter of fact, but her body suddenly seems tense.

"Not a big deal? People have been speculating for at least a decade about your identity. You've sold paintings for excessive sums, yet you've never made an appearance or done an interview. You're like an enigma. I don't even know much about art and I've heard about you." I'm stunned, my brain struggles to process what Isabella has just revealed to me. Isabella, on the other hand, seems uncomfortable.

"While what you say is true, I must ask you not to tell anyone. Very few people know this secret. I would prefer to keep it that way." I turn to face Isabella and take her hands in mine.

"I'm sorry if I sound a little star struck, I didn't even know that you paint, much less this. I promise your secret is safe. Why the secrecy though?"

"I don't want fame or notoriety. I enjoy a simple, quiet life. I paint because I enjoy it; when I feel inspired to do it. When I started, it was just a hobby, I never signed anything. Then one year a tourist from New York saw some of my work. That was how it started. Torres was my grandmother's maiden name. Her parents didn't want her to marry my grandfather, but they were in love. So when she married him, she broke with tradition and dropped her last name when she took his instead of hyphenating the two." I let the information from the last couple of minutes sink in, the revelation seeming so unreal.

"So you have an ownership stake in the resort and you have a über successful alter ego as a painter? Why are you moonlighting as a bartender?" Isabella lets out a heavy sigh before answering.

"I didn't for a long time. I make enough from the resort, much less the paintings. I've donated over half of what I've made from my paintings, and I still have plenty for the rest of my life. I started bartending again after the breakup as a means of passing the time and a distraction. I actually enjoy it and it allows me to contribute to the business without getting involved in the mundane aspects of it." I can tell Isabella is growing tired of talking about this. I still hold her hands in mine, but she is uncharacteristically antsy.

"I'm sorry for all the questions. You just levied a huge shock on me is all. I kinda feel like Bruce Wayne just told me he's Batman. I want you to know that it doesn't change how I look at you, it just adds another layer to who you are. I don't care about the money or the notoriety of your alter ego." Isabella wears a small smile as I brush the hair back from her face and plant a light kiss on her forehead. "For the record, I'm glad you took up bartending again." She laughs, dispelling the tension that had surrounded us.

"I'm glad too," she says as she wraps her arms around my waist and kisses me again. "So doctor, what are your plans for the rest of the day?"

"If you keep calling me doctor, I'm going to have to call you Torres."

"You wouldn't." I raise an eyebrow, daring her to try me. "Ok, maybe you would." Her smile assures me she knows this is just playful banter.

"No plans. I need to go back and shower though."

"Do you really need to? You could come inside." Isabella starts kissing me along my neck, working to bend me to her will.

"Oh, could I?" I'm not fooling anyone, we both know I'm not going back to my suite for a shower right now.

"I think you should, you're already all sweaty."

Chapter 18

"How do you want to spend your last two days here?" Isabella and I lay holding each other in her bed. I can hear a certain sadness in her voice, the same sadness that echoes in my body. The last week and a half flew by, Isabella and I spending as much time as possible together. I've grown unexpectedly close to this beautiful, intelligent, talented, warm-hearted, passionate woman. Punta Cana was meant to be a balm on a burn. Instead it offered me something more, like gaining the ability to regenerate new skin instead of waiting for it to heal. No matter what, the truth is that I've barely thought about Katrina since my first days here and when I have it has lacked the sadness and confusion that it did when I first arrived.

"When do you work?" Isabella softly runs her fingers up and down the length of my spine, the action threatening to lull me to sleep.

"I covered my shifts." Her words pull me out of the sleepy haze her fingers were sending me into.

"You did?" I ask lifting my head off of her chest to look her in the eye. She brushes the hair from my face, letting her fingers caress my cheek and chin.

"I want to spend the time with you; if that is what you'd like." I lay my hand over hers and turn my face, planting a soft kiss on the inside of her palm.

"I would like that a lot." I lay my head back on her chest and sigh, her words increasing the sadness I feel about leaving. "You're going to make it harder for me to leave, aren't you?"

"I would like it if you didn't have to, but I know that you must." I think about my time with Isabella, how it was only meant to be a distraction for both of us and how quickly it morphed into something more. Meals shared every day, surfing lessons, the market, the lagoon, time spent cuddling and watching movies, late night walks along the beach and times like this, where we just lay with each other and talk. Somehow the woman meant to be a vacation distraction found a way into my heart, despite constantly reminding myself that she and I are from different worlds and I would be leaving hers sooner than later. I want to tell her that I wish I could stay, but saying the words out loud would give them life, making any attempt to repress those feelings impossible.

We spend the morning in the ocean, the waves too calm for surfing. We swim and goof around like children, trying to dunk each other. Our playfulness quickly turns serious and before I know it, Isabella is pushing my top up over my breasts. I nervously look around for anyone else, but the beach is deserted, not that Isabella would mind if it weren't. I lose the few inhibitions holding me back when Isabella's lips meet mine and her hands grasp my breasts.

*****

"What else would you like to do?" Isabella smirks at me over our brunch table before popping a piece of fresh pineapple in her mouth. "Mmmm," she quietly moans as she chews, closing her eyes and tipping her head back slightly. I clear my throat and Isabella opens her eyes as she starts sliding her foot up the inside of my leg.

"There is that," I utter, feeling my pulse pounding in my neck. "I'd like to go back to your lagoon, see it in the daylight." Isabella doesn't hesitate. She takes out her phone and sends a quick message, leaving it on the table when she's finished. "Anything else?"

"I want to dance with you." Isabella eyes me with skepticism.

"Here? Now? This music isn't very good." I can't help but laugh.

"No, not here and now."

"Hmm, the discotecas here are not that great. There may be an act here either tonight or tomorrow night that would work. I will check." Isabella's phone vibrates on the table. She checks the message and smiles at me. "The lagoon is ours for the day." I smile back at her, feeling a warmth spread through me seeing her happy.

"No discoteca or show tomorrow night. I have other ideas for my last day here." Isabella's raises her eyebrows as she leans across the table.

"Care to fill me in?"

"No, but I'll give you a hint: none of it will involve clothing." Isabella bites her bottom lip as she sits back in her chair, then allows her seductive smile to join the lust filled look in her eyes.

"You plan to be mine all day and night?" I feel a thrill travel through my body as she claims me as hers. I wish that it could be.

"Maybe you'll be mine," I challenge. "I don't think this has ever only worked one way."

"I agree," she answers, although I'm unsure if she means my plans or my statement regarding the dynamic of our time together. The waiter comes over to take our empty plates and glasses. Isabella has a brief conversation with him in Spanish before he leaves.

"What?" Her question alerts me to the fact that I've been staring at her.

"Nothing," I tell her, looking away. I can't tell her that I wish this could be real and of the sadness I feel when I think about leaving. I see her tilt her head slightly out of the corner of my eye. She doesn't believe me, but thankfully she doesn't press. The waiter returns and gives Isabella a bag. She gives him several bills and he leaves.

"I need to go back to the bungalow before we leave. Ready?" We walk back to her place along the beach. "What will you do when you go back?"

"Work, a lot. I had the surgeries and patients I should have seen over the last two weeks rescheduled. I'm hoping to catch back up in the next two weeks or so. Going to have some long days ahead of me."

"What will you do about Katrina?" Her question stops me in my tracks. Why is she asking me about her?

"Nothing. I haven't thought about her since early last week." Isabella tugs on my hand, encouraging me to move my feet. "Why, what will you do?"

"I don't know. Paint, bartend, surf, the things I usually do." We climb the stairs and enter the bungalow. "I'm just going to grab a few things. I'll be back in a minute."

I look around me and remember the time I've spent here, the memories made. Dancing with Isabella the first night we slept together, drinking coffee in the morning on the deck, watching Isabella paint, meals and conversations shared, all the places we fucked and made love. Made love? That can't be the right phrase for it, even if our unions have become dominated by a certain slowness, tenderness and level of emotion people often associate with love, it can't be that. I'm still not sure that I've ever actually been in love, but this can't be it. I know my heart feels heavy when I think about leaving, but this was never intended to be about love. It isn't practical, was never the agreement, nor could the universe ever be that cruel. I've never been carefree with my emotions, have never thought myself a hopeless romantic, yet somehow my vacation fling has come to mean more to me than she was ever supposed to.

"What are you thinking about?" Isabella whispers against my ear as she presses herself against my back, wrapping her arms around me. Her lips brush against my cheek as she holds me and I feel my confusion from moments ago slip away, replaced by contentment.

"You. Just remembering our time here." Isabella loosens her arms just enough to allow me to turn and face her. She brushes her lips against mine, intending the kiss to be a brief, chaste peck, but my hand moves up to her face and gently pulls her lips more firmly against mine, drawing the kiss into one that is anything but chaste.

Isabella finally pulls away, "This is difficult for me too." She plants a soft kiss on my forehead as I feel her arms release me and my hand slip from her face. We each grab a bag and head for Isabella's Jeep, neither of us saying a word. She slips her hand into mine as she pilots us towards her family estate and I silently admonish myself to enjoy the time I have left with her.

We pull into the estate and exit the Jeep, each of us grabbing a bag. Isabella slips her arm around my waist as we walk down the path, my arm automatically wrapping around her. I feel cold when we reach the stairs and our arms fall from each other's waists, despite the heat of the late morning sun. I take in the lagoon in the light of day, the colors more vibrant, the water even more inviting.

When I reach the base of the stairs, I take two long strides and pull Isabella to me with my free hand. I wrap my arm around her and gaze into her eyes that remind me of the rich homemade hot chocolate my grandmother used to make. "Thank you for bringing me back here." I press my lips to hers and yield without hesitation when her free hand finds the back of my head, gently holding me in place. The kiss is long and deep, sucking the air out of me as I try to pour all the emotions I've been feeling into it. We're both gasping for air when we finally part.

"I love that you wanted to come back here." Her fingers gently caress my face, the touch as soft as a faint breeze blowing over your skin. She draws me to her, and our lips meet again, Isabella guiding me toward one of the lounge chairs as the kiss lingers on but doesn't intensify.
"Sit," she orders as she deposits her bag next to the chair. My body tingles with excitement as I obey her order, sliding back until I'm reclining in the chair properly. Isabella walks up the side of the chair and swings her leg over it, lowering herself to straddle me. Her hands cup my face as her thumbs caress my kiss swollen lips. She closes the distance between us, reconnecting our mouths and I feel her hands drop lower, slowly skating over the fabric of my top. My skin burns to feel her flesh pressed against it as she softly continues running her hands over the contours of my torso. I release a soft groan into Isabella's mouth as her thumbs lightly skate over my nipples. I feel her smile in response. I know she's teasing me, half of me wants to sit back and enjoy it, the other half urges me to seize control and ravish the amazing woman astride me. Curious as to how long she plans to make this last, I fight the urge to take control and let her continue, gripping her ass and pulling her as close to me as possible. She brushes her thumbs more firmly over my

nipples, and I realize that this has become a chess match of sorts. We continue to kiss as our hands explore each other through the soft fabric covering us. Isabella bites my lip and bucks her hips as my fingers make contact with her sensitive nipples. I smile as I repeat the action and elicit a moan from her. I slip my hands under the fabric of her top and slide them up to her breasts, directly teasing her nipples. Isabella's head tips back as she arches her breasts into my hands and she grinds her sex against me, her moan causing a wave of desire to pulse through me. I pull her to me and capture one of the taut nipples with my mouth, lashing my tongue over it before sucking it hard as I withdraw. Isabella moans again as she continues to grind herself against my stomach. Her fingers grip my hair and direct my attention to her other nipple. I happily oblige and circle my tongue slowly around it before flicking it repeatedly. My hands continue caressing the rest of her exposed flesh as I pull her nipple between my teeth as I withdraw my mouth. Isabella's pace intensifies as she crushes her mouth against mine, the pulsing feeling in my own sex growing stronger. I push myself against her, wanting to pleasure her, to see her come undone. She stops without warning and pushes me back against the chair, her breathing heavy.

"Did you just come?" I know there's a mask of confusion on my face. If she just climaxed it was the weakest, quietest of our time together.

"Not yet," she informs me, kissing me quickly before directing her attention to the bag she left next to the chair. In seconds she withdraws a pair of leather cuffs, separated by a short length of chain. "I warned you that I would pay you back." Anticipation floods through me as I wait for her next move. She refocuses on me and slowly lifts my top over my head, smiling down at me with a look that is equal parts impish and adoring. She lifts my right hand and kisses the inside of my wrist and palm before securing the cuff around it. I willingly let her guide my arms, directing my hands behind the chair, refusing to fight as she secures my free wrist in the second cuff. Isabella sits back and admires her work before kissing me again as her hands resume caressing and teasing my exposed torso. I long to touch her but fighting the restraints is pointless. She pulls out of the kiss and turns back to the bag, this time withdrawing a blindfold. "I know how much you love to look at me and touch me. You won't be enjoying either of those things right now." She slides the blindfold over my eyes, causing an instant blackout to take place. I feel the heat of her body near mine as she connects our lips once again, this time kissing me fiercely, claiming my mouth with hers. I try to push our flesh against each other, but the restraints stop me, my shoulders only able to withstand so much. I feel Isabella's nipple drag over my face as she stands, but I'm not fast enough to capture it with my mouth. Her hands trail down my sides, and her fingers tug down on the waist of my shorts, so I lift my hips allowing her to pull them off. I sit there naked, bound and blinded, waiting for her to return to me. Instead, I hear varying noises a few feet away.

"I wish you could see how you look right now, with the sun glistening off the light coat of sweat on your body. So beautiful." Sweat isn't the only fluid on my body, I can feel my own wetness against my thighs, so I drop a leg over each side of the chair, exposing myself to her. "Mmm, that's nice." The sound of her voice grows stronger, I know she's returning to me. I feel the sensation of smooth glass against my lips and tilt my head back accepting Isabella's offer of what is surely wine. I drink her offering and feel the contact of the warming liquid as she intentionally spills some down my chest. I feel her tongue connecting with the trail, stopping to take my nipple in her mouth, sucking and tonguing it. "Mmm, salty and sweet," she whispers as she repeats her actions on the other side, causing me to arch my hips upwards, my sex starting to pulse with need.

The bottle returns to my lips, and I once again drink what is offered before feeling Isabella pour a heavier stream down my chest and over my sex, the sensation pleasant, but not enough. She trails her mouth and tongue down, licking at the trail left by the wine, stopping to lick and suck it out of my navel, teasing me even more. She follows the trail to its end, and as I arch slightly upward, she runs her tongue slowly over my lips, using only the tip the first trip but broadening her stroke on the second. I try to push myself against her face, but the restraints won't allow it. She continues teasing me, adding more wine as she pleases, her long slow licks inching further inside my lips with each stroke.

"You are so wet for me already. I love it." Her tongue finally finds my core, and she slowly drags it upward, delicately circling my clit, causing me to rock my hips and gasp. "So sensitive already?" she teases before repeating her actions again, this time gently sucking my aching nub before removing her mouth. I smell her scent a second before she presses her fingers against my lips and I greedily suck them in, cleaning her juices off of them, groaning as the unfulfilled desire courses through me. I refuse to beg though, at least not yet. I sense Isabella's presence hovering over me and gradually feel my body being shaded from the sun as she lowers herself. The sensation of silicone trailing down my stomach only adds to the fire raging in me. We've used her toys before. I have no idea which one she has on, but it doesn't matter, I want her inside of me. I hear her set the wine bottle down seconds before she crushes her lips against mine, wine seeping from her mouth into mine. I drink it and her greedily, wanting everything she will offer. I feel the tip of the dildo being guided over my sex, teasing me, lubricating itself for what comes next. Isabella rests her forehead against mine as I pant with desire.

"Is this what you want?" She presses the tip of the toy against my entrance with the smallest pressure, just enough to stimulate the nerve endings. "Do you want me to fuck you?" She wants me to ask for it, to beg for it, and with her perched at my entrance, I will.

"I just want you," the words come unbidden, shocking me. Instead of giving me what I want, she withdraws, and there is nothing.

I feel the cuff on my wrist being loosened, and my heart drops. "I can't fuck you right now," she says as I pull my stiff arms back around, my shoulders protesting the return to their natural position. I lift the blindfold to see Isabella, drinking deeply from the bottle, her double headed dildo still in place. I stand as I remove the second binding, letting it fall to the deck.

"What just happened?" My desire has been dampened by concern, but not extinguished.

"What you just said, I don't want to fuck you, I want..." She leaves her thought unfinished. I don't need her to finish it though, it's the same thing I've been feeling, I want what she does at well. I close the gap between us, reaching up to caress her face. I know she's with me when she leans into my touch. I wrap my arms around her neck and kiss her, the toy pinned between us. This time I lead her to the chair and guide her down to it. Our lips part and she relaxes against the cushion. I slide up until the protruding toy makes contact with me and kiss her again, letting it slowly build to reflect my desire for her. When we finally part I rest my forehead against hers and move my hand down to the toy. Eyes locked on hers, I softly roll it over her sex looking for any sign I should stop.

"Yeah?" I whisper the question. She bites her lower lip and nods. I slowly insert the toy inside her, loving the view of her eyes rolling back and fluttering as she lets out a long, low moan. I wait for her to recover and steady myself as she guides the other end into me. "Fuck," I groan as she slowly fills me. We lock eyes before I start working myself on the blue shaft, knowing that every time I push downward it drives they toy further into Isabella. Her hands lock onto my hips, and I pull her to me, melding our lips together again as the steady rhythm slowly builds until we are grinding ourselves against one another. The electricity of our connection rips through me, and I know I can let go soon, as soon as I know Isabella is there with me. Our lips separate, and I glance downward at the sight of us working the length of the toy and Isabella's breasts as they bounce with our forceful motions. I take one in each hand and work her nipples as my eyes reconnect with hers. My body surges, demanding I let myself go, but I deny it, wanting Isabella there with me. Her moans and grunts tell me she is close. "Let go with me," I pant and she smiles slightly before tipping her head back. I feel my orgasm crash over me, and hear Isabella's ecstasy escape her body. When my trembling finally stops I lean forward and kiss her softly before allowing my body to fall against hers, the sweat pouring out of both of us. I kiss the side of her neck and along her shoulder as I raise my hips enough to slide the toy out of me. I feel Isabella reach down and do the same for herself before she wraps her arms and legs around me, clutching me tightly against her.

"No quiero que te vayas," she whispers. I have no idea what she said, but tears threaten to spill out of my eyes when I hear the sadness in her voice. I push them away, not wanting my memories of this place to be sad ones. Instead, I inhale her scent, the smells of sunshine, sweat, cucumber melon soap, her fruity shampoo and sex implant themselves in my memory. This is how I want to remember her. We sit wrapped around each other for a while, communicating how we feel without words.

"I really need to get this harness off," Isabella whispers. I can't help but laugh, a welcome respite from the sadness that has settled over us. I feel Isabella start to laugh as well and know that things will be fine. I plant a soft kiss on her forehead as she releases me and I help her up. She removes the harness and tosses it and the toy into the water. When she sees the look of horror on my face she tells me, "Relax, it's water proof." She kisses me quickly before bending to pick up the bottle of wine, offering it to me first. We finish off the bottle before nature calls, and I have to head into the nearby foliage for relief. I hear a splash and know Isabella is in the water, the image of her swimming under the full moon fresh in my mind. I walk back to the deck and look down at the water, the sun reflecting brightly off of the surface, casting a heavy glare back at me. I spot Isabella near the recession in the wall, watching me. She smiles and tilts her head slightly, the sun reflecting off her water slicked hair. Without further delay, I dive in and swim towards her.

We spend the day swimming, chatting, basking in the sun, and feasting on one another, simply enjoying being together. We don't discuss anything of dire consequence, and we both avoid the subject of my leaving. By dusk we've finished the second bottle of wine and most of the water, both of us feeling tired and hungry. As we dress to return to the resort, I look around and remember our first night here. Was it that night when things started to shift between us? Had it been those first tender kisses that had sealed my fate?

We have dinner at the restaurant, stopping at the sound of blues music coming from the performance hall. "Do you want to stop?" I pull Isabella through the doors in answer. We stand towards the back and watch the band, Isabella behind me, wrapping her arms around my waist, her breath tickling my ear as she kisses my neck. "I didn't know you liked blues music," she whispers. A petite woman with a voice that sounds too big for her body, belts out the lyrics to *Hoochie Coochie Man* as the band maintains the beat behind her. I start swaying my hips with the music, giving Isabella little choice between letting go of me and joining in. "Something tells me you don't just like blues music, you love it." I feel Isabella join me, her body swaying with mine as she presses against me.

"What's not to love? Everyone can relate to the lyrics and the beats are often hypnotic." I feel Isabella's smile against my cheek.

"You certainly present proof of your second argument," she coos against my ear. The song wraps up, Isabella's hands separating long enough to clap along with me.

"We don't cover a lot of modern music since it never seems to have the same feeling as the classics." The singer takes a long drink from her glass before continuing. "The first time I heard this song, I knew we had to cover it, so bear with us, we haven't done this one live too many times." The opening chords of *Love on the Brain* fill the room.

"Turn around and dance with me," Isabella demands, whispering the order in my ear. I turn around smiling at Isabella. She wraps her arms around my neck as I lock mine around her hips. Our eyes lock before Isabella lightly kisses me. "I really like this song." I halfway stifle my chuckle. "You don't think it's good?"

"Well, it's up for debate whether or not it's about her abusive relationship with her ex. So maybe it isn't all good. But I can't deny that the beat is amazing, and if you ignore the potential negativity, it's an incredibly sexy song." Isabella presses a finger to my lips, silencing me.

"Ssh. Just shut out the negativity and live with me, be in the moment. Pretend if you have to." Her lips briefly replace her finger before she rests her forehead against mine, her eyes close as we move with the music.

"Is that what you're doing? Pretending?" Isabella's eyes snap open.

"Does it feel like I'm pretending?"

"What did you say to me at the lagoon?" Isabella's eyes close.

"You heard that?" I nod against her forehead. Isabella sighs, "I said that I don't want you to leave." I feel something in my heart as I process her words, a flutter or a skip, I'm not sure. Whatever the feeling is, it conflicts with or compensates for the ever present ache I feel when I remember I have to leave in a day. Isabella opens her eyes and they bore into me, waiting for some response to her confession.

"I don't want to leave you," I whisper, reaching up to cup her face with my hand. I close my eyes and just follow the rhythm. Isabella presses her lips to mine. I presume it will just be a lingering press, but when her tongue rolls over my lips, I don't deny it entry. The kiss is long, filled with the emotions neither of us can or want to express. We continue dancing to a song that's no longer playing as we kiss.

"I'm gonna dedicate this one to the couple in the back since it looks like they've already found it. Looking good ladies." Isabella and I both start laughing when we realize she's talking about us, putting an abrupt end to our kiss. Her voice fills the room as she begins belting out the opening line of *A Sunday Kind of Love*. Isabella closes the small gap separating us, wrapping her arms protectively around me as I rest my head against her shoulder. She turns her head and plants a tender kiss on my forehead before turning it back to rest her cheek in the spot her lips just vacated. We dance with our bodies pressed together, holding each other, my fingers tracing small circles on her back. Our lips meet again as she belts out the closing words and part when the music stops. *Feeling Good* starts as I glance around the room at the other couples. My eyes stop when I see the two women from our first night here. They aren't staring tonight, but they seem to alternate making quick glances in our direction.

"Do you want to get out of here?"

"Only if that is what you want. I'm not worried about them." Of course she already saw them, she seems to notice everything. I remember our first night here, when we saw them watching us dance together, and how Isabella basically shut down, cutting our evening short. She told me the next evening that she was over it, but is she really? I don't want to leave the comfort of her embrace but if I don't enjoy their prying eyes, how does Isabella really feel about it?

"Come on," I urge her, "let's go for a walk." She tightens her arms around me as her eyes meet mine. I give her a slight nod, and we release each other, our hands clasping as I lead us out the door.

"I enjoyed dancing with you, we could have stayed." Isabella starts the conversation as we slowly amble along the beach, the moon reflecting off of the ocean, giving some extra light on this quiet night. I don't know how to broach this conversation, but hope we can have it without any major issues.

"I loved dancing with you too. I just want to be sure that you're alright, I didn't want you to feel uncomfortable with them there."

"I told you, I'm over it." Isabella's bungalow is in sight, so I keep quiet until we're on the beach in front of it. I turn to face her, clasp both of her hands, and slowly take a seat, gently tugging downward on her arms, encouraging her to join me. We sit facing each other, our hands still linked, as I contemplate how to continue. "Esme and I were over long before I caught her in bed with Camila. We were never truly compatible. She likes to go out every night and be wild, isn't all that responsible, is a bit of a slob, and doesn't have a charitable bone in her body. We drove each other crazy, but somehow we thought it was a good idea to get together. By the time she and Camila started sleeping together, Esme and I had basically stopped. But she knew my secret, and even though I knew on some level we would never work, I still felt obligated to try. I looked into moving to New York, where there would be more things that she would enjoy. She was already sleeping with Camila by then and refused to go. I'm over Esme, have been for a while, but I didn't just lose that relationship. I lost my lifelong best friend, which hurt a lot more. I can't explain it, but I still miss Camila at times, even though I will never be able to trust her again, nor do I know if I will ever be able to forgive her for betraying my trust. When we saw them staring at us that first night I was angry. I don't feel like they have a right to be privy to my private affairs, even if it is the first time I've been with someone since the breakup." She's shared more with me than I had anticipated, and my heart aches for her. I can't imagine what it would be like to lose Abby, Catherine or Alex, my three closest friends. But one tidbit seems to stick out the most.

"You mean the first woman they saw you with, right?" Isabella's eyes lock unflinchingly on mine.

242

"No, I mean the first woman I've been with. I've had opportunities but I didn't take or want them."

"Why me then?" I don't ask out of some need to have my ego stroked, I'm truly curious why this remarkable woman chose me.

"Because you're beautiful, you seemed genuine, I knew you were hurting, and I knew you would be leaving. It seemed safe; that we could have this affair and it would be over. But you are far more than I anticipated you would be, and now the thought of you leaving makes me ache." These are likely the sweetest and most honest words any woman has ever spoken to me. Unable to formulate a verbal response, I follow my gut instinct, lunging forward, knocking Isabella into the sand and crushing my mouth against hers. Our tongues mingle as Isabella locks her legs around my waist. I let the kiss linger on before finally rolling my hips against her, causing her to moan into my mouth. I kiss her for a while again before allowing myself to roll against her, again she moans into my mouth, causing me to roll my hips once more. This time it sounds more like a groan as she slides her legs down, hooking them around mine and flipping me onto my back. "We shouldn't start this here." I bite my swollen lower lip trying to convince her that she's wrong. "Trust me, you'll get sand in places you don't want it." I can't help but laugh, I know she's right, but even the slightest touch from this woman causes me to lose all control. Isabella extracts herself from me, stands up and offers me her hand, I sit up but don't take it.

"Can we just sit here a while longer?" Isabella answers by sitting down behind me, her legs extended around me, her arms enveloping me as she pulls me back to recline against her chest. We sit and watch the water and the moon, not saying a word.

"What are we going to do?" Isabella's words escape her in a hushed tone. A heavy sigh escapes me as I pose a question my overly analytic brain feels it needs answered.

"Do you think it's just all the sex?"

"Is what just all the sex?"

"These feelings. Do you think it's just because of all the sex we've been having?" Isabella squeezes me tight before answering.

"No. I know it was supposed to be casual fucking, but we moved beyond that long ago. Is it still just sex for you?" I can hear the underlying hurt in her voice, so I pull away slightly to turn and look her in the eyes.

"No, it isn't. I've had a few casual flings, none of them have ever been like this. In the past I've been able to easily separate lust and my feelings, never letting them overlap, but this…I don't know how it happened. I care about you, when I go home, out of sight is not going to mean you aren't on my mind. I'm certain of that." Isabella presses her lips against mine, letting them linger there before pulling back. I return to my reclining position, and Isabella holds me a little tighter than before.

"Any ideas then?"

"I guess we have a few options. We can just decide that when I leave here, we are done. No contact info exchanged. We simply move on and try to forget about each other."

"I don't like that option." I smile at her answer, even if she can't see it. I don't like it either, but no other option seems practical.

"Well, we could exchange information and take it day by day. Video chatting is free and easy. I think it will require total honesty if we want to go that route. Honesty about how we are feeling, if either of us meets someone else, anything. We could take it from there, see if we even want to see each other again after a while."

"This option is better, but…" I wait for Isabella to answer but she stays quiet.

"But what?"

"What about Katrina? What will you do when you see her?" I sigh, knowing I can't give Isabella the full reassurance she wants to hear. I remove myself from her embrace and turn around to face her, the least I can do is look her in the eye. Her legs remain spread, so I sit and extend mine to loosely drape around her waist, sitting as close to her as I can.

"Honestly, I don't know. I haven't thought about her or missed her, I can tell you that. I think I'm good on that front, but who knows what will happen when our paths cross. We have mutual friends, and there aren't a lot of gay-friendly spaces where I live, so we will inevitably see each other. The only thing I can promise you is transparency. I won't keep you in the dark about anything. If something happens, I promise I will tell you. There's always the chance that you'll meet someone else. I'm trusting you to be honest with me." Isabella searches my face, looking for any clue that I could be lying or leading her on. I'm not, I wouldn't, especially knowing what she went through with Esme and Camila.

"Life never makes it easy."

"No, it doesn't. Look, I'm curious if there is something between us. The circumstances are far from ideal, but I'd still like to know. I know that when I leave here Saturday morning, I'm going to be hurting more than I was when I arrived. I'm leaving the decision up to you. Take whatever time you need to think about it. I can give you my information before I leave, and you can use it or throw it away." I hate this option, will hate the not knowing as I wait to hear from her, but I know where I stand and don't want to pressure her into making a choice without thinking it through.

"I don't need time to think about it. I want to know what this is." I smile at her as her hand finds the back of my neck, pulling me to her to share a kiss. While things are far from guaranteed, and they certainly won't be easy, I feel a modicum of relief knowing when I leave here Saturday I won't be leaving Isabella as well. My body is on fire with the combination of this knowledge and the kiss, I want Isabella now. I pull out of the kiss and run my thumb over Isabella's lips as I take in the burning in her eyes.

"Let's go inside before we get sand where we don't want it."

*****

I come to and quickly realize Isabella isn't in bed with me, I don't even have to open my eyes. "Don't move," I hear her command as I begin to stretch. I open my eyes and rotate them in the direction her voice came from. Isabella sits on top of the dresser, her back against the vanity, with her legs crossed under her. Her hand works feverishly over the large sketch book perched in her lap.

"What are you doing?" I ask, trying not to smile.

246

"You normally sleep longer, I only need a few more minutes." Her eyes dart back and forth between me and the sketchpad.

"You know, I'm going to need to use the bathroom soon." I'm playing with her, teasing her, but she's so focused on her work she doesn't seem to hear me. I hold as still as I can and watch her work, my bladder protesting more with each passing second.

"Ok, I'm done." I can't spare a second to look at the work, I jump out of bed and bolt down the hallway to the bathroom. I can hear Isabella chuckling, but it doesn't stop me. My bladder gladder, I head back to the bedroom to find Isabella sitting on the edge of the bed holding the sketchpad.

"May I see it?" I ask as I sit down next to her, much closer than the available space requires. She hands me the book and I carefully open it. The first few are landscapes, the view of the ocean from her deck under the full moon, the lagoon, her family estate, then a picture of me sunbathing on the beach, followed by a picture of me reclining on the rocks at the lagoon, a picture of me sleeping in Isabella's bed with the sunlight pouring into the room, and finally a picture of me sleeping in her bed with the moon outside the window, the shadows much heavier than in the previous sketch, my sleeping position exposing much more of my body. I slowly examine each of the sketches, letting the details of each sink in. Even the beach sketch is shaded to reflect the tan lines Isabella had teased me about.

"I'm sorry." I look at Isabella, but she doesn't want to look at me. I set the sketch book down on the bed beside me and squat down in front of her, forcing her to meet my eyes.

"Is that how you see me?" The woman in the sketches is beautiful, not just physically, but she seems to have an inner beauty that oozes out of her as well. It can't be me, even if it looks like me.

"It's who you are."

"But that woman is beautiful." Isabella reaches up and strokes my face with her fingertips.

"Sara, I've told you before that you are beautiful. Are you upset?"

"Why would I be upset?"

"Esme forbade me from sketching her when she caught me."

"I'm not upset, I'm flattered that you see me like that," I say pointing to the open book. "This is who you are. I would never ask you to stop, it would be like cutting off your hand in my opinion." Isabella leans forward and kisses my forehead, letting her lips linger just below my hairline. "Do you display your sketches?"

"Just my paintings. Why?"

"Because there is no way I want that last sketch hanging up anywhere. You can see everything!" Isabella laughs, and I can't help but join her.

Chapter 19

I wake up just before sunrise, Isabella wrapped around me, spooning me as she continues sleeping soundly. If only I could wake up every morning to this, but I leave tomorrow, not knowing if I'll ever see her again. This has never been me, I've never been one to fall quickly for anyone or to even feel much romantically for anyone before. I've often wondered if that part of me was missing or broken, yet as I lay here with Isabella curled around me, thinking about leaving her, I feel hot tears stinging my eyes. I slowly extract myself from Isabella's embrace and head to the bathroom. I blow my nose and splash cold water on my face, before crossing into the kitchen for a glass of water. I stare out at the ocean under the lightening sky as I drink the water, willing myself to keep my emotions in check. I practically tiptoe back to the bedroom, trying not to wake Isabella. Even if I can't sleep, simply laying in bed with her will be enough. I stop and lean on the door frame, looking at Isabella lying there on her stomach, the sheet barely covering her perfect ass, her naked back facing the ceiling as it steadily rises and falls, her black hair slipping around her neck, pooling above her shoulders. She looks so beautiful and peaceful that I just stand here, watching her sleep.

"Are you ever coming back to bed?" Her voice is husky, still filled with sleep, yet she lays perfectly still. I smile to myself as I cross the room and slide back into bed. I find a comfortable position on my back and as soon as I stop moving Isabella nestles in against me, kissing my cheek before resting her head on my chest. I lazily run my fingers through her hair as she drifts back off to sleep. Yes, to wake up to this every day, minus the sadness, would be amazing.

As promised, Isabella and I spend the day together naked. We have our meals delivered to the bungalow and manage a few short naps between our intense, emotionally charged intimacies. Isabella wraps a sheet around us as we watch the sunset from her deck and again as we watch the sunrise, the reality of my departure hitting both of us. We feast on each other one last time before I leave Isabella to shower at the bungalow while I return to my suite to shower and pack. Despite my protests, Isabella insists on driving me to the airport. We share a few brief kisses and a long embrace at the airport, both of our eyes red and puffy from the tears that neither of us hold back. She promises that we will talk soon before we share one last kiss and I'm forced to board my plane.

*****

I unlock my front door and step into my home, releasing a heavy sigh. It isn't the typical sigh I release when I get home, one where you finally get to let go of the breath you've been holding all day and just relax. This is a sigh of feeling a heavy burden weighing down on me. It's early evening, and I have a million things I need to get done before I get back to my usual grind on Monday morning. I drop my bags and head to the kitchen for a glass of water. I find my mail in a neat pile on the counter along with a note from Abby letting me know that the pool is finished, my phone is plugged in on the bedside charger and that she picked up a few groceries for me. Abby takes care of me at the office, in the OR and now at home. I grab a glass from the cupboard and fill it before opening the refrigerator. I chuckle and shake my head, a few groceries. Abby bought me enough food for the next two weeks. Excited to see the pool, I head in that direction. I'm not disappointed, it looks even better in person than it did in the virtual rendering. As I stand there taking it in, a mental image of Isabella slicing through the water hits me, causing my sadness to conflict with the lust the image conjures. Without thinking, I strip off my clothes and jump in the water. Shock hits me initially, the water is still a bit cooler than where the temperature controls will maintain it, and much cooler than the water at the lagoon. It doesn't matter though. I'm in the water to work out, and I do, pushing myself to the point of exhaustion. I shower and order Chinese food before settling down in the den to get through my missed calls, text messages and emails. I groan as the phone finally catches up and I see the number of voice mails and text messages I've missed. I grab a pad of paper and a pen as the messages start playing over the speaker. Thankfully there aren't any urgent calls that I must return tonight. I turn on the TV and quickly find *Four Rooms* playing. I start it from the beginning and start weeding through the text messages. Finally satisfied that I've made a full list of people I must contact, I open up my laptop and get to work on my emails, the delivery guy interrupting me before I can get too far into them. I pay him and settle back in on the sofa, opening my lo mein as I start clearing out my inbox. An alert pulls me out of a response I'm composing. The second time I hear it, my heart leaps into my throat. I quickly switch to my home screen and see an invite from Isabella.

"Hey, beautiful." God her voice, I miss her voice, and her eyes, and just her. I miss her so much, and it's only been half a day.

"Hello gorgeous," I whisper and smile at her. I honestly didn't expect to hear from her so soon, but I'm thrilled that she's contacted me already. "What are you doing?" She sounds sleepy and looks worn out as well.

"Thinking about going to bed soon. I didn't get much sleep last night," she says with a giant grin plastered on her lips. "What about you?"

"Having a late dinner while I try to get caught up on correspondence."

"Should I let you go?" I can't help but think of another way that question could be intended.

"Don't you dare!" Oops, I hadn't meant to answer so sharply, but I got distracted by my brain. Isabella just smiles. "Do you care if I eat while we talk?"

"Of course not, I like watching you eat." We talk for nearly an hour, the credits rolling on my movie and Isabella's eyes slow to open after each blink.

"I should let you go to bed, you look spent."

"Ok, will I talk to you tomorrow?"

"I hope so." Isabella flashes me a sleepy smile.

"Me too. I miss you beautiful."

"I miss you too baby. Goodnight." Baby? When did I start calling her baby? I honestly don't recall ever calling her baby, but I find that I actually don't feel uncomfortable with it, and the smile Isabella's face lit up with tells me she doesn't either.

"Goodnight." She blows me a kiss before disconnecting our chat. I switch back over to my inbox but feel totally deflated. There isn't anything here that can't wait until tomorrow. I switch off the TV and lights, brush my teeth and curl up in bed, wrapping my arms around one of the extra pillows, as if the cold lifelessness could replace Isabella.

*****

I wake up at 6 am feeling physically refreshed, but still missing Isabella. I get out of bed and head downstairs for my morning workout, I need to get back into my routine.

I push myself hard, despite feeling fatigue earlier than I typically would. My diet and laziness over the last two weeks are certainly impacting my performance. I cool off with a quick swim in the pool, remembering how great it felt to dive into the ocean after running on the beach. I shower and make breakfast before settling at the table with my laptop, preparing to respond to all the messages I missed. I manage to get through my emails from the last few days and check my surgery schedule for tomorrow. I'm surprised to see that Dr. Westland has been added on as secondary on my cases. The passage of time has slipped by me, but I'm pleased that she's part of the team now, and happy that she will be scrubbing with me the next couple of weeks. Between Westland, Abby and I, we should be able to get through the cases much faster, hopefully making the catch-up schedule I'll be on much more bearable. I'm happy that I'll be so busy, it will allow me to focus on something other than missing Isabella. I close the applications I have running and spot the video chat icon on the task bar at the bottom of my screen. My finger directs the mouse over it, and I hesitate. Is it too soon? How often is too often? It doesn't matter though, my desire to talk to Isabella is too strong, I click on the icon and then tell it to connect me to Isabella.

"Good morning," she purrs, her beautiful smile lighting up my screen. Her hair is wet and pulled up into what I know will be a messy bun. I can see the shoulders and neck of her work shirt.

"Hi," I whisper, smiling like a school girl with a crush. "What are you doing?"

"Heading to the bar, I've decided to stay busy."

"Why busy?" She flashes me a look of pure skepticism.

"Because I miss you. My bed still smells like you, I thought you were here when I woke up this morning." I can see her sadness as she tells me this. I feel it too.

"I know, I just looked at my schedule, I'm going to be so busy the next few weeks catching up from being gone."

"I want to come see you." Her words catch me off guard, but send a tidal wave of excitement through me.

"You do?"

"Yes. I would get on a plane today if you told me to." I want to tell her to do it, to get on the next flight here, but she wouldn't see me, she would see how life is for me currently, my schedule over packed, my workaholic nature.

"Just a second." I pull up my schedule on my phone and look at the coming weeks. I have a Friday coming up in early October with one fast case on it that I could move to the end of my day Wednesday. My Thursday clinic has some rechecks in the morning but no new consults. With a late evening Tuesday I can see all of those patients in office then. The following Monday I took off as Abby is going to be returning from a PA conference, the very thing that has made this long weekend possible. I'm not on call. It's a perfect opportunity. I can see Isabella watching me, amusement on her face. "I have a long weekend coming up, a Thursday through Monday free."

"Give me the dates." I tell her the dates and look at my Wednesday surgery schedule. If I bump that Friday case to the previous Monday instead of Wednesday, I could be out of surgery by 5. She could fly in Wednesday evening, giving us a few more precious hours together.

"See if anything comes in Wednesday evening. I should be done in the OR by 5." Isabella's smile is like nothing I've ever seen before. The happiness I feel knowing that she might be coming to visit is nearly overwhelming.

"I will look into flights at work. I have to get going, but I will talk to you later."

"Can't wait. Have fun at work." Our chat disconnects but I feel giddy knowing that she will be visiting soon. I check the time and decide it's late enough to start responding to the missed calls and texts. Most are easy enough, just a quick response saying that I was sorry to miss their invitation but I had taken an impromptu vacation. I send Abby a text thanking her for everything and Catherine one letting her and Alex know that I'm back. The only person I don't respond to is Katrina. Aside from her initial messages from the weekend that I left, there was nothing. I know it's because they told her I was gone, but I'm still unsure what to say to her.

I busy myself getting things done around the house. The service was here Friday, so the house is clean, but I still have laundry to do, mail to sort through, and financial things to take care of. I'm sitting in the den a few hours later, working on paying my bills when the doorbell rings. I set my laptop next to my phone on the coffee table and head to the front door, where Katrina waits on the other side.

"Hi," I say as I open the door and step aside to allow her to come in. She hesitates momentarily, and I close the door behind her as she slips off her shoes. I hadn't responded to her messages because I wasn't sure what I would say or how I would feel when I saw her, and I wanted to be sure. Now that she's here I don't feel anything really. I feel like I'm being visited by a good friend, much like I would if Catherine, Alex or Abby randomly stopped by. She makes her way into the den and sits in one of the arm chairs. I sit back down on the couch in front of my laptop and complete the payment I was in the middle of making.

"Is this a bad time?" She seems nervous, but I don't want to push her to talk; or have this conversation end up starting an argument.

"No, just paying the bills. How are you?" Her brow furrows; as if my asking how she is might be the most ridiculous thing in the world.

"I'm fine. You?"

"I'm good." This is awkward, I hate it. "Look, I feel like you came over here because you have something to say. I'm not trying to start another argument, but I can't stand it being awkward between us."

"Me either." She sits quietly for a moment, fidgeting uncontrollably. "I, uh, just wanted to apologize to you. I've been an asshole, I know I have. Running out on you at Velvet, ignoring your calls, then showing up here trying to get you into bed." She shakes her head a little as she looks at the floor. "I'm really sorry. You were right though, I'm not ready for the whole relationship package. I'm just really lonely and I miss physical intimacy. I think some part of me thought it would be easier to sleep with someone that I care about instead of a stranger. I never stopped to think about what it would do to you. I'm sorry if I hurt you." She looks up at me with tears spilling from her eyes. I know her apology is genuine, and I appreciate it, but that's all. I don't feel the urge to cross the room to her, to comfort her, or kiss her.

"I appreciate that, I really do. I know that couldn't have been easy for you to admit." She smiles a little before looking back at the floor. "I'm fine though, really. Maybe we're just really good friends who got a little confused because of all the time we were spending together." She looks up at me with a mixed stare of shock and confusion. I have to stifle the giggle I feel threatening to escape.

"So you're ok?"

"I am."

"But you ran away. I don't even know where you went, but guessing from that tan it was someplace nice." I laugh then, because it was far more than nice.

"I went to Punta Cana. After you left that night I'd had enough of life. It was the first place that popped up with a cheap all inclusive deal, so I took it." She raises her eyebrows at me, clearly not believing what I've just told her.

"You, who had not taken a vacation in a decade just spur of the moment booked a two-week vacation and ran away?"

"Yes. It might be the best decision I ever made." She sits there and stares at me, her lips parted slightly, but nothing coming out.

"You seem different." I can't tell from her tone if she thinks whatever change she senses is positive or not.

"Well vacation is supposed to relax you, maybe that's what it is." I know that is definitely not what it is, but I don't feel I owe her the details. "Look, why don't we forget what happened, write it off as a drunken mistake and move on. Just be friends like we were before."

"Yeah, that would be nice."

"Great, would you like something to drink?"

"Just an ice water." I nod as I grab my glass and head to the kitchen. I'm filling two glasses when Katrina calls out, "Who is Isabella?" My heart leaps as I realize Isabella is likely trying to get me on video chat. I bolt out of the kitchen, leaving the glasses of water behind. I quickly hit the connect key on my phone without picking it up, hoping I'm not too late.

"Hey baby, are you there?" A thrill surges through me at the sound of her voice and hearing her call me baby.

"I'm here," I inform her as I fumble with my phone, struggling to get a hold of it.

"Hey beautiful," she purrs as I finally take control of the phone. I feel that ridiculous smile creep onto my face as I stare at her beautiful eyes.

"Hey, yourself. How's work?" I can see the bright sunshine and the bottles on the bar behind her.

"It's picking up. Matt says hello." Matt pops into the frame and waves before disappearing again. "I think he's still a little salty that you never called him."

"Do you want me to call him? You could get his number for me." I hear Katrina clear her throat as I challenge Isabella. I completely forgot that she's here. I see Isabella's brow furrow.

"Do you have company?"

"I do, just a second." I look at Katrina. "I really need to take this, just make yourself at home." I head down the hallway to my bedroom and shut the door. "Sorry, I forgot I wasn't alone when you called. Katrina is here." I see hurt, insecurity, and a few other emotions flash through Isabella's eyes. "Hey, it's ok. She came over unannounced. We're just talking, clearing the air. That's all. Whatever I thought was there before I left isn't there now. I'd like to be friends with her if it's possible. We were just discussing it." Isabella relaxes a little, but her smile isn't there.

"Do you still want me to visit?"

"More than anything!" Isabella's face lights up, somehow reaching across the 2,000 miles between us, making me feel warmer.

"Good. I booked my flight. Where are you right now?" I barely hear her question over the hammering of my heart. She will be here in just over two weeks!

"Sitting on my bed, why?"

"Can I see?"

"Can you see what?"

"Your bedroom." It seems an odd request, but I slowly rotate my phone around, giving Isabella a complete scan of my bedroom. "Very nice."

"What are you up to?" I know her well enough to know that she has a motive for that request.

"Just wanted to start fantasizing about the place I'm going to fuck you in 17 days," she whispers into the microphone. Just those words caused a flood in my panties. Thankfully I have a bathroom and a fresh pair within reach.

"What if I fuck you?" I challenge her and watch as her eyes close. I can imagine the quiet murmur she is releasing, too quiet for the microphone to pick up.

"I'll imagine that too." I can see the desire in her eyes.

"Me too. I don't want to go, but I have a visitor." Isabella smiles, but it isn't full like the one she had earlier. "Hey, I promised you transparency, and I'm telling you the truth. Nothing has happened, nothing is going to happen." She smiles and nods.

"Will I talk to you later?"

"Yes, please." We stare into our phones for a moment, just enjoying the connection. "I'll talk to you before bed tonight. I miss you."

"Miss you too." The video disconnects but I can't feel sad. Isabella will be here soon, and I'll be so busy playing catch up at work that the time should fly by. I quickly clean myself up and change my panties before heading back to the den.

"Sorry about that. I wasn't expecting that call." I wasn't expecting it, but I sure wasn't going to ignore it.

"No problem," Katrina says eyeing me. "That's what the difference is, you met someone."

"I did," I inform her, I can feel the smile consuming my face. I search Katrina's but can't determine her reaction.

"I'm happy for you." She says the words, but they don't seem entirely sincere.

"Are you?"

"Of course I am. You're a remarkable woman, you deserve to be happy. Plus she's gorgeous, and that accent. So you met her in Punta Cana?" I'm still smiling like an idiot, I know I am, but I can't help it.

"I met her my first day there. She was working behind the bar at the resort. It was only supposed to be a vacation fling, we both agreed to it from the start, but somehow something altered the plan. I spent every moment I could with her. She showed me around the area, taught me to surf, she—."

"She rocked your world."

"Yeah, she did. She's intelligent, caring, talented, fierce, compassionate, altruistic." I close my eyes and picture Isabella.

"Wow, you're in deep." I've tried to deny it, tell myself that it's too fast, too soon, but I know what Katrina said is true.

"Yeah, I am," I whisper as I open my eyes. "It's scary how much I miss her. It feels too quick. We haven't promised each other anything but the truth. We know if we're going to make this happen it won't be easy. She'll be here in 17 days for a long weekend."

"Wow. Bartenders there must make really good money." I detect a certain hit of sarcasm in Katrina's voice.

"She isn't just a bartender, she has an ownership share in the resort. She bartends because she enjoys it." I deliberately leave out the fact that she is also secretly a famous painter who has more money than she could ever possibly need. I would never reveal Isabella's secret.

"Sounds like she has it all." I realize then that our glasses of water are still in the kitchen. I get up to retrieve them but when I turn the corner Katrina is putting her shoes on. "I've got to get going."

"Ok." Clearly she's upset about the Isabella situation, but there isn't any solace I can offer her.

"Talk to you soon?"

"Yeah, we'll talk soon." She gives me a weak smile before leaving.

An hour later Catherine calls to inform me that they're picking me up for a late lunch. I'm happy to catch up with my friends. When we arrive at the bistro, I see Abby and Katrina already seated with drinks. I can't help but feel like I'm walking into an ambush, or an intervention. Katrina was clearly not happy to learn about Isabella earlier today and Catherine's call an hour after Katrina left my place suddenly feels a bit too coincidental. Abby wraps me up in a big hug before I take the vacant seat next to her, putting me between Catherine and Abby. To my relief, lunch really is just friends catching up. Katrina looks slightly uncomfortable when I tell them about Isabella, but doesn't say anything. It's clear that she's trying to be friends, which is all I want from her.

I'm in bed reading that night when the alert finally goes off. "Hello beautiful," I say as soon as I see her sleepy face.

"Isn't that my line?" she teases me. "Sorry it's late, I fell asleep."

"Long day at work?" She looks so cute when she just wakes up, her eyelids heavy, her hair mussed, and her sleepy grin.

"No, work was fine. I went for a walk and a swim after dinner, then came home to take a shower. I crawled into bed to message you, but I still smell you on my sheets, and since I miss you touching me I had to do it myself." My body catches fire as I imagine Isabella pleasuring herself. I can hear the noises she makes in my head; like she is laying next to me making them in reality. My body responds, and I feel the wetness between my legs. "How was your day?"

"Good," I choke out. I clear my throat before continuing, watching Isabella's grin grow. She knows what her confession has done to me. "I told my friends about you."

"You did?" She sounds surprised.

"Of course I did. They're excited to meet you."

"Even Katrina?"

"Well, I don't know how she feels. We talked about you after our chat earlier. She knows that I only want to be friends with her. I don't think she was pleased, but she joined the rest of us for lunch, so I think she's willing to try."

"That's good." I can't tell if Isabella is worried about Katrina or not. She doesn't press further, and there isn't anything to tell. "What were you doing when I called?"

"Reading, waiting for you to call."

"You should've called me." I had thought about calling her but wasn't sure how late she was working.

"I thought about it, but it sounds like you were busy." Isabella's grin turns sinister; like I've walked straight into her trap. Little does she know I willingly did and hoped she would join me. "You aren't wearing any clothes right now, are you?" She slowly inches her laptop away from her, revealing inch after inch of her bronzed body. "Oh my god," I whisper as she leans back on her elbows, spreading herself wide for me.

"I showed you mine," Isabella challenges. I slide the laptop away from me, revealing the tank top and mesh shorts I have on. "Mmm, I get a strip tease tonight. Take it off…slowly." If anyone else had ever suggested, much less demand that I strip for them on video chat I would have refused. But Isabella is different, when I see the desire in her eyes, I cannot deny her. I kneel on the bed and slowly tease the bottom of the top up my abdomen, inching it higher and higher, lingering on my breasts to run my fingers over them and tease my nipples a few times. Isabella bites down on her lower lip, and her ass presses down into her mattress, but she doesn't touch herself. I know she's waiting for me. I slowly lift my top off the rest of the way and let it fall to the floor. Instead of dropping my hands I lower them to my shoulders and slide them down my body, once again stopping to tease my breasts. I can see the moisture on Isabella's slit as she refrains from touching herself.

"You know what I'd be doing to you if you were here to remove these?" My thumbs hook in the waistband of my shorts, and I pull lightly on them for emphasis. Isabella quickly wedges a few pillows behind her back and allows her hands to make contact with her highly sensitive nipples. Another bout of wetness spills from me as I watch her and hear her moan. "That's right baby," I encourage her. When her eyes finally flutter open I slowly inch the shorts and my panties down, shifting back once they reach my knees, and unceremoniously letting them join my top on the floor. I slowly lean back the rest of the way and reveal myself to her, the cool air colliding with my moist folds. "I'm already so wet for you."

"Mmm, you always are. Touch yourself, imagine that I'm there and touch yourself, just like I would." I slowly slide my hand down my abdomen and start to caress my outer folds, groaning as I inch closer to my throbbing clit, knowing Isabella wouldn't give me the satisfaction just yet.

"You know how I would lick and tease you, I want to watch you." Isabella grins as she watches me rubbing myself and drops her right hand down from her breast, bypassing her outer lips to slip straight into her slit. I can see the juices on her fingers as she slowly rubs up and down, slowly circling her clit with each stroke. My own fingers slip between my folds and start teasing my clit as I watch Isabella groan and grind against her hand, her other still teasing her erect nipples. We watch each other masturbating, encouraging each other, our pace ramping up, our breathing heavy, our moans more frequent. I know we're both teetering on the edge, but when Isabella turns her face away from the camera and inhales from the pillow next to her, my pillow, I lose the little remaining control that I had. "Fuck, Isabella," I moan as my muscles tighten, and my heart bursts. I watch her come on the monitor as she inhales my scent from the pillow once again. A tinge of jealousy hitting me that I can't smell her right now.

"Do you have any idea how much I miss you?" she asks as she turns her face back toward the camera.

"Yeah, I do," I inform her. We both slide our laptops back into our laps.

"You know, I wasn't planning on that." I lift my eyebrow, showing her nothing but disbelief.

"What exactly did you think would happen after you told me you masturbated thinking about me?"

"Ok, so maybe I hoped it would happen." Isabella grins, a satisfied, proud grin that reflects the cockiness she occasionally lets free. I can't help but grin back, while her cockiness comes out in the bedroom, it isn't who she really is at all. We chat for another hour before I tell her I must go to bed. Her lower lip protrudes in an adorable pout, but she doesn't pressure me to stay awake. She does, however, make me promise to message her in the morning, despite the fact that it will be 7 am there, and she would have no reason other than surfing to be awake.

Chapter 20

The next week flies by in a blur. I'm so busy trying to play catch-up at work that I barely have a chance to breathe. That doesn't mean that Isabella and I don't chat every chance we get. I wake her every morning while I'm on my way to work, contact her at lunch (if I get one), and she contacts me every night before bed, even if she's working late at the bar. Katrina and I exchange a few messages, mostly checking to see how the other one is doing.

Dr. Valerie Westland is a pleasant surprise, and a godsend. Not only does she help shave a few hours off each of my OR days, but she has a great sense of humor, seems to fit right in with the staff and utilizes the same approaches that I do for my operations. I'm glad we were able to snag her when we did. By the end of the first week, I'm more than comfortable allowing her to take on some of the overwhelming case load I've been shouldering for years.

Friday evening we're wrapping up the last case around 6:30. I'm exhausted and want to go home, but Abby suggests we see if Catherine and Alex want to meet up for a drink at Velvet. So instead of going home, Abby, Valerie and I head to Velvet from the hospital to have a drink or two. I park at the bar and loiter in the car to connect with Isabella. I've nearly given up when she finally answers. I can see she's working and kick myself for not remembering.

"Hey, beautiful. Everything alright?" Her smile instantly eases the tension from the chaotic week.

"Everything's fine. Just wanted to let you know I'm meeting some friends for a drink or two before heading home. I forgot you're working late tonight."

"It's ok baby. We're busy though, can I call you when I finish up here?" I smile at her, knowing she needs to hang up sooner than later.

"I hope you will."

"I promise I will, have fun, be safe." The chat disconnects and I head inside to join my friends.

I stop and order a whiskey sour from Sandra on the main level before locating everyone upstairs around a pool table. Catherine and Alex are battling Abby and Valerie in what looks to be a close game. I join them and watch the action, striking up a conversation with whomever winds up near me.

"Hey Sara, you didn't tell us you hired a sister." Alex grins at me. "Abby, I think you're destined to be our token straight girl." Alex laughs as I choke on my drink. I look at Valerie, I had no idea.

"Sorry, I didn't know," I stammer. Valerie laughs.

"Why would you? It isn't a big deal. I've been meaning to come here, so this is great. You guys come here every weekend?"

"No. The thought alone exhausts me. Alex and Abby usually have their own Friday night dinner thing. Usually by the time the week is done, I can't wait to get home and relax."

"I know how you feel. I do like knowing I won't feel so isolated here though. I had no idea there were so many of us at work."

"You've clearly never seen those two within 10 feet of each other then." Valerie and I look at Catherine and Alex. Even though they aren't touching, the sexual tension between them is palpable.

"I haven't, but they seem pretty great together."

"What are you drinking? I owe you a drink for helping me get out of the OR at a reasonable hour all week. You've been a real lifesaver."

"It isn't a problem. I'm drinking a dirty martini, but wait until you finish yours to order me another. I'm not trying to get drunk."

"Understood. I think you're up."

"Hey girls, didn't know you were coming out tonight." I look up to see Katrina, a very tipsy Katrina. Abby introduces her to Valerie, who doesn't seem that impressed. Abby, Catherine, and Alex chat with Katrina while Valerie takes a seat next to me.

"So that's Katrina." It isn't a question. I look at her, and she releases a soft chuckle. "Sorry, they sort of gave me a brief history when we walked in. Said there was some sort of mess between the two of you, but then you went on vacation and met someone else."

"Ouch, that makes me sound like a horrible person. I don't know what they told you, but she lost her long time partner seven months ago. I didn't really know her before the accident, but happened to be in the OR the night it happened. Long story short, we became good friends and the last time we were all here for a friend's moving away party we both got really drunk, and she kissed me before running away. I thought that maybe I had some feelings for her that I had been in denial about or had been

269

ignoring. She showed up at my place claiming to have feelings for me and trying to get me into bed, but the way she was saying things, it was clear she was looking for something casual. I was confused, frustrated and exhausted from too much work. Everything just seemed so damn impossible at that point, so I found the first all inclusive resort trip I could and hopped on the first flight out the next morning to Punta Cana for two weeks. I met Isabella while I was there." I can't deny the smile that always swallows my face when I think about Isabella.

"You're quite smitten aren't you?" I laugh, the smile never leaving my face.

"Yeah, I think I am. She'll be here in a week and a half, I can't wait to see her."

"Let me guess, Katrina hasn't taken the Isabella news very well." We both turn our eyes toward Katrina and watch the woman she's with seemingly hold her up.

"I guess not. We haven't really talked about it, but given the way she abruptly left my place after I told her and how drunk she is right now…I don't know what I'm supposed to do about that though."

"Nothing you can do other than just be honest." I see Valerie's eyes flit over in Katrina's direction. "Who is that with her? Is she even old enough to drink?" Katrina's companion is a woman who appears to be all of 20. Katrina sees my gaze and pulls the woman in my direction, everyone's eyes behind her growing in size.

"Hey, Sara."

"Katrina. Who's your friend?"

"This is…" Katrina is so drunk I don't know if she is holding the other woman's waist in order to stay vertical or because she wants to.

"Sam," the younger woman says, extending her hand to me. I feel embarrassed for Katrina, she can't even remember the woman's name.

"Nice to meet you, Sam, this is Valerie." We chat for a few minutes with the slurry Katrina and her companion before Sam drags her back downstairs to dance.

"I think you dodged a bullet with that one," Valerie says.

"I don't know, maybe. She's been through a lot. I don't want to judge her." Valerie eyes me but doesn't say anything. "What?" I finally ask.

"You're one of the nice ones, aren't you?"

I shrug in answer as I head towards the bar to buy another round. When I return, I see Alex looking over the balcony to the dance floor below.

"What is she doing?" Everyone in our group leans against the rail and looks down. Katrina is staring up at the balcony. When her eyes lock on me, she stares for a moment before crushing her mouth against Sam's. I simply shake my head and turn my back.

"You alright?" Catherine asks.

"Yeah, I'm good. I feel sorry for Sam though. Katrina couldn't even remember her name earlier, and now it's like she is putting on a show down there."

"Oh, she's certainly putting on a show." Catherine shakes her head as well.

"Is this where you tell me that I'm obligated to do something?"

"The only thing you are obligated to do is be happy. Katrina doesn't know what she wants right now, she certainly isn't ready for you. Besides, you seem quite taken with Isabella, I'm looking forward to meeting her." Just like that the smile is back.

"I'm looking forward to you meeting her too. I'm glad she isn't here to see that," I say hooking my thumb over my shoulder. "I think she worries about it, even though she has nothing to worry about."

"No, she doesn't. I can tell." Catherine squeezes my hand as she gazes at Alex. I've finished my second drink and am ready to go home. "Now, I think I'll bow out of this evening and take my lady home." I raise a skeptical eyebrow at her.

"Alex, a lady? Who are you trying to fool?" Catherine chuckles.

"Who among us is anyway?" We both laugh then. We all walk out of Velvet together, each of us exhausted from the week and ready for bed. We say our goodbyes in the quiet parking lot and head our separate ways.

*****

The next week breezes by, well not breezes, that makes it sound like it was easy. With Valerie's assistance we manage to finish cases at a decent hour, and by the time I leave my office Thursday evening, I will be caught up at clinic. I buy my office staff lunch on Thursday to thank them for their hard work over the last two weeks. I'm finishing up my charting when Abby knocks on my office door. "Hey Abby, come on in." She comes in but doesn't sit. Instead, she seems anxious, a sign that her bonus has finally been deposited.

"So I, uh…" Abby never stutters, nor does she use uh or um in a sentence. This is how I know she is about to broach a subject she's uncomfortable talking about.

"Sit down Abby." I continue when she finally manages to seat herself. "Look, you earned it, every penny of it. Probably more honestly. I won't negotiate this." Abby and I do this every time I give her an unplanned bonus, she never wins.

"That was a lot of money though. My bank thinks I'm a drug dealer or something."

"Like I said, you've earned it. Do something nice for yourself, put the money in a college fund for Stella, donate it. It doesn't matter to me, you're keeping it though." I make sure my tone conveys that this isn't something I'm willing to budge on. I can't wait until my proposal to the partners is complete, the one where I suggest that we grant Abby a percentage of the cosmetic clinic profits, given she pretty much runs it single handedly. Abby shakes her head but stops arguing. She gets up to leave before I stop her. "If things go well next week with Isabella, I plan on taking the week of Thanksgiving off along with the Thursday and Friday before and Monday after. I want you to take the time off as well." Abby opens her mouth to protest, but I stop her. "No arguments about money, you're salaried, and you've earned it. Valerie has already agreed to cover any patient concerns while we're off."

"You're the boss," she says before stopping in the doorway. "Thank you."

Our last patient on Friday presents an unexpected challenge, but with Valerie's help, we are out of the OR before 8 pm. I make the trip home thoroughly exhausted from the marathon the last two weeks have been. I crawl into bed after taking a long hot shower and start to put together a list of things to buy and do before Isabella's arrival Wednesday evening. I'm working on a list of places I might take her when the alert finally goes off.

"Hey baby," I say trying to smother another yawn. She flashes her knowing smile, the one that I could look at for hours.

"Did I wake you?"

"Not quite, but I'm pretty wiped."

"You want me to let you go? You should get some sleep."

"Not just yet. I want to hear about your day." The smile Isabella gives me radiates exactly how I feel about her. We talk for a short while before it becomes clear to her that I can barely hold my eyes open anymore.

"Go to sleep beautiful, we will talk in the morning."

"Five more sleeps," I tell her, giving her a sleepy grin, my eyes half closed. Five more sleeps before I can wrap my arms around her and press my lips to hers.

"I know baby, I can't wait. Sweet dreams."

*****

The doorbell followed by a loud banging wakes me up. I roll over and look at the clock. It's nearly 3 am. I stumble out of bed and head toward the front door, thankful I'm dressed because I was too tired to have video sex with Isabella tonight. I flip on the porch light to see Katrina on the other side of the glass, a drunk, very unsteady Katrina. Headlights illuminate my driveway. I open the door ready to tear her a new one for drunk driving but a taxi backs into the road as I stand there with my mouth open.

"I think I left my keys at Velvet. I need a place to stay." Irritation boils my blood.

"Naturally my B & B was the first place that came to mind." I get bitchy when I'm irritated, add to the fact that she just woke me up at 3 a.m. and I'm bordering on being livid.

"Please, Sara." I've never been one to turn my back on someone who needs help. I know that in this instance I should, but I stand aside and let her in. She has to put both hands on the wall in order to not fall over while kicking off her shoes.

"Just go to the guest room," I order her as I head to the kitchen to get her a glass of water. I enter the guest room to see her struggling to get her jacket off. I deposit the water on the night stand and help her remove her jacket, hanging it on the closet door handle. I toss back the covers, and she sits on the bed, taking the glass of water and downing most of it. She lays down, and I flip the covers over her, then take the glass back to the kitchen to refill it. By the time I return, she has passed out. Grateful, I put the water on the nightstand and leave one of the lamps on low, closing the door as I leave.

I'm deep in a dream about Isabella when I feel her hand caressing my breast and her lips against my neck. "Mmm, Isabella," I murmur, slowly being pulled from sleep. The hand hesitates but resumes its work. That's when I know, Isabella would never hesitate. My eyes snap open, but even in the dark I know that it isn't Isabella touching me, the nauseating smell of stale booze hits me. "What the hell?" I scream, sliding to the other side of the bed and turning the light on. Katrina sits there, wearing nothing but a pair of boyshort underwear and a t-shirt, confusion on her face. "What are you doing?" I ask, pulling my shirt back down to cover myself.

"You were moaning, I thought you were enjoying it." I'm beyond pissed at this point.

"I was sleeping. I thought you were Isabella!" She flinches, but I'm unsure if it's because I'm screaming or because I thought she was someone else. I don't really care either. I slide out of the bed and glare at her. "Go back to the guest room Katrina." When she doesn't move, I round the foot of the bed and grab her arm, ready to escort her if necessary. She stands and tries to kiss me, but I'm expecting it, and she's still intoxicated and slow, making it easy to dodge. "Get out of my fucking room or get out of my house," I order her through clenched teeth. Everything about this is wrong, and I want her gone. She finally gives in and slumps back to the guest room. As soon as she's out of my bedroom I shut the door and lock it, knowing I should have done so earlier. I feel angry and dirty, but mostly I feel scared, because I know that Isabella has already been worried about Katrina, and I know I have to tell her. I glance at the clock to see that it's only 6:30 on a Saturday morning in Punta Cana. I know Isabella is asleep, but I also know that I can't wait. I have to tell her now. With dread coursing through me, I open my laptop and request the connection, hoping she hears the alert from her phone. I'm about to give up on connecting with her when she finally answers.

"Hey gorgeous, can't sleep?" Her voice is a sleepy murmur. Fear has a hold on my tongue. I can't speak. It must be clear on my face, as Isabella is quickly alert. "What's wrong?"

"I'm so sorry," I whisper, as the tears spill from my eyes.

"Sorry?" I take a deep breath and tell Isabella the events of my night after I spoke with her. I can see the anger in her eyes, but I tell her everything. When I finish she doesn't say anything, but I can see the muscles in her jaw clenching.

"Baby, I'm so sorry. I swear I didn't want it, I didn't invite it or ask for it." She remains quiet as I wipe the tears from my eyes with the heels of my hand.

"Are you ok?" She finally breaks her silence.

"Physically yes, but I know that I've just hurt you, even if I never wanted that to happen. I know you've been worried about her."

"Why did you tell me then?"

"Because I promised you honesty. I won't lie to you, even if it means I'm going to lose you, I won't lie." My heart aches, knowing that I've likely lost Isabella.

"I hate that she was touching you, that she just assaulted you." I can see her anger as she closes her eyes and tries to stay composed. I think to myself that assaulted might be a bit harsh of a word. When she finally opens her eyes something has shifted. "Do you still want me to come see you?" I feel my heartbeat speed a little just knowing she is willing to consider it still.

"More than anything, but only if you want to." Isabella's eyes close again, and I sit there waiting for her to tell me she doesn't want to. "Isabella, please come."

"You didn't do anything wrong," she says opening her eyes. "I'm just very angry right now. Not at you, at her. I will still come if you really want me to." I feel the smile blossom on my lips.

"Yes baby, I want you here more than you can imagine." She smiles as well, but it doesn't totally eclipse the anger I see in her eyes.

"Now tell me, are you really ok?"

"Yeah. It was just the initial shock and then the fear of how you would react, that you would cancel your visit, stop speaking to me. I'm ok now." I slide back into my bed and lay down with my head next to my laptop. "You should go back to sleep, I woke you up."

"Not until you do. I wish I was there to hold you right now."

"Me too, so much." I reach out and touch my fingertips to the image of her face causing her to smile. We each lay in our beds, chatting with one another, both refusing to disconnect and go back to sleep. Eventually one of us must have fallen asleep, as I wake up next to my laptop, the clear light of day coming in around the edges of the blinds. I roll over to see it's nearly 9 am.
Remembering the events from a few hours ago, I feel dirty and a bit afraid of where things stand between Isabella and I. I quietly unlock my bedroom door and find the door to the guest room open, the bed empty. I check the house to

find a note on the kitchen counter saying *I'm sorry.* I climb in the shower and stand under the steaming stream of water long after I've finished my cleansing routine. The sound of the chat alert pulls me out of my own head. I shut the water off and run for my phone pressing the connect key. Isabella's face greets me, her mouth hanging open, desire replacing the anger that had been in her eyes before. I smile back at her, aware that I'm naked and dripping water all over my carpet.

"See something you like?" I tease as I head back into the bathroom to grab a towel.

"Yes. Am I interrupting?" My brow furrows.

"No. Just finished taking a shower. Are we ok?"

"Yes. Is she gone?" I can hear the anger in her voice when she asks about Katrina.

"Yeah, she was gone when I woke up a bit ago. Left a note saying she's sorry." I can see Isabella's jaw clench.

"She should be."

"Isabella, does it bother you that she was here? That I tried to be her friend?" Isabella sighs as I wait for her to answer me.

"No. I was worried when you left that you would see her and remember your feelings for her or forget about me. You've been honest with me about everything though, so I trust you. I'm just really pissed about what she did last night."

"I know, I should've seen it coming."

"Don't blame yourself. You didn't put her in your bed, she came there uninvited."

"You're right." I hesitate to ask my next question but I must. "You haven't met anyone since I left, have you?" We never promised to be monogamous, but we did promise to be honest.

"No, I haven't even flirted. Matt keeps teasing me because we chat all the time." I smile because of her answer and because I can see Matt teasing her.

"When did you fall asleep this morning? I can't remember much."

"You fell asleep and I sketched you before disconnecting and going back to bed."

"I'm sorry."

"Don't be, you haven't seen the sketch yet." Isabella grins, and I know that we're ok.

"Why, was I drooling?" I can't help but tease her.

"You drool?" she asks with complete sincerity.

"I'm sure I have, I'm sure we all have."

"Hmm, perhaps I should add that to the sketch later."

"Perhaps. What are your plans for the day?"

"I'm going to work in a little bit, then packing. I think I'll paint later if I get the chance. What are you doing?"

"Running errands mostly. Do you have warmer clothes? It isn't freezing here, but it's cooler."

"I have some things, I'll be fine." She smiles at me as I sit on the bed, still wrapped in my towel. "I know you just showered but want to get dirty with me?"

"Yes please," I answer, knowing that my errands can wait.

Chapter 21

Wednesday finally rolls around, and I walk into the OR to find Alex setting up my room. "Thank god you're my tech today." I know that Alex will keep the room moving along like she always does, not just because she knows that Isabella arrives tonight.

"Good morning to you too. I sorta lied to the bosses and told them I had a request case in here today. I know how important tonight is to you." Her mask prevents me from seeing her smile, but I know it's there, I can see it in her eyes.

"Thank you. If they ask I'll be sure to back your story." We both chuckle as we get ready for the day.

Thanks to the combined efforts of everyone in the room, I'm walking out of the OR at 4:30. I check Isabella's flight information and see that it's still on time for the 6:05 pm landing. I rush home and shower before heading to the airport, arriving at 5:45. Her flight is still listed as being on time, so I stand at the door of the small airport and wait. I try reading to distract myself, but nervous energy prevents me from concentrating. Instead, I find myself pacing up and down the small entryway that leads outside from baggage claim. I look up each time I complete a lap, waiting to see her. When I finally do, we both freeze momentarily before she passes beyond the security gate, drops her bag and wraps her arms around my neck. I wrap mine around her waist and we stare into each others eyes before finally kissing each other, a long passionate kiss that I swear will result in my clothes turning to ash. When our lips finally part she pulls me tighter to her.

"Hey beautiful," she whispers in my ear as I inhale her scent of sunshine, saltwater and cucumber melon soap.

"You're here," I respond, stating the obvious.

"I am," she says pressing a kiss to my temple. We finally break our embrace and I grab Isabella's suitcase as she takes my hand. I lead her to the small open lot where I left my car. When we reach it, she presses me against the hood and kisses me deeply again. Her lips are swollen when we part, my heart thundering in my chest. "How long until we're at your place?" I don't have to ask why, it's taking all of my willpower not to tear her clothes off where we stand.

"Ten minutes or so."

"Drive fast," she commands. She needn't have given the order, I already planned to.

The ten longest minutes of my life pass by agonizingly slow. I'm convinced they've installed at least a dozen more stoplights between the airport and my house, and that each of them are red. Of course I'm being irrational and impatient, but Isabella's hand trailing up and down my inner thigh will do that to me. I park in the garage and open the door, letting Isabella enter before me. She drops her bag before pinning me against the door as soon as I close it, her mouth crushing mine, the urgency we both feel causing us to abandon all romanticism. I tug on her shirt as her hands slide under my sweater.

"You want a tour?" I ask as she pulls my sweater over my head, letting it fall to the floor. She grins as she presses her mouth to mine once more, her hands landing on my breasts, causing me to moan into her mouth.

"Dinner?" I ask, as I pull her shirt over her head. She tilts her head slightly at me and grins.

"You all night tonight. Everything else can wait until tomorrow." It's all I needed to hear. I pull her back to me and our kiss resumes. She smiles against my mouth as I slide my hands under her ass and she locks her legs around my waist. I quickly realize that I won't make it to the bedroom, I need to feel her naked flesh against mine. I sit her down on the table and unclasp her bra. Our kiss breaks as I pull the black lace down her arms and press her down onto the table.

"So this is the kitchen and dining room," I inform her as my hands caress her liberated breasts. She smiles up at me but doesn't break eye contact, not even as I pinch both of her nipples and she gasps. My hands trail down her stomach moving to unbutton her jeans. I pull the offending barrier down along with her panties, the scent of her sex greeting me. My mouth waters as I chew my lower lip and start to trail kisses down her neck, trying to rush to the place my mouth desires most.

"No," she intones, pulling me back up to her. She locks her mouth on mine before wrapping her legs around me again, her sex leaving a moist spot on my abdomen where they connect. Her fingers quickly reach down and unhook my bra. "Bedroom," she orders as I help her remove the garment. She kisses me as I pick her up off the table and carry her into my bedroom, sitting her on the side of the bed. Her hands quickly slide down to the button on my jeans, and I help her remove all of our remaining clothing before she slides back on the bed, allowing me to slither on top of her, the connection of our naked flesh once again pressed against each other spurring me on. I stare into her eyes, seeing my own longing reflected back at me. She pulls me down and locks her lips on mine as I slide between her legs, grinding my sex against hers. The overwhelming need to hear her climax, to feel her come undone under my touch is too strong. Our hips roll with much more urgency than the night on the terrace, as we work ourselves against one another. In minutes we're both tensing, our orgasms sending us both into the abyss. It may have been a quickie for all intents and purposes, but we both know it's simply the appetizer to the feast the rest of the night has in store.

*****

I wake up in the morning and revel in the feeling of Isabella's arms wrapped around me. I watch her sleep, a smile playing on my lips. When I can't ignore the screaming from my bladder any longer, I kiss her forehead. She doesn't stir. I carefully slide out of her arms and grab a set of clothes. Isabella is still sound asleep when I leave the bathroom, so I head to the kitchen to make breakfast. Fresh fruit prepped, veggies for omelets diced, and turkey sausage browning, I work on whisking a little bit of milk into the eggs for our omelets.

"I think you're overdressed," Isabella whispers in my ear as she slides her hands under my shirt, slowly caressing my abdomen. "Why did you leave me alone in bed?" she asks between the soft kisses she peppers along my neck.

"I wanted to make you breakfast," I moan leaning into her, starting to forget the task at hand. No one has ever had the effect on me that Isabella does. Her fingers slip between the waistband of my shorts and my skin, teasing me, threatening to sink lower.

"What if I want you for breakfast?" Isabella's hands grip my hips as she pulls my ass into her pelvis. My right hand drops the whisk as my left switches the burner off. Last night had been filled with tenderness and emotion as we physically reconnected with each other. With the forceful pull, Isabella has unleashed a savage hunger in me, one that I know she shares, the only common thread between our never ending night and this morning being each other. I quickly spin around and crush my mouth against Isabella's, pushing her back to pin her against the refrigerator. My hands grip her hips as I bite down on her lower lip and tug on it roughly. Isabella shudders as I nip my way along her jawline to pull her earlobe between my teeth.

"You're right, breakfast can wait until after I fuck you." Isabella groans as I bite down forcefully on her shoulder. I dip my head down to her breast and roughly suck and bite one nipple as my fingers pinch and pull on the other. She grabs two fistfuls of my hair, but instead of pulling me away she presses my head against her breast as he arches her back into me. I can hear the hissing as she pulls breaths between her teeth each time I clamp down on her protruding buds. She finally pulls me off of her nipple and back up to her mouth. She claws at my shirt as I back her down the hallway. Our lips separate as she tugs my shirt off and we pass into my bedroom. I steer her to the side of the bed and push her down onto it. Without hesitation, I latch my mouth onto her exposed sex and attack her clit. I want her warmed up and ready, this is going to be rough, something I know she will enjoy as much as I do.

"Fuck, Sara," Isabella moans as her hips buck against my mouth. I smile as I tentatively direct a probing finger around her entrance and find it soaking wet. I withdraw my finger and my mouth and stare at Isabella lasciviously.

"On your knees in the middle of the bed, facing the mirror," I order her. I see her eyes dilate with excitement as she flashes her cocky grin back at me. I drop my shorts to the floor as I turn to my closet to get the storage bin that houses my toys. I grab my harness and the dildo I feel appropriate for this situation, one that will stimulate me as I drive it into Isabella. The vibrating ring that slips over the purple shaft catches my eye as I step into the harness, so I grab it and slide it on. I hear Isabella gasp behind me and catch her rubbing herself, exciting me even more. "I never told you to touch yourself," I snap. Isabella's hand freezes before she slowly lowers it back to the bed in front of her, a disgruntled expression filling her face. I slowly walk over to the bed and lean in, grabbing her chin with my right hand and angling her face towards mine. "I'm going to have to punish you for that. You know that, right?" Her eyes drop to the strap-on before moving back to meet mine. She flashes me a defiant look, a silent challenge. "I can see you aren't the least bit repentant. You leave me no choice but to spank you." Isabella and I have never played this roughly, have never crossed this line. Yet something tells me that it isn't a line she will be afraid to cross. If she says no, I won't do it, but she doesn't.

"Do your worst," she challenges, her eyes betraying her excitement. I allow my thumbs to caress her cheekbones as I stare into her defiant stare. I kiss the top of her head before moving around the bed, kneeling on the mattress behind her. I see her reflection watching me as I roughly knead her ass cheeks, tenderizing them before I punish her. She pushes back into my hands, causing the toy to slide along her slit. Eventually, I've had enough teasing, it's time to play. I line myself up behind her, positioning the head of the toy against her entrance. She can feel it there, threatening to invade her as I lock eyes with her in the mirror.

"This is your last chance to change your mind," I warn her. She grins back at me, giving me permission to do as I please. "Canvas will be our safe word, ok?" Isabella's reflection nods at me before flashing me her cocky grin. I windup my right hand and bring it down hard on Isabella's ass, the electric shock of skin slapping skin almost as sweet as Isabella's pleasure filled moan. I tenderly rub the affronted area and smack it again, the crack as flesh meets flesh like a thunderbolt. Isabella groans, her right cheek red where I struck it. I turn my attention to the other cheek and smack it as hard as I can, the impact forcing Isabella's breath to leave her. I rub it down and smack it all over again. Isabella's fingers curl into the sheets as she arches back into the touch. I gently caress both of her aching, red cheeks while watching her in the mirror. When her eyes meet mine, I ask, "Are you ready?" She nods that she is, so I switch the vibrating attachment on and position myself directly behind Isabella, teasing her slit with the tip of the toy. "I'm going to fuck you now, and it's going to be rough. Are you ok with that?" Isabella silently responds by biting down hard on her lower lip and gripping the sheets in each of her fists. To my surprise she forces herself back onto the toy, trying to wrest some of the control from me. In order to regain the upper hand, I clamp my hands firmly on Isabella's hips and guide the remainder of the shaft inside her, burying it. I inch back out before slamming the full length of the toy back inside her. I withdraw as Isabella catches her breath, pounding into her once she does. The impact combined with the vibrator providing both of us great stimulation. The sensation of her ass repeatedly beating against my hips is amazing, only adding fuel to the fire that she creates. In no time, Isabella and I have our rhythm worked out, Isabella leaning back as I pound into her, and then we both withdrawal, to only repeat the process over and over again. I pound my hips against her ass over and over, watching the pendulum of her breasts, the rise and fall of her chest as she fights for air, searching for any sign that this is too much for her. I reach around with my right hand and play with her clit, adding even more stimulation to the pounding I've been giving her. She moans loudly at the additional teasing, so I keep it up as I continue to fuck her. Sweat begins to bead on both of our bodies as our pace becomes frantic. I know Isabella is close, that all I need to do is to continue what I'm doing. The combination of the clitoral stimulation and the penetrating toy are too much for her, and she falls screaming over the edge in a matter of minutes. She lays splayed on the bed after, as I slowly lick and kiss the red handprints on her ass cheeks before finding myself sprawled out on top of her kissing and massaging her back. "Was that alright baby?" I ask, whispering in her ear. She rolls over underneath me and wraps her arms around my waist. Her eyes are red and puffy like she has been crying. Fear plummets through me. "Baby are you ok? Did I hurt you?"

"No one has ever fucked me like that. I'm very much ok." She pulls me down to kiss her and locks her arms around me. "Did you come though?"

"No, but I'm good." Isabella isn't one to take no for an answer, so I'm not surprised when she flips me over, wrapping her arms around my thighs to pull me to the edge of the bed. She slides the harness off of me and steps into it, securing it tightly on her hips. She stands between my legs as I wrap them around her midsection. She slides in easily and quickly starts rolling her hips against me. As soon as I display the smallest amount of excitement her thumb joins the game and begins teasing my pulsing clit. The combined sensations of being filled and teased by Isabella at the same time ripple through my body. In mere minutes, my breathing is heavy and my muscles are starting to clench. She brings me to an explosive orgasm that I'm certain is going to leave me blind. When my body finally comes back to Earth, I pull Isabella into my arms and just hold her there for a few minutes. Isabella softly plants kisses along my shoulder, as I sleepily trail my fingers along her spine. She nuzzles her face against my neck and for a moment she's so still and her breathing so even that I wonder if she has fallen asleep. "Are you really ok?" Isabella lifts her head to stare into my eyes, a quizzical expression on her face.

"I am. Why are you so concerned?"

"I just want to be sure I didn't overstep or force you to do something you weren't comfortable with. That wasn't exactly gentle, and we never discussed spanking or the like before." She presses her finger against my lips, stopping my train of thought.

"We never discussed it, but you asked for permission several times. I could have said no and you would have stopped. No more worrying about this, we both enjoyed ourselves." She presses her lips to mine; as if she's presenting her closing argument. "Do you still want to make me breakfast baby? I'm famished."

"Me too," I inform her after I stop laughing. "Come on, I'll finish breakfast then give you the tour."

*****

I've never really seen the point of giving someone a tour of your home. In a way, it's always felt like a mode of bragging to me. 'Look what I have here,' or 'Look what I've done with this,' neither of which have ever been me. But Isabella is here and I want her to feel comfortable, to feel at home. Her presence has stirred something in me, it feels right, it makes me happy versus the usual claustrophobic feeling I get when I have guests. So after cleaning up the kitchen, I start by leading Isabella down to the basement, causing a slight sense of guilt to stir in me for not working out this morning. She looks around taking in all of the assorted equipment, while I lean against the wall, watching her.

"So this is where you got that body," she teases as she makes her way over to me.

"I thought you liked my body," I tease back. She pulls the cord on my bathrobe and watches as it falls back and drapes off of my reclining form.

"Very much," she purrs as her hands find my abdomen and slowly inch upward. She leans in and kisses me as her hands caress my curves, leaving goosebumps in their wake. She separates our lips to work her way over my jaw, to my earlobe and then down my neck. I've already lost at this point, but I decide to put up a mock resistance.

"Is your plan to do this in every room in the house?" My voice is already throaty and my breathing has picked up, the sensations this woman elicits with even the simplest of touches is more than I can resist.

"That sounds like a good idea to me," Isabella whispers before running the tip of her tongue along my collar bone. Her hands find my breasts and slowly start to tease my nipples. My body involuntarily arches into her. She knows she had me long before this, but I feel her cocky smile against my shoulder anyway.

"We'll miss dinner with the girls tonight if we do." Right now I don't care about dinner with the girls, I have no desire for Isabella to stop.

"Don't worry, I know how to make this quick." Her right hand slips down my torso and finds my already throbbing pussy. Her mouth latches on the nipple her hand abandoned as she strokes her fingers inside my folds, lubricating them before teasing my clit. I'm already panting when I drop my own hand down to Isabella's and encourage it to slip inside me and apply more pressure.

"Yes," I rasp as she complies, my hips already swaying forward to swallow the length of her fingers. She works inside of me, teasing my g-spot, swirling along my walls, withdrawing and entering again and again. The cool air against my moist nipple hardens it even more as Isabella lowers herself to her knees. "God, Isabella," I moan as her mouth connects with my clit, her tongue slowly swirling around it before she gently sucks it. She continues working me with her fingers and her mouth and proves that she was right, in no time my fingers are coiled in her hair, pressing her against me as my hips work in time with her fingers. I feel the ripples start to course through me and my muscles start to tense. My head falls back, no longer able to enjoy the view of Isabella making my body sing. The world goes black as I allow myself to ride the waves of ecstasy Isabella has called forth from my body. When my muscles finally relax I watch again as Isabella withdraws her fingers from me and slowly licks and sucks them clean, the sight stoking the desire that had just been fed.

"I told you I could make it quick," she teases, making me laugh as she kisses her way back up my body.

"Have you always been this insatiable?" Isabella chuckles as she embraces me, her breath tickling my ear.

"No, but I've never missed anyone the way I've missed you." She plants a soft kiss on the side of my head, and her words echo in my mind. I wrap my arms around her a little tighter.

"Me either." We stand there holding each other, time no longer mattering. Even just standing here clinging to her, I feel things I can't explain. My heart feels full, it beats faster, my skin tingles, and I feel free, free to let go, to let my guard down with her, to let her see me, all of me.

The feeling scares me to death though. I've shut off and hidden so much of myself for fear that I would become another woman's puppet again that I'm scared to let it all out. But Isabella makes me want to feel those emotions again, makes me want to be a whole person again, even if the prospect of liberation is the most frightening thing I can imagine.

"Where are you right now?" Isabella's voice brings me back to the moment. My arms have slipped down, hanging around her waist as she eyes me with concern, her thumbs brushing under my eyes, wiping away the tears I didn't know I was shedding. "What happened?"

"Nothing," I murmur, clearing my throat. "We should head upstairs, continue the tour." Isabella gives me a look, I know she isn't happy that I just shut down on her. Instead of protesting she nods and takes one of my hands, leading me back up the stairs. I lead her to the den next, where the gift I've forgotten about waits on the coffee table in a pre-wrapped black gift box with a silver bow. I've never considered myself good at giving gifts, and I feel that insecurity creeping in as Isabella spots the package. "That's for you," I inform her, leading her over to the sofa, where she'll be able to sit and open it. We both sit, and she plants a tender kiss on my forehead before turning her attention to the gift. She releases my hand and lifts the lid off the box, revealing the two sets of sketching pencils and the sketch pad. Isabella turns back to me, the sight of pure joy radiating from her eyes, her smile unlike any I've seen from her.

"Sara these are expensive," she whispers as she picks up one of the sets. Of course, Isabella knows her supplies, she would know how much I spent, but the money didn't matter to me. I just want her to be happy.

"I told the woman at the store that I wanted the best. If they aren't right, we can exchange them." Isabella places the set back in the box and turns to me. "I just wanted you to be able to be yourself while you're here. You seem to love sketching. I didn't want you to not have that." Isabella's hand finds the back of my neck, and she pulls me forward to meet her lips.

"They're perfect, thank you," she says after the quick kiss. Her lips find mine again, and she slowly presses me down on the sofa as our tongues mingle. Her body presses against mine as we kiss, causing anticipation to build within me. She separates our lips and stares into my eyes. "Do you know what I really want?"

"Hmm." I meet her gaze with lust filled eyes and a silly smile. At this moment I'm eating from the palm of her hand and we both know it.

"I want you to tell me what happened in the basement." My features shift completely as I start to feel trapped. Isabella removes her weight from me and returns to a sitting position. I take a deep breath and slowly release it as I sit up and face Isabella.

"You scare me." Isabella looks at me and I know I haven't phrased my feelings properly, she looks frightened. "Sorry, how you make me feel scares me."

"Tell me," she whispers as her fingers stroke my cheek.

"My last serious relationship was bad. She was selfish, manipulative and controlling. I foolishly allowed it, thinking that I was in love. I changed into a person I didn't recognize, a person I couldn't stand. When I finally ended it, I shut down parts of me, the parts that I was certain led me down the path to not recognizing myself in the mirror.

I've kept them closed off. I've had flings and casual relationships but haven't gotten attached. Sure it could get lonely at times, but I couldn't trust myself with anything serious, couldn't trust myself not to become that person I didn't like again. But then I met you. Somehow you've snuck in. I think about you too much, I spend each day waiting for our next chat, and worst of all I want to feel those things with you that I told myself never again. I feel free to be myself with you, to have feelings for you, to let you in and it's terrifying. I'm so happy that you're here, I want you to meet my friends, and they want to meet you. These aren't things I've felt in quite a while." I've never readily expressed or been great at expressing my emotions. With every word that spills out of my mouth, more worry sets in that it will be too much for her, that I will have opened up only to scare her away. Instead, she looks at me with a warm smile on her lips, one that feels like it's hugging me, comforting me.

"It's the same for me. I know we said we would talk, get to know each other better, but I never expected that I'd need to talk to you every day, that I would miss you as much as I do. I didn't think that I would smell you on my pillow and feel happiness at your familiar scent coupled with a deep ache of wishing you were next to me. I didn't expect for you to wind up here," she takes my hand and places it over her heart, "but you did. I spend all day waiting for our next chat too. I'm painting more than I have in a long time because I need something to do with everything I've been feeling. I had to come see you, I couldn't wait for you to come back to me." She presses a kiss to my lips as she cradles my face in her hands. "So you see, it's the same for me, only I'm not scared. I'm curious and excited. I need to discover what this is." Now it's my turn to smile at Isabella as my heartbeat rages out of control and emotions that I've denied myself access to flood my system. I lean forward, and Isabella meets me halfway as we slowly lock lips. The kiss is slow and deep, my hands eventually dropping to untie the robe I gladly let her wear. She does the same, and we each push the fabric off of the other's shoulders and let them fall. I press my body against Isabella, and she slowly lowers herself back. We may check another room off of the list, but this will not be fast. Everything else can wait, right now we simply need to enjoy the emotions we're feeling, to revel in the confessions we made. This is real, and no matter how much it scares me, I want it.

*****

"Are you ready?" Isabella and I sit in my car outside of the Italian restaurant that Catherine and Alex love. Somehow we made it a few minutes early, despite only leaving the pool and the hot tub for another time. Isabella looks at me, and it looks as though I'll have to pull her from the car. "Wait, are you nervous?" Never in a million years did I think I'd see this woman, who is always so confident, a big bundle of nerves about meeting my closest friends.

"I am. This is a big deal. What happens if they don't like me?"

"Baby, it's going to be great. They're going to like you, I promise. Why wouldn't they? Plus they're going to see how happy I am with you." I lean over the center console and kiss her. "Do you want me to cancel? We can go somewhere else by ourselves."

"No. This is important to both of us. I will be fine." She kisses me again before we exit the car. We meet at the rear of the car and Isabella takes my extended hand. I try to lead us toward the restaurant's entrance, but a slight resistance from Isabella stops me, forcing me to turn around. She closes the space between us and wraps her free arm around my waist. "How about a kiss for good luck?" I smile at her before softly planting my lips against hers. Her hand quickly drops mine and reaches up to cradle the back of my head. I feel her tongue slide over my lips, asking permission to enter, and feel my own lips part to allow it. We stand there and share the passionate kiss, our hands never straying anywhere inappropriate. I feel the tension melt out of Isabella's body as we pour our feelings into one another. When we finally part Isabella leans her forehead against mine, her swollen lips tempting me to claim them again. I know we will never make it inside if I do.

"Ready now?" Isabella smiles, she still seems a little nervous but better than she was. We enter the restaurant, and the hostess leads us to a table where Catherine, Alex, Abby and, to my surprise, Valerie wait for us. I introduce Isabella to everyone and am not at all shocked when Abby gets up from the table and hugs Isabella instead of shaking her hand. Isabella looks at me surprised but then focuses on something. I can hear the murmur of Abby's voice but can't make out what she's saying. Whatever it is, Isabella visibly relaxes and smiles broadly at me as we take our seats.

"It's about time Sara, we were just about to draw straws to see who was going outside to pull you out of the parking lot." Alex has never been one to not voice her every thought, but I had no idea that we had arrived before everyone.

"So you saw—." Isabella's hand grips mine under the table.

"Oh, we saw alright. It was hot. Catherine and I would have never made it inside."

"We do not act like that in public," Catherine protests, but fails to hide her mock indignation behind her own chuckle.

"Yeah, and fish now live without water," Abby chimes in. Everyone is laughing at this point, any tension that had existed has now been vanquished.

"In all seriousness though, welcome Isabella. Anyone who makes Sara smile as much as you do is very welcome with us."

"Thank you," Isabella responds before looking at me. We smile at each other and share a quick kiss.

"They are so the new you two," I hear Abby say. I don't have to look away to know she's talking to Catherine and Alex. The waiter comes and takes our drink orders and a quiet falls over the table while we all examine our menus. By the time the waiter returns with our cocktails, we're all ready to order, and the conversation resumes as though it never ended. Isabella excuses herself to use the restroom, softly kissing the top of my head as she slides her chair back to the table.

"Good grief Sara, you never said how hot she is." Catherine shoots Alex a look, one we all know is in jest. "What, like I don't have eyes. You aren't worried are you?" Alex wiggles her eyebrows at Catherine.

"Hardly, you aren't going anywhere." They both smile.

"No, I'm not." They share a quick kiss and a quiet whisper that I'm unable to decipher.

"She seems lovely, and as taken with you as you are her," Valerie adds. Isabella returns to the table, lightly running her fingertips across my shoulders as she sits. The getting to know you questioning continues from all angles and by the time the waiter brings our meals I know Isabella has won each one of them over.

"They adore you," I whisper in Isabella's ear under the pretense of feeding her a bite of my Cajun chicken Alfredo. She accepts the offered bite and loads up a bite of her lasagna to offer me.

"Would they still adore me if they knew what I plan on doing to you in that hot tub later?" I feel the warmth between my legs as I take the offered food, my mouth suddenly dry. Isabella grins and goes back to her meal as I roughly swallow the food she just fed me.

"So Isabella, where did Sara take you today?" Valerie's question is innocent enough, but Isabella and I both struggle not to laugh as the last 24 hours flash through both of our minds.

"I knew it, they never even left the house!" Damn that Alex and her all knowing grin.

"I don't remember any of us giving the two of you a hard time when you finally got together."

"That's because we—ouch." Alex's counter argument is cut short by Catherine poking her in the ribs. I hear Abby and Valerie chuckle in response.

"No, we didn't. We holed up at the house and were shut ins. We still are." They smile warmly at each other before Alex turns her attention back to us.

"So Velvet Saturday night then?" Her enthusiasm is infectious.

"If Isabella would like to, then sure."

"What's Velvet?" I would answer, but Isabella wisely addresses Alex, the woman who brought it up.

"Our local lesbian bar. It isn't super fancy, but they have pool tables and we can dance." Alex flashes Isabella her best you know you want to smile. She clearly has yet to learn that Isabella won't be swayed by that.

"Mmm, I do like to watch Sara dance. I'm in."

"Yes," Alex exclaims. "We should invite Derrick, Dahlia, Shannon, Kevin, Nate, Jeff, and Katrina." I feel Isabella stiffen next to me, but she keeps her facial expression static, ensuring that I'm the only one to notice. "Abby you should invite Blake." I rest my hand on Isabella's thigh and squeeze it lightly. She looks over and smiles at me, but I see the anger still burning in her eyes.

"I think I will," Abby responds. I look at her and see her beaming.

"So things are still going well with Blake?" I spend more time with Abby than perhaps anyone else, yet I have to ask the question, I've been so wrapped up in my own head recently that I hadn't thought to inquire.

"Very well. I really like him, and Stella likes him, which is big." I'm happy for Abby, she might be one of the kindest people on the planet, she deserves all the happiness she can find.

"Isabella before I forget, we would love it if you would join us for Sunday brunch as well." Isabella looks at me.

"It's sort of become our tradition, we all go to brunch on Sunday morning. We have a drink, eat too much and just relax before the start of another week. Totally up to you."

"We should do it," Isabella informs me before giving me a quick kiss. Her hand lands on my thigh, and unlike my well behaved, stationary one, hers is anything but.

"Ok ladies, I hate to do this, but I have to get home to Stella."

"Yes, and some of us have to operate in the morning," Catherine says fixing me with a grin.

"If memory serves, you guys always used to tell me I needed to take a vacation or even a day off. Well, I finally listened."

"Yes, and we have Isabella to thank for it." Catherine gives Isabella a warm smile, which Isabella quickly returns. At least she has calmed down some. We settle our check and exit the restaurant en masse. Isabella is quiet on the short ride home. I know what's bothering her, but I'd rather deal with it when I'm not driving. As soon as we enter the house and have kicked off our shoes, I head for the kitchen. I hear Isabella follow me and as I open the cupboard to get a pair of wine glasses, I decide to break the ice on the topic that sits untouched between us.

"So, do you want to—." Isabella has the same idea, and we both start speaking at the same time. "Go ahead," I tell her, hoping she's going to talk about the issue at hand.

"Why haven't you told your friends about Katrina?" Well, at least we're on the same page. I set the glasses down on the counter and take Isabella's hand, leading her over to the dining room table. I turn two of the chairs to face each other and motion for her to sit as I take the other.

"Look, my friends were all there when Katrina kissed me. They all saw what happened, so they all know about it. I haven't really told them anything else, though I'm sure Catherine and maybe even Abby suspect something else transpired at some point. They're both smart, and both know that I wouldn't have just run off to Punta Cana like I did without a reason. I haven't specifically told them anything else because Katrina needs all of the friends she can get right now. What good would it do her for me to tell our mutual friends the gory details? What good would it do me to waste energy on maintaining that negativity? Who wins? I've told you everything. I've been honest with you. When she pulled that stunt that night, it was you that I contacted, because it was you that I wanted to talk to. I'm asking you, please do not tell them. It won't do anyone involved any good." I rub my thumbs over Isabella's knuckles while she processes what I've just asked of her. Finally, she sighs and squeezes my hands.

"You're right, it won't do anyone any good if I reveal this. That doesn't mean that I'm not going to be upset about what she did."

"Thank you. I can't ask you to not be angry, but I wish you could find a way to not be so upset about it. I'm here with you because I want to be with you."

"It isn't that I worry about losing you to her. I just don't like that she disrespected you in that manner."

"I know baby. Do we really want to let this put a damper on our night though?" Isabella's smile is all the answer I need. I stand up and she rises with me. I pull her into my arms and kiss her on the cheek. "My friends adored you tonight."

"I like your friends too. Catherine and Alex are quite the couple." All I can do is laugh because this seems to be everyone's reaction when they meet Catherine and Alex. "What?"

"Nothing, just everyone feels that way. They have quite the story. I'll tell it to you someday." I kiss Isabella quickly before breaking our embrace to retrieve the chilled bottle of wine from the refrigerator. I uncork the bottle and feel Isabella's arms wrap around my waist.

"Why not tell me now?" I set the bottle down before turning around in Isabella's arms. I pull her to me so that I can whisper in her ear.

"I can tell you now, if you'd like. Or you can take me out to the hot tub and do whatever it was you were planning to do." I pull her earlobe between my teeth for added effect.

"Mmm, hot tub please," Isabella moans as she presses her body against mine.

"Good," I whisper, "because I want you." I quickly turn around to grab the wine and the glasses. Isabella groans as she leans into my back before kissing and biting along my neck. "Come on, this isn't the hot tub." Isabella's hands stay on my hips as she follows me out of the kitchen.

Chapter 22

"Baby are you almost ready? I still need to arrange a ride for us." I know that any minute my phone will start going off, asking where we are, plus I feel like I'm starving. I pull my sangria hued v-neck on and button my black jeans. A quick look in the mirror to smooth my hair again and I'm ready to go. Simple has always been my way, even on a night when I'm going out. Besides, the only woman I care to impress is getting ready in my bathroom. I grab my phone and send out the ride request. Isabella isn't one to primp and preen for long, she doesn't need to.

"I'm ready," she informs me as she steps out of the bathroom. My jaw drops when I finally see her in a pair of black skinny jeans and an amber top that snugly fits her form, the fabric crossing over itself at her stomach, the thin straps that show off her clavicles and the plunging neckline that pulls my attention to her perfect breasts. "I take it I look alright." I can hear the slight tone of smugness in her voice, she knows she looks better than alright, but she does enjoy teasing me.

"You look amazing," I observe as I move towards her. We share a quick kiss before heading to the den to wait for our ride. As we head to the entrance, I stop and grab two of my black leather jackets. Isabella looks at me, questioning my actions. "It's warm out now, but by the time we leave Velvet, you may want this." She simply smiles and takes my hand, leading me to the waiting car.

We arrive at the restaurant and are escorted to the side room where they seat larger parties. I introduce Isabella to the friends she has yet to meet and fight off the chuckle I feel when Derrick and Kevin see her. We take our seats, and I realize that I'm relieved that Katrina isn't here.

"What have I gotten myself into," I hear Shannon lament as the waitress walks in with a tray of shots. "I'm way too pregnant, can't drink and now I'll be dealing with you drunken fools all night." She laughs and smiles as a few of us start giving her a hard time. Catherine stands once the waitress has dispersed the shots and taken her leave.

"To our chosen family and all of us being here tonight. Where would we be without one another on the crazy ride called life?" Alex bolts up, stopping us from drinking.

"And welcome to our family Isabella, who seems to have stolen our Wizard of Ta-tas heart." I feel the blood rush to my face as I try to cover it with my free hand. I would crawl under the table right now if I could. I hear the laughter of my friends and feel Isabella's lips connect with my cheek.

"Wizard of Ta-tas?" she whispers in my ear. All I can do is groan.

"You've told everyone haven't you?" I'm not surprised that Alex doesn't show the least bit of remorse.

"Well, now I have. Let's drink!" We all raise our glasses and down our shots.

"It's the nickname Alex gave me long ago," I explain as I lean against Isabella. "I've also been dubbed the Breast Whisperer buy some of the locals."

"Mmm, you certainly know how to talk to them," Isabella murmurs back. I drop my face against her shoulder, trying to bury it from sight. Thankfully the rest of dinner passes without further embarrassment. By the time we leave for Velvet, Isabella is more than holding her own with my friends, and we both have a pleasant buzz going.

We step into Velvet a little later than we intended. It's busy, but we manage to find a table a few seats shy of accommodating all of us. It won't be an issue as we are off to the bar for a drink before we start dancing.

"Hey Sara, who's your new friend?" Sandra asks as she prepares my whiskey sour. Isabella has her arms wrapped around my waist as she jokes around with Alex. My hands fall over Isabella's, and her fingers curl around mine.

"This is Isabella." I squeeze Isabella's fingers pulling her attention back to me. "Baby, this is Sandra."

"Hello. May I have a Manhattan please?"

"Sexy and polite. She looks good on you Sara." Sandra shoots me a wink as she quickly mixes Isabella's drink. "Have fun," Sandra orders as she passes me our drinks. I give her my card to start a tab and grab our drinks, leading Isabella back to our table, where we wait for the rest of our group to join us.

"Come on beautiful, I want to see you dance." Isabella and I both down half our drinks before she leads me to the dance floor. Alex, Catherine, Nate, Jeff, Abby, and Dahlia all follow, and we manage to carve a space out on the floor for ourselves. We dance and dance some more, buzzing around in our group like bees trapped in a hive. We swap partners, laugh and joke, but only Isabella's touch sets my nerve endings ablaze. When the upbeat tempo finally slows down, Isabella and I quickly grab onto each other, neither of us letting the opportunity pass us by.

"Are you having a good time?" I ask, my lips pressed to her ear.

"Yes, I love watching you dance." Her teeth nip at my earlobe, sending a surge of warmth through me.

"Mmm, and I love seeing you in that top."

"If you like the top, you're going to love what I have on underneath it." I nearly lose my footing as she whispers in my ear, but somehow keep from dragging us both to the floor.

"Is that a promise?" Isabella simply rests her forehead against mine and smiles. I gently pull against the back of her neck and meet her halfway, stealing a kiss, extinguishing the feeling that it's been too long since out lips last met. "We need to do this more," I inform her when our lips finally part.

"I agree," she responds, pulling me tightly against her. "Who is that dancing with your friends? She's been watching us all night."

"Our friends," I correct her, spinning us around so I can see who she's referring to, not that I don't already know. I glance over at the rest of our group to see Katrina's gunmetal eyes locked on Isabella and me. I sigh, hoping to not have a situation brewing on my hands.

"That would be Katrina." Isabella's body instantly goes rigid against mine. "Hey, relax. Don't let her ruin our night." The song switches to *Love on the Brain,* and I hope that it helps me diffuse this. "Listen." I wait for a few beats of the song to play out. "Please just be here with me." Isabella locks eyes with me, and I watch some of the fight go out of her. I lock my arms around her neck and pull her lips to mine. She responds by gripping my hips and pulling me into her. I smile against her lips as we continue to kiss, knowing that I've won her over, that right now it's just her and I, it doesn't matter who we came here with or who is watching us. When the song ends, the up-tempo music resumes, and I drag Isabella from the dance floor, needing a drink. We finish our now watery drinks, and I head to the bar to order another round as Isabella heads for the bathroom. There's a short line for her to wait in though, so I take advantage and head to the DJ booth after getting our drinks to make a request.

"Hey, Sara!" Kelly gives me a big hug in greeting before turning back to her equipment. "Don't think I've met your new friend but she certainly has a positive effect on you."

"Thanks, I'm quite fond of her. I was wondering if you could do me a favor though." Kelly smiles as I make my request and promises me she will make it happen. I head back to our table just as Isabella makes her return from the bathroom. She leans in and kisses me as I hand her the fresh drink. We make quick work of them and return to the dance floor, the combination of the alcohol and our hormones making us a little more handsy than we've been thus far. We aren't alone though, Alex and Catherine are positively plastered to one another. Finally, the tempo slows down again, and Etta James starts belting out *A Sunday Kind of Love*. Isabella smiles at me and pulls me closer to her.

"You made this happen, didn't you?" She rests her head on my shoulder, her lips against my neck.

"I might have," I reply, the feeling of Isabella smiling against my neck sending chills along my spine. I squeeze her tight and close my eyes, letting my head fall onto her shoulder, absorbing everything the moment has to offer. "You know, I think Alex may have been right. I think you've stolen my heart." It's sappy, romantic and not at all like me. I could blame the alcohol, but it wouldn't matter, it's true and I know it. Isabella's head leaves my shoulder, and her hand finds my face, lifting it from hers, cradling it, so we are starting into each other's eyes. Her thumb brushes over my lips and then my cheekbone as her eyes bore into mine, searching for my truth.

"I promise to take good care of it," Isabella vows before kissing me. My heart melts, flowing with the rest of my blood throughout my body. "I will be leaving mine here with you," she whispers against my ear. Now it's my turn to back up a little, to force the eye contact.

"I swear it will be safe." We finish the song in silence, clinging to one another, just being together.

"Will everyone be upset if we get out of here?"

"I don't think so, why are you not having fun?"

"I am, I just want to get you home so we can be alone." I'm sold on the plan and have no problem ordering a ride to take us home. "It will be about half an hour. I'll get us one last round to drink while we tell everyone good night."

"Thank you," she says wrapping her hand around my neck to pull me in for another kiss. Our drinks in tow and my tab closed we head over to the table, where, unsurprisingly, most of us are ready to call it a night. We finish our drinks and head outside to wait for our rides and say our goodnights. Everyone hugs Isabella goodbye, telling me that they all loved her.

We share a ride back to the house with Catherine and Alex since their stop is a few minutes before ours. This driver is used to us and therefore isn't thrown by seeing two pairs of women being overly affectionate in the back of his SUV. Isabella and I occupy the very back seat, giving us the slight illusion of privacy.

"About what you said, what we said, I want you to know that I meant it. If I truly have your heart, I swear I will take care of it. Either way, I will be leaving mine here when I leave."

"I meant it as well. You have it, and I trust you to take care of it, just as I promise to keep yours safe. I don't want to see you hurt."

"Mmm, that is very sweet, but it doesn't exactly fit with my plan for the night."

"Oh?" I question, grinning at Isabella.

"Definitely not, tonight I plan to get a little long overdue revenge for that incident at the lagoon." Her words cause heat to surge through my body and moisture to leak from between my lips.

"Mmm, I'm happy to let you fuck me tonight. Do your worst." Isabella arches an eyebrow at that challenge, she recognizes it.

"You should be careful, I've had time to plan this." I have yet to find my body not ready for Isabella. I feel like I'm always aching for her at the simplest touch. Yet she hasn't touched me, just her words and the piercing stare full of intent are enough to cause what feels like a flood in my panties. When her lips claim mine, I'm certain that I will come undone as a moan escapes my mouth to be trapped in Isabella's. I can feel Catherine and Alex's eyes on us, and vaguely hear their soft giggles as Isabella wraps me in the spell she is so deftly weaving, her fingers never leaving the sides of my face. When she finally pulls away from me, tugging my lower lip with her, I'm left panting and wanting more. "See baby, I don't even have to touch you and you're burning for me," she murmurs against my ear, the soft caress of her breath giving me gooseflesh. Isabella is right, I don't bother trying to deny her claim. Instead, I try to satisfy the urge tearing through my body, not caring about the driver or that Catherine and Alex are sitting just a few feet in front of us. I take one of the hands Isabella has pressed to my face and lower it downward, pressing her fingers against the seam of my jeans, grinding my hips slightly, trying to encourage her to touch me. Isabella pulls her hand away and flashes me a fiendish grin. I decide to try another tactic and place my hand against the crotch of her jeans. Without hesitation she begins working herself against my hand, slowly moving her hips as she chews her lower lip. Her free hand reaches up and pulls me to her, placing my ear in front of her mouth. "Do you want me to come for you baby, because I will," she gasps, her hand dropping over mine, forcing more pressure against her sex. She begins to work herself more firmly against the press of my fingers, and her panting picks up in my ear.

"Ahem," Catherine clears her throat. Clearly, she and Alex have some inclination what's happening behind them. I realize we've stopped, that we have finally made it to Catherine and Alex's place. "You two have a beautiful night," Catherine winks at us as she and Alex exit the ride.

"See you at brunch," I manage to articulate, happy that my voice isn't as throaty as I imagined it would be. Alex wiggles her eyebrows at us, but Catherine shuts the door and pulls her away before she can say anything. Just a few more minutes and we will be back at my place. Somehow we manage to behave during the short ride, but as soon as the driver stops in my driveway, I practically pull Isabella into the house. I barely have the door shut behind us when I pounce on her, pushing her against the wall and clamping my mouth on hers, my tongue demanding entry. Isabella allows it, but her hands grip my wrists when I try to slide them under her shirt.

"I'm in charge tonight, remember?" She pushes herself off of the wall and slides the leather jacket from her shoulders. I do the same and return them to the closet. Isabella has made her way to the kitchen where I find her filling two glasses with water. I coil my arms around her waist and run my nose along the nape of her neck, her messy bun allowing me access. I take in her scent, now mixed with sweat from dancing for hours. I feel my heart expand and know I'm totally falling for this woman, despite our initial intentions or the fact that our situation feels impossible at times. I grab two fistfuls of her shirt, and her hands close over mine.

"I can't take you rejecting me much longer," I protest before lightly running the tip of my tongue along the back of her neck, making Isabella moan. Her hands tighten over mine as she arches herself into me.

"I'm not rejecting you, I'm making you wait. Drink this and follow me," she orders, handing me a glass of water and heading towards the bedroom. I anxiously follow her, dying to get my hands on her body. She finally pulls me to her and kisses me, it starts soft and slow but quickly evolves into the two of us hungrily attacking each other. Isabella raises the bottom of my shirt separating us to pull it off. My nipples already protrude against the fabric of my bra when Isabella's hands land on my breasts as she kisses me again. I try to lift off her shirt, but she stops everything, her hands on my forearms as she stares at me and shakes her head. She backs me up to the bed as she unbuttons my jeans and presses them downward. When I feel the mattress against the back of my thighs, I sit down and allow her to pull them off. "If you need to take care of anything, do it now. You won't be free for a while."

Isabella unhooks my bra and guides the straps off of my shoulders.

"I'm good," I whisper. Isabella grins and presses me backward, laying me on the bed. She hooks her fingers in the waist of my silk panties and slowly slides them off, the cool air connecting with my soaked sex. I slide back onto the bed, and she glides her fully clothed body over my naked flesh, her clothing feeling abrasive against my extra sensitive skin. She straddles my waist and skims her palm up my abdomen and between my breasts. Her thumb brushes my lips as she gazes down at me, the lust in her eyes mixed with adoration.

"I looked through your toys the other morning. It took me a minute to figure out where you secure these." She leans forward, her breasts landing near my lips. I greedily tongue and bite at her nipple, wishing she at least wasn't wearing her top, no matter how sexy she looks in it. She grins down at me as she pulls my hand off of her waist, securing the leather cuff around my wrist, the soft lining a welcome sensation against my flesh. I hear the rattle of the chain as she reveals the second cuff and secures my other hand. She grins at me again before pressing her lips to mine, her hands reaching down to tease my nipples, making them harder than they already were. I struggle against the restraints, a useless fight. I placed the eyebolts in the head and footboards of my sleigh bed, I know they won't yield. Isabella laughs as she pulls away from me, sliding down to the foot of the bed, where she secures my feet, spreading me out as if I'm about to be drawn and quartered. My body hums with anticipation, awaiting Isabella's next move, only she just stands at the foot of the bed, staring at me.

Isabella grins at me, cockiness rising to the surface. "Do you have any idea what it does to me to see you like this?" If she is half as wet as I am then yeah, I do.

Isabella licks her lips before slowly raising the amber colored top over her head, revealing a black lace bra underneath. The straps are so narrow they barely exist and the fabric so thin I can see the dark pigmenting of her areolae under it. If she comes near me now, I know I will try to chew through the lace to get to her nipples. She smiles as my jaw clenches. I've clearly given her the reaction that she was hoping for thus far. "Do you know what the sensation of your hands on my body feels like to me?" Isabella slowly glides her hands up her sides and stops on her breasts. She slowly kneads them and teases her nipples through the thin lace, her lips parting and soft gasps escaping as her ministrations grow more intense. "Do you know that when we are apart, I think about your hands on me?" She becomes more aggressive with her breasts, eliciting a soft cry from herself. Her hand slides down to the button of her jeans and opens it, allowing her fingers to slide inside and downward. "Do you know that I think about you licking and fucking me when I pleasure myself?" This time I groan as I feel my own moisture start to trickle between my cheeks. Isabella withdraws her hand and undoes the zipper of her jeans. She slowly pushes the black denim off of her hips revealing a black garter belt set, the waist strap no more than an inch wide, the black lace forming a tapering triangle downward to clasp the black stockings, her underwear more barely there black lace. All I can do is stare at the breathtaking woman before me and marvel at what I ever did to deserve her here with me. She turns her back to me and heads to the closet, revealing the two matching triangles in the back and the thin thong strap resting between her cheeks. I can see her muscles working with every step. She obscures her selection from my view and deposits it at the foot of the bed, folding it underneath the comforter to keep the identity secret. Her fingernails drag up my leg and over my stomach as she makes her way to the head of the bed, where she releases all four clasps on the stockings and smoothly drags the thong downward, stepping out of it once it falls to her ankles. "I know you're dying to touch me right now," her fingers trail downward, and she rubs them through her folds, "to see how wet I am, to taste me." She brings her fingers to my lips and rubs her moisture on them like lip balm. The scent of her sex hits me, and I instinctively lick my lips, tasting her there. She's right, I want more, but when I open my eyes, she's already retreating to the foot of the bed. She climbs on the bed, positioning herself between my splayed legs, opening herself wide so that I can see all of her. My arms fight against the restraints, I long to bury my fingers deep inside her as I lick at the pool of mana I know is there. Isabella's right hand reaches over and grabs the toy she secreted away, one of my vibrators. "Do you know what it does to me when you look at me like that?" She drags the toy along her folds a few times, spreading her juices, before switching it on. This is a whole new level of tangled pleasure and torture. Watching Isabella pleasure herself is so damn hot, but seeing it within arms reach, if my arms weren't bound, is borderline cruel. Her head tips back as she starts teasing herself, slowly running the tip up her folds before circling her clit and repeating the pattern. Her breaths come faster and her hips start undulating, the more excited she becomes.

"Isabella," I growl, fighting the restraints. She tips her head up and looks at me, but doesn't stop the work she is doing with the toy in her hands.

"Do you know what would be better than this?"

"My tongue in your pussy?" She smiles at my retort and pulls the toy away. I'm secretly praying to deities I don't believe in that she will smother my face with her sex, and when she starts crawling up my body, I'm certain that she will. Only Isabella stops her progress with her sex lingering over my pubis. She angles the vibrator downward and starts grinding herself against it as she stares down at me. I was wrong before, this is worse than simply watching her. Now her skin is making contact with mine, and she is close enough that I can smell her excitement.

"Oh Sara," she moans as her hips work faster, her nipples straining against the bra, her head dropping back and her eyes closing. Her free hand starts pinching and twisting her nipple, and that is when I know, she's close, and she fully intends to make herself come while she straddles me. I'm powerless to help or stop her. Her muscles tighten, and her hips arch forward, but she's much quieter than what I'm accustomed to her being.

"Sounds like I do a better job," I taunt her when she finally opens her eyes. She presses the vibrator to my lips to further tease and silence me. I gladly clean her juices off it, desperate to taste or touch her by any means that I can, even if it's indirectly. I groan as her flavor fully hits my taste buds, and Isabella greedily withdraws the toy. She switches it back on, and I think she will start pleasuring herself again, but she rolls it over one of my nipples and then the other, drawing them both to attention. She alternates between the two until my hips arch upward into her. My clit is throbbing when she finally climbs off of me. I watch her retreat back to the closet where she pulls on the harness and navy blue dildo, but when she turns back to me, I see that isn't the only thing she's bringing with her. In her right hand she holds my black leather riding crop. She drags the smooth leather along my leg, giving me playful swats as she moves higher and higher. She brings it up to my face, tilting my chin upward with it before resting it against my lips. I lock eyes with her making sure she knows that I'm not afraid, that nothing about this scares me. She slowly lowers the crop, letting it skim my flesh until she reaches my right nipple. She brushes the leather over my erect flesh before bringing the crop down on it. She moves to the left side and repeats her actions, causing me to groan as more moisture leaks out of me. She repeats this three times per nipple, until I am gasping for breath and bright red patches stand out against my areolae. She allows me to catch my breath as she teases my abdomen and sides with the leather, only giving playful swats here and there. Without warning, she winds up and smacks the side of my ass. The sting of the leather causing me to suck air through my clenched teeth, the pain only escalating my level of arousal. She does it again, and even though I can't see her handiwork, I can feel the welts throbbing on the tender flesh. She trails the crop even lower, teasing it along my thighs and I know where she's headed next. I don't object. The soft taps of the leather against my labia echo through my body as my head falls back, the sensation of lightning shooting through my clit.

"Please, Isabella." I can't finish the thought, I'm so turned on that my synapses refuse to fire, my speaking ability has been disabled. Isabella smiles as she climbs back onto the bed, once again straddling me, the dildo lying against my stomach. Her hand reaches up and cups my face as she leans down to kiss me. It isn't a rushed hungry kiss like I would expect. Instead, it's slow and almost apologetic, which isn't necessary. She slowly works her way down to my nipples and gently runs her tongue over them, as if it were leaving a soothing balm in its wake. She kisses her way lower and gently blows on my sex, causing me to lift my hips towards her mouth. Then she pounces, locking her mouth on my sex, rolling her tongue around my clit. I could come now if I allowed myself to, but I fight it, wanting this to last longer. Her tongue slides into my pussy and swirls. She moans as she tastes my desire and it reverberates through my body. My hips arch upward again, and Isabella knows to pull away. She turns and frees my ankles. My pussy pulses knowing she is finally going to fuck me. "Slow," I tell her when she locks eyes with me, she doesn't ask for clarification, she knows how turned on I am and anything but slow will end this too soon. Her fingers connect with my slit, gathering lubricant for the dildo. When she's satisfied, she positions it at my entrance and looks at me.

"Ready?" I smile at her and nod that I am. She watches as she slowly slides the toy inside of me then drapes her body over mine, kissing me once she rests on her elbows. She breaks the kiss, rests her forehead against mine and slowly rocks her hips, pulling the toy out and then pushing it back in. Even the slightest movement of Isabella inside me has me on edge. She must sense it because she waits a few moments before doing it again. My nerves have calmed enough that it doesn't threaten to end this, so I kiss her. She slowly builds her rhythm, our eyes staying locked on each other the entire time. The fire quickly rages in me, and this time I have no desire to fight it.

"Yes baby, more," I command as I hook my legs around her ass, pulling her further into me each time I thrust my hips upward to meet her. I can feel the sweat drip off of her abdomen onto mine as her gaze blazes into me, her grunts turning me on even more. "Don't stop," I gasp as I feel the first signs of my orgasm set in. Isabella starts pounding into me, relentlessly bringing me to my peak, my body arching into her as I come, screaming out my bliss as she watches me. When I finally come down enough to comprehend what's happening, Isabella is plying light kisses on my cheeks, lips, nose, and forehead. She gazes at me when my muscles stop twitching, withdrawing the toy without breaking our eye contact.

"I…," she starts but stops herself or loses her thought. Her expression one I haven't seen before. I want to encourage her to finish her thought, but I still haven't found my voice. Her eyes leave mine as she frees my hands, and I can't help but feel like a moment has been lost. I wrap my arms around Isabella and pull her to me, holding her as I try to regain some of my stamina. I feel totally spent, but there's no way I plan to sleep before I give her a proper orgasm. Isabella is so still, her breathing so even, I wonder if she's fallen asleep on top of me as my fingers trace a path over her back.

"Are you awake baby?" I whisper, not wanting to disturb her if she fell asleep. I feel the slight shake of her torso as she giggles against my shoulder. She turns her head and kisses me just below my ear.

"Of course. That just feels so good I don't want to move." She picks up her head to look me in the eyes, where I see pure mischief. "Plus I like having you underneath me," she teases as she wiggles her hips, the toy still resting between my thighs.

"Alright Lotharia, time to let me up," I announce, slapping her ass. She groans in protest but rolls off of me, sliding the harness off as I leave the comfort of the bed.

"Where are you going?" Isabella is crazy if she thinks I'm leaving her. I head to the closet and pull the french vanilla scented massage oil from the shelf. I turn and see Isabella reclining on the bed in the lingerie she wore for me, the lamp light casting a soft glow over her bronzed skin. I gaze upon her for a minute before turning back to the closet and grabbing a dental damn. There are few things at this point Isabella and I haven't tried, but this is one of them.

"You look amazing, but I want you to take that off." Isabella reaches behind her back and unclasps her bra, slowly sliding it down her arms and casting it aside as I slide back onto the bed, kneeling between her feet. I reach up and unhook the belt from the stockings before slowly sliding each one off, the sensation of my fingers against her skin feels electrifying. With the stockings off

319

the only thing remaining is the belt. I run my fingertips up the outside of her legs as I make my way to the belt, my eyes locked on Isabella's. Her lips part slightly as my light touch inches up her legs and runs over her hips. She lifts her bottom off of the bed as I slide my hands around her and unclasp the hooks, removing the belt. I slide my body up over hers, letting our flesh connect at every opportunity.

"Why is the feel of your skin against mine so intense?" She whispers the question in my ear, sending chills down my spine.

"I don't know," I briefly plant my lips against hers, "but I feel it too." I kiss her again, allowing this one to intensify when Isabella traces her tongue over my lips. "I thought it would dissipate, but it only seems to grow." I skim my fingertips over her lips before kissing her one last time. "Roll over," I instruct her. She smiles at me and obeys, allowing me to straddle her just below her shapely ass. She releases a soft murmur of pleasure as I run my hands over her back, depositing myself against her as I reach higher and higher. I pepper kisses over her exposed shoulder and up her neck until I reach her ear. "Don't fall asleep on me baby," I whisper.

"I won't," her muffled voice informs me. I slide back up to a sitting position, slowly working my hands down her back. I squirt some of the massage oil into my hands and rub them together to warm it before starting to massage Isabella's shoulders.

"Mmmm." Is the only sound that escapes Isabella. I keep rubbing her exquisite flesh, now glistening from the oil, and enjoy the sounds of her moans. I slowly work my way down her back, adding more oil when necessary, the vanilla scent of the oil mixing perfectly with her natural aroma, her moans letting me know she appreciates my efforts.

"You still with me baby?" I ask as my hands return to her shoulders. I lean down and kiss along her neck as my hands continue massaging her. She surprises me by turning her head and taking a handful of my hair to guide my lips to hers. Our kiss is drawn out, filled with emotion that reverberates throughout my body. Isabella tries to roll over, but I prevent it, wanting to continue what I had originally planned. Our lips part and I give her a shy smile before focusing my full attention on her back once again. I take my time working, this time rubbing the oil into her buttocks, causing Isabella to arch them into my hands. I lean in to run the tip of my tongue along the base of her spine, the scent of her excitement overtaking the sensual scent of the oil. I sit up and watch as I finally allow my hand to fall between her legs, gently caressing her outer lips. I repeat the tease time and again, loving the sounds of Isabella's moans and feeling her try to push harder against my fingers. I finally relent and slip my fingers inside her folds where a large puddle of her desire greets me. She releases her loudest moan yet as I draw some of her fluid down, circling her nub a few times before softly flicking it.

"Yes," Isabella pants as she arches into my fingers. I quickly switch to my left hand, which feels foreign yet necessary, and easily slide two fingers inside of Isabella. "Please fuck me," she groans, as she pushes back, drawing my fingers further into her. I smile even though she can't see it and slowly withdraw my fingers, collecting as much of her juices as I can. She groans in protest and attempts to move, but I steady her with my hand on her lower back. I slowly draw my soaked fingers up over her taint and gently massage her anus. I feel her tighten as she looks back at me.

"Relax. I'm going to fuck you, but what if I give you a rim job first?" I slowly lower my fingers down over her taint and draw them up again to circle around her tight hole, maintaining eye contact with her. "I'll never do anything to you that you don't want me to. If you aren't ok with this or ready for it, just tell me, and I'll stop." Isabella turns and lowers her head again, a low moan escaping her as my fingers continue their gentle onslaught. Accepting this as consent I grab one of the pillows and reposition myself between her now spread legs. "Lift your hips," I instruct. She quickly obeys, allowing me to slide the pillow beneath them. I unwrap the dental dam and spread her cheeks a little further with one hand as I place the barrier with the other. I place one hand on each of her cheeks as I lower myself, my shins resting on the footboard of my bed. I slip my tongue between Isabella's folds, groaning as I taste her, continuing to lick upward over her taint and around her anus. I take my right hand and use my fingers to spread more of her juices on the barrier, wanting to taste Isabella as I do this. When the latex glistens with her mana, I reapply my tongue, savoring her flavor enough to moan against her. I feel her press back against me and know that she's enjoying this. I continue my assault, gradually increasing my pace and the pressure I apply. When I can no longer taste Isabella, I move lower, licking upward again starting at her clit, stopping to stick my tongue in her pussy. "You taste so fucking good that I'll never get enough of you," I inform her before running my tongue back over her taint. This time when I reach her hole I run my tongue around it a few times before probing inward as I dig my fingers into her cheeks.

"Oh god," Isabella purrs as she arches into me. I swirl my tongue around before withdrawing and inserting it again. I repeat this over and over and Isabella's pelvis rocks back meeting my strokes. I quickly sink down again and lavish some brief attention on her clit before lapping up more of her juices and refocusing on her ass. This time I'm relentless, I want her to come so I can roll her over and fuck her. Her moans of pleasure have worked like a shot of adrenaline on me, I no longer remember feeling spent, now I just want to pleasure her time and again. I run my tongue over her repeatedly, letting her movements, moans, heavy breathing and words of encouragement fuel me. She buries her face in the mattress when she finally comes, her ass arching up as I continue probing and swirling around her. When her hips fall back onto the pillow, I toss the dental dam on the floor and lay my body over hers, linking my fingers through hers above her head. When her breathing steadies, I climb off of her and head to the closet grabbing the large red marbled dildo with the clit tickler extension. I return to the bed and grab the harness, dropping the previously used dildo to the floor and inserting my selection before I slip the harness on. Isabella eyes me as she rolls over, tossing the pillow from under her hips out of our way. I position myself between her spread legs and lower my mouth to her, needing to taste her again. I lavish attention on her clit, only stopping when I know she will come if I don't. I sit up and start rubbing the head of the toy along her slit, her flooding juices providing ample lubrication, the tickler stimulating my clit with even the slightest movement of the dildo.

"I want to come with you baby," I whisper as I position the tip against her entrance.

"Then lay down," she orders, sitting up and putting her hands on my shoulders. I don't even pause to think about it. I love watching Isabella ride me as I fuck her and she knows it. I feel a surge of wetness escape me as she swings her leg over me and positions her entrance over the toy. I grip the shaft in one hand as I run my fingertips over her torso. I watch as she slowly lowers herself onto me, the toy filling her. She leans down and kisses me once she is fully astride me, allowing herself to adjust to the fullness. The kiss continues as she slowly starts working herself on the shaft, the movement stimulating my clit, causing us to moan into each other's mouths as our tongues probe and swirl. My hands grip Isabella's hips as I slide my knees up allowing me to thrust into her a little more, each thrust increasing our pleasure.

"Hold on baby, we can make this better." Isabella is panting as she slides off of the toy. I quickly get on my knees and pull her to me. She wraps her arms around my neck, and I guide the toy back inside her.

"Mmm, Sara," she moans, her nipples rubbing against my lips. Each of her thrusts sends a shockwave into my throbbing clit. I work my hips with her, grinding over the tickler as she raises and lowers herself on the shaft. When I know I'm getting close I start stimulating her clit with my thumb as I pull one of her bouncing nipples into my mouth. "Fuck baby, don't stop!" Isabella starts working the shaft even faster, and I feel my own orgasm threaten to take hold. She lowers her hand to my breast and starts roughly pulling and twisting my nipple. "I'm going to come, baby. Fuck me harder and let go with me." I drive into her as hard as I can while continuing to stimulate her clit. Her nipple slips free from my lips as my climax sets in. We scream each other's names as we both come, our muscles clenching as we cling tightly to one another. We hold each other until the trembling stops, neither of us saying a word.

"That was amazing," Isabella whispers as she loosens her grip on me, rising up off of the toy. I slip off the harness and lay back as Isabella smothers my body with hers, her head nuzzled into my neck as I stare at the ceiling. Her fingers stroke my face as I lose myself in thought. I'm not sure if my heartbeat betrays me or my muscles stiffen, but Isabella sits up and looks at me with concern in her eyes. "What is it baby?" She continues to stroke my face as I try to formulate an answer that won't sound crazy. I've known for a while but admitting this to myself, much less Isabella is frightening.

"I'm completely falling for you," I tell her, never looking away from her beautiful eyes, the ones I see in my dreams.

"I've already fallen for you," she whispers. My heart feels like the real life version of the Grinch's when it grew three times its size in one day. I can admit that I'm scared of this feeling, but I don't want to run from it. I can feel tears threatening to spill from my eyes, so I press my lips to hers and pull her tightly against me. We lay there clinging to each other, sharing tender kisses and talking until one, or perhaps both of us, finally falls asleep.

Chapter 23

I arrive at the office earlier than usual on Tuesday morning. I miss Isabella with a ferocity that I didn't think possible. We attended brunch on Sunday as planned before quickly retreating back to my house where we made love continuously until I had to take her to the airport on Monday. Now I see reminders of her everywhere, I smell her on the pillowcase I refuse to launder, and her sketchbook and the art within it do little to fill the void I feel. I won't see her until Thanksgiving, which I've already had Abby clear and have booked my flight. Several long weeks stand between now and our reunion. I decide to cope the only way I know how, by working and exercising even harder. I'm looking over the schedule to see where I can bump some things up and add on additional cases when Abby finally strolls in.

"Good morning! How was the rest of your weekend?" She smiles at me before taking a sip from her travel cup, which I assume contains her usual tea.

"Amazing." I return her smile before I feel my forehead contract. "Why do I have another long weekend booked in October?" I stare at the schedule trying to figure out why I only have one case in the OR that Wednesday and nothing until the following Tuesday in the office. I don't remember having a conference.

"Over your birthday right?" I check the dates again and realize that it indeed is over my birthday.

"Yeah." I look at Abby hoping she knows why.

"Catherine told me to block it off, said they're taking you to Chicago for your birthday. I figured you knew." I sigh as I sit back in my chair. "Ok, you didn't know. Are you upset?"

"No. It's hard to be upset when someone wants to do something nice for you." I feel guilty for wishing I could use the time to go see Isabella instead of going to Chicago.

"It isn't like you to look more than a week or so ahead. You're going to throw yourself into your work again aren't you?"

"Yeah. You won't be obligated to stay late though. I just need the distraction."

"Alright. I'll look into it for you. You know you're always welcome to play soccer mom with me while I tote Stella around to her games." I should make it to one of Stella's games soon, it's been too long.

"Did you book a vacation for yourself?"

"Not yet. Blake and I are talking about it though." Her smile is infectious. Despite feeling sorry for myself, I can't help but return it.

"Sounds like you two are getting serious."

"We are. I really like him. Plus he survived a night out with our little clan and had a good time." I smile because I'm genuinely happy for Abby. "My parents said they'll watch Stella, we just have to pick a destination." I start concocting a plan in my mind, helping me to maintain my smile. "Ok, I've got a few things to set up in the cosmetic clinic. I'll let you know what I figure out as far as rearranging things goes."

"Abby." She stops in the doorway and turns to look at me. "Don't worry about it. Exhaustion isn't the way for me to deal with this." She steps back into the office, closing the door behind her.

"Are you ok?"

"I won't see her for nearly two months. I already miss her." Abby sets her cup down and moves around my desk. She pulls me in for one of her comforting hugs. I never had a sibling, but I think of Abby like a sister.

"Isn't love great? It might be the only thing that can leave you feeling totally full and empty at the same time." I feel my body tighten when Abby tosses out love like that. "Relax, I know you don't use that word, but we all saw it. You love her." Abby releases me, picks up her tea and heads out of my office. I need to see my first patient of the day, but I delay, hoping to connect with Isabella.

"Twice in one morning!" Her smile lights up my screen.

"Hey, gorgeous. I wish I could stay and chat, but I need to ask a favor." Isabella arches an eyebrow but continues to smile.

"Is this where you ask me to take off my shirt?" She teases, but I can see her hands lowering, she'll do it if I don't stop her.

"I wish," I groan. "I was wondering how the resort looks over Thanksgiving. I need a suite for two." Isabella's hands drop, and her smile disappears.

"For two? Why do you need a suite for two? I thought you were coming to see me over your holiday."

"I am baby, it's the one thing I'm looking forward to." I smile at her and her smile returns. "I told Abby to take a vacation while I'm gone. She and Blake are talking about taking one together, they just need to figure out a destination. It's pretty romantic at your little paradise. I'd like to take care of it for them. If you have something, make the arrangements and I'll give you the payment information."

"No problem. Do you really have to go?"

"I do, I'm late for my first patient." I try to smile but feel it falter.

"Ok. I miss you."

"I miss you too. I'll talk to you later. Have a good day." I disconnect the chat, hopeful that something will work out at the resort.

*****

I manage to get out of the office just after six. I'm exhausted, so I stop for some falafel and hummus take out on the way home. I eat while I go through my mail and finish charting for the day. I try to connect with Isabella once I've caught up, but she doesn't answer. Suddenly I feel like I have too much pent up energy, so I go for a swim, hauling my laptop and phone with me. The only message waiting for me when I finish is a text from Catherine asking if I'd like to get dinner tomorrow night since Alex will be working late. I double check my surgery schedule for the day and let her know that I'd love to, that I should finish up by six a the latest, that we can touch base in the morning. I try connecting with Isabella again but get no answer. I take a quick shower and blow dry my hair before curling up to read. It's nearly 10 when I check the clock again. I try Isabella one more time but get nothing. My heart sinks. This is the first night we haven't spoken since we started this. I switch off the lamp and find myself tossing and turning, the scent of Isabella on the pillow next to me a constant reminder of what I'm missing. I pull it tightly to me trying to pretend that I'm holding her but the lacking body heat and heartbeat make it impossible.

I wake up when the alarm starts blaring out the annoying beeping buzzing hybrid sound that's so irritating that I always jump out of bed to silence it. I immediately open my laptop and try to reach Isabella, again getting no answer. I start to wonder if I've done something wrong, or if something is wrong. I go for another swim in an attempt to clear my mind. It doesn't work. I shower and eat a small breakfast before forcing myself out the door.

"Still want to get dinner tonight?" Catherine asks as I head towards my locker.

"Yeah." I'm still distracted by the Isabella situation.

"What about Thai food?"

"Sure."

"And drinks of course."

"Ok."

"Afterwards we can go back to yours, Alex doesn't need to know."

"Sounds good."

"Sara." I feel Catherine's hand on my shoulder. I'm standing in front of my open locker just staring into it. "Have you been listening to anything I've asked you?"

"Uh…" Catherine starts laughing.

"I thought not when you agreed that we could have sex at yours tonight." I feel the blood rush to my face. "Everything ok?"

"Yeah, I'm being crazy, I'm sure." Catherine raises her eyebrows at me. "I haven't spoken to Isabella since early yesterday morning. It's the first time we haven't spoken before bed or in the morning. Just being paranoid and dramatic, panicking that I did or said something wrong."

"I'm sure everything is fine. Maybe she just went to bed early or wasn't feeling well. You'll talk to her today."

"You're probably right," I agree, even though my unease doesn't fade a bit.

"Stop driving yourself mad. She's crazy about you, trust me." I smile at Catherine before turning back to my locker to get changed. "So is Thai food really ok tonight?"

"Sure, sounds good. I'll text you when I finish up."

*****

Catherine and I deposit ourselves in the booth the server leads us to. I order a whiskey sour, Catherine orders a martini and two ice waters. "Thanks for driving."

"Of course. I figured you might want to have more than one while we're here. Still no word?"

"None. I tried between cases and before you picked me up." I glance at my phone, willing it to light up. I know it's rude, but I can't help it.

"Did you argue about something?"

"No. I talked to her before going into the office yesterday morning, like we do every morning. I talked to her again before seeing my first patient to ask her for a favor, she said she missed me and that was it." My mind wanders, thinking of the dozen scenarios that could have happened and I would never know. Is Isabella hurt, did something happen to her, have I upset her in some way, did she meet someone else? The waitress brings our drinks and we both order spicy Pad Thai, mine with chicken, Catherine's with beef.

"Whatever you're imagining is probably far worse than the reality. I'm sure you'll talk to her tonight."

"I hope so." I sigh as Catherine reaches across the table and squeezes my hand. "How did you know that you were in love with Alex?" Catherine takes a sip of her martini before answering.

"That's tricky. Looking back I'm certain that I was in love with her well before I would even admit to myself that I had feelings for her. It took me too long to realize that. I could have lost the best thing to ever happen to me before I ever accepted its existence." Catherine takes a bigger sip from her drink, likely remembering things she'd rather forget. "I know this is terrifying for you to admit, but you love her." I down half my drink in one go, signaling the waitress for another.

"I know I do." I feel deflated, not only do I have no clue where Isabella is, but I've also admitted that I love her, giving life to the feelings that I've been trying to rationalize.

"Well at least you don't deny it. Honestly, everyone could see it at dinner and Velvet. You look at her differently than any of us have ever seen you look at someone before. You should tell her."

"Yeah. I guess when I see her over the holiday. I don't want to do it over video the first time." The waitress deposits my new drink on the table and informs us our food should be right out.

"You won't see her before then?"

"No. We have the women's health expo next weekend, then you guys are taking me to Chicago. I can't schedule any more time away before then."

"Thanksgiving will be here before you know it," Catherine reassures me as she squeezes my hand again. The waitress delivers our food and confirms things look correct before leaving us. "I'm curious, so please forgive my asking, but what happened between you and Katrina?" I sigh as I force myself to eat another bite of the food I have no appetite for.

"I'll tell you if you promise you won't change how you treat her. You're my friend, and you've become friends with her, which I'm fine with. I don't want anyone taking sides here."

"Of course." I unleash a heavy sigh before rehashing the gory details for Catherine. She listens attentively as she continues to eat, allowing me to pause occasionally to take another sip from my drink. I've completely forgotten about my meal at this point and know I'll have it boxed up for lunch tomorrow.

"Good grief. You didn't tell anyone about any of that?" she asks when I finish recounting the gory details.

"Just Isabella. I promised her transparency and honesty, so she knows everything. I haven't spoken to Katrina since I threw her out of my room. Honestly, I don't want to. I feel like she's back sliding or something. I don't know. Am I concerned for her? Absolutely. But I can't make her my problem like I did before."

"Understandable. It won't change anything, but I think she does care about you, she just can't handle those feelings right now. She's lashing out in her own way. We're trying to convince her to go back to Dr. Sutton. She says she will, but I'm not sure if she has."

"I'm glad you guys are looking out for her. I hope she accepts some help." I finish my second drink and want a third but refrain, knowing I'll regret it tomorrow if I do. "Gods this is the most depressing dinner ever." Catherine and I both start laughing, the way great friends can even when things truly suck. "So tell me about this trip to Chicago. Don't be cross with Abby, I questioned the time being blocked out on my schedule."

"Not to worry, Abby is a gem. You know, it's Chicago. We'll have a ladies weekend, food, drinks, dancing, shopping, meet some of my friends, just go have fun like we have before. Did you have other plans?"

"No. I appreciate you thinking of me. It's nice to be thought of." Catherine and I chat a little while longer before I have the waitress box up my barely touched meal and we depart. She drops me at home and I brush my teeth before crawling into bed. I want to try connecting with Isabella but I can't take another empty attempt, so I simply shut off the lamp and try to sleep.

*****

Like a glutton for punishment, I try reaching Isabella again before heading into the office. I trudge through my morning appointments, trying to inject some happiness into my demeanor. Abby knocks on my closed door during lunch while I play with my leftovers, not bothering to eat. "Want to talk about it?"

"Not really," I respond, not bothering to look away from the takeout container. Thankfully Abby doesn't press. I see her leave my office in my peripheral view, and hear the door click shut behind her. The afternoon drags on and I become certain that the energy expenditure required to fake some level of happiness with my clients is a bigger drain than my personal concerns. Once I've seen my last patient, I shut myself in my office again and finish my charting instead of doing it at home over dinner. I look at my scheduled cases for tomorrow and realize that we're only doing one case due to needing to be at the convention center to prepare for the expo. A knock on my door pulls my attention away from staring at the monitor. "Come in," I call out wondering who it is. I thought I was alone in the office at this point.

"You staying over night?" Valerie leans against the doorframe and smiles at me.

"No. I'll probably head home soon." I realize it doesn't matter if I stay here or go home, I'm still going to be fixated on why I haven't spoken to Isabella.

"Everything ok?" Valerie's face shows nothing but concern as she makes her way toward the chairs in front of my desk.

"Fine. How are things going for you?"

"Great. Looking forward to getting a regular caseload going, getting back to the OR on a regular basis. Want an extra assistant in the morning before we take care of the expo stuff?"

"Of course, you're welcome to scrub with me anytime."

"Thanks," she says as she gets up. She hesitates before heading to the door. "See you in the morning then." I nod and power down my computer as she leaves, at least I can have a drink at home.

*****

I still haven't heard from Isabella when it's time to scrub in for my case the next morning. Alex, Valerie and Abby are having a lively conversation while we wait for pre-op to finish prepping the patient. I pretend to listen, but I have no idea what they're discussing. The looks Alex keep giving me are enough to know that Catherine has shared with her what's bothering me. Our nurse finally arrives with our patient and I feel a small relief knowing that for a few hours I'll be able to focus my attention on the task at hand.

We're an hour into the panniculectomy when I hear the familiar tone of the video chat alert. I look up at the nurse hoping it's my phone. It takes her a second to show us which of the phones was ringing. It was mine, but the alert has since stopped and my focus has been disrupted. She's finally contacting me and I can't help but wonder where she's been.

"If you go down the hall towards the fire exit there's an old equipment room just to the left of it. Everything in there is a backup, so no one ever goes in there." Alex is whispering in my ear as my hand freezes with the cautery suspended over the patient's exposed rectus muscles. "Dr. Westland and Abby can handle this for a few minutes. Why don't you break and try to contact her."

I turn to Alex and look at her. "How do you know it was her?" I'm hoping our conversation is quiet enough that Abby and Valerie haven't heard us.

"It might have been the way you just lit up, plus Catherine and I use that app when she travels to conferences, it's the default tone." I turn back to the patient and try to refocus but I can't. I need to know what's going on with Isabella.

"Dr. Westland, will you and Abby be alright if I break for a few minutes?"

"Absolutely, take whatever time you need." I step away from the field and pull off my gown and gloves, wondering if Abby and Valerie know what's bothering me. I grab my phone and follow Alex's directions, easily finding the room she sent me to. I reluctantly send the chat request, hoping that Isabella isn't about to shatter my heart.

"Sara, thank god, I've been going insane." Isabella practically glows as she says the words, all I feel is more confusion.

"I've been trying to reach you for days." They're the only words that I can manage, the anxiety of not knowing has a firm hold on my tongue. My stomach is in knots and my heart is pounding against my ribs as I wait for an explanation.

"I know baby, I'm so sorry. There was a storm and the wi-fi and phone services were knocked out. They just finished repairing them. Can you take that stuff off, I want to see you?" It takes me a second to realize I'm still wearing my tinted safety glasses and surgical mask. I push the glasses up and rip off my mask. "Baby this is going to come out wrong, but are you alright?"

"Why do I look that bad?" I know that I do. I've been contemplating naming the bags that have formed under my eyes.

"Of course not, I always think you look beautiful. It just doesn't look like you've slept or eaten." Isabella looks concerned as she waits for me to speak.

"I haven't really. I've been going out of my mind. We haven't gone half a day without speaking then suddenly I can't reach you for days."

"You were worried?"

"Yes!" I know that I'm getting overly emotional and I need to get back to my OR. "I had no idea what happened. Things were fine when I spoke to you that morning, and then there was nothing. I didn't know if something had happened or if I had said or done something wrong." I let out a deep sigh, trying to release my pent up anxiety.

"Sara, I'm sorry. I was going to get on a plane today if they didn't think they would have it fixed. It was only supposed to be down one day, but the company had to wait for a part. It was a service provider issue, so I couldn't connect anywhere. I can get on a plane today if I need to." I love that she's willing to do that for me and I want to see her more than anything, but I'm tied up for most of the day today and all day tomorrow. I have a full schedule next week, so there would only be one day available for Isabella.

"As much as I'd love to see you I have obligations today and tomorrow. Are you working this afternoon and evening?"

"I work until around 11 tonight. I'd like to talk to you tonight, if you want to." I already feel my exhaustion weighing on me, but there's no way I'm going to let this be the only conversation I have with Isabella in three days.

"Ok. I'm in the middle of an operation, I've got to get back to my room."

"You left in the middle of an operation to talk to me? Are you crazy?" She smiles, and I can't help but smile back, her effect on me can't be contained or limited by distance.

"Mad about you and going insane, yes. I've got to go though."

"Ok. I really am sorry. I was going crazy too."

"It wasn't your fault. I'll talk to you tonight." Isabella blows me a kiss as I pull the phone away to disconnect our chat.

"Wait," I hear her call. I stop and wait for her to continue. "I want to see you in your scrubs, show me." I back the camera up giving her what she asked for. "Mmm, now let me see your behind." I swing my phone behind my back and bend over slightly. "Damn, even in that outfit you look sexy. Next time I visit I want to see you wearing those in person." I chuckle a little as I bring the phone back to my face.

"I've got a patient on the table that Valerie, Abby, and Alex are taking care of. I have to go. I'll talk to you tonight." I quickly disconnect before she can delay any further and head back to my OR. Alex meets me away from the field to help gown and glove me.

"Everything ok?" she whispers as she opens my first glove for me.

"Yeah, a storm knocked the wi-fi and phones out. Sometimes I don't know how you and Catherine do it."

"Quite well, explosive actually," Alex winks at me once she finishes her joke. "Honestly it's easy though. Well, getting together wasn't, but once we did it's been easy." I process Alex's words as I return to the field. Things are so easy when Isabella and I are together, but when we're apart, they are harder than hell and only seem to become increasingly difficult to handle.

Thanks to Valerie's help during the panniculectomy we are able to finish up early, allowing us to head over to the convention center earlier than I anticipated. It takes us roughly an hour to set up our informational booth. I head home in the early afternoon, exhausted and ready for a nap. I start stripping as soon as I reach the doorway to my bedroom, dropping my clothes in a trail between the door and the bed. I crawl into bed in just my underwear and am out seconds after my face hits the pillow.

*****

I slowly come to hours later, still feeling the effects of not sleeping well the past few nights. It takes me a minute to realize that I'm not alone, that there's an arm draped over my hip and body heat radiating against my back. I jump up, my initial panic being that Katrina has decided to cross another boundary. My eyes fix on Isabella, but she can't be here, I must still be dreaming. I sit down on the bed completely confused as to what's happening, if this is another dream or if she's really here. I reach out and gently stroke my fingertips along her jawline, the familiar torrent of excitement stimulating my nerve endings when I touch her.

340

"Hey beautiful," she grins as she comes to. "You were out cold."

"What are you doing here?" I'm still exhausted, so the question comes out sounding a bit harsh. Isabella's eyes snap open and inspect me.

"Aren't you happy to see me?"

"Of course I am," I assure her as I lean over to brush my lips over hers. I try to sit up, but Isabella pulls me onto the bed, deepening the kiss. "I'm so confused," I confess after I pull out of the kiss. "What are you doing here? How did you get in my house?" I sit up once again, facing Isabella, my hand resting on her hip, hers on my thigh.

"It seemed like you were upset earlier. I don't like that you haven't been sleeping or eating. Plus, I missed you. It seemed like a good enough reason to come here so we could see each other. I covered my shifts and got on the first flight out. I messaged Alex when I was in Miami to get your address, but she said she left work early and would pick me up. She let me in. She also told me that you've been a mess since we last spoke. Why?" Isabella's eyes are full of concern as she answers my questions.

"I'm happy you're here, but Alex talks too much. When do you have to leave?" Isabella sits up, positioning herself in front of me. She takes my hands in hers and gazes into my eyes.

"I fly out first thing Tuesday morning." She keeps staring at me and squeezes my hands. "Sara, I never push you on anything. Please don't avoid my question. Why were you so upset?"

341

"I don't know," I take a deep breath and release it before I continue. "Things seemed great when I asked you for that favor, then it was like you disappeared. My imagination started working overtime the longer I couldn't connect with you. I was worried you were sick, or hurt or that there had been an accident, or..." I shake my head feeling especially foolish now that Isabella has made an unplanned trip here. "I was scared that I lost you." Catherine's words echo in my mind, but I shut them out for the time being. Isabella uses her hands to encourage me to spread my legs. Once I comply she scoots between them, wrapping her long legs around my waist. Her arms pull me into a tight embrace, and we hold each other, Isabella stroking my hair and frequently kissing me on my temple. It doesn't matter that we're both only wearing underwear, that our naked skin is connected at so many levels. This is about comfort and reassurance, things I'm not sure I've received from anyone before. After spending several minutes like this, Isabella finally backs up far enough that we can lock eyes again.

"We will work out a system. I'll give your contact information to my sister or someone who will reach you if something were to ever happen to me. As far as whatever else you were thinking, I promise that I would never be cruel and just disappear. I would at the very least give you an explanation." She places a soft kiss on my lips before continuing. "Do you doubt how I feel about you?" Her eyes search my face as her thumb caresses my cheekbone.

"No. I trust you, it's the distance that sucks." I take a deep breath and slowly release it as I explore Isabella's eyes. They are filled with compassion, concern, tenderness and what I hope is love. My heart rages inside my chest as anxiety shreds through my nerves. My mouth goes dry when I try to speak. I clear my throat and try again. "I'm in love with you Isabella, and it scares the shit out of me." Isabella smiles and slides closer to me again, pressing her lips to mine. I pour myself into the kiss, releasing my fears and anxiety, trying to tell her I love her without words. Our tongues softly stroke the other's lips, slowly probing and twirling inside the other before retreating and starting over again. I'm not sure if I've ever kissed anyone with this much emotion, or this passionately before. I've certainly never kissed anyone for this long without escalating it to something more. As much as I know I love Isabella and I always physically desire her, right now this is enough. My lips feel numb when we finally separate. She plants a kiss against my temple and holds me tightly against her.

"I love you too," she whispers, "in case that wasn't clear." I smile as I turn into her neck and pepper a few soft kisses on it. "I've known for a while but waited to tell you. I could tell you struggle with your feelings, I didn't want to scare you by saying it too soon. I love you Sara." I revel in hearing Isabella proclaim her returned love for me, holding onto her tightly. Her fingers stroke my hair and travel down my back over and over again. Her lips graze my temple as her stomach grumbles loudly. I snigger against her bare shoulder as mine announces its own dissatisfaction, echoing hers.

"Have you eaten?" I ask, refusing to release her.

"Not since breakfast. I'm guessing you haven't either." I shake my head no, letting her feel the motion against her clavicle. "Do you have any food or do we need to order something?"

"I'm sure I have something. Want to help me make dinner?"

"Absolutely." She presses another kiss to my lips before sliding back so we can exit the bed. Remembering our talk from this morning, I grab a pair of scrubs and slip into them. She quickly pulls on a pair of shorts and a shirt and closes the space between us, her lips stretched into a wide grin as her eyes roam up and down my body.

"First you admit that you love me and now you're wearing that? This must be my lucky day." She wraps her arms around my neck and kisses me.

"Just wait until after dinner," I warn her, pulling her out of the bedroom.

I open the refrigerator and find the leftover chicken I baked for lunches this week. "Chicken Waldorf salad?"

"Sounds good. What can I do?" I pull out the chicken, some grapes, celery, onion, and a head of romaine lettuce, depositing everything on the counter. We busy ourselves with cutting everything up, both of us in a hurry to eat so we can move on to other things.

"Tell me about your thing tomorrow."

"The expo? It's a very relaxed event that I collaborate on with physicians from all specialties to help educate women about the importance of healthy choices, exercise, routine exams and other factors that impact women's health. We started it a few years ago and have seen attendance grow exponentially every year since its inception. Valerie, Abby and I will staff an information booth where we present our services, answer questions and help educate women on how to conduct proper breast exams, genetic factors, and other things. I'm letting Valerie take more of a lead this year as I'd like to get her name out into the community so I can start sharing the workload with her." Isabella's hand freezes with her glass of water halfway to her mouth. "What?"

"So this is a foundation that you started?"

"No. Just an idea that a few of us shared. A lot of women neglect their health in favor of taking care of their families, working or trying to juggle both. Early detection and preventative measures are key with a number of common diseases among women. So we host this event every year to help educate the community. I won't lie, it's also a great networking tool for all of us, puts our names and the services we provide out there a little more." Isabella smiles at me before going back to work.

"Does it last all day?"

"No, from 10 until 4. Do you want to go?" Isabella smiles at me. "Seriously?"

"I'd like to see you in your element, doctor." Isabella's little tease makes me laugh.

"Very well. If you get bored, I can always arrange a ride back here for you." We continue chatting as we prep and eat dinner. I think about how Alex said things with Catherine are easy, and since our talk earlier, this has been easy. But I know Isabella is about to get a glimpse into what actually being with me is like. Working on a Saturday, an OR day on Monday. Will she be ok with it once she knows how much I work? Then I realize in a way she already does know, we've always arranged our talks around our work schedules, so maybe it won't be as big of a shock for her as I think.

"What are you worried about right now?" Isabella's question pulls me from my moment of concern. She reads me so easily at this point that it would be fruitless to try to deny her anything but the truth.

"Just wondering how you will handle being with me when you realize how much I work. It's always become an issue in the past."

"But I already know how much you work, and you still make sure you carve out time for us. Besides you've already said you're working on cutting back a little. Maybe you won't feel so stressed about it once Valerie takes on some of the cases."

"I know, I just need you to be patient while we get Valerie's client based established. I can't just shuffle my patients over to her, it doesn't seem right." Isabella's hand glides over the surface of the table and grips mine.

"Relax Sara. It will be ok. I knew how much you worked when you told me you hadn't taken a vacation in over 10 years. Look at you now. You took a vacation, then you took more time off for my visit, and now you're taking a week off for your holiday. I'm not concerned." Without releasing Isabella's hand, I move around the table and straddle her before she can rise, our hands parting as I cup her face in both of mine and she wraps her arms around my waist, linking her hands against my lower back.

"I can't believe you flew here just to make sure I'm ok. I love you, Isabella." As soon as the words leave my mouth, I press my lips to hers. Isabella moans into my mouth as our tongues meet. She grips my hips firmly as she slides me further up on her lap, my sex dangerously close to pressing against her abdomen. She trails her fingers over the outside of my thighs, lightly runs her palms up my sides, and softly traces my abdomen, deftly avoiding my most sensitive areas. When I can't take anymore, I withdraw from the kiss and rest my forehead against hers, trying to catch my breath.

"It was worth it just to hear that," Isabella purrs as she continues exploring my body with her hands. She slowly runs her fingertips along the inside of my thighs, and my body releases an involuntary shudder.

"I want to make love with you," I whisper the request as I extract myself from her lap. She rises and presses her body against mine, pinning me against the table. Her hands continue roving over my body, eliciting sparks from my nerve endings as our lips collide for another sensual kiss. I feel the gooseflesh claim Isabella's skin when I slip my fingers under her shirt and lightly trail them over her abdomen. She intensifies the kiss a little as her hands find their way under my scrub top and start caressing a pattern over my abdomen, sides, back, and hips, each repetition causing the need to grow within me. Isabella breaks the kiss, her breathing heavy as she stares at me. "So was that a yes?" I tease as her eyes burn into me. She laughs as she clasps my hand and leads me to the bedroom where she pulls me to her and instigates a more fervent kiss. Our hands immediately resume their under the shirt action. I finally give in and brush my fingers along the underside of Isabella's breasts, causing her to gasp and pull out of the kiss.

"That was a yes," she pants as she lifts my top over my head and drops it to the floor. I slowly free Isabella of her top and pull her to me, her already erect nipples pressing against me, adding to my own excitement. Our tender caresses escalate to heavy petting as our fiery kiss fills with much more urgency. It's only a few moments before I can't tolerate Isabella wearing a single thread of clothing anymore. My hands fall to the waistband of her shorts, hooking them and her panties and pressing them downward, never parting our lips. As soon as they fall to the floor, I run my fingertips along her inner thighs, up and down so slowly, inching closer to her apex with each stroke. Isabella's hands grip my shoulders, pushing me back a step, breaking the kiss and my contact with her thighs. She steps out of her shorts and panties as her hand slowly falls from my shoulder, her fingertips tracing a path between my breasts and down my abdomen to the drawstring of the scrub pants. She slowly twirls one end of the tie around her finger and pulls it away from my body, allowing them to easily fall to the floor. I move to push my panties down, but Isabella's hands quickly close over mine, stopping me. "Slow down my love, we have all night." She releases my wrists as she snakes her hands inside the waist of my panties and grips my cheeks, pulling me back to her. Her tongue glides over my shoulder as she kneads my behind, each movement of her hands pushing the black silk lower. "I love you, Sara," she coos in my ear as she finally liberates me from my silk constraints.

"I love hearing you say that," I inform her as I press my body against hers, starting to back her up to the bed.

"Good," she smiles as she wraps her arms around my neck, allowing me to direct her. "I plan on telling you often." I begin peppering butterfly kisses along Isabella's neck as my hands tease up her torso to her breasts. I feel the small impact of the bed against her backside, and she deftly slides away from me onto the bed.

"Come here beautiful," Isabella beckons me with an outstretched hand as she kneels in the middle of the bed. I loiter, allowing my eyes to study Isabella, her dark locks and deep brown eyes, her beautiful breasts with the pert nipples, her smooth stomach, and toned thighs. I crawl onto the bed and plant soft kisses on her abdomen until her hands gently pull my head upward. Our eyes lock as we eliminate the space between us, our hands gripping the other's body as our lips meld. Isabella's knee presses against my thighs opening me a little further. Her hands steady my hips as she slides her leg between mine and positions her sex against my left thigh. We both groan as our sexes connect with the other's thigh, Isabella's moisture allowing her to easily grind against me. We writhe against each other as we share passionate kisses and our hands tease and explore. Isabella's pleasure quickly escalates, causing me to grip her hips to slow her down.

"Slow baby, remember?" I remind her, sucking her earlobe between my lips. She groans but accepts the conditions, slowing her pace. We continue regulating one another, knowing the other's responses so well that detecting the signs of impending climax is easy. Continually denying Isabella her pleasure is not. My entire body is on edge, I feel like the slightest breeze on my clit will send me into the abyss, but I deny myself, waiting for Isabella to concede. Her head tips back and I quickly grab her hips to slow her. "Look at me baby," I order her. She tilts her head up and gazes into my eyes, her desire written painfully across her face, her hazy, half lidded eyes oozing need. She relocates my hands from her hips to her breasts, her hands quickly darting to my hips to slam me against her. Isabella has finally given the green light, and my hands quickly start manipulating her nipples as she forcefully grinds herself against me. Isabella wraps one hand around the back of my neck, pulling my forehead against hers. My eyes close as I feel my own climax threatening, as the friction against my clit is nearly too much.

"Look at me Sara." I open my eyes and gaze into hers. Her breath is a hot tickle on my lips and her fingers dig into my hip, the sensation causing my orgasm to begin, there is no turning back.

"I love you baby," I pant, our eye contact never faltering.

"Sara," I hear Isabella moan as the world fades and my pleasure takes control, my muscles tighten and I finally have release. When I regain my bearings, Isabella and I are slumped against each other, sweat beading our bodies, our breathing still heavy, my body still trembling from our shared bliss. I pull her against me and slowly lay back on the bed, her body covering most of mine as her tremors finally fade. Her palm skims up and down the length of my body, the slight touch leaving small sparks in its wake. Every few trips she inches closer and closer to my breasts and my apex, rekindling my previously sated excitement. Her palm inches between my legs and she softly caresses my labia, causing me to spread myself wider for her. She lifts her head and watches me as I squirm, trying to increase the strength of her touch, but she refuses, bringing her hand back up where she starts tormenting my nipple. My breath catches as she pulls the other into her mouth, lashing it with her tongue and sucking on it oh so gently, causing me to release a quiet moan. She stops her ministrations, and my eyes find hers.

"Sit on my face baby," I rasp, my desire to taste her outweighing my need for her to touch me. Isabella slides up to her knees and positions one of the pillows under my head. I feel more of my own excitement escape me as I wait for her to mount my face. She flashes me a devious smile before pivoting herself over me, wrapping her arms around my thighs and angling my hips upwards and my legs apart. Her sex sits just out of reach, the sweet smell of her excitement taunting me as she lowers her head and administers a slow, deep lick, setting me on fire. I pull at her hips, but she refuses to back up the last inch or so. She licks me again leaving me little choice but to run two fingers along her slit. Her juices quickly coat my fingers, allowing me to easily slide inside of her. For every swipe of her tongue, I administer equally slow strokes with my fingers, being sure to tease her g-spot each time. Isabella finally relents and latches her mouth over my clit, lowering herself in the process. I burry my fingers inside her and finally taste my prize, flicking my tongue over her clit as I feel hers slip into my pussy, swirling around the entrance before withdrawing. I moan against her nub and feel her hips buck against me. I add a third finger and start steadily stroking in and out of her, causing her to start rocking her hips with my rhythm, drawing my fingers in deeper. Isabella sucks on my clit as she inserts her fingers into my dripping sex, causing me to raise my hips so she can bury them. She builds her rhythm quickly, and I realize she's set on making me come first. I give into to her while my fingers maintain their own torturous rhythm and I occasionally tease her clit with my mouth. My body burns as my hips pump faster, pulling Isabella into me as deeply as I can, grinding my nub against her working mouth. I pull my fingers out of Isabella as I feel my orgasm coming on, clamping my hands down on her thighs as she sucks me hard into her mouth. "Oh fuck," I scream as the lightning shoots through my body and my thighs tighten around her. She slows her musings as I come down and when I finally open my eyes, I can see the indentations my fingers have left on her thighs and her juices glistening on her pussy. "On your back," I order as I playfully slap her ass. She quickly obeys and I spring up and press my body on top of hers, grinding my hip against her pelvis, causing her to arch upward. "No more going slow?" I ask as I grind against her again. Isabella only grins in response. "I think you want something. What is it?"

"I want you inside me," she pants. I grind against her again causing her to arch into the motion.

"But baby, I was inside you."

"I need all of you inside me." I've done it before, and I certainly know that she's excited enough I shouldn't have an issue doing it again. I remember our first night at the lagoon and the earth shattering orgasm Isabella had when I fisted her.

"Well since you need it," I grind against her one last time before removing my hip and running my fingers through her dripping sex. I straddle her left leg and watch her carefully, looking for any sign that it's too much. I slowly insert two fingers and meet no resistance, so I up it to three. I stroke her a few times and she rocks with me, four certainly will not be an issue tonight. I withdraw and slowly insert four, stroking her with slow deliberation as she adjusts to the fullness.

"Yes, fuck me, Sara." Hearing Isabella talk dirty, gasp out my name, and seeing her like this turns me on, so I start working myself against the leg I'm straddling, allowing the undulations of Isabella's hips to dictate our pace. "More," she finally demands, and I withdraw far enough to add my thumb to the mix, slowly working my hand into her deepest folds, allowing her to relax around the intrusion. When she starts slowly moving her hips again, I resume the slight movements inside her as she presses her thigh against my own eager slit. Isabella rides my hand faster, and I feel my own orgasm closing in again. I reach back for the pillow I had under my head and quickly slide it under the leg I'm grinding against. Isabella's hands finger her hard nipples and start roughly pulling them. I know she's close and so is my own grinding climax. I quickly latch my mouth onto her clit and lick and suck on her with abandon as I pump my fist inside her. Her hips buck wildly at the sensation. "I'm close. Sara, don't stop!" I can feel her walls starting to tighten, I didn't need the warning, but her ecstasy is a massive aphrodisiac, eliciting a moan from me as my own climax sets in. I lock in my focus sucking her clit hard as her walls finally crumble and she screams out in pleasure as her juices cascade over my wrist and down my forearm. My body goes limp against hers as I come down and wait for her walls to relax enough to allow me to withdraw my hand. She's still trembling when I can finally withdraw from her relaxing folds. I quickly pull her into my arms and hold her tightly, pulling the sheet around us.

"Sweetheart are you ok?" I'm confident that Isabella's tears are from pleasure, but I have to be certain.

"Yes," she finally whispers. I plant kisses on her forehead and hold her. "Mmm, that was even better than the lagoon, watching you get off while you were inside me. I really enjoyed that."

"I got that," I respond as I grin with my lips pressed to her forehead.

"That really just happened, didn't it?" Isabella's cheeks grow a little darker.

"It did." Isabella turns and props herself up on her elbow, her fingers running along my cheek as she gazes at me with her half lidded eyes.

"I love you, Sara," she whispers before leaning up to brush a soft kiss on my lips.

"I love you too," I confirm as she settles her head on my chest. I wrap my arms a little tighter around her and succumb to the exhaustion seeping through my bones.

Chapter 24

"I thought you said this is a small event." Isabella's eyes shift around the exhibition hall as she tries to take everything in. I lead us away from the entrance and stop so she can process everything. "You helped create this?"

"I was one of many. It took a lot of effort to get sponsors, space, and advertising the first year. It's been a lot easier since." I get lost in the memory of how we had to practically fight for everything the first year we held the expo. Isabella's lips pressed to mine bring me back to reality. "What was that for?" I ask, unable to suppress my smile.

"This is a good thing, look at all of this." She sweeps her hand across the expanse of booths and displays in front of her. "I'm proud of you."

"Thank you," I say as I pull her to me for another kiss, one arm wrapped around her waist. "I think with the number of years that I've done this I've forgotten how it must look to people not involved in maintaining it." I quickly kiss her again as I realize that I could stand here with her all day and be perfectly content. "Come on, we should go see if Valerie and Abby are here yet."

"Isabella!" Abby abandons whatever she was doing on her phone to welcome her with a hug. "I didn't know you were going to be here."

"Me either," I inform her, as I smile at Isabella.

"It was a surprise." I think about waking up and finding her spooning me yesterday, it certainly was a surprise.

"Isabella, very nice to see you," Valerie greets her as she approaches our booth. They exchange a quick hug before Valerie deposits her bag behind the table.

"We're going to the coffee shop. Do either of you want anything?" I take their requests and we make our way back outside.

"More coffee?" she teases me as she squeezes my hand.

"Baby, I practically live on coffee. Plus I need something to eat, for some reason my shower took longer than usual this morning." A lot longer actually. We barely had time to brew a pot of coffee before running out the door.

"Is that a complaint?" Isabella winks at me as she grins.

"Not at all. I do need something to snack on though. Alex and Catherine won't be here with our lunch until noon at the earliest. They probably won't stay until it ends if you want to leave before I finish up." We enter the coffee shop, and I give Isabella a few minutes to determine what she wants. Beverages, muffins, bagels and yogurt parfaits in tow, we head back to the convention center.

"This is nice," Isabella purrs as she squeezes my hand.

"What's nice?"

"Just doing something routine like this with you, walking in the city, getting coffee." She smiles at me before brushing a quick kiss against my temple.

"It is. What do you want to do tonight? The girls will probably go out if you want to." Isabella stops, tugging on my hand to stop me. I turn to face her, wishing I could set the drink carrier down, the cardboard handle beginning to dig uncomfortably into my flesh.

"I'd like to be selfish tonight if I may. I have to share you all day, I'd like to be alone with you tonight. We could go to brunch tomorrow." I smile at her because her plan already sounds perfect.

"Sometimes I think you can read my mind. Want to go to dinner?"

"Are you asking me out on a date?" She eyes me playfully as she leans in for a kiss.

"I'm sure I could come up with something last minute if you're going to say yes."

"Then my answer is yes." I smile before leaning in to kiss her again.

"We should get back before everyone has cold coffee." I tug on her hand, and we continue on our way. "You should sign up for a massage before the doors open. There are other pampering activities you could try as well."

"Maybe I'd rather have you give me one later."

"I'm sure that could be arranged." We step back into the center and return to our booth where we eat our yogurt parfaits and sip our drinks. I send two quick text messages off, hoping to utilize a few of my connections for our impromptu date this evening. In what feels like no time at all, the doors to the center open and the expo is underway. Isabella dismisses herself when the crowds filter over to our booth. I watch her disappear into the masses before focusing my attention on our guests. Talking shop passes the time quickly, and before I know it, Alex and Catherine show up with lunch. Valerie and I let Abby sneak away to eat as we continue greeting our visitors.

"Dr. Hudson?" I have my back turned to the crowd to retrieve my bottle of water. I take a quick drink and replace the cap before turning around to discover Katrina standing behind me. I haven't spoken to her since the night of her inappropriate behavior, and I certainly don't want to speak to her in this setting. The fact that Isabella is somewhere in the building doesn't help my nerves either. This is a work function as far as I'm concerned, my conduct and demeanor must remain professional.

"Katrina. If you have any questions, Dr. Westland would be happy to answer them." Valerie is talking to a small group of women in front of the table, yet she still turns when she hears her name. I see her expression shift, the smile slipping off her lips briefly when she sees who I'm addressing.

"I don't have any questions, I just wanted a word with you." Her demeanor is timid, but my blood is starting to boil.

"This is a work function for me," I inform her, my voice dropping in volume.

"I know, and I'm sorry about that. I wasn't sure if you would take my call or talk to me at your place though." I'm clearly not going to be able to get rid of her so I grab a few of the information pamphlets and direct her to the side of our booth, away from most of the visitors.

"Take this," I command her as I shove one of the pamphlets into her hand. "Keep your voice down and make it quick. This is highly inappropriate." I plaster a fake smile on my face, I can't see it but I can certainly feel that it's strained at best. "Open the damn pamphlet and at least look like you are asking me questions related to it!" I'm practically hissing at her at this point.

"I wanted to say that I'm sorry. What I did…it was unacceptable. I'm trying to get better, I really am. Sometimes I just have no idea what I'm supposed to do or feel. I have all these conflicting emotions…I don't know. I'm back at the grief counselor and I've started going to a support group."

"I'm glad you're trying to get some help. I'm not sure what it is you want me to say though." I point to a random spot in the brochure trying to make it look like this chat is business related. I glance around to see if we've attracted any unwanted attention and spot Abby returning to the booth, with Isabella in tow. They're laughing about something when Isabella's eyes find me. I feel the genuine smile spread across my face, a reflection of hers, until Katrina turns to see what I am smiling at. Isabella's smile is quickly replaced by her lips pressing into a firm line as her eyes darken with anger. "She knows what you did and she isn't happy about it."

"You told her?"

"Of course I told her. I contacted her the second you were out of my bedroom." I feel my own anger return as I recall the situation. Isabella is only a few feet away now. I quickly step around Katrina and place myself between them.

"Hello love," I say as I wrap my arms around her. She quickly reciprocates, pulling me tightly against her, silently claiming me as hers. Even though I can't see her face I know that her stare is locked on Katrina. "Baby this is a work function for me. Please calm down." She relaxes into our embrace allowing me to relax as well. "Thank you. Is she still there?"

"Yes."

"Come on, you may as well officially meet her. She knows that you know what she did." Isabella eases her embrace enough to lean back and kiss me before grabbing my hand and allowing me to lead her to Katrina.

"Isabella this is Katrina, Katrina meet Isabella." Katrina extends her hand, but Isabella refuses to acknowledge it.

"I deserve that," Katrina mutters as she drops her hand. "I guess I owe you an apology as well."

"I do not want your apology, nor do I trust you. You took advantage of Sara's generosity and then tried to take advantage of her." Isabella keeps her voice level, and Katrina blanches at her words.

"You're right, and I'm very sorry about that. Sara, I hope that one day we can be friends again. I'm glad that you met Isabella, you seem very happy."

"I am, thank you. We'll talk soon, ok?" Isabella squeezes my hand, and I know that we are going to have to discuss this.

"Ok. It was nice to meet you, Isabella." Isabella stares at me as Katrina drops her head walks away.

"Why don't you two take a few minutes for lunch," Abby interjects. I'm grateful for the suggestion. Abby hands me the bag containing our food, and I lead Isabella outside, to one of the tables along the side of the convention center. Thankfully the area is empty, likely due to it only being 60 degrees out. The sunshine makes it feel slightly warmer, making it a very nice afternoon for late October.

"Are you really planning on forgiving her?" We haven't even managed to sit down yet.

"Sit down please," I request as I pull a chair out for her. Isabella takes the offered plastic patio chair, and I grab the one to the immediate left and turn it to face her. I deposit our lunch on the table and lay my hand on her forearm. She finally turns her chair to face me, allowing me to clasp both of her hands in mine. "I'm not asking you to like her or to forgive her. She is a good person though. She's just going through something neither of us can fully understand. That doesn't excuse her behavior, I know that. However, we have a lot of mutual friends, and we're going to run into one another at Velvet and other functions. I don't want it to always be strained and awkward. I don't need her to be my best friend, but I would like to be friends with her again at some point. I'm sorry if that upsets you."

"What if she tries something again?"

"What if she does? I'm not going to put myself in a situation where she can. Even if she does try, it won't make any difference, I'm already in love with someone else." Isabella smiles but doesn't say anything. "Do you never talk to Esme or Camila?"

"No. They tried for a long time, and I eventually gave in and met with them. But they both betrayed me, I had nothing to say to them. I still have nothing to say."

"Fair enough. Katrina didn't betray me though. I can forgive her and move on. Do you want to be there when I talk to her?"

"No, I trust you. I just want you to be careful."

"I will. I'll meet her in public, a coffee shop or something. Ok?" Isabella gives me a small smile.

"I'll never tell you what you can or cannot do Sara. That doesn't mean that I have to like this though."

"Are you doubting my feelings for you?" I lean forward a little bit more and lay my hands just above her knees.

"Not at all," she whispers as she leans forward and kisses me. Despite being in public, I lift my hand to the back of her neck and hold her in place, deepening the kiss. When we finally part I rest my forehead against hers with my eyes closed, fighting the surge of desire within me.

"Still want to go on that date tonight?" I whisper as I open my eyes to look into hers.

"Yes," she whispers before kissing me again. When we part this time, I plant a lingering kiss to her forehead. When I open my eyes, I see Katrina on the sidewalk watching us. She shakes her head before walking away. My phone vibrates, pulling my attention away from Katrina's retreating form. I check it and smile. "What are you smiling like that for?"

"Everything's all set for our date tonight. Dinner at 5:30."

"Where are we going?"

"You'll see," I smile at her and unpack our lunch, happy that things are relaxed between us again. We quickly devour our meal while watching the ducks play on the river bank and the occasional kayak pass by.

"This is amazing, Sara. Look at how many people are here!" We've reentered the packed exhibition hall. I once again find myself chuckling.

"Thank you. We expect to top 30,000 guests this year." Isabella gives me a look of shock. "Well not all at once obviously, people don't spend the entire day here, I don't think." Isabella unexpectedly pulls me to the side and kisses me. "Not sure what I did to deserve that." Isabella grins at me but says nothing. "Come on, I've got to relieve Valerie so she can eat."

"Before I forget again, I took care of that favor you asked me for. You might want to let Abby know soon, she and Blake are close to booking something."

"Thank you. What do I owe you?" Isabella shoots me a funny look.

"Nothing. I said I took care of it. They'll be considered my guests."

"You know I didn't ask for your help so that I wouldn't have to pay, right?" I appreciate her generosity but still dislike feeling like I've taken advantage of her.

"I know. I like Abby, and it didn't cost anything. Just let me take care of it."

"Thank you," I answer as I squeeze her tightly to me. "You off to explore some more?"

"Yes. I'll see you later." She gives me a quick kiss before letting go of my hand and disappearing into the crowd.

By the time we have everything cleaned up and packed into Abby's car it's just after 5. "Give my brother a hug for me," Abby orders me before climbing into her car. I grab the emergency blanket from the trunk of my car, take Isabella's hand and lead her away from the parking lot. She hesitates, but follows me as I guide her down the street to the bistro Abby's brother and his wife own. It's known for the wine selection and romantic atmosphere, the menu designed so that most items are considered sharable. The hostess immediately leads us to a semi private table in the back, where lit candles, wine, and fresh bread with herbed oil wait for us. We've barely taken our seats when Greg appears with a Caprese salad for us. I greet him with a hug and introduce him to Isabella. He pours our wine for us and informs me that everything has been taken care of. I'm happy to hear this as we have an appointment at 7.

"Out to impress, doctor?" Isabella's smile is radiant as she teases me.

"No, but I didn't exactly have a lot of time to plan a date did I?"

"I'd say you do well under pressure." I bite my lower lip to keep from laughing, hoping she feels the same way about the rest of my plan.

Greg gives us plenty of time, waiting 20 minutes before bringing out our entrees, seared chicken breasts with a garlic cream sauce, bacon wrapped asparagus and a wild rice blend. He told me via text that he was considering adding it to the menu and would love some additional opinions. The meal is amazing, and Isabella seems equally satisfied. We share a sizable portion of tiramisu before Greg checks on us one last time as we finish the wine and prepare to leave. I let him know everything was amazing before leading Isabella back outside.

"Baby, I don't know if I can make it back to the car. I'm so full."

"Not to worry, this is our ride," I tell her as I lead her to the horse drawn carriage. Our driver lowers the ladder and helps us up to our seats. I sit next to Isabella, wrapping my arm around her shoulders. She leans into me as the driver takes his seat and commences our ride.

"You did all of this after getting coffee?"

"I did. This is a service offered in the city. He'll take us through the city gardens and around some of the historic architecture." Realizing that Isabella is probably cold, I grab the blanket, and together we situate it over ourselves. Isabella snuggles in against me as we make our way into the gardens where the fall flowers are still in bloom, their muted colors visible thanks to the dim lights placed along the paths.

"This place is beautiful. I'd like to see it during the day."

"Anytime," I say before planting a kiss on her forehead. We complete the ride nestled against each other, keeping our conversation whispered in an effort to maintain some level of privacy. The carriage drops us off at the convention center, and we head home.

"I'm going to change into something comfortable," she informs me.

"Ok. Stay in the bedroom until I come get you." She gives me a look but doesn't protest. I head into the den and start the fire before grabbing my set of oversized floor pillows. Isabella and I could easily share one, but I pull out all three so we have the additional space. In the kitchen I open a bottle of wine and grab two glasses, leaving them in the den before starting some quiet music. With everything set, I head to the bedroom to change and retrieve Isabella.

"I loved our date tonight," she whispers as she pulls me into her embrace.

"Who said our date is over?" She leans back and eyes me questioningly as I smile at her. "Let me change really quick." I move to step out of her arms but she holds fast and presses her lips to mine. I fall into the kiss, even though I know we're in danger of not leaving the bedroom the longer it continues. I pull away, and she finally releases me to change, her eyes radiating desire as she watches me strip down to my underwear before pulling on a set of shorts and a shirt. I lead her into the den and feel her arms wrap around me when she sees the transformation.

"What have you done?" Her breath tickles my ear before she plants a kiss on the side of my neck.

"I didn't know what you'd want to do, so you have options. We can just relax in front of the fire, we can watch a movie, or we can dance." I rest my hands over hers to hold them in place as I slowly lead her into the open space I've created in the den. She pulls me tightly against her and begins swaying us to the music.

"What if I want to do all three?"

"Then we'll do all three." Her hands slide free of mine and grip my hips, turning me to face her. Her lips meet mine as her arms close around my neck. I pull her closer, and we fall back into swaying in time with the music. Isabella strokes my hair and neck as we dance, sending chills down my spine. I slip my hands under her shirt and run my fingertips over her lower back, slowly forming small circles.

"Mmm, that feels nice."

"Did you get your massage at the expo?"

"No, I was holding out for you." I smile against her shoulder.

"I'm hardly a professional. Why don't you get ready and lay down, I'll get the oil." I give her a quick kiss before heading back to the bedroom. I return to the den to find Isabella lying on her stomach, sipping from a glass of wine, wearing nothing. I stand frozen in place, watching the flames reflect off of her black hair and her bronzed skin, an image I'm certain I'll never forget.

"I poured you some wine." The sound of her voice pulls me from the trance. She looks over her shoulder at me, smiling like she knows I've been standing here, drinking the sight of her in. I return her smile, knowing at one point I might have felt some level of embarrassment at having been caught, but not now. I cross the room and kneel on the pillows next to Isabella, accepting the offered glass. She drapes her arm over my lap, her hand resting on my hip as she gazes up at me. I reach down and brush my fingertips down the length of her face and then back up to brush a stray strand of hair away. I feel her plant a kiss just above my knee as I lean over to deposit my wine glass in a safe location. She folds her arm in front of her and rests her head on it when I pump some of the massage oil into my palm. She releases a quiet groan as I start the massage, focusing on her lower back and working up to her shoulders. Her moans continue as I work her muscles, tending to her from her neck to her feet. I take my time,

366

enjoying this intimacy, the soft music playing nothing more than the quietest of background noises. I work my way down and back up several times before realizing that her moans have ceased, Isabella has fallen asleep. I shut off the music and start a movie before slowly easing myself down on the pillows next to her, hoping not to wake her. I try to focus on the movie, but find the steady rise and fall of Isabella's respirations more entrancing.

The soft whisper of Isabella's voice drags me from my slumber, her words incomprehensible as the Spanish oozes from her lips. I stay perfectly still as I listen to her before finally smiling and opening my eyes, stopping her speech. "Why didn't you wake me?" Her fingers push my hair out of my face before she trails them down my arm.

"You need your rest too. I never had any expectations, I'm happy just having you here next to me." Isabella leans in and kisses me. "What were you whispering?"

"I was telling you why I love you." This time I lean in to steal a kiss. "Did you really not have any expectations, even after everything you did for our date?"

"I did not. I just want you to be happy and to know that I love you. I'm happy to just have you here, to be able to hold you and wake up next to you." Isabella's lips meet mine, my mouth opening to admit her tongue as she presses me onto my back and shifts herself on top of me, the kiss picking up momentum, adding fuel to my seemingly unending desire for her.

"What if I have expectations?" The seriousness of our conversation has been replaced by playfulness.

"I'll try to not disappoint."

Chapter 25

I call Abby into my office during lunch on Tuesday. After dropping Isabella off at the airport this morning I need something to lift my spirits. Being away from her is becoming increasingly difficult, and I find myself researching plastic surgery practices and the possibility of starting a practice there. It isn't practical, nor does it make any sense given I'm fully rooted here. It would be at least a year before I could move, given the patients whose treatment I feel obligated to see through to the finish. I quietly curse as Abby enters my office.

"Everything alright?" Abby asks as she takes a seat on the other side of my desk.

"Yeah. Just researching a problem without a clear solution." I close the web browser and pass Abby her half of our delivered lunch. "That isn't why I wanted to talk to you though." I pull the envelope out of my desk and pass it to her. She gives me a funny look before taking the envelope and opening it. "If you need to change the resort dates let me know."

"Sara this is too much. I can't accept this."

"Yes, you can. Consider it an early Christmas gift if it makes you feel better. Things with Blake seem to be going well for you. You deserve to be happy and have a nice vacation." Abby's eyes take on a glassy appearance, she's often emotional and easily expresses those emotions.

"This is amazing, thank you." She double checks the dates on the resort booking. "Isn't this when you'll be there?"

"It is, but the resort is plenty large enough and there is so much you can do that we won't cross paths unless we want to."

"Is that your way of saying you don't plan on leaving Isabella's place." Abby shoots me a smile. She rarely makes jokes with sexual connotations, but every once in a while she surprises me.

"I'm sure we will, but the best spot is on her family's estate." I smile as I think about the lagoon.

"Are you leaving?" Abby's question quickly snaps me back to reality. I can see the concern written on her face.

"No. Probably not. I don't know. That's the problem without an easy solution. It makes little sense for me to leave here, yet I can't ask Isabella to sacrifice her life to move here if I'm not willing to do the same. But I want to be with her. I don't know what's going to happen." I sigh, trying to release my growing frustration. "You'll be taken care of no matter what. One of the other partners would take you on in a heartbeat. Don't worry about your position here."

"I'm not concerned about my position, just wondering if my friend is leaving."

"There is one other thing." I pull the legal document out of the pile of papers on my desk. "I'd like you to look this over when you have some time. If it's agreeable then sign it and get it back to me."

"What is it?" Abby asks as she reluctantly takes the document from me.

"That would be your partner's contract. It will grant you 10% off the cosmetic clinic profits and a few other perks. No buy in, just a guarantee of commitment to the practice." Abby does cry this time. "You've earned this Abby. Everyone here knows it, has seen the work you've put into this place. You developed and run the cosmetic clinic practically on your own in addition to everything else you do for our patients. I certainly couldn't do this without you." Abby comes around my desk and hugs me.

"I don't know what I'm supposed to say."

"You don't have to say anything. I promised when I hired you that I'd take care of you." Honestly, there's still a part of me that feels like I owe her more. She's been my right hand for years now, and I know without a doubt I probably would have cracked ages ago if it weren't for Abby.

*****

Time passes quickly, and before I can blink, I find myself walking out of the OR after a quick case to prepare for my birthday trip to Chicago. I've been busy enough that I haven't had a chance to pack. Catherine and Alex are picking me up in less than an hour. They will likely have to wait a few minutes for me to get my things together. As soon as I walk in the door, I grab my laptop and connect with Isabella. No reason I shouldn't be able to chat with her as I frantically pack.

"Sara are you ready?" I hear Alex call from the entryway. I didn't hear them pull in or Alex open the door.

"I need a few minutes," I call out as Alex appears in the doorway.

"Hey Isabella!" They exchange greetings as Alex surveys my work. "We'll be in the car." Alex heads out as I try to gather the last few things I need.

"Baby I've got to get going." I hate having to disconnect so quickly, but I know I need to get out the door.

"I know. I'm sorry I won't be there for your birthday."

"Don't be. It isn't that big of a deal. I still want to talk to you while I'm in Chicago though."

"Of course. I love you. Have a nice trip."

"Love you too. Talk to you soon." I close the laptop and my suitcase and head out the door. We pull into the airport and Catherine pulls directly up to the departures terminal.

"Uh Catherine, they don't have valet parking here."

"Oh, thank you for that." I can see her smirk in the rearview mirror. She turns around and hands me my ticket. "You aren't the only one capable of booking unexpected trips." I check the ticket and discover that my flight is to Miami with a connection to Punta Cana.

"You guys..." I feel my own tears threaten to make an appearance. "Thank you, really, thank you."

"We'd love to spend the weekend with you, but we all know you'll be happier spending it with Isabella. Go, have a good time." Catherine gives me a genuine smile.

"I don't have my passport. I'm packed for colder Chicago weather, not Punta Cana." Alex steps out of the car and pulls a suitcase from the trunk. She opens my door and hands it to me.

"Isabella packed this while she was here. You're all set."

"Honestly Sara, you have a house without a safe. You keep your passport in your sock drawer." Catherine turns and gives me my passport. "You should get going." I quickly switch my toiletry bag from the suitcase I packed over to the one Isabella prepared. I'm happy to see something other than underwear in the suitcase. I give Catherine a quick hug between the front seats and Alex one once I exit the car.

"Thanks you guys. You have no idea what this means to me." I shut the door and head into the airport. After checking in and heading through security, I settle in outside my gate and connect with Isabella again.

"Were you surprised?" she asks, her smile beaming.

"I was. I didn't even realize I was missing those clothes. How long did it take you to find my passport?" Isabella laughs.

"It was a lucky find. We thought we would have to tell you so you'd have it. I can't wait to see you."

"Same here. I was surprised to see you packed something other than underwear for me."

"Why would I want you to wear underwear?" She arches her eyebrow before my laughing causes her to breakdown in a fit of her own.

"Fair point. So do we have big plans?"

"I may have told my father I need the lagoon. He did have a condition though." I feel my eyes grow larger when she reveals the next bit. "He wants to meet you when you're here at the end of November. Not just meet you, he wants you to have dinner with the family."

"Uh..." Meeting the family isn't something I've done before. I feel nervous just thinking about it, and now I'll have nearly a month to work myself up about it. "Ok."

"Are you ok?" Isabella's forehead wrinkles as her concern grows.

"Yeah, it just makes me nervous is all."

"You'll be fine Sara. They're going to adore you. I've told them all about you, I think they already adore you." If I'm being honest with myself, I'm curious to meet the people who brought Isabella into the world and raised the amazing woman that I love.

"Don't raise their expectations too high," I tease her. "I'm going to get a bite to eat. I'll see you soon."

"Very soon," she reiterates before blowing me a kiss and disconnecting our chat.

*****

"Nice trip?" Abby's smile is nothing but mischief and happiness as she enters my office and sits down a coffee for me before taking a seat.

"It was perfect. You guys are better friends than I deserve. Thank you."

"Says the woman who just gave me a dream vacation and an unexpected partner share." Abby's smile never falters, even when she's sitting alone it lingers, but this smile is one I've seldom seen, and it looks remarkable on her.

"One was a personal gift, the other an earned business reward. Never forget you earned that share."

"I won't. Speaking of earning it, I better go set up for my first appointment. We're still on for dinner tonight right?"

"Of course." Abby heads out of my office, leaving me to prepare for my first few patients of the day.

*****

Days pass and one week bleeds into the next as I fall into what has become my new normal. Wake up, work out, shower, video with Isabella while I prepare and eat breakfast, work, try to connect with Isabella during lunch, finish work and take care of evening events, and chat with Isabella before bed. Even though I ache for physical proximity to her, this is our normal, how our relationship is, the only way I can see it being. I can't abandon my patients, and I can never ask her to leave her family. Two more weeks and I'll be back on a plane to see her.

"Dr. Hudson." Abby's voice pulls me from my mental countdown, as she approaches me in the hallway. "I'm headed out to pick up lunch, can I grab you anything?"

"That would be great, thank you. I've got a few patients left before then, but I'll get you some cash when you get back." I'm only half paying attention to Abby as I review the patient information for my current appointment.

"Don't worry about it. I'll be back." Abby heads out as I knock on the door to recheck a reconstruction we did a week ago. An hour and three appointments later I find myself with a stomach that's raging with hunger. Hopefully Abby is back by now.

"I left your lunch on your desk," she informs me as I pass her while escorting my last consult to scheduling.

"Thanks, Abby." My salivary glands kick into overdrive as I head towards my office. As soon as I open the door the scent of the Mediterranean take out hits my nose, which is buried in my tablet, reviewing my next patient's information. I shut the door, so I can privately chat with Isabella and walk the familiar path to my desk, not bothering to look away from the images I'm flipping through.

"I thought we could have lunch." I jump, dropping my tablet as I look up to find Isabella sitting in my chair grinning at me, the bag of take out perched on my desk in front of her. My heart soars as a wide grin takes over my expression. I retrieve my tablet from the floor and deposit it on the corner of my desk as I round it to gather her in my arms.

"What are you doing here?" I pull her against me like a child holding on to the teddy bear they have no intention of letting someone take from them.

"I was in the neighborhood." My face is buried in her neck, but I still detect the teasing tone in her voice.

I back up and kiss her as my hands sweep her hair away from her face. "In the neighborhood? Your idea of a neighborhood is much larger than mine." I let my eyes take her in, how the black power suit she is wearing amplifies her usual sex appeal. The smell of the food hits me again, and my stomach makes its desire to be satisfied known.

"You need to eat. Sit down." I begrudgingly release her and sit on top of my desk, a slight pout on my lips. "I had a meeting in New York first thing this morning, I rushed it along and flew here. Abby picked me up." I smile as Isabella leans in for a quick kiss before unpacking our lunch.

"I'm so happy you're here." I open my shawarma meal and stop the fork as it approaches my mouth. "Wait. Meeting in New York?" Isabella grins as she pushes a forkful of her own meal between her parted lips. I refocus on eating and dig into my meal, happy for once that I have the now innate ability to inhale a meal in under 10 minutes.

"I have an opening after the first of the year." She says it so matter of factly; like this information isn't great news for her, or important at all.

"Baby that's wonderful! Congratulations!" I forget my meal and pull her to me, pulling her between my spread legs that dangle over the edge of my desk. Our lips meet, and I can taste the seasoning of her kabobs and rice as my tongue flicks over her lips.

"You look very sexy today, doctor. I could have you for lunch, but you need to eat." She pulls away from me, leaving me wanting. I know she won't bend on this issue, she doesn't like it when I don't eat. "I know you're capable of eating fast though." She throws down the challenge as she takes another bite of her food and smirks at me. Challenge accepted.

"I still want to know more about your opening." I watch her to see if she gives any reaction to my prying, but her look doesn't change.

"I want you to be there with me, to blend into the crowd with me." She smiles, knowing that I would deny her very little in this life.

"I'd love to. Just tell me when and I'll be there." I keep shoveling food into my mouth as quickly as I can, barely tasting it, hardly chewing it before swallowing. An ingrained habit of working in the fast paced environment of human medicine.

"I've already mentioned to Abby that I'd like you to be free for a few days in January. She's taking care of it. We'll spend some time in New York together." She watches me inhaling my food as she takes another meticulous bite, demonstrating restraint and the proper way to consume a meal.

"How long are you here for?" I toss my fork into the mostly empty container, signaling that I'm done eating. Isabella watches me before sipping from her straw and moving around the desk, away from me. I watch as she locks my office door and her long, graceful legs carry her back to me. She stands between my legs once again, her fingers tangling in my hair as I fall into the depths of her piercing stare.

"We'll talk later," she advises me, before drawing me to her. "How much time do we have?" The whispered question with it's implied intent is enough to elicit a gush of juices from me. My eyes dart to the clock on the wall, it's 1:11.

"Fifteen minutes tops," I pant into her ear, my fingers winding in her hair as she moves along my neck, alternating between her lips and tongue.

"Mmm, what do you think doctor? Up for the challenge?" She already has me. At this point I couldn't care less if it takes an hour, I won't be leaving my office without touching her, without making her come.

"If not I'll be late," I rasp before my lips crush hers, our eager tongues invading each other, our hands pawing at one another like a pair of out of control teenagers. Isabella pulls on the drawstring of my scrub pants as I work to unbutton her trousers. The door is locked, but the glass panes along the side of it are hardly opaque. Despite the small voice in my head alerting me to this, I do not care. All caution has been thrown to the wind, as Isabella and I frantically work to get each other off.

"We have to be quiet," I warn her before latching my lips back onto hers. We slide our hands into each other's pants, and our fingers start exploring in unison. We both moan into the kiss, refusing to break contact, trying to stay quiet. Isabella is soaking wet and ready. I moan into her mouth again as she quickly inserts two fingers inside of me. I coat my fingers in her juices before sliding up to stimulate her clit. Isabella starts fucking me as I slip my fingers into her pussy, feeling her hips push into the invasion. I slide forward a little allowing her better access as my fingers stimulate her g-spot, ensuring my palm connects with her clit on each upstroke.

"Fuck I've missed you," she pants as her forehead rests against mine. My hips work to meet her fingers as her thumb glances against my clit with each of her thrusts. Isabella's hips rock harder against the desk, sending my tablet to the floor. I don't care. I can feel my climax coming on and sense that Isabella is close as well.

"I'm close baby. You better kiss me until we're done." Our lips collide, and our tongues swirl as we fuck each other, our hips thrusting, as our bodies yearn to fall into oblivion. The room fades away as I fall, letting the darkness swallow me up as I moan into Isabella's mouth, her fingers working inside me until I finally come down. My fingers are still buried in Isabella, her hips still working herself on them. I resume fucking her with little abandon. I need her to come the same way I need water and air. Her walls finally start contracting around my fingers, pulling them in as she achieves her release, my mouth swallowing the sounds of her pleasure as hers did mine moments ago. When her spasms stop, I withdraw from her, pulling my fingers into my mouth to lick and suck them clean. I open my eyes to see Isabella doing the same, the sight of her devouring my juices sending a fresh bout of lust through me. I check the clock to see it's 1:28. I'm running late.

"Best lunch ever," I inform her. I'm tying my pants up when I realize that I have no idea what Isabella is going to do while I'm working. "Uh, do you want me to get you a ride to the house?"

"How late is your last appointment?" she inquires as she zips up her pants and attempting to straighten out her jacket.

"Four. This is my early day. I have class Thursday nights. I can cancel though."

"Or you could go and let me watch," she purrs as she sidles up to me to help make me presentable again. "I'll wait for you. Can I use your computer?"

"Yeah, of course." This isn't an issue since all patient information is stored in a database that we're required to log into in order to access. "Are you sure though? It isn't an issue to get you a ride."

"I'm sure. I have a few things to do, plus I can always sketch something or read. It isn't that long." I lean in and kiss her again before unlocking my desktop for her.

"If you need anything, have someone find me. The bathroom is down the hall on the right. I've gotta go." I kiss her quickly one more time before picking up my tablet and opening the door.

"Hey, Sara," Valerie greets me as I pull the door behind me, leaving it slightly ajar.

"Hi. Isabella's in my office if you'd like to say hello." She looks me up and down before giggling.

"You don't say. I think you might want to use the bathroom before you see your next patient." I quickly drop my head and do my walk of shame to the bathroom, grateful that our offices are on the back side of the building, away from the consult rooms.

*****

"What has gotten into you?" I pant, trying to catch my breath. Isabella is suddenly insatiable, taking me in my office again before class and pouncing on me as soon as we pull into the garage when we arrive home. I lay on the hood of my car with Isabella on top of me, still staring at me after watching me come.

"Is that a complaint?" She lowers her head and starts kissing her way down my exposed abdomen. As badly as I still ache for her, I stop her.

"What aren't you telling me?" She tries to stop my questioning by lowering her mouth, but now I'm extremely curious. I slide my bare ass across the hood, the resistance of my flesh against the polished metal not

381

stopping me from moving beyond her reach. I grab my underwear and sweatpants from around my ankles and lift my hips to pull them back into place. Isabella stands up with a defeated look on her face.

"Come on, let's make dinner."

"I'm not going to eat until you tell me what's going on." It's my one piece of leverage, I know I won't be strong enough to deny her sex all night. Isabella stops and shoots me an incredulous look. "I'm serious Isabella. Do you think I'm going to have any kind of appetite knowing that there's something that you're avoiding talking to me about?"

"I do want to talk to you. Let's go inside." Isabella grabs her suitcase from the back seat and extends her hand to me. I take it, but it does little to alleviate the anxiety that's closing in on me with every passing second. I've never seen the confident, self-assured Isabella reduced to the uncertainty and nervousness that stands before me. "Please sit in the den, I will be right in." I seat myself on the sofa and wait, my leg bouncing up and down, my hands seeking anything to fidget with. My anxiety mixes with fear, tightly coiling around my stomach and chest, making every inhalation a struggle. Unable to sit anymore, I start pacing, massaging my tightening sternum, so lost in my own head that the sound of ice hitting glass makes me jump. Isabella enters the den with a drink in each hand. We stop and stare at each other and I see Isabella taking in the emotions that I'm certain are laid bare on my face. I watch as she deposits the two tumblers on the coffee table before eliminating the space between us, enveloping me in a tight embrace.

"Baby, please calm down. I love you." I wrap my arms around her but can't release the tension from my body. "Sara, please take a deep breath." I fight the mental

constraints and manage to suck a lungful of air in.
"Please, come sit with me." I let her lead me back to the
sofa and accept the offered drink once I'm seated, downing
half of it in one go.

"Please Isabella, what is it?" She takes a deep
breath as her eyes search mine, the anxiety and fear
quickly returning. Every conversation that begins with 'we
need to talk' or 'I need to talk to you' always ends with the
earth falling out from under your feet. 'I care about you,
but,' 'maybe if you focused on work a little less,' 'your
mother is sick.' Nothing good ever comes from someone
telling you that they need to talk.

"Is what we have enough for you?" There it is.
This is how it begins, or perhaps ends. I feel the tears well
up, distorting my vision, as I fight to stay composed, to
keep breathing. Isabella starts rattling off words in
Spanish, her palm on her forehead between her eyes.
She sounds frustrated, but I have no idea what she's
saying. "Shit, I'm sorry. That did not come out right.
Come here." She wraps her legs around my waist and her
arms around my neck and holds me. "You're not making
this easy for me. I need to say this. Please just listen with
an open mind and let me speak." I nod my head against
her shoulder, trying to calm myself. "I love you, Sara.
Perhaps a part of me has known since you sat down at my
bar that day. I'm never happier than when I'm with you.
I'm also never more depressed than when one of us has to
leave. I cry in the parking lot when you leave, I cry in the
airport bathroom when I leave. It tears me apart every
time. I thought it would get easier, but it doesn't." Isabella
stops speaking, and I'm unsure if she's waiting for me to
say something or just organizing her thoughts. I can't
speak right now, even though I know how she feels, it's the
same for me every time. So I do what I can do, I wrap my
arms around her a little tighter, hoping she will continue. "I
want to be with you, Sara. Not like we are now, but really

be with you. I hate not knowing when I'll get to hold you again, to kiss you good morning, to simply reach out and be able to touch you. It's so difficult not having the simple things that most couples get to take for granted. I want to move here to be with you. I don't want an answer now, I want you to think about it." All of her words and sentiments coupled with my anxiety slow my processing of what she just said. My head jerks off of her shoulder as I look at her in disbelief when I finally catch up.

"You what?" I must have misheard something.

"I want to move here to be with you." She says it again, and I know there's been no mistake. I sit there, speechless, trying to process what she just laid on me. "Why do you think my parents want to meet you?"

"I…I don't…" My synapses have suddenly taken a leave of absence, refusing to formulate thoughts into words.

"Oh Sara, my frequents trips here, taking extended days off at the bar, hiring a new bartender and getting her trained, taking you to the lagoon all those times. My family isn't blind, plus we're very open. They know all about you."

"They do? The lagoon? New bartender?" My mind is suddenly on information overload. I'm amazed I can form sentence fragments at this point.

"Of course they do. Do you think I take random women to my family estate? There have only been two women that I've taken there. Esme never appreciated it the way that you do, she never wanted to go back. They're very intuitive, they put all the pieces together when I hired the new bartender and had her trained right away." So much information is coming my way right now that I feel overwhelmed, thrilled and sad all in the same breath.

Isabella looks at me, concern clearly written on her face. "Is this not something that you want?"

"I do, of course, I do. I've even thought about it, but..." I trail off unable to give voice to all my concerns.

"But what?" Isabella now looks slightly frightened, unsure of what I'm thinking.

"I thought about moving there, opening a practice, starting over, but I can't see it. I'm selfish, I know, but when I try to picture that part of moving I can't. I can see myself living there with you, but I can't see myself giving up my work here. The images never line up. For that reason alone I cannot ask you to give up everything to be with me here." I drop my head because I know I'm likely closing the coffin on our relationship.

"You did not ask me, I asked you, I wanted to see if you feel the same. It seems that you do. I could buy a place and move here next week without telling you. What would you do then?" She pauses, waiting for me to answer, yet my words still elude me. "I'm not giving anything up. I'm not losing anything. My family is there, I'm not losing them. It's easier to be away from them than it is you, that is what I know. I'm not losing my ownership of the resort, and I can paint anywhere. I really want to paint near you, for you to be the first person to see my work. I'm not losing anything, but I stand to gain a great deal."

"But how can you be ok with that decision after I just told you that I can't make the same choices to be with you?"

"Sara, you are a dedicated woman who is passionate about her work. I saw it with my own eyes at the expo that day. You will never be done with your work, even if you tried to be, it won't happen. You could reduce your patient load and finish your obligations here, but there will always be that next person who needs your help, and I know you won't be able to say no. Your compassion and dedication are two of the things I love the most about you. To take that away from you would kill off a part of who you are. I never want to see that."

"What if you miss your family? What if something happens and we don't work out?"

"If I miss them I'll go visit. If we don't work out then, I'll move back there. What if I don't move here? Is this going to get easier for you?"

"No." I know with absolute certainty that it will only get harder.

"Have you thought about the fight we will have to get you a green card, or a visa, or to have you naturalized?"

"That will not be an issue." How can she believe that it won't be an issue? Does she not understand that they are monitoring illegals more and more every day? "Sara, I was born in Texas. My parents came here to visit some family while my mother was pregnant. I was their first child, and they knew things would never be the same after I was born. It was a last hurrah sort of trip. She was supposed to be fine to travel, and everything seemed to be in order. Then something happened, and things were not ok anymore. The pregnancy was suddenly deemed high risk, and she was placed on bedrest until I was born. So you see, I'm already a citizen, I never renounced it. How do you think I was planning to move to New York?"

"I hadn't thought." I really hadn't. That piece of knowledge was given as part of a larger picture, I never stopped to dissect the entire scenario.

"I want this Sara, but I want you to want it as well. I don't need an answer right now. I want you to think about it."

"How long do I have? How long are you here?"

"Take as long as you need. I've already started looking into a few places for ideas, but nothing more. As for how long I'm here..."

"Please tell me you aren't leaving tomorrow." Right now I know I can't handle Isabella leaving so soon.

"I don't have a return flight booked. I was going to see how you felt about me flying back with you for the holiday."

"That would be like a whole month together!"

"Close. It would also allow us to see what this looks like in the cold light of day, when you're working, and we each have other things going on."

"What happens if I can't say yes. Are we over?" I might as well know what I'm looking at, have all the information to make a decision with.

"If you say no then we keep trying like we have been, and I'll rack up a lot of frequent flyer miles. I don't want to be away from you." I should be on the moon right now with joy, yet I can't shake the feeling that I'm taking her away from her family, asking her to give up everything, even though she's offering and has thought about it. "I know I just threw a lot of information at you. Please just consider it."

"I will, I promise." I already know that I can't say yes, I can never put my happiness above hers.

"Do you want me to go?" The question sends a bolt of panic through me, making me clutch Isabella tightly to me.

"I want you to stay. Fly back with me." I know I'm being selfish, that this is a mistake. It will only give Isabella the idea that I'm going to say yes, and show me what it would be like to have her here permanently, making it that much harder for me to tell her no.

Chapter 26

We pull into Catherine and Alex's house for their early Thanksgiving party. Given that they will be in California visiting Taylor and Nikki, while Abby and I will be in Punta Cana on our own vacations, everyone agreed we should hold it early. Isabella and I grab our pie and pumpkin roll contributions as well as our overnight bag and head inside. Catherine promptly greets us and takes my keys, as expected.

"Katrina is planning on being here. I hope that won't be an issue." Catherine looks between Isabella and me, waiting for one of us to answer.

"It'll be fine," Isabella answers. I can tell she's irritated, but the anger that usually accompanies the mention of Katrina isn't there.

"Good. Alex." Alex quickly heads towards us, wrapping her arms around Catherine's waist when she joins us.

"Hey ladies, welcome." Catherine gives Alex a brief kiss before taking the desserts from me.

"Alex, could you put them in one of the guest rooms please?"

"Yes dear," Alex teases her before directing us to follow her, even though I already know which of the guest rooms she's leading us to.

"Can we have a minute Alex? We'll be right out." I make the request as we deposit our bag in our room for the night.

"Sure. Just don't do anything I wouldn't do." She winks before turning for the door.

"That doesn't exactly take much off the table then, does it?" I can't help but play the game with her.

"Nope," she responds as she closes the door. I immediately turn to face Isabella and wrap my arms around her waist.

"Are you really ok knowing Katrina will be here?"

"I've had time to think about this. You two were friends before things happened. If nothing had happened maybe I wouldn't be with you right now. All of your friends call her their friend. I'm going to trust everyone's judgment and assume there's a decent person in there somewhere. All of you can't be wrong."

"Thank you." Has Isabella really thought about everything while we've been apart?

"That doesn't mean I'm ready to be her friend, I'll simply tolerate her presence for now. Besides, if I do end up living here it seems I'll be seeing plenty of her." There it is, the topic we haven't mentioned since last week when we talked. It sits like a giant pink elephant in our silences, mocking me, taunting me for what I'm certain I'm going to lose, the one person I've been happier with than anyone else, ever.

"We should probably join the others," I whisper, feeling the stress creeping toward the surface.

"Not just yet," she informs me before pressing her lips to mine. Things have shifted this week. Our lovemaking, while just as frequent, has a certain sadness to it, like each time is a countdown to the end. It's tender and emotional. I can't help but wonder if it's the same for Isabella. If it is, she hasn't let on. I kiss her with everything that I have, I want her to know that I love her, to know that the decision I haven't given her isn't one I've made lightly.

"I can't promise you we'll make it out of this room if we don't leave now." Isabella smiles before releasing me and leading us back to the party.

The party is in full swing, and in typical fashion, there's plenty of alcohol for everyone. Isabella makes us each a drink, and when I take my first sip, I realize it's the first drink she ever made for me, the unnamed masterpiece. "We need to stock your bar like this," she whispers against my ear before kissing my cheek. We each have an arm around the other's waist as we half dance with the song that's playing.

"Would it be possible to speak to Sara for a few minutes?" Katrina is behind me, Isabella's body language never betraying that fact.

"That's up to Sara," Isabella informs her, allowing me to turn around to face Katrina.

"Give me a few minutes," I whisper to her before kissing her and letting go of the hand I had grabbed. I follow Katrina to a quiet corner and notice she isn't drinking as I wait for her to speak.

"I'm sorry if I interrupted your moment, I just thought it would be better to do this before dinner."

"It's ok Katrina." I nearly reach out to place a comforting hand on her shoulder, but after everything, I stop myself.

"I want you to know that I'm very sorry for everything. I wasn't honest with you, and I tried to manipulate you. I'm not proud of any of it. I do hope that one day we can be friends again." I can see the sincerity in Katrina's expression.

"I do too. How are you doing?" I really do hope we can be friends again one day, but I can't just jump back to being best friends with her, part of the trust is gone.

"Better, I think. Trying to live life one day at a time. Regretting some of my recent decisions, but learning to live with them." Is that what I will have to do with Isabella? Regret my decision to not take her away from her family and learn to live with it? I can't imagine living without her, yet there's a strong likelihood that it will soon be my reality.

"Is she living here now?" I follow Katrina's eyes to Isabella whose back is to us as she animatedly chats with Abby and Blake.

"No, but she would like to."

"Really? That's great news! Why aren't you celebrating?" I want to believe that Katrina is being sincere, but that little bit of trust that evaporated has me second guessing her sentiments, even if talking with her again is nice.

"We're still discussing it. You and I once talked about being able to see our futures. I can see mine with her. I don't see how I can take her away from her family though." My eyes loiter on Isabella, wishing I could find the answer stamped on her back. Catherine briefly cuts off my eye contact with her and gives me a concerned look.

"You know, relationships are about sacrifice sometimes. It sounds like she's willing to be further away from them to be with you, you aren't taking her away. There are planes that go there everyday." Katrina's words aren't anything that I haven't told myself at least a hundred times this past week. They don't change a thing.

"I know." It's the only answer I have.

"Some regret is nearly impossible to live with. You two have that same something that Catherine and Alex have. I've seen it. A part of me will always have regrets when it comes to you, this conversation might become one of them. You two clearly love each other. That isn't an easy thing to find, nor is it guaranteed to be there tomorrow. Seize it while you can." I nod because I don't know what else to say to her. "Maybe we can get a coffee sometime soon. Before we do, think about what I've said. There isn't a day that goes by that I don't wish I could have stopped Jill from going for that run." She pats me on my upper arm before walking away.

I stand there watching Isabella, savoring the drink she made me. She fits so seamlessly with my friends, she easily fell in with them like they had known one another for years. They have their own jokes and even their own schemes to get us in the same place at the same time.

"Are you alright?" Catherine's inquiry cuts my line of thought. "Sweetie, you look about as stressed as I've ever seen you. Is everything ok?"

"Do I really? Shit!" I've been trying to hide my stress level from Isabella ever since our talk last week. If Catherine sees it, surely Isabella does as well.

"Meet me in the garage. I'll fix us each a fresh drink and you can tell me all about it." Catherine heads toward the bar as I make my way through the kitchen and into the garage, where I pace around waiting for Catherine to join me. "Tell me what's going on," she demands as she hands me a new drink. I take a sip and find the whiskey sour to be strong, but not comforting like the beverage Isabella made me.

"Isabella wants to move here."

"That's wonderful news." Catherine flashes me her full, radiant smile. "Why are you so upset?" I fill Catherine in on everything Isabella and I have discussed. "Well, there really is only one answer."

"I have to tell her no." Genuine shock registers on Catherine's face. Clearly, she and I are not on the same page.

"Gods Sara, why would you tell her no? Have you lost the plot?"

"It doesn't matter what will make me happy, I can't take her away from her family." The tears I've held back for a week break free and burn their way down my face.

"Sara, I know your family history. You can't take someone from their family though. Taylor is across the country, and either of us would be on a plane for the other in a heartbeat if needed. My parents cavort around the world, yet I know if we needed them they would be back here on the next flight. That's how family works. Your grandmother raised you. Was she less of your family when you went off to college? When you moved away for residency?"

"No. She would have been there no matter what."

"Exactly. She wants to be with you, Sara. You didn't ask her or pressure her into this decision. Relationships aren't about you or me, they're about us.

Being together is going to make both of your happier; otherwise, she wouldn't have offered."

"Yeah but—."

"There is no but, Sara. Some problems can't be solved with logic. Life doesn't fit neatly into a bag or a box. It's messy and complicated. There are times you have to follow your heart instead of your head. If I had listened to my head, I probably would've never wound up with Alex." I can't help but scoff at this idea.

"Yeah right, you were destined for each other."

"And you and Isabella are not? I ignored my heart for a long time when it came to Alex, too afraid to admit or acknowledge how I felt. My heart won in the end anyway. Besides, I think Katrina is right, if you let her go, you will regret it for the rest of your days. You're happier with her than I've ever seen you. Don't throw it away because you think you know what's better for her than she does." Catherine hugs me as more tears make their escape. She holds me as I cry, still not convinced I can tell Isabella yes. The stress is killing me, putting up a fake front exhausting every last drop of energy I have. "You've got to get out of your head Sara. The answer isn't there." She plants a quick kiss on my forehead. "I've got to get back inside. Stay out here as long as you need to."

"Thanks," I whisper and squeeze her hand before she walks away. I sit down on the hood of Alex's car and stare into my whiskey sour, like I'm reading tea leaves. I hear the door open and close and look up to see Isabella making her way to me. She takes my cup from me and deposits it on the roof of the car before placing herself between my knees and wrapping her arms around me. "How did you know I was out here?"

"Catherine told me," she informs me before kissing the top of my head. "I know that you plan to tell me no." Isabella doesn't let go of me. Instead, she holds me tighter.

"How? Did Catherine tell you?" Fresh tears fall from my eyes, I know that this is the beginning of the end for us.

"No. I'd have to be blind not to see how stressed you've been this week. Plus you're sad when we make love; like you are trying to say goodbye to me." I hear Isabella's soft sniffle near my ear.

"I'm sorry. I'll cancel my trip." I try to let her go, but Isabella refuses to budge.

"No, you won't. I have no intention of making this easy for you. I love you. I know that you love me. I want to be here with you. I know that's what you want as well, otherwise this wouldn't be so difficult for you. I don't care if it takes a year, I'm not giving up on this." I wrap my arms back around Isabella. "Why no though? Is it still because of my family?"

"Yes," I whisper, not wanting to cry again.

"Come back with me. You don't have to meet them if you don't want to. Just come be with me."

"Ok." I can't deny her request. If we really are nearing the end, I want to spend as much of time with Isabella as I possibly can.

"And stop trying to tell me goodbye. I won't let you." We hold each other in silence for the longest time, the elephant out of the room, leaving the two of us with our emotions laid out like cards on a table. "We should get back inside. Derrick and Kevin are getting hangry." She leans back and looks at me, as she runs the back of her fingers over my face, attempting to erase any tear trails that might still be there. "Are you ok?"

"Yeah." I know that it's a half truth at best.

"I never thought it would be this difficult for you. I'm so sorry." I can see the love and concern in Isabella's eyes and it tears at my heart knowing that I stand to lose her.

"It's only difficult because I want you here with me. I just can't allow you to give up your family for me."

"It isn't a you or them deal, Sara. I won't lose them by moving here to be with you. I wish you could see that." Her fingers continue to stroke my face as her eyes bore into my soul.

"Me too." My words are barely an audible whisper. I'm not even sure if Isabella actually hears them.

"I love you," she whispers before kissing me. "We should probably rejoin everyone." Despite her words, she still holds me tightly.

"Just a few more minutes. I need to be here with you right now." I grab two fistfuls of the back of Isabella's shirt, not giving her a choice. "I love you so very much. Please know that."

"I know baby." Her hands slowly stroke my back as she places soft kisses on the side of my head. "How was your talk with Katrina?"

"It was fine. She apologized again, only this time she seemed sincere. She would like to be friends again some day. She basically told me I'd regret it forever if I didn't agree to let you move here."

"She did?" Isabella's surprise is evident in her tone as she lifts her head to look at me. I nod to confirm. "What did Catherine say?"

"To get out of my head and follow my heart, not to let you go." She kisses my forehead again before resting hers against it.

"You're friends are wise." I lean in and kiss her this time, a real kiss, one that is anything but me letting her go. Isabella looks into my eyes when our lips part and I see a hint of her own sadness there. "I wish you would talk to me about this. You aren't going to lose me."

"I hope that's true." I break our stare as I take a deep breath. "The family stuff. My father died before I even knew him. I lost my mother when I was young. I never had any siblings, I'll never have nieces or nephews. I don't want you to not have those things. I know they're important to you." Isabella's fingers caress my faces as she studies me.

"They are, but so are you. They want me to be happy, Sara. We can visit them, they can visit us. There are video chats. There are weeks when I don't see them, and I'm fine. I miss you as soon as one of us has to leave. Do you think that I haven't considered these things?"

"No. I know you wouldn't make this decision without thinking it through. I'm worried that you'll grow to resent me when you miss things or if something happens and you aren't there."

"Sara, I'm making this choice knowing all of the what ifs. It's what I want, only now I think it would have been better to just move without talking to you first. Then this wouldn't be eating you alive and we would be here enjoying ourselves. Please just give it some more thought. Think about what your friends said. Meet my family and talk to them, see how they feel."

"Ok." Isabella presses her lips to mine, but when she tries to pull away, I stop her, forcing the kiss to deepen when I run my tongue over her lips. For the first time since we initially spoke of Isabella moving here, I forget the stress of feeling like I'm making this decision for her and live in the moment. I focus on our love and put everything that I have into the kiss. Isabella senses it and slowly presses my back down onto the hood as we continue to share one of our most passionate kisses yet. I coil my legs around her waist and pull her further into me, savoring the feeling of her body on top of mine.

"Ahem. When you two have quite finished, dinner is ready." I hadn't heard the door open before Catherine spoke. Isabella pulls her lips slightly away from mine as we grin at each other, neither of us moving.

"Five minutes," I call to Catherine. I hear the door close as Catherine retreats back into the house.

"Welcome back. I've missed you," Isabella whispers as her nose brushes against mine. "We should head inside." She tries to extract herself from my limbs, but I refuse to let her go.

"Not before you kiss me like that again."

"If I do we might not make it for dinner."

"That's a risk I'm willing to take," I inform her as I pull her lips back to mine.

Chapter 27

I sit at the foot of Isabella's bed, watching her moonlit form sleep, the question of if I will say yes still weighing heavily on my mind. I love her, of that, I have no doubt. I still can't bring myself to agree though, despite feeling my resolve starting to weaken. I dread flying home without her, nor can I imagine going back to having our relationship exist primarily over video chat, but the worst will surely be waking up without her that first morning back. The last three weeks have given me a taste of what a life together could be like, and it's something that I know I want more than anything. How cruel is fate to lay this choice at my feet? I wonder if Isabella knows that I still cannot say yes.

"Will you please lay back down or do you wish to watch me all night?" Isabella doesn't move an inch or open her eyes. I had no idea she's awake. Isabella rolls over and holds out her arms, summoning me. I slide up the bed and lay my head on her chest where I can hear her heartbeat. Isabella's fingers caress my hip as I try to collect my thoughts.

"I feel like no matter what my answer is someone will get hurt. If I say no I feel like I'm hurting us. Saying no feels like I'm trying to cut out my own heart with a butterknife. But if I say yes I feel like I'm harming you by taking you away from your family." I take a deep breath and close my eyes against the tears threatening to escape.

"I will hurt too if you say no, not like the possible or imagined harm if you were to say yes." Now I know that no decision I make will be the right one, either way Isabella stands to be hurt. A tear escapes, dropping down onto Isabella and rolling down her abdomen. "Baby come up here please." I lift my head and slide further up the bed as Isabella rolls onto her side to face me. In the moonlight her eyes appear to be black as we stare at each other. "I hate seeing you cry." She brushes her thumb under my eye before planting a soft kiss on my cheek. "Is it getting harder to say no?"

"Yeah." Isabella's smile is unmistakable, even in the dark. "What does it look like when you picture us being together?"

"It's beautiful. You're the first thing I see in the morning and the last thing I see at night. I get to ask you how your day was in person and hold you if it was bad. We get to go on regular dates and spend time with your friends. I can make dinner on the evenings you have to work late and on the others we do it together. I get to show you my paintings and sketch you whenever I want. We get to do all the little things together most couples take for granted. It's what I want."

"What would you do though? Wouldn't being alone all day while I work get boring?"

"No. I can paint, find a job, volunteer. I have options." Isabella seems so sure of herself, of her desire.

"When you picture all of this, do we live together?"

"I suppose so."

"Then why were you looking at places?"

"I don't know. Inviting myself to live at your house would have been rude. I wasn't sure if you even wanted me to move." Her fingertips softly brush along my cheek as she pushes a few stray hairs behind my ear. "You asked me to picture us being together, that is what I picture."

"I promise you that I would love nothing more than to be with you every day." I caress her face as I lean in to kiss her. "What happens if we try it and you figure out that you can't be away from your family? Do you honestly think we could go back to being together long distance?" I know I'm fairly certain that we could not. It's already hard enough thinking about being away from Isabella after three weeks together.

"I have no idea, but I would rather try and know for sure. We can reevaluate if that time comes. Until then I'd much rather live life and be happy than sit and second guess things, never really experiencing them to see how they actually would be."

"Ouch. That was a little bit direct." Even if it's direct, there's some truth to her words.

"I'm sorry." Isabella sighs and closes her eyes for a few seconds. "I just know that I want this, I don't have any doubts. I wish it were the same for you, because I'm ready. I want to see how amazing life could be if we were together." I hadn't realized how frustrating this has become for her.

"Me too. I'm just trying to sort this out. This is a big sacrifice you want to make." I trace her hairline from the peak of her forehead to the nape of her neck, our eyes fixed on each other. "I do love you." I take Isabella's hand and place it over my heart. "This is yours." Isabella's eyes slowly close as the corners of her lips curl upward slightly.

"What would you have done if I had just gotten a place and moved without asking you about it first?"

"Honestly? I would have been thrilled. I doubt I would have questioned the family thing like I am. But being given the power to say yes or no makes it feel like

I'm making the decision for you. Having lost that, knowing what it feels like to not have that, I don't want that for you." I see a glimmer of moonlight reflect off a tear that escaped from Isabella's eye. I reach up and wipe it away with my thumb before slowly tracing her cheek. "Why the tears?"

"I love that you are concerned about this. That you are willing to sacrifice your own happiness to protect me. Even if what you're trying to protect me from is something that may never happen." I can't tell Isabella that eventually, it will happen, that one day something will happen to her parents, expected or not. "Which one feels better to you, saying yes or saying no?"

"Saying yes. I am so much happier when we're together."

"Then Sara I am begging you to be selfish just this once. Please say yes. Choose us." Isabella's words are brimming with emotion. This is what she wants, there isn't a doubt in my mind. She emphasizes them by seizing my lips with hers, gliding her tongue across my lips until I yield and permit it entry. "I love you, Sara," she breathes, temporarily separating our mouths. "Please let that be enough."

*****

Isabella leads me through the front door of the impressive house, and the hamster using my stomach as an exercise wheel goes into double time. She turns back to face me, but I can't be sure if I physically started to drag my feet or if my sweaty palms communicated my nervousness to her.

"Relax. They're going to love you." She gives me a quick kiss and chuckles.

"Well that isn't helpful."

"I just find it amusing that you face life and death everyday at work, yet meeting my parents freaks you out."

"I'm glad you find this amusing, but to be fair my patients are typically undergoing elective procedures, which means they're hardly in dire straights."

"No matter. Come on." Isabella resumes leading me through her family home, her excitement evident. We pass through the house so quickly that I don't have time to take anything in. Finally we arrive in the spacious kitchen, where a petite woman slightly shorter than myself works at cutting up peppers and onions, her hair pulled up into a familiar looking messy bun, the dark color showing the first signs of grey at the temples.

"Isabella, you're early!" She looks up from her task and I see the striking resemblance that Isabella shares with her. She quickly steps around the island she's working at and pulls Isabella in for a welcoming hug and kiss on the cheek.

"Mamá this is Sara. Sara this is my mother, Adelita." Adelita's smile radiates warmth as she quickly assesses me.

"Sara, it is so lovely to finally meet you." I hold out my hand to shake hers but she steps right through it, pulling me into the same hug and kiss she gave Isabella moments ago.

"It's nice to meet you as well." Her hug eases a little bit of my nervousness, but deep down I know Isabella is daddy's little girl. "You have a beautiful home, thank you for inviting me."

"Of course, of course," she assures me as she waves her hand and heads back around the island to finish her work. "You're welcome here anytime." I quickly find myself drawn to the openness of her family and wonder if my relationship with my parents would have looked like this if things had been different.

"Thank you." Isabella's smile glows enough it might be capable of lighting a small room on its own.

"Isabella tells me you love fajitas, I hope this is true." Adelita smiles at me as she continues working away.

"I do. Is there anything I can do to help?"

"You're our guest, I won't hear of it. Things are almost taken care of. Isabella, would you take these to your father while I get Sara something to drink?"

"Yes, mamá." Adelita watches us as Isabella wraps her arms around my waist and brushes her lips against mine, her adoring smile never leaving her face. My anxiety ratchets back up as the reality that I'm about to be left alone with her mother quickly sinks in. I begin to panic, wondering if the warm welcome I've been given thus far will quickly disappear once we're alone.

"I need pictures of the two of you before you leave," she calls to Isabella as she exits the room. "What may I get you to drink?"

"Water would be fine, thank you." I watch as Adelita retrieves a glass and fills it. She walks it around the bar to me as I anticipate the facade falling away at any moment.

"Isabella has told us a great deal about you, including what happened to your parents. I'm very sorry that you had to go through all of that. Please know that you're always welcome here." How very wrong I've been. This woman is nothing but warmth and honesty, which shouldn't come as a surprise when I consider that she raised Isabella.

"Thank you. That really means a lot to me, Adelita." I smile at her before she pulls me into another hug. "I hope Isabella hasn't set your expectations of me too high," I joke, managing to garner a laugh from Adelita.

"Nonsense. She told us that you are intelligent, compassionate, benevolent, beautiful and honest."

"She made me sound like a saint. I'm not sure I can compare."

"You don't have to. Isabella isn't perfect either. If you love her, respect her, and treat her properly then I will be happy." A commotion from the front of the house filters into the kitchen. "That will be Gabriela and the girls. Promise me one thing."

"Of course."

"Don't ever break her heart the way that Esme did." The twins burst into the kitchen before I can answer. I watch as Adelita wraps them both up in her arms and kisses each of them on the cheek.

"I promise that I won't," I vow to her when she looks at me again.

"I believe you." She smiles at me before greeting the woman just entering the kitchen. I recognize Gabriela from our brief meeting during a video chat one time.

"Sara, nice to meet you in person." She greets me in the same manner that her mother did earlier. "Please don't mind the girls, they're a little hyper right now."

"It's great to finally meet you as well." I feel Isabella's familiar arms wrap around my waist.

"How are you doing my love?" she whispers in my ear. I turn my head toward her and smile, causing her to kiss me.

"Are you Aunt Izzy's new girlfriend?" one of the twins questions immediately after the kiss.

"Yes, she is. What do you think?" Isabella squats down next to her niece, and they both look up at me.

"I think she's pretty," is the little girl's reply.

"So do I. Should I keep her?" The little girl nods before taking off in the direction Isabella exited earlier. Isabella grins at me as she stands to greet Gabriela. I hear a pair of male voices heading towards us, so I turn to locate their origin. Two sets of eyes are busy assessing me as their conversation continues. I quickly do my own appraisal of the pair, noting Mateo's full head of thick black hair and his thickset build. He smiles warmly at me as he and the man I assume to be Hector enter the kitchen.

"You must be the lovely Sara," he says as he deposits the tray of grilled meats and veggies on the island. He pulls me into a strong hug. "Welcome to our home."

"Thank you for inviting me."

"Anytime. Did you get something to drink?" Up close I finally see where Isabella gets her eye color and her nose.

"I did, thank you," I answer, picking up my glass of water.

"Very good. Have you met Hector yet?" Hector approaches and offers me his hand. I shake it, happy to not have to hug one more stranger.

"Dinner will be ready soon. Help me get this stuff onto the table." Adelita issues the order, and a hush falls over the room as everyone listens. I attempt to grab a dish or two to help, but Isabella stops me.

"They will get that, come with me." She clasps my hand and leads me outside to a patio area with a full bar. "I'm responsible for making drinks. Margaritas since we're having fajitas?"

"Sure." Isabella stops and faces me, her free hand reaching up to brush the hair out of my face.

"How are you doing? Is it as scary as you thought it would be?" Isabella grins, clearly still feeling amused by my earlier discomfort.

"It's been a lot all at once, but your mother is very lovely. She only made me swear to one thing, so I suppose that's good." I chuckle, but Isabella's look stops me.

"What did she make you promise her?"

"That I would never hurt you the way that Esme did. It was an easy promise to make." Isabella smiles but seems relieved. "Wait a second, you were worried?"

"After everything that happened with Esme I couldn't be certain they would trust everything I told them about you."

"Yeah well, you made me sound like I'm perfect from what your mother has told me. Those are expectations I'll clearly never be able to live up to." I give her a smile as we both start laughing.

"Now that I have you alone," Isabella lowers her voice as she pulls me into her arms. Her lips find my neck as she trails kisses along it.

"Promises, promises," I tease her.

"I'll give you more than a promise," she warns as she backs me up against the side of the house, slipping her leg between mine, causing my body to explode as her thigh presses against me. Her hands slip under my top and quickly make their way to my breasts.

"Isabella wait." My body is cursing my brain, wanting what Isabella is offering. She can play my body like a virtuoso though, resisting her is nearly impossible. "Isabella, we can't," I pant, finally planting my hands on her shoulders and forcing the smallest of spaces between us. "Everyone is waiting for us. Plus, this is your parent's house." Isabella's eyes appear unable to contain her desire. She slowly releases me and busies herself making drinks. Two pitchers of margaritas in tow, we head inside and rejoin the others.

"Sara, please forgive the informal setup. We've found buffet style serving to work best with fajitas." Adelita sounds embarrassed.

"No need to apologize, Adelita. It looks amazing. Thank you for all of your hard work preparing all of this."

"My pleasure. It isn't often we're able to get everyone here for the same meal. Someone is always working, traveling or otherwise engaged. I should be thanking you." She shoots me a warm smile before scanning the room. She finally grants permission for dinner to begin. We prepare our plates and seat ourselves at the table, Isabella on my right and one of her nieces on my left. Dinner passes with lively conversation and a lot of laughs. I feel so included that if I didn't know better, I would think I'd been dining with this family for years. Isabella cannot contain her joy, her smile never fades. Her joy turns to sadness in me though. Seeing her like this only reinforces my belief, I cannot say yes.

"Where's the bathroom?" I lean over and ask Isabella. She turns to tell me and her smile finally falters.

"I'll show you." I open my mouth to protest, but Isabella is already leaving her seat. "We'll be right back." She takes my hand and leads me down the hallway and around the corner, pulling me into the bathroom and closing the door. "What just happened?" She leans against the sink, her fingers hooked around mine.

"You're so happy tonight, here with your family. As happy as I've ever seen you. It just reinforces my concern, the reason I can't say yes. The reason you can't leave them." Isabella's radiant smile is gone, sadness flooding her eyes.

"It isn't always like this. You heard my mother, it's rarely like this. My father works constantly, as do Hector and Gabriela. The girls are often with their nanny or my mother when they aren't in school. This wouldn't even be happening if you weren't here right now. Everyone is here

411

to meet you. Yes, I was very happy out there, with everyone I love seated at the same table, enjoying a nice meal together. The same way you're always happy at Sunday brunch."

"I'm sorry," I whisper as I lean into her, resting my forehead on her shoulder. There's nothing else I can say, my heart feels fractured. "We need to get back." I rotate my head to kiss Isabella's cheek at the same time she turns into me, resulting in our lips meeting unexpectedly. She pulls me to her, demanding more before spinning us so that she has me pinned against the sink. Her lips leave mine, and her eyes bore into me, searching for my feelings.

"I'm not done fighting for us." The weight of her body leaves me as she finds my hand and guides us back to the dining room. I glance around and quickly assess the room. It seems no one is aware of the emotional issue suspended between us. No one except Mateo, whose demeanor has shifted ever so slightly, showing a hint of concern. I shouldn't be surprised that he noticed or that he's able to conceal it so well, he would likely have to possess keen powers of observation and a decent poker face. Dinner concludes, and the lively conversation continues while Adelita brings out a small cake, cutting it and serving each of us a piece. I'm physically stuffed from the drinks and delicious meal, but I accept the dessert out of politeness.

"You're going to love this. It's one of my favorites." Isabella smiles at me, the hint of sadness still visible in her eyes, no matter how she tries to conceal it.

"What is it?" It looks like a typical white cake with white frosting, but clearly must be something more.

"It's called tres leches. Just try it." I watch as Isabella lifts her fork to her mouth and takes her first bite. Her eyes close as the morsels connect with her taste buds, her smile growing broader. I wait for her eyes to open before picking up my fork and trying a bite. The cake is incredibly sweet and super moist, yet somehow it practically dissolves in my mouth, the whipped cream frosting a perfect compliment to the gooey sponginess of the cake.

"This is amazing," I compliment Adelita before feeding myself another forkful.

"Thank you, Sara. Do you bake?" Adelita's smile is full of warmth. I wonder how she isn't exhausted from preparing everything.

"I can bake fairly well, but I don't do it that often."

"I'll have to give you the recipe for this. Isabella practically begs for it every month. You know how difficult it is to deny her once she decides she wants something." I have to force my self to swallow and plaster on a fake smile as I allow Adelita's words to sink in. Does Isabella's family believe her moving is already a done deal? Am I reading too far into Adelita's words? Her manner conducts nothing but kindness and adoration for her family, yet I still can't stop the nagging feeling that her intent was something more.

"I would be very grateful, thank you. Isabella's happiness is my biggest concern." I've chosen my words carefully, aware of their hidden meaning. I have no doubt that Isabella's family is aware of my conflicted feelings regarding her possible move. Isabella leans in and kisses my cheek. "I love you," she whispers.

"I love you too," I whisper back, our eyes locked on each other, ignoring everyone else in the room.

"It makes me very happy to hear that. It's easy to see how much you mean to each other." Adelita oozes happiness at us from across the table. Mateo has been consumed in a somewhat heated debate with Hector about baseball, yet I catch him watching us, listening to our conversation as well. "I hope you will join us for dinner again before you leave."

"I'd like that, thank you." The conversation continues in every direction as the twins take off to play somewhere in the house. I join in when I'm able to focus enough to contribute, but more and more my thoughts keep shifting back to Isabella. As if possessing a sixth sense, her hand reaches over and squeezes my thigh. I give her a strained smile as I rest my hand on top of hers.

"Hector, we should probably be going. We have a busy day tomorrow." Hector nods his agreement to Gabriela and finishes his conversation with Mateo. "Sara, perhaps we can find time for lunch while you're here."

"Absolutely, let us know when you're free." Gabriela smiles at us before heading off to find the girls. I take her exit as a cue that dinner is over and rise from my seat and start to gather the dirty dishes.

"Sara, please leave it. You're our guest. We will handle the clean up." Adelita smiles at me as everyone stands.

"Sara, come have a drink with me," Mateo suggests. With no reason to refuse the offer, I kiss Isabella and follow her father outside, for a conversation I've known is inevitable ever since Isabella and I excused ourselves to the bathroom earlier. I watch him as he makes us each another margarita, generously pouring the tequila before adding the triple sec and lime juice. "Sit," he says as he hands me my drink. I sit in one of the chairs, and Mateo takes the seat directly across from me. The seat affords him a direct view of my face, allowing him to gauge my reactions, to try to determine if I'm being genuine or not. "I'm not known for beating around the bush, so I apologize in advance if I start to seem a little pushy."

"No need to apologize. I can appreciate getting straight down to business, so to speak." I'm fairly certain why we're out here anyway.

"Yes. Isabella told me that you're a partner in your practice. How is that? So much for not beating around the bush, I guess.

"It's good. I have more opportunities than I have the ability to handle, so we recently added another partner. She'll be able to help with the cases I don't have the time to take on as well as do additional procedures. It'll be good for our growth."

"That's good. It's funny how it never ends, isn't it?" He releases a soft chuckle as he considers the idea.

"You're right, it never does. I remember when we started the practice, it was just the two of us. Thankfully my partner enjoyed the business administration and numbers side of things. I much prefer to be in the operating room." I take a sip of my drink, trying to relax. "That first year felt like pure chaos. Establishing a brand, garnering name recognition, getting ourselves out there. It felt so impossible at times. Then we finally got to a point where things were just smooth, and we thought we were where we needed to be. It just keeps growing though, even without an added effort, it just grows. Don't get me wrong, I'm grateful for what I have. I just never imagined it would become what it is." I take another sip as Mateo appraises me. "I guess you understand this better than most though." Mateo laughs as he nods his head.

"Yes, it sounds very familiar indeed. I think there were times when I didn't sleep for days." He chuckles before enjoying a taste of his margarita. "Can you imagine doing it all over again?"

"Heavens no! The thought alone is exhausting." Mateo unleashes a hearty laugh.

"It is. It took our entire family to start the resort. We were doing everything at first, working the desk, the bar, doing the books, turning over the rooms. We were all exhausted. Like you said though, it grows and evolves with little help sometimes. So are we blessed or have we earned it?" I sip my drink as I consider his question.

"Both, I think. We certainly worked hard for what we have, so I wouldn't dismiss it all down to a stroke of luck. At the same time, there has to be a need for what you're offering, which would be out of your hands." Mateo smiles.

"Isabella has told us many things about you. I can see that she speaks the truth. You cannot imagine how much of a relief this is." Mateo takes a drink as he measures me. "I'm sure she has told you about Esme. I never really cared for her, even when Isabella first brought her home. I could tell that Esme wasn't what my daughter needed. She was wild, selfish, rude, opportunistic, and even disrespectful at times. Of all the times she was in our home, I can't recall one occasion where she tried to help Adelita in the kitchen or tried to help clean up after a meal. It's always the little things that show you who a person truly is. When she spoke she never used us to refer to them as a couple, everything was somehow related to her as an individual. For the longest time, I wondered if Adelita and I had somehow failed as parents. We knew that our children had a more privileged life than most, but we still tried to raise them to be kind, generous, and respectful. We kept asking ourselves how Isabella could be so attracted to someone who didn't represent any of the values we raised her with. Then Esme betrayed her in one of the worst ways possible and broke my baby girl's heart. It was hard to be happy that she was out of our lives when Isabella was so broken." Mateo pauses to take a drink, but I see the glassiness of his eyes. Remembering Isabella that way has nearly brought him to tears. "It took a long time for her to heal and it wasn't always pretty. I was surprised when she first brought you to the estate, she hadn't mentioned anyone specific but her mood the few days before that had inexplicably shifted. She was smiling and talking more. I was certainly curious, but didn't want to spoil it, so I didn't ask questions. Then she started painting again and brought you to the lagoon a second time, but the next time I saw her she had changed again. I could tell that something was on her mind, so we talked, and she told me about you. Naturally, I was worried for many reasons, worried that she found someone like Esme, that she would have her heart broken again. She's been a different person since she met you, she's been euphoric. When she told Adelita and I that she wanted to move so you could be together we supported her decision, but were concerned. What would happen if you were to hurt her? Would we know? Who would take care of her? I'm no longer worried about those things now that I've met you."

"Thank you, it means a lot hearing that. I love your daughter more than I can explain to you. For what it's worth, you raised an extraordinary woman who is all of those things you wanted her to be."

"Thank you, but the thing we want most is for her to be happy." He pauses and finishes his drink. "Isabella tells us that you haven't agreed to her moving yet. Why is that?" I toss back the remainder of my drink and sigh. Mateo stands up and extends his hand, requesting my empty glass. Without a word, he retreats back to the bar and refills our drinks, returning to his seat when his task is complete.

"Honestly, there is only one thing keeping me from saying yes. I can't ask her to leave you guys. She has something I've never had, that I'll never have. Now I've seen first hand how happy being with all of you makes her. How can I selfishly ask her to give up that part of her life for me, when I can't even give up my practice and my commitment to my patients for her? It isn't that I don't love her. I've seen the sadness in her eyes, and it tears me apart. I just keep searching for the perfect solution, and I can't find it." Tears stream down my face as I ramble. I don't bother attempting to conceal them, I'm certain Mateo has figured out how difficult this is for me. Mateo collects a few napkins from behind the bar, and seats himself in the chair next to mine when he returns. I lean forward in my chair, placing my elbows on my knees and resting my forehead on my palms. I let everything out, my frustrations, fears, and anxiety all seep forth from my tear ducts.

"Sara, life doesn't have perfect solutions. Choices are always about sacrifice, we can't have everything." The sound of the door opening is as loud as a thunderclap in the ensuing silence. Mateo and I both turn to see who it is. Isabella is making her way towards me, her concern evident. She stops when Mateo shakes his head. They exchange words in Spanish, Mateo's tone staying calm while Isabella becomes increasingly agitated.

"Sara?" Her eyes and face show nothing but concern when she looks at me.

"I'm ok. We're just talking." Isabella sighs before giving up and retreating back into the house.

"Isabella told us this has been difficult for you."

"I just feel like if I say yes, then I'm being selfish, but if I say no then it will hurt her. I don't want to hurt her, but my indecision is already doing that."

"No one is entirely selfless Sara. Besides, Isabella will be happy if you say yes, which would make it an unselfish decision as well."

"You're ok with your daughter moving thousands of miles away?"

"I'm ok with my daughter making the decision to be happy. She's happy with you. Yes, we will miss her, but we don't see her every day now. It's easy to take people for granted when you see them all the time. I couldn't tell you the last time both of my girls, my granddaughters and Hector were all sitting at the table with us. This is a rare occurrence. Everyone has a life, a job, or somewhere else to be. We all made time so that we could meet you, so thank you for that." Mateo sips from his drink before continuing. "I've always known that the day would come when they would leave. When Isabella was planning to move to New York, I wasn't thrilled. Esme's true colors had shown long before then. But this, with you, it has our blessing. We want Isabella to be happy, to feel alive again like she has since meeting you." He smiles at me as he squeezes my shoulder. "Besides, I might get more of these dinners when you visit." He winks at me after saying it, causing me to smile.

"Thank you," I whisper to him. He pulls me in for another of his bear hugs, nearly squeezing the breath out of me.

"You have to promise to take care of my little girl."

"Isabella is good at taking care of herself, but I promise I will." Mateo laughs.

"I believe you will. She told us your first gift to her was some art supplies." I remember the gift but have no idea where this is heading.

"It was."

"You have no idea how much that really meant to her. When she told us about that, I knew she found someone who finally understands her, who had figured out what is important to her and what she needs to thrive." Hector smiles at me and gently squeezes my shoulder. "You know Isabella can be stubborn. Even if you tell her no, I wouldn't be surprised if she just shows up one day and gives you her new address." We both chuckle before turning to our drinks. "Do you want me to send her out to you now?"

"Actually, I need some time to think. Would you mind if I walked down to the lagoon for a bit?"

"Not at all. Are you ok to get there on your own?"

"I am. Thank you, Mateo."

"Of course. Grab something to drink from the bar before you go. There are bottles of water back there as well. I'll make sure Isabella gives you some time." Mateo chuckles and shakes his head. "She has never spoken to me the way she just did. I think she was ready to club me with something to get to you. I'll find a way to stall her." He heads inside as I grab two bottles of water from behind the bar and make my way to the lagoon.

Chapter 28

I sit on the side of the deck and look down at the water, letting it calm me. I pull my knees to my chest and wrap my arms around my legs as I start the internal debate. I know that I want Isabella with me, there isn't a doubt in my mind. But does having her family's blessing change anything? I recall my question to Isabella, my asking her if we tried and she missed her family, could she go back to being long distance. I think about living by video chat, not waking up next to her, having to count the days until we see each other again, working longer days at the office and in the OR so I can carve out time off to see her, everything that I've adapted or changed to have her in my life. It's been worth it, but is that how I want it to be for as long as we're together? The thoughts swirl through my mind like a tornado as I finish one bottle of water and start the second. Time has lost all meaning as I sit here trying to fit the pieces together.

"Sara?" Isabella whispers my name, startling me. "I'm sorry I frightened you. I thought you would hear me coming down the stairs." Isabella sits a bag down near me and kneels at my side. Her fingers gently brush the hair from my face as I turn my face to her, resting my cheek on my knees. "Are you alright? My father wouldn't let me sit with you earlier."

"I am. We were just talking, he was perfectly nice, it was more than civil." I smile as her eyes examine me, searching for some hidden piece of information that isn't there. She reaches out and takes the bottle from my hand, I had no idea it was empty. "Can I kiss you?" Her voice sounds more like a plea than a question.

"Since when do you have to ask?" I feel my brow knit, I have no idea where this is coming from.

"Since I have no idea what's happening with us. My father prevents me from seeing you, you've been out here for over an hour and all my father would say was you needed space to think." Isabella is in full on panic mode.

"We're fine," I assure her as I pull my stiff legs down so I can turn to face her. I guess I have been out here for a while, my muscles are letting me know I've sit still for too long. I manage to pivot my body to face her, my legs forming a perimeter around her.

"Am I losing you?" Her voice trembles as she asks the question. I lean forward and pull her to me, our lips finally connecting, Isabella's kiss teeming with desperation. My fingers repeatedly caress her face, trying to reassure her that she isn't losing me. I pull away when my fingertips meet moisture, Isabella's tears finally escaping. I wrap my arms around her and hold her against me, my hand slowly rubbing her back.

"I love you. Why do you think you're losing me?"

"It just felt like it. First, you were upset during dinner, then I see you sobbing while you were talking to my father. He wouldn't let me talk to you, wouldn't tell me what had upset you and then he made me leave you out here alone. I've been going crazy." Isabella's hands clutch my shirt as she squeezes me tightly.

"Sweetheart, we're fine. Your father and I had a nice talk. I just needed some time alone to process. I asked him if I could come here to do that. It's my fault."

"I was worried he said something…I don't know. He never liked Esme. I was afraid he was trying to get rid of you." I laugh because she has no idea how our conversation went.

"It was nothing like that. Well except the Esme part. He wanted to know why I couldn't say yes. We talked. It released a lot of pent up emotions. He gave me his approval." Isabella pulls back and searches my eyes.

"He did?"

"Yeah, he did. Actually both your parents did." She presses her lips to mine and quickly pulls back.

"So you came here to think?" I nod before resting my head on her shoulder. "Do you want me to leave you alone? I can go back to the house."

"No, stay here with me. I can think later." Her hand rests on the back of my neck, holding me against her as I cling to two fistfuls of her shirt.

*****

"When will we see each other again?" Isabella and I stand outside the airport, locked in a desperate embrace. It's the Sunday after the holiday, and I must return home, without Isabella.

"I have another meeting in New York in two weeks. I can come to you after that. I could stay until you come here for Christmas, if you'd like." Two weeks without Isabella, then we could be together for a month. But what happens after that? There aren't any other major holidays for months following Christmas and New Year's Eve. The thought of only seeing her for the occasional long weekend depresses me.

"What would you like?" I whisper into her shoulder, my voice failing me. Isabella remains silent, her only answer a sniffle she fails to conceal. In all the times we've parted, I've never seen her cry. I'm aware that she does, she has admitted as much to me, but knowing that it has happened and seeing it happen are two entirely different things. "Isabella," I manage to utter as I pull away from her shoulder to look at her. The sight of her glassy, reddened eyes causes my heart to falter and my breath to catch. Isabella sighs, a tear slipping out and trailing down her face.

"That isn't a fair question, you know what I would like." I cast my gaze to the ground, unable to see the faint shimmer of hope fade from Isabella's eyes when I can't give her the answer she so desperately longs to hear. "It's ok Sara," she assures me before pressing her lips to the top of my head. "I did warn you that I wouldn't stop fighting for it." I release a soft chuckle before stepping back into her arms.

"I love you, you know."

"I do," she whispers before squeezing me tightly to her. "Will you message me when you get home?"

"Of course. I have to get going though." Isabella's arms constrict around me, refusing to relinquish their hold.

"I already miss you," she murmurs, the sadness heavy in her voice.

"Me too," I whisper, leaning back to kiss her. "I'll talk to you in a few hours," I promise as I rest my forehead against hers, stealing a few extra seconds of closeness until I have to walk away from her. I walk towards the entrance determined to hold back my tears until I've completed my check in. I turn back when the automatic doors slide open and steal a glance at Isabella to find her openly crying, not bothering to attempt to hide her grief.

The sight of her in such a state stripping away yet another layer of my resolve and tearing out a chunk of my heart.

Chapter 29

Two weeks has never felt more like a lifetime. These two weeks feel longer than the entire summer vacation I spent in a cast, my seven-year-old self sulking around, unable to participate in swimming, baseball, basketball and a litany of other activities while healing from my broken ulna. Weeks during which I find myself struggling to get out of bed, make it through my usual morning workouts, enjoy Sunday brunch, or pretty much anything else in life. I feel lethargic and unable to shake the shroud of perpetual sadness that clings to me. Insomnia makes the lonely nights feel infinitely longer and my empty bed three times as large. I've never felt this low after a breakup, only Isabella and I haven't broken up, we're simply separated by 2,000 miles and the haunting memory of Isabella's heartbreaking visage as I entered the airport.

"What's gotten into you lately," Catherine asks as we sip our coffee while we wait for our first cases of the day to get started. I stare mutely out the window, absorbing the city's familiar skyline as I try to articulate everything on my mind. "Does it have to do with Isabella?"

"In a nutshell," I answer and nod, knowing Catherine will expect elaboration.

"Please tell me you didn't end it."

"I didn't. I don't think I ever could. I just wish I could get over my hangup about her being away from her family." I continue staring out the window, wishing Abby would hurry up and text me, longing for the distraction of operating, anything to erase the memory of the sorrow etched on Isabella's features the last time I saw her in person. "The look on her face…so much sadness… knowing that I caused it…" I shake my head as I continue staring out the window, Catherine's arm now wrapped around my shoulders providing little comfort.

"So you're this despondent because Isabella was upset?"

"It isn't that simple. We were together for weeks. I know what that feels like now. This will sound cliched, but I don't know how else to phrase it. I feel like a part of me is missing without her here." I release a half-hearted chuckle before shaking my head and looking over at Catherine. "Listen to how absurd I sound," I mutter, more to myself than Catherine.

"You know I think you're mad for not saying yes already." Catherine sighs as my phone goes off, I know it will be Abby letting me know they're ready. "Think about how many people you know that actually still live within 20 miles of their parents. The world didn't end simply because they relocated. I know you lost both of your parents when you were young, but you won't prevent Isabella from going through that in the future simply because you don't agree to her moving here. Besides, Isabella is a determined woman, she may suffer through this for the time being, but she knows what she wants. There will come a day when she'll just show up here and tell you it's settled. You won't be able to stop her."

I sigh as I turn toward the elevator, I know Catherine is right on all fronts, even Mateo told me I wouldn't be able to stop her. Hadn't I had the thought myself that Isabella was a woman that takes what she wants? The elevator chimes its arrival, and we enter to head down to the basement, the doors closing but not ending our conversation.

"You know that no matter which choice you make you're being selfish right?" I feel my eyebrows knit together as I glare at Catherine like she has lost her mind. "You tell her no so that she isn't away from her family, insulating yourself from your fear that she'll resent you someday if she's not on their doorstep the second something happens. You tell her yes, and you'll be happy. So will she. Sara, there are few opportunities in life to actually seize something that has the potential to increase your happiness for years to come. Don't waste time denying something you both want."

"You've been talking to her, haven't you?" I ask as the doors open, depositing us in the OR.

"Alex and I have video chatted with her, yes. She isn't faring much better than you are I'm afraid, although I'm sure you both put on a good front when you chat." Catherine's revelation is like an icepick to my heart. I can deal with my emotions, but knowing Isabella isn't handling this well has my stomaching suddenly rolling. "Are you alright? You've suddenly gone a bit pale."

"I'm fine," I lie, able to taste the bile laden coffee in the back of my throat.

"You'll see her soon. Only two days before she'll be here." I nod, too afraid that if I try to speak my coffee won't stay down. Catherine gives me a quick hug before heading to her OR, leaving me to deal with an unappealing image of a dejected Isabella struggling to get through her day.

*****

Pre-op pages me as I'm on my way to the hospital. I call the number as I wait at a red light, knowing that whatever they're about to tell me, it likely won't make me happy. I shake my head in disbelief when they inform me that my first patient experienced car trouble and will be there as soon as possible. I'm fully irritated at this point. Isabella's plane is set to arrive at just after 2 pm today. With this delay, there's no way I'll be able to pick her up from the airport. The pre-op nurse assures me they will fast track my patient as soon as she arrives. I thank them before hanging up and trying to sort out what to do about Isabella. I honestly could just cancel the case, but it isn't something I would do on any other day, and this patient is always early, so I know that the car trouble isn't just an excuse.

Knowing I have plenty of time, I pull into the coffee shop and order my next coffee fix. I call Catherine, but she informs me that both she and Alex will be at the hospital today. I already know that Valerie also has cases this morning too. Katrina has a key to my place but she and I are just starting to reconnect and placing Isabella in a car with her is not a hornet's nest I desire to kick. I decide my best remaining option is to send Abby, despite the fact that sending her on this errand will take her out of the OR for at least an hour, meaning even more time lost. I dial Abby's number and let her know about the issue and ask if she would mind picking up Isabella. Abby assures me she doesn't mind but says that Blake is free for the day and he would probably help me out. We disconnect our call, and I wait impatiently for Abby to text me to let me know the plan. Her message comes in a few minutes later, letting me know she is meeting Blake to give him my house key and that he will take care of it. I sigh, partially relieved that at least that problem is solved.

"Hey gorgeous," Isabella purrs when she connects the chat. "What's wrong?" she asks as her smile slips from her face.

"Nothing major. My first patient had car trouble, so I'm delayed. I'm not going to be able to pick you up at the airport. Blake will be there though and will take you to the house."

"It's alright Sara. I'll be there when you get home. How late do you think you'll be?" I can see the disappointment in Isabella's eyes, along with the dark circles around them. Catherine wasn't exaggerating, Isabella hasn't been doing much better than I have.

"I'm really hoping to be home by four. I'm sorry."

"It isn't your fault. My flight is boarding. I'll see you when you get home. Love you."

"Love you too. See you then."

*****

"Dr. Hudson, you aren't going to believe this," Brittney, my nurse for the day calls over to me. I stop suturing and look over at her as she holds the phone against her shoulder.

"What is it?" I ask, barely able to contain the irritation in my voice.

"Apparently our next patient is in pre-op, sharing a soda with her husband." I momentarily close my eyes thinking about the blatant stupidity of some people when it dawns on me, anesthesia will cancel the case and I should be out in time to pick Isabella up from the airport. A glance at the clock confirms this, banishing all of my remaining annoyance.

"Ok. Just have the pre-op nurse inform her she needs to call the office to reschedule her procedure. Thanks, Brittney." I glance at the clock again, 12:32 and we're almost closed. I should be able to get out of here and to the airport with a few minutes to spare.

"I can finish running the 4-0 and do orders if you want to dictate and speak with the family," Abby offers. I foolishly smile at her, despite wearing a mask.

"Thanks Abby, what would I do without you?" Abby nods as she comes around the table to take over for me. "Thanks everyone for your hard work today. I appreciate it." I break scrub and debrief with the nurse before heading to the dictation room to hasten my exit from the hospital.

*****

"Excuse me, I'm looking for a woman name Torres," I call from behind Isabella. The large bouquet of flowers coupled with leaning against the wall a few feet down from the exit somehow made for a perfect cover. Likely that and the fact that she was looking for Blake. I giggle when I see her confused expression as she turns around, a huge smile blossoming on her lips as I lower the bouquet and reveal myself.

"What are you doing here?" she asks as she quickly closes the distance between us. I barely have a chance to move the flowers to the side before she is crushing me in her arms, her nose buried in my hair as she takes a deep breath. "I've missed you so much," she murmurs against my ear, the warmth of her embrace welcome in the cold December air.

"I've missed you too," I inform her before leaning back far enough to kiss her.

"Are those for me?" she asks when we finally separate.

"Nope, they're for the other girlfriend I'm picking up."

"There better not be another girlfriend," Isabella scowls. I suddenly remember too late what she went through with her ex and immediately feel like an ass.

"I'm sorry. I promise you there isn't anyone else. Of course, these are for you," I assure her. "Trade you." She smiles at me as she passes me her suitcase before taking the bouquet.

"These are beautiful," she whispers as she takes in the arrangement of orchids, lilies, and irises. I know nothing about flowers, I've actually never bought flowers for a woman before. I ran into the shop with only 20 minutes to spare, told the florist what I needed them for and that I'd rather not have roses because they seem so generic. She smiled and assured me she could throw just the thing together quickly. Gauging Isabella's reaction, she did well.

"You're beautiful," I remind her. "Can we please get in the car though? No matter how long I live here I'll never get used to the cold weather." Isabella laughs before clasping my free hand and allowing me to lead her to the car. "Did you have a chance to grab something for lunch?"

"No. I guess you haven't eaten either," she gives me a disapproving look from over the roof of the car as I place her suitcase in the back seat.

"I didn't," I inform her as we settle in our seats and close the doors. "It was a stroke of luck that I was even able to come get you, that or a stroke of stupidity."

"You mean you really weren't coming to pick me up?" she asks giving me a confused look.

"I wasn't, right up until my last patient decided to split a soda with her husband in pre-op. Anesthesia canceled the case."

"I'm sorry about your case," Isabella says, smirking at me.

"No you're not, and neither am I," I inform her, leaning over to steal a kiss. "Want to stop somewhere for lunch?" I ask as we rest our foreheads against one another.

"Not really, but we probably should. Are there any good Thai places around here? I've had a craving lately."

"Absolutely," I inform her before stealing a quick kiss and leading us away from the airport.

Chapter 30

I wake up just after 4:30 am on Saturday morning, brimming with energy. Isabella still slumbers beside me, unaware of my growing restlessness. I quietly slide out of bed and put on a pair of shorts and a shirt in the dark before slipping downstairs for a run. It doesn't take me long to realize that the lethargic dead weight I've been shouldering these last two weeks is gone, the only difference between yesterday and today being Isabella's presence. I run as I contemplate this simple fact, realizing that to continue on as we are would mean dealing with the emotional peaks and valleys of being together and being apart. Given the last two weeks, I feel certain that the emotional rollercoaster isn't one I can continue to ride. By the end of my workout, I've come to the conclusion that we only have two real options. Either we end things or Isabella moves here. Ending things isn't on my radar, nor do I think I could do it or that it would help. I would still know Isabella is out there, would still love her and would only be swallowed by a pit of depression I'm not sure I could climb back out of. *I have to say yes*, I realize as the hot water of the shower cleanses the workout induced sweat from my body. Hypotheticals can no longer control my happiness. I must take this leap and deal with the consequences.

"You smell like soap," Isabella murmurs when she nestles against me after I fail to stealthily slip back into bed.

"I couldn't sleep, so I went for a run," I whisper before kissing the top of her head. "Go back to sleep."

"You ok?" Isabella mutters, already halfway back to being out cold.

"Yes," I whisper before angling my head to press a soft kiss to hers. She releases a soft sound of contentment, her breathing already having leveled back out. I revel in the comfort of holding her in my arms as she slumbers, yet my mind refuses to rest. Does my emotional state relying on proximity to her make me some kind of co-dependent? *I was fine before Isabella came into my life*, I tell myself. *Ok, I wasn't fine*, I quickly amend. I know I was pushing myself way too hard, devoting at least 90% of myself to work and leaving little for anything else. I was physically drained, emotionally stagnant, and incapable of dealing with the slightest addition of stress in any form. I know with certainty that Katrina was the catalyst I needed to make me realize I was not on a sustainable path. Isabella is the one that pushes me to be better. I'm also certain that if I had not met Isabella, I would have simply reverted back to my old habits upon my return from Punta Cana. The fact that my stubbornness willing yields, allowing me to make alterations for Isabella that I've never considered making for anyone else, reinforces what I already know, Isabella is the one. I can no longer tell her no, my answer is finally yes.

I come to sometime later and quickly realize that Isabella is no longer pressed against me. I hear the soft sound of her sketching and know she is near. Opening my eyes, I ignore the urge to stretch and locate her sitting on the foot of the bed, working away.

"You were smiling in your sleep," she informs me, never halting the steady movements of her hand.

"Must be because you're here," I whisper, forcing myself not to reach for her. Even if she just started, I know the sketch won't take her long. I watch her work, feeling contentment and love coursing through me.

"Done," she says as she drops the pad and pencils to the floor then rejoins me under the sheets, kissing me good morning before settling in.

"Will you ever tire of sketching me?"

"I don't think I will. There's always something different. Today you were smiling." She flashes me her grin before giving me a quick kiss. "They're like my photographs. Do you want me to stop?" she asks, her brow slightly furrowed.

"Never," I reassure her, pulling her against me.

*****

I'm finishing wrapping things up on Tuesday when Valerie taps on my door. "Hey, come on in," I call out as I power down my computer and put my tablet on the charger.

"I thought you'd be running out of here as fast as your legs will carry you," Valerie jokes as she deposits herself in one of the chairs in front of my desk.

"Alex had the day off and invited Isabella to hang out with her for the day. Something about Christmas shopping or whatever they're getting up to." I shrug, vaguely remembering their conversation at brunch on Sunday and clearly remembering encouraging Isabella to join her.

"So what are you getting Isabella?"

"Shit," I mutter, shaking my head. "I've been so focused on other things I haven't even thought about it."

"Everything alright?" Valerie asks, concern written on her face.

"Everything is fine. Just had a few epiphanies recently and I'm working on addressing them." Valerie shoots me a look, I'm not the only one who realizes I'm being incredibly vague.

"Ok. Well, you still have time to figure out the perfect gift," she reminds me, mercifully giving me a pass on diving deeper into what I'm not telling her. It isn't that I don't want my friends to know, I just feel Isabella and I should talk first.

"Thanks. What about you? How are things?"

"Good. Things are starting to pick up nicely. That was actually part of the reason I stopped in?"

"Oh?"

"I was wondering what your thoughts were about trying to find another Abby. It doesn't seem like you've really cut back that much and I keep finding myself increasingly booked."

"I haven't cut back too much. Seems like we still have plenty of work to keep the two of us busy for the foreseeable future. I would like to drop a day or even a half day somewhere once Isabella moves here—." I stop myself by slapping my hand over my mouth when I realize the mistake that I've made while distracted thinking about gifts. Valerie's eyebrows shoot skyward, and she dons a giant grin. "I haven't spoken to her about it yet, please don't repeat that."

"I won't. I wondered if that was what your "epiphany" was," she informs me, making air quotes when necessary. "I'm happy for you."

"Thanks. Back to you hiring a PA, I think it's a good idea. Abby is increasingly busy in the cosmetic clinic as well, so perhaps you can find someone who has the training to help her there too. I don't think the other partners will be hard to convince, especially if the applicant possesses those skills. That clinic makes us a lot of money."

"I'm well aware. Do you think Abby would know of anyone?"

"She might. If she doesn't off the top of her head, she does have a lot of contacts and goes to a few conferences a year. She might make a good headhunter. Plus, if we're going to have them working side by side in the clinic we'll need to hire someone that she'll get along with."

"Is there anyone she can't work with?"

"Not that I know of. The choice would ultimately be yours, but it may be wise to seek her input."

"I agree," she tells me as she rises from her seat. "I'll let you get going, I'm sure you're anxious to get home."

"Thanks. I'm sure they're still out and about. Just mention it to the other partners. I don't think you'll meet any resistance."

"Will do. Good luck with your other thing," she calls as she steps out of my office. I quickly glance at the time and realize it's early enough that I have time to make a quick stop on the way home.

*****

I arrive home, grateful that Isabella is still out with Alex. I sent a message asking Alex to drag her feet for a while, buying myself time. I make the few trips from the garage up to my office, or the room that was always intended to be my office, yet still stands empty. The sales woman at the art supply store remembered me from my first trip there. She seemed surprised when I asked for help with the top of the line painting supplies, but was happy to assist me with everything. As with the pencils and sketchpad, she assured me that she would exchange any of the unopened items if they weren't what Isabella was looking for. I quickly organize all of the supplies and make a few adjustments, trying to arrange things I know nothing about into a perfect display.

"Sara are you home?" I hear Isabella call from the entryway. I quickly dash out of the room and close the door before she turns the corner.

"Only just," I tell her as she turns the corner and wraps her arms around me. "Did you have fun with Alex today?"

"I did. She has no idea what to get Catherine for Christmas, so it took longer than I anticipated." Glad I'm not the only one who has no idea what to get her girlfriend.

"You don't have a curfew. I want you to have fun when you're here, not sit in the house waiting for me to come home every day."

"I know you do. The two weeks we were apart were difficult though. I want to spend as much time as I can with you before we have to go through that again." I squeeze her a little tighter, knowing exactly how I felt during those two weeks, remembering Catherine telling me Isabella wasn't doing much better. "Why don't you have a Christmas tree?"

"I've never needed one. It's always just been me for the most part."

"You spend Christmas alone?"

"Not always. I get plenty of invitations every year. Sometimes I join Abby and her family, others I volunteer at the homeless shelter and then stay home. It always makes for a good catchup with work day. We always have a holiday party every year so it isn't as though my life has been void of holiday celebrations."

"You're not spending this year alone," she whispers into my neck before pressing her soft lips against it.

"No, I'm not," I agree, smiling against hers. "Would you like to get a tree?"

"Only if you would."

"Sure. Let's go to dinner then we can go to the store and the tree lot." I give her a quick kiss as she releases me before stepping around the corner, where I immediately freeze, my eyes locked on a pile of bags left in the entryway.

"I may have bought a few things to put under the tree already," Isabella whispers as she locks her arms around my waist.

"A few?" I choke out. "Those are all for me?"

"Mostly. I did pick something up for everyone else as well."

"You really like Christmas, don't you?" I ask, my eyes still glued to the pile near the door.

"I love it. You don't?" she asks, turning me to face her.

"I remember I did when I was a kid. But the year my mom passed, it was so close to the holiday that we didn't really celebrate it. In fact, we never really celebrated it after that."

"Oh Sara, I'm so sorry. I didn't even think. Is that what has been bothering you the past few days?"

"What? Oh, no. Don't get me wrong, I miss her terribly and I'll always wonder if she'd be proud of me, what she would make of my choices, even what she would look like now…but I'm not upset."

"I can return that stuff, I'm so sorry."

"No. Maybe it's time to start celebrating the holiday again. There isn't anyone I'd rather do that with than you." I pull Isabella into my arms and press a kiss to her forehead. "I didn't realize I needed so much stuff though," I whisper, chuckling softly.

"You probably don't *need* any of it. I just picked up anything that made me think of you."

"Looks like you think of me quite a bit," I murmur into her neck.

"You have no idea," she replies, not knowing how very wrong she is.

*****

"Baby, why are you so tense?" Isabella and I sit snuggled up in front of the fireplace, admiring our tree craftsmanship. I realized at dinner the possible flaw in my plan. I already set everything around in the room I plan to offer Isabella as a studio. It isn't that I think she goes snooping around the house when I'm not home, I just don't want her finding everything before I present it to her. That leaves my only option being to tell her tonight. I'm not sure why I'm nervous, Isabella has made clear her desire to move here time and again.

"Am I?" I ask, knowing I'm keenly aware of the tension in my neck and shoulders. "Look, it's starting to snow," I inform her, pointing toward the window.

"It's snowing!" Isabella excitedly exclaims. I lean back and examine her, she looks as happy as a kid in a candy store.

"You've never seen snow?"

"Nope. I thought they would have some when I got to New York but they didn't. Then I thought there would be some here but nada." I watch her as she smiles broadly and gazes out the window.

"Want to go outside?" She nods her agreement but doesn't move. "Come on," I instruct her as I get to my feet, extending my hand to help her up. We pull on a pair of my warm jackets, hats, scarves, and boots before exiting the front door. Once outside I clasp Isabella's hand and lead her into the yard where she tilts her face upward and allows the falling flakes to settle and melt on her flesh.

"It's beautiful," she exclaims as she looks at the flakes that have collected on the sleeve of her jacket. "I didn't think you'd actually be able to see the structural differences of each flake." Despite the chill in the air, I feel a warmth spread through me as I watch Isabella get excited about something as simple as snow. I feel a satisfied smile spread across my lips as I allow Isabella her explorations. "Why are you smiling like that?"

"Because you see the beauty in something that a lot of people have grown sick and tired of. Because having you here in moments like this, it's priceless."

"You know," she says closing the space between us, "I've never kissed anyone in the snow before." She leans into me, and I gladly assist her in closing the distance between our lips. I greedily cling to her as her silky tongue slides into my mouth to meet mine. The kiss is leisurely, yet the heat it produces has me convinced that when we break for air, we will somehow find ourselves transported to the beach outside of her bungalow.

"How was that?" I whisper as I rest my forehead against hers, still not opening my eyes.

"Even better than I imagined."

"Isabella," I utter as I tip my head away from hers, waiting for her to open her eyes. "When we were apart I was miserable, I felt like I had somehow been fractured, that a part of me had been cleaved away. Now that you're here though…it's like that certain joie de vivre has returned." I have no idea if I'm making any sense, I feel like I'm mucking this up already.

"I know," she whispers as her cold fingertips caress my cheek, her eyes reflecting nothing but love at me.

"I need to show you something," I inform her as I take her hand and lead her back into the house. She waits patiently as I return our jackets to the closet, neither of us saying a word. I clasp her hand as I lead her down the hallway to the closed door. "Open it," I tell her, standing aside. She gives me a confused look before twisting the knob and swinging the door open. I watch as she looks around at my handiwork, still not saying a word. "I think that's the paint you prefer. The sales lady said if I thought that's what the label looked like then it was the one, that the packaging is unique." My stomach is doing summersaults as I wait for her to say something.

"It is," she assures me as she looks around the room again, her eyes containing a glassy sheen. "What is all of this? I thought you said you didn't have any idea what to get me for Christmas."

"This isn't a Christmas gift," I inform her.

"What then? Do you want me to paint for you?"

"No. I want to inspire you to paint." Isabella turns her focus on me, the corners of her mouth turned upward, the tears starting to escape from her eyes. "I want you to paint here, with me." Still, after everything, I have no idea if I'm making any sense. Why am I incapable of making a grand gesture?

"Are you implying what I think you are?" she asks, hope brimming in her eyes.

"I need you here with me. I don't want to be away from you, not knowing when I'll see you again." I snap my mouth shut, if I don't stop myself, I'll just keep babbling.

"What about your reservations about taking me from my family?" I sigh and take a moment to compose my thoughts.

"I was miserable the two weeks we were apart. I barely slept, I didn't have the energy to workout…honestly it sucked. If our options are to keep going through the emotional ups and downs, end it, or for you to move here, then I chose you moving here. If you're willing to take that chance, then I want us to be together." Isabella doesn't say anything. I barely catch the corners of her mouth inching further upward before she launches herself at me and claims my mouth with hers. She slowly backs me up against the wall as her hands slip under my sweater.

"Mmm, as much as I want to continue this, I need to put the fire out," I inform her stopping her hands before they can erase logical thought from my mind.

"Not just yet you don't," she says as she withdraws her hands, clasping mine in hers as she guides us out of her studio. "I think it's time you welcome me home properly," she informs me as she leads me towards the den.

Author's Note

Thank you for taking the time to read Providence. The Velvet series was never supposed to exist. Fusion was meant to be a stand alone novel, but after completing it, Catherine & Alex's world continue to call to me. It came to me then that I could easily incorporate them into a story involving their friends, and thus the Sara's story began to take shape. Providence wasn't always kind to me. She refused to tell me her name for months and even forced me to change my original outcome well into the writing process. I'm pleased with where she ended up and hope you were as well. Book 3 in the series will be coming, although a definitive timetable has yet to be determined. I can share with you that it will focus on Valerie's story following the conclusion of Providence.

If you enjoyed this story and would be kind enough, please leave a review. For independent authors such as myself, reviews are critical in helping to spread the word about our work.

To stay up to date on my future releases please follow me on Facebook and Twitter.

Email: dianakanebooks@gmail.com

Made in the USA
Monee, IL
26 November 2022

18534302R00260